Becoming Mariella

Becoming Mariella

A Novel

JANET CONSTANTINO

SHE WRITES PRESS

Published 2025

Printed in the United States of America

Print ISBN: 978-1-64742-768-9
E-ISBN: 978-1-64742-769-6
Library of Congress Control Number: 2024918947

For information, address:
She Writes Press
1569 Solano Ave #546
Berkeley, CA 94707

Interior design and typeset by Katherine Lloyd, The DESK

She Writes Press is a division of SparkPoint Studio, LLC.

For Larry, for always

For Jason

For the Sicilians

How many Sicilian mothers does it take
to change a light bulb?

"Change? Don't talk to me about change!
Things are fine the way they are.

And don't think I'm falling for that old line
about sitting in the dark."

—*Yolanda Russo*

"[As Chevally says,]
'Sicilians never want to improve for the simple
reason that they think themselves perfect.'"

—*Frances Maye*

Chapter One

Mariella gripped the scrub brush so tightly her fingernails dug into her palm. She kept her eyes down, avoiding her mother's dark accusing gaze, and concentrated instead on one of the many chips in the old cast-iron sink's enamel, a black scar in the shape of a crescent moon.

"A marriage to such power—for us, for our family," Mamma chanted, in her sing-song voice, the one she used when she prayed or slipped over into what appeared to be a trance. Which was at least fifty times a day.

"*O Dio,* who can believe," Mamma intoned. "*La Famiglia Russo,* so blessed. Only the saints can say why Matteo chose you, but . . ." At this Mamma raised her eyes to the statue of Saint Agatha in the niche of the Russo kitchen, and slammed a cleaver—Whack!—straight down onto the neck of the handsome russet-feathered chicken she'd held captive on the thick wooden butcher block. She threw the head into the nearby garbage bin, and with the back of her arm, swept the chicken onto the floor. The bird circled the kitchen, spraying blood, its red fleshy wattle flopping as it ran, and bolted straight into Mariella's bare legs. There was a terrified and noisy flapping of wings and a final squawk before the nerves in its spinal column gave way and the headless creature collapsed at her feet.

"*Ayyy!*" Mariella clenched her jaw and silently screamed. Chicken blood spattered her ankles and toes, her new tan leather sandals, the back of her calves, and the wooden kitchen

1

cabinets and seeped into the grout of the terra-cotta tiles on the floor. It was only a small amount of blood, but it spread like a bucketful.

That does it! she inwardly fumed. She refused to give her mother the satisfaction of a reaction. Mamma had engineered this beheading just to incite her daughter's revulsion. It was one of the conditions Mariella had insisted on, time and again, if her mother wanted her help in the kitchen: no slaughtering of chickens here. There was a washroom in the basement of the building, with a big sink, and a big workbench, perfect for chicken bleeding and plucking.

". . . *Grazie, Madrona, grazie!*" Mamma, acting all innocent and unaware, lifted her arms to Saint Agatha. She quickly bagged the chicken in plastic, leaving a few feathers and the blood behind on the tiles as she carried the chicken off to the basement for plucking.

"You knew I was breaking in these sandals for the beach," Mariella muttered under her breath. She wiped away a tear with the back of her hand. "You know I can't afford another pair."

She gritted her teeth and scrubbed at the skin of that evening's stuffed sardines seared onto the bottom of the blue speckled roasting pan, the residual odor of the oily fish wafting into her nostrils.

"I'm a prisoner," she whispered, although no one was there to hear. As baked into her family's expectations as that poor fish stuck onto the pan.

She recited to herself the litany she'd memorized as a young child: *Agatha, martyr and patron saint of all martyrs, of the city of Catania, of wet nurses, fire, earthquakes, and eruptions of Mount Etna.*

Mamma's outbursts were as capricious as that volcano, endlessly rumbling in the background and framed through the Russo's dining room window.

"And I'm not cleaning the floor!" Mariella yelled, knowing her mother was out of range, four stories down.

She didn't *want* to be a housewife. She didn't want to marry Matteo, even though she loved him. She didn't want to marry *anyone*. She scrubbed even harder at the fish's remains.

Two days later, at one o'clock on Sunday afternoon, the doorbell chimed at the Russo apartment.

Papa laid down the weekend edition of *La Sicilia* on the lamp table next to him in the living room. He rose to his feet from his favorite leather armchair and opened the door to their guest.

"Come in, Matteo, come in," he said, sweeping his arm in a gesture of welcome.

"And a good afternoon, Signor Russo. It looks like we both got the memo," Matteo said, looking down at his outfit and then at Papa's. An instant, mutually affectionate smile at the coincidence: oxford cloth shirts with the sleeves rolled up. Matteo's shirt was white, with khaki-colored chinos over his taut and younger frame. Papa's shirt moss green with a slight pull on the buttons at his thickening middle, the color reflecting his green eyes, a legacy handed down from Nonna, Papa's mother Giuseppina Russo, and to Mariella as well. Nonna called their eyes "A gift from the Norman Invasion." Matteo's eyes were as jet black as his hair; Papa's wiry hair was golden brown and shot through with gray.

"Catania's finest!" Matteo proclaimed, holding out a bottle of the prized local red to Papa, a Nerello Mascalese from Mount Etna's arid and rumbling slopes. In his right hand, a small bouquet of white plumeria with the fragrance of jasmine, in a delicate blown glass blue vase.

Papa accepted the wine, perused the label, and nodded approvingly. "*Grazie*, Matteo, *grazie!*"

Mariella emerged from her room, still reading as she walked, the latest iteration of Harry Potter, *The Goblet of Fire*, deliberately in English to keep practicing what she'd learned in high school and university. "Reading for pure fun," she'd told one of her university girlfriends when the friend asked her what she'd be doing over the summer now that their undergraduate studies were finished.

Matteo kissed her on the forehead. She stood on tiptoe to greet him—his six feet to her five foot two—and pulled him further into the living room. Before she could receive the bouquet, her mother dashed from the kitchen, wiping her hands on her apron, squeezed Mariella aside, and snatched the flowers from Matteo's hand.

"You spoil us," Mamma crooned, as if Matteo were *her* suitor and not her daughter's. "Flowers in a vase so we don't have to fix them ourselves—so thoughtful." In the background, Papa looked at the floor and shook his head, resigned to his wife's antics he'd witnessed a thousand times.

"No, it is you who spoils *me*," Matteo insisted, kissing Mamma on both cheeks. "Everyone knows you're the best cook in Catania."

"Tch," Mamma said, and tilted her head coyly. Behind her mother's back, Mariella sighed and rolled her eyes.

The aroma of chicken—that recent unfortunate bird—roasting with rosemary, along with the rich meaty Sunday ragu, permeated the apartment. Matteo sniffed the air. "Ahh," he said and closed his eyes in an exaggerated display of ecstasy.

"Why do you always humor her?" Mariella asked Matteo after her mother disappeared to place the flowers on the dining table, and Papa to the kitchen to open the wine.

"You know I like your mother," he said. "I think she's a real kick, unpredictable, like *Zia* Mame." Auntie Mame, the flamboyant Rosalind Russell character from the 1950's movie, with subtitles in Italian, a favorite classic for Sicilians, who had a penchant for slapstick and corny.

"A kick for you but not for me," Mariella said. "You don't

have to live with her. I hate it when you're so nice to her." She turned from him in a pout. "Besides, it makes me feel like you're on her side and not mine."

"I will be on your side until the day I die," Matteo said, nudging her around to face him and gently pulling her closer. "But I want your Mamma on our side too." He looked down at Mariella. "Can you imagine what it would be like for us if she had it in for me?"

"Hey, dude!" Olimpio, Mariella's eighteen-year-old brother, burst through the apartment door and grabbed Matteo from behind in an awkward hug. He was out of breath from running up the stairs, three at a time, his usual manner of entry. "I heard you were coming for dinner. Cool!" Matteo had become a frequent Sunday guest at the Russo's table.

"Hey, yourself," Matteo said, reluctantly releasing one arm from around Mariella and patting Olimpio on the back with his free one. "Oh, before I forget, Isabella made me promise to say hello." Isabella was Matteo's youngest sister, seventeen years old, with curly light hair and a sweet air of innocence, who'd confessed to Mariella that she had a mad crush on Olimpio. Many girls had crushes on Olimpio, handsome as a movie star and with coal black eyes, like his mother.

"Say hi back to Isabella," Olimpio said, without much apparent interest. "So hey, what're you gonna do now that you're finished university? I heard you're going to law school."

"You heard right," Matteo said. He glanced sheepishly at Mariella. "Siracusa International Institute."

"When?" she asked. "Why didn't you tell me you were accepted?"

"I wanted to surprise you." He searched her face for a long moment. "We'll both be in Siracusa during the week now, with your internship starting there at the American embassy in September. I thought you'd be pleased."

"Oh no . . . I am pleased," she said. "Pleased for you . . . I mean for both of us. It's just that I *am* surprised." The Institute was the perfect place for Matteo, specializing in Human Rights, Criminal Justice, and International Law. He wanted to save the world, and especially *Sicilia* from the Mafia.

"This way we'll be able to see each other every day," Matteo said. "We can drive back and forth together."

Whatever dream of independence, whatever bit of control she'd clung to was just shot through, delivered like a death blow. She swallowed back a wave of nausea rising in her throat.

"That's great," she said, a feeble attempt at enthusiasm. But she was hobbled now, beyond escape. Along with any hope of freedom, gone as well was the train ride to Siracusa she'd so looked forward to, an hour each way and time to herself, away from everyone who wanted too much from her, including Matteo.

The only sound for a moment was the ticking of a wood framed mantelpiece clock.

Nonna made her quiet appearance in the living room and lowered her head, with its crown of gray braids, in a slight bow toward Matteo with a smile of warmth. She held out her hands to him, and he took them and gazed fondly back. Always, as now, she sported her regular costume of a rayon floral print dress, this one aqua blue, and old lady black lace up shoes. Never the eternal black garb for her, the standard for widows and husbandless women on the island. Once five-foot-two, like Mariella, she was shorter now at seventy-three, and the wisest person in Mariella's life. Nonna was the only one who understood Mariella's need to escape.

"Welcome to another adventure at the Russo's," Nonna said with a laugh. Mariella had invited few friends to their table over the years. She hadn't wanted to risk the humiliation of Mamma's erratic belittling, nor of having her friends see Mamma as a crazy woman.

"With you here, everything makes sense," Matteo said, still holding Nonna's hands. He knew how much Mariella loved and relied on her grandmother, how Nonna was Mariella's anchor in a sea of unrest.

"So you two leave tomorrow for Licata?" Papa said, addressing Matteo and Mariella part way through the meal. "And tell me again, you're both staying with a university friend?"

"Yes, at the Fiducci's. Benno's my good friend who lives there, and Mariella knows Angela and Gabriella, his sisters, so the girls will have their own sleepover. A slumber party," he said. "Benno and I will stay in a separate cottage on the property, away from the main house."

Nonna's look told Mariella she knew better, but Nonna only inclined her head, her gesture of secrecy, and approval.

"You're welcome to talk to my mother if you want reassurance," Matteo said. "She and Papa have known the Fiducci's forever."

"Oh, no, no," I trust you completely, Mamma said, flashing him her most ingratiating smile. In fact, she'd fawned over both him and Olimpio all through dinner: *"Have more chicken, Matteo . . . more penne . . . more insalata with the fresh fennel, you too Olimpio, you need to stay strong."* With the boys, Mamma was always charming, obsequious even, they could do no wrong, and so Olimpio's friends, unlike Mariella's, were frequent and welcome visitors.

Chapter Two

"I think our parents *wanted* to be convinced," Mariella shouted, laughing, as Matteo drove against the wind the following morning, her dark auburn corkscrew curls bouncing around, as untamable as she was. They took the winding coast road west, the long way around the southern tip, with the top down in his shiny yellow Alfa Romeo convertible.

Suffocation always nagged at her like Mamma, but it was relegated for the moment to the back of her mind, with the wind in her hair and so much beauty impossible to ignore, the air balmy and fragrant with citrus, and musk from dark Nero d'Avola grapes ripening in vineyards. All over the island, late spring wildflowers—rock roses, red and orange poppies, and valerian the color of fuchsia—were at their riotous, most bountiful peak.

She'd only wanted a few easy, unfettered days at the sea with Matteo before graduation.

They roamed the ancient harbor town of Licata and ate a leisurely late lunch under a maroon umbrella at a trattoria on a cobblestone alleyway: pasta pomodoro with the freshest sauce of small, round Pachino tomatoes; whole roasted sweet, delicate branzino that they fed to one another, along with the promise of desire, as they locked eyes and licked small bites from one another's fingers. The wine, a bottle of fruity white Inzolia. A panzanella salad of arugula and cubes of focaccia soaked in rich, spicy olive oil and tart red wine vinegar.

They took provisions back to their seaside pensione for a light, late supper on the tiny veranda. A teardrop shaped bulb of caciocavallo, a good loaf of *muffuletti*, the local bread with spices and sesame, a straw basket of fresh figs, and a second bottle of the Inzolia.

Under the velvet night sky with stars that poked through like diamonds, they made love on a hidden, deserted pocket beach, safe from prying eyes, making believe they were the only souls on the planet. Moonlight illuminated their bodies as if outlined and glowing from within. Nearby, the heady perfume of orange and lemon groves, and the sound of the sea. And, even closer, the warm scent of one another's bodies.

"What do you say, *tesoro mio?* Let's forget the church and just get married tomorrow morning. Right away," Matteo said, and tickled her cheek with a blade of beach grass.

"How do you know some dog hasn't pissed on that?" she asked.

If she hadn't been naked, she'd have run from him, but she never allowed herself such free rein, the indulgence of impulse or drama. Mamma commanded that territory.

"Matteo. I'm not ready to be a wife." Even if he'd only been trying to make light, to make her understand how much he loved her, he'd turned their little getaway unpleasant, at least for her, and their road trip into a reminder of a betrothal she had neither asked for nor wanted.

"What does that mean?" he asked. "Don't you love me? Don't you want us to spend the rest of our lives together?"

She heard the appeal, the plaintive cry in his voice. She closed her eyes so she couldn't see his expression: hurt, disappointment, perhaps anger.

The night was humid and warm enough to sleep outside without clothing if they'd wanted to, but now she felt a chill, a shiver, and the urge to cover herself.

She laughed, as if even an abbreviated sound would banish her wedding goblins into the night.

The evening after their return from Licata, she lay in her single bed for hours in a tangle of sweaty sheets, staring at her bedroom ceiling. Not even a slight breeze stirred the filmy curtains in front of the wide-open window. Everyone was counting on her to marry Matteo. Maybe she'd be lucky and drop into a spontaneous coma and not wake up for five years. Matteo would surely have moved on by then, and she'd still be young enough to make some kind of life for herself. Maybe he'd be whisked off to somewhere in Africa for political asylum, maybe Tripoli or some other Libyan city. He was going to get himself in real trouble someday with his frequent and far left proclamations at university political rallies, and sometimes on street corners prior to local elections, his voice rising distinctively above a smattering of cries protesting against the conservative candidate for regional President: *Power to the people! Democracy rules! Stand up to the Nationalist Right!*

Sometime in the sleepless night, she remembered the lectures *Professore* Maldonado, her beloved psychology instructor, had given about brain plasticity. About adaptability and the capacity to learn and to grow, about changing habitual ways of thinking, even recasting a crisis from a disaster into a challenge. Like when she was a child and pretended she was someone else's daughter when Mamma made her feel bad, or that she had a twin sister who would always stand between her and anyone who hurt her feelings, or that her stuffed dog and bear were real and could talk and hug her in return.

She'd simply change Matteo from her fiancé to her "affair." Even with the diamond ring on her finger, which she absentmindedly twisted around and around.

Oh, she knew she couldn't change *him*. Only the way she thought about him. Her little secret, in her mind. She wouldn't tell anyone; they'd accuse her of magical thinking. Something else she'd learned about from *Professore* Maldonado. And maybe it was crazy magical thinking on her part. But never mind.

It made her calmer, thinking of Matteo as only her affair.

Adaptability, a mantra, a secret benediction she carried in the weeks before graduation.

Chapter Three

On her and Matteo's sweltering commencement day, Mariella and her family were released, after the ceremony, along with several hundred others, into the University of Catania's main courtyard. The circular black-and-white pattern mosaics beneath their feet now worn to a matte dark gray where the ancient stones were once the color of jet. The Department of Humanities graduation had taken place in the stuffy *Aula Magna*, the Great Hall, replete with *professori* in pompous ceremonial robes and medieval-looking head gear. Somnolent speeches had been endured, from both faculty and valedictory students, including Matteo, whose delivery was singularly lively and blessedly short.

"*. . . and it will be our generation, the class of 2000, that brings our beloved Sicily back to its once glorified distinction as a cornerstone of civilization and culture . . .*"

Once outside, Mariella unzipped the front of her black graduation robe, hoping, to no avail, to bring a modicum of relief from the oppressive heat.

Mamma and Nonna sat apart from them, apart from each other on separate benches along one of the courtyard's sheltered walkways. Matteo's eyes sought out Mariella. In return, she watched him from a distance: intense, beautiful, tender Matteo. He stood across the crowded courtyard with his parents and his two sisters. The older one tall and blonde, the younger with light brown curls framing her face; her mouth was sensuous and full, like her brother's.

Matteo and his parents smiled and waved as they made their way to Mariella. She called on the adaptation she'd chosen in the middle of the night, silently addressing him as her "affair," tucking her left hand, the hand with the ring, into the folds of her graduation gown.

Here, in front of her, stood Matteo's parents, the Gamberinis: rotund Bruno, in his expensive beige summer suit, embracing her, at least a foot shorter than his wife, like old photos she'd seen of Carlo Ponti and Sophia Loren. Bruno smelled of sandalwood and lime.

"*Mariella, ciao bella*, my sweet third daughter. *Complimenti!*" he said, wiping perspiration from his brow with a crisp white handkerchief, and shaking hands with Papa. And Olimpio, in turn, punched Matteo lightly on the arm before grasping him in a congratulatory hug.

"Grazie, Signor Gamberini—I mean Bruno. Grazie," Mariella said, taking his hands in hers. She hoped Papa hadn't heard Bruno say, "My daughter." As much as she cherished the inclusion, the genuine fondness from Matteo's parents, she didn't want to be anyone's daughter but her father's. Mostly, she didn't want her father's feelings hurt.

Sylvia, Matteo's gracious mother, elegant in a pale pink silk sheath and pearls, exchanged kisses with Mariella on both cheeks. His parents had insisted she call them by their first names, had made clear how much they approved of her, how happy they were for their son to find someone of her intellect and potential, how glad they were she was more than a young woman "... *con la testa vuota* ..."

If only Mamma treated her like she was more than an "empty head."

His mother had cried during the valedictorian speech Matteo delivered.

Their darling Matteo, so vociferous and liberal. He, who was jailed twice overnight and threatened by the Mafia more than once. The first time, Mariella had followed him to the jail as quickly as she could get there, "borrowing" (she couldn't risk the chance he'd say no) her brother Olimpio's prized lime-green Vespa. She'd begged to stay overnight, sitting in a chair in the tiny, stark waiting room with metal walls. But the fierce *carabinieri* guard, an officer of the paramilitary, barred her from even seeing Matteo.

Still, she had no doubt: because of his fierce passions, because of his wealthy family and its influence, and in spite of his extreme leftism, no door of public office would ever be closed to him. Though how unlikely her beloved Sicilia would rise again, Mariella had thought earlier as Matteo had spoken his prediction to thunderous applause.

She watched, now, as the Gamberinis chatted politely, even enthusiastically, with her father. *Noblesse oblige?* Did they like her sweet workaday father, or were they only pretending? No, her beloved Sicilia wasn't likely to rise as Matteo had proclaimed it would, not unless the powerful Mafia underground could be routed out. Or some miracle of fortune would restore the war-torn buildings, clean up the grime, and fix the toothless grins of so many who called this island home. The people she passed every day on the streets, the out-of-work and the poor.

Out of the corner of her eye she saw her mother pushing her way through the throng of visitors and graduates. Of course, Mamma wouldn't stand in public with her own daughter, though she'd never miss an opportunity to be seen alongside Matteo and his parents. Mariella had her suspicions about their "business" connections—olive oil and exports, Matteo told her—and how they garnered their political power and amassed such wealth, but they were never spelled out.

"*Scusi, scusi,*" Mamma said, bursting into their little circle. She was breathing hard and patting her chest, trying to act composed and delicate, as if she hadn't just run a foot race. She lowered her head, nearly bowing to Sylvia and Bruno.

Shamed and indignant, Mariella watched her mother fawn over Matteo's parents. Mamma was good-looking and plenty smart, and if only she understood her own worth perhaps she wouldn't be so mean to Mariella. She thought her mother was beautiful, black shoulder-length hair and fierce dark looks set off as dramatically as Mamma's temperament, against her crisp white blouse and lipstick the color of blood.

"Aren't we just so proud of our *due bambini*?" Mamma said, flashing her dark eyes and that ingratiating smile, back and forth between Mariella and Matteo.

Mamma had never before told her daughter that she was proud of her.

Matteo sidled up next to Mariella, the golden tassel from his mortarboard falling over her eyes. "I don't ever want to be without you," he whispered.

She raised her face to him from under the square brim of her own cap, and forced herself to laugh, as if he were only making a joke. *Affair*, she told herself, her heart pounding in her ears. *Affair, affair, affair.*

"Affair" had a beginning, a middle, and while she didn't necessarily wish it so, it also, potentially, had an end.

"Why are you laughing?" Matteo asked. "Like you have a secret—or maybe," he suggested, slyly. "You just broke wind."

"You're bad," she said. She nudged him, playfully, keeping up the charade. They both smiled and appeared, she imagined, for anyone who cared to notice, like the perfect young pair.

At the *al fresco* graduation dinner that evening, Matteo insisted she sit next to him at the head of the table, the way married couples were seated at important public or social events: local district elections, confirmations, anniversaries. Weddings too, but she pushed the image of *sposa e sposo* from her mind.

Sure, everybody knew they were engaged, everyone saw the ring on her finger. She knew he was only her affair.

His parents took the seats at the long granite table's other end. Sylvia Gamberini beamed at Matteo and Mariella and held up her wine glass to them. Sylvia's pearls shone under the little white lights that were strung overhead through grapevines, entwined in an arbor. Her hair was dark brown, streaked with gray, and swept back from her temples in a modern, sophisticated coif. Mariella touched her red dangly earrings—beaded garnets, her birthstone—a graduation gift from Sylvia, and Sylvia inclined her fashionable head in return.

Her parents were seated on Mariella's left, and Olimpio, the handsome one, at Papa's left, and Nonna, her beloved Nonna Giuseppina, in one of her pink floral housedresses, her old lady lace-up shoes and a big straw sun hat, next to Olimpio. As far away from Mamma as she could be, Mariella guessed, without appearing obvious.

Aunts, uncles, cousins, mostly Gamberinis, family and close university friends of both Mariella and Matteo filled out the forty remaining seats at the main and two smaller round adjacent tables.

"Your mother likes me," Matteo said, leaning toward Mariella. "And I think she only pretends not to know we're sleeping together."

"My mother likes you because she thinks you're going to be important. She thinks you're going to be mayor or . . . what? President of the town."

"Maybe I will be," he said, stretching himself up in his chair and puffing out his chest like a victorious gladiator.

Imagining herself a politician's wife, the claustrophobia of a private life made public, always putting on a false face, caused the sweat to break out on her bare arms. The night air was heavy and warm, but she felt chilled. She sought out her grandmother's eyes and nodded at her. Nonna blew Mariella a silent kiss. Nonna understood Mariella's restlessness. Nonna understood every-thing. She'd broken away to her own dreams when she was even younger than Mariella. When it was even more revolutionary for a young woman than it was today.

Her mother scowled, just as she had all through the gradu-ation ceremony. Mariella suspected her mother was intimidated, more nervous than usual, her dramatics silenced now by the Gam-berinis' social standing, and their easy assumption of paying for and hosting the party. Mamma felt entitled to preside at this event marking her daughter's and Matteo's accomplishments—"It should be *our* party!" she'd complained to Papa. But neither she nor Papa were consulted about the evening, merely included and informed.

Bitter, envious Mamma who married at seventeen and treated her daughter like she was lower than dirt on the floor. And yet clutched onto her, enslaved her, and, Mariella swore, lay awake nights inventing chores for her, instead of sleeping.

Only yesterday, Mariella had overheard her mother fretting to Papa: "Salvatore, maybe our daughter isn't good enough for the Gamberinis. Maybe they'll open their eyes one day and real-ize their son has married beneath them." Mariella translated: her marriage to Matteo was Mamma's last chance to be good enough, to vicariously live out everything *she'd* missed. While at the same time, Mamma's envy made her dream up reasons to keep her daughter housebound, like *Centerentola*. But if she was Cinderella, where was her glass slipper, her prince to spirit her away? Her friends would have said Matteo was her prince, but even with his privilege, he was caught in the same snare of family and tradition as she.

Olimpio, the chosen one, the *Bambinone* could shit on the floor and Mamma would say it was manna from Heaven.

She saw Papa pat her mother's hand. Forever there, to calm Mamma's nerves. Papa was . . . well, her sweet Papa, a simple accountant, and she adored him. He was a big kind-hearted man with those green eyes, like hers and Nonna's, and his unruly head of wiry, curly, golden-brown hair, tinged with gray. Her father, always giving the impression of rumpled even if, as now, the dress shirt he wore was pressed and starched.

She felt the sting of tears, remembering how Papa had stood up for her when Mamma insisted that going to university was a waste of time. Even after Mariella had been awarded a scholarship.

"You only have to think enough to marry higher than yourself," Mamma had argued. "No man wants a smarty-pants wife. Even for a *non eccezionale* girl like you, it's the only way!" So desperate to get through to Mariella, her mother had squeezed a glass so hard it shattered in her hand.

"No, *bella*," Papa had said, gently wiping Mamma's blood and binding her hand with a towel. "Our Mariella gets to go because she *is* exceptional." Papa had spoken calmly but stayed firm.

"Thank you for tonight, *cara* Mariella," Bruno Gamberini said, rising and toasting her from the other end of the table. Mariella waitressed here, at the Trattoria Inglese on weekends. In return, the chef had given her the night off, with pay, in honor of their celebration. She'd simply planned and ordered the menu for the dinner.

"The pleasure is mine," Mariella said, blushing at Bruno's compliment, and raised her glass in return. It was so rare she had a moment in the spotlight when Mamma was in the room.

"Grazie, Bruno!" Mamma cried out suddenly, on cue, her voice raspy and harsh. "Say something, Salvatore!" she whispered, loud enough for everyone to hear. "Remind them that we're important, one big family now." She nudged Papa in the ribs. Papa shook his head and pressed a finger to his lips. Mamma touched her cheek as if she'd been slapped and looked at Papa like a child who didn't know why she'd been punished. Nervous titters rang out around the tables. If Mariella's chair had a lever to open the floor beneath her, she would happily have fallen through. Nonna rolled her eyes, and Olimpio stared at his plate.

"*Salute!*" Bruno quickly declared.

"*Salute!*" the assembled guests proclaimed in response, lifting their glasses to both Mariella and Matteo. Mariella swallowed several mouthfuls of the dark Nero d'Avola to dull the burn of her shame.

Under the calming influence of the wine, she let go of the breath she'd been holding and surveyed the faces on both sides of the table, including a handful of beloved young women friends and their parents, dear people she'd known practically since birth. Like family.

Except for Mamma, who muttered under her breath to Papa, the mood was once again convivial, guests' cheeks aglow from the alcohol, the soft lighting, and the heat of the summer night air idyllic.

The antipasti was nearly as good as Nonna's: roasted red peppers dressed with olive oil and sea salt; eggplant *rolatini* with ricotta and basil tucked inside; astringent black olives and sardines, quickly sautéed to a golden toasty crisp, netted only hours before, so fresh Mariella imagined them still wiggling on the plate.

Her eyes lingered again on Matteo's mother, admiring, with a twinge of envy, Sylvia's obvious affection for her children, her warm, down-to-earth manner, despite her wealth. Matteo was the middle child between two sisters, Isabella and Leonora, both of whom sat near his parents, one on either side. Mariella was especially fond of Isabella, the youngest, who had a big crush on Olimpio and grilled her about him whenever Mariella visited the Villa Gamberini: "Does he have a girlfriend?" "What does he like to read?" "Invite me over sometime when he's going to be home, okay?"

Mariella turned to Matteo as he leaned over and spoke to his cousin, Rodolfo, on his right—Rudy, for short—who was still in high school. So handsome, her Matteo, though not in a traditional way: his lean, intense face too poetic for that. Eyes so dark they were nearly black. She felt a throb of desire, felt the wetness between her legs, remembering their lovemaking in his apartment bed. Only yesterday.

My Matteo. That's what she'd called him out loud, in the throes of sex. *My brilliant Matteo.* Her first, who'd taught her the art of making love, taught her to relish and enjoy the curves of her body. He'd taken her to tango clubs where she'd mastered the sensuous, gliding movements of a panther. And now he kept hold of her hand, placed it with his in the lap of her white cotton eyelet dress, while he spoke with his young cousin.

Affair, she reminded herself, as Matteo nodded at whatever Rudy was saying. *Affair, affair, affair*, and she thought of herself as sinful, and Matteo both forbidden and, because of that, even more desirable.

She lifted a forkful of the ribbed pasta tube to her lips, the *penne alla norma*, the specialty of the house: glistening chunks of ricotta *salata*, the capers, the cubes of eggplant, exactly the right amount of red pepper flakes, the minced vegetable *soffritto* that made the base for the spicy *salsa pomodoro*.

Bruno Gamberini stood and tapped a butter knife against his water glass. He waited for silence, with the indulgent smile of someone used to commanding an assemblage. The collective chatter and high-pitched laughter subsided, in staggered succession, as guests turned toward their host. Bruno's gaze came to rest on Mariella.

He cleared his throat, and she raised her eyebrows at him. She attempted to stay composed, even as the heat rose through her body, turning her neck bright red—she could feel it—and perspiration broke out along her hairline and under her arms.

"Mariella," he began. "Our dear girl." He regarded her with

genuine affection. More than fifty faces shifted their attention toward her.

Her heart surged and skipped a beat. Whomever or whatever in the universe one could ask favors of, let it be that Bruno was only going to thank her again for "Caring for our son." For "Standing by his side when his youthful politics got him into trouble," because, above all else, that is what both he and Sylvia had told her they were most grateful for. Surely Bruno wouldn't betray her trust. Both families had finally agreed to keep the wedding date secret until after graduation, until she was settled in her internship. Even Mamma had ultimately relented, though not without a struggle. What was the point of her daughter marrying someone important, she'd insisted, if she had to keep it to herself?

Bruno continued to smile fondly at her. "What is in our hearts—and we speak for our son when we say it's foremost in his heart too—is our joy for the day when you will become part of our family."

At this he nodded a sheepish apology to Mariella's mother and father, while Mariella's stomach churned in somersaults.

"Not only as a daughter-in-law," he went on. "But as a *vera figlia*." He paused once again, appearing happy and assured, as if what he was about to say was certain to please her. "Yes, as a true daughter, because when you are the beloved wife of our only son, we will welcome you even more than we already do, as a loyal Gamberini and one of our very own."

Guests waited silently for her response.

Mamma's loud raspy voice soared. "What? What, Salvatore? What did he say? She belongs to us first. I don't believe my ears!" Now Mamma was on her feet. "*Ascotare! Attezione!*" she cried, waving her arms.

A rapid high-pitched giggle hit the air and Mariella realized it was her own.

"Bruno! Bruno," Mamma said breathlessly, turning to Matteo's father, as if they were in accord. "It's okay now to tell them, it's all right to tell them . . ."

Mariella's father sat with his head down. The fragile restraint on Mamma's internal dam had broken, and Papa had no way now of stopping the torrent.

Bruno Gamberini stood with his mouth agape, frozen in mid-speech.

The others in the room no longer existed for Mariella. Mamma, Papa, Matteo: now only animated blurs. Was she going to pass out? She fixed her gaze on Nonna's eyes, her calm and steady regard an anchor.

"Yes!" Mamma forged ahead. "I tell you now, we have the biggest church for our *cara bambini*—*Il Duomo*—and so you have the time to make the plans, we have the date of just six months. Isn't that so, Bruno? Yes, you tell them, our babies will be married on the Sunday of December the seventeenth!"

Mariella had hyperventilated before, but the foreign sound that came out of her now was the gagging a cat makes, its body heaving and convulsing before it vomits up a fur ball. Could it be that she could produce such a noise, this alien voice that seemed to have taken up residence in her?

She downed a glass of water in nearly one gulp.

After breathing deeply, she willed herself to stand. Matteo stood with her and attempted to hold onto her arm, but she pulled it away. He was shaking his head, as if defeated, as if he'd always realized the inevitability of her moving beyond his grasp.

"No," she whispered, barely audible, and speaking softly, only to him. "Why can't you understand? Why is everyone in such a hurry? I'm sorry, but I don't *want* to get married!"

She backed away from Matteo, from all of them. As she fled from the restaurant, it was only Nonna's voice that reached her, a firm voice, commanding Mariella's father. "Let her be, Salvatore. Let her go. She needs to be alone."

Chapter Four

*I*t was *her* bench, the baroque one at the end of the marina, away from the other plainer benches, the one with the statue of the dwarf elephant behind it, facing out to sea.

She slumped miserably onto it, out of breath. She bent over, rocking and holding herself, moaning in shame as her outrageous behavior replayed itself again and again in her mind's eye. Every surge of memory brought with it a fresh wave of nausea. Never before had she displayed such open rebellion, lost such control of herself, although God knows how many times she'd fantasized throwing herself on the floor, kicking and screaming in mutiny against her mother.

She'd run straight here from the trattoria. She was grateful for the scattering of palm trees that made the bench more private.

After several minutes of panting, she began to relax and breathed a little deeper.

She could see out, between the trees, and she wanted to believe, in spite of the bright moon and the path illuminated by ornate, carriage-style streetlamps, that no one could see in. That even if someone from the graduation dinner did come for her, they'd never find her, even though the trattoria was only three street corners away. She couldn't imagine why anyone *would* want anything to do with her, after the fool—no, the spectacle—she'd just made of herself.

To this small, sheltered grove—she thought of it as her personal haven—is where she escaped whenever she wanted to steal time alone, away from Mamma, away from Matteo, and away from her other part-time job at a travel agency, the *Agenzia Turistica* on *Via Finocchiaro Aprile*. She worked at the *Agenzia* late afternoons, when she'd finished with classes. And occasionally on weekends, if the restaurant didn't need her.

Usually, being on this bench brought her a sense of peace. But not tonight. Nothing brought her peace tonight, not even the soft lapping rhythm of the sea.

At the *Agenzia*, at least she was free to daydream, which was partly the reason she'd presented herself over a year ago, to the proprietor, Signora Luisa Romano. A middle-aged woman with cropped, frizzy, bleached hair and a slick of red lipstick, who'd listened to Mariella's proposal, read her credentials, sighed, and said, "I suppose I could use some help. It's just me here, and I hardly ever close in case someone comes in. But I can't pay you much."

It wasn't only the extra money, but a sense of wanderlust that had driven her to the *Agenzia's* door in the first place, and that sense of wanderlust, of something beyond herself, had only been confirmed and amplified during her time there. Mariella helped the ones who could afford to travel—usually professional men and women, mostly couples—plan their honeymoons or excursions to places whose names she'd only read about or seen on maps, places she longed to see: Australia, Egypt, New York, Russia, the Caribbean, Chicago, Switzerland, San Francisco— the city that pulled on her the most. She'd never really been far from home. Even *Roma* was too much like what she already knew, and the rest of Europe too close to home, as well. She couldn't say exactly why San Francisco held such allure, except that it was by the sea, like Catania. And it wasn't so big and overwhelming, like New York, and besides, through the *Agenzia's* computer, she'd found hundreds of Russos, people with *her* last name, living in San Francisco. *Molti Italiani* who'd been brave enough to make a life for themselves, out there, across that vast ocean. In America.

The bay was calm tonight, deserted except for the festive lights of a late-night pleasure boat in the distance, and an empty fishing trawler making its silent, careful way to dock. Fluorescent buoys offshore marked the entrance to deeper water.

She'd lost all sense of time, and when she checked her watch, a numberless face held in a thin black lizard band, she was surprised that nearly an hour had slipped by. The watch had been a lavish gift from Matteo on her twenty-first birthday last year, a Movado with only gold hands and a gold dot at the top for twelve o'clock. They'd be worried about her at home; at least Papa would. She trusted—hoped—that Nonna would know she was all right.

As she stood, reluctantly, to leave, she absentmindedly fixed her gaze on a teenage couple strolling toward her. They both wore all-black, and punk-style tight jeans, their arms wound desperately around each other's waists, as if hanging on for survival. The streetlamps' reflected glow twinkled in their numerous and similarly studded ear piercings and metallic chains.

"What are you looking at?" the boy hissed at Mariella through clenched teeth, as they drew near. "Who are you? Some kind of old maid busybody?" A slight breeze lifted his silky, sandy brown hair from his forehead, a soft, boyish contrast to his scowl and tight jaw.

Mariella was stunned, felt the blow as sharply as if he'd slapped her in the face. No one had ever before accused her of being a busybody, a designation that belonged to her mother. She unblinkingly stared at the young man.

"Sorry, sorry," the girl said, patting her boyfriend's hand, muttering something inaudible to him and simultaneously pulling him along. "He didn't mean anything."

Mariella's pulse raced. What if she did end up an old maid,

like the boy called her? After her performance tonight, she deserved the insult.

Still, wasn't that better than giving up her life?

After midnight, when she let herself into the apartment, it was Papa waiting for her in the living room, in his leather armchair. The glow from the floor lamp behind him bathed him in a dim triangle of shadow and light, as if he were captured in a film noir. He'd removed his jacket and tie and unbuttoned the top of his white shirt, but he still wore his slacks and good shoes.

"*Mia*, thank God you're home," he said, rushing to her. He crushed her small body against his ample chest. "I was giving you fifteen more minutes before I called the police."

"I'm sorry if I scared you, Papa." She raised her chin as best she could, engulfed in his big protective hug. "I'm sorry if I hurt you."

Papa held her and rocked her and when he started to say, "Your mamma . . ." she stopped him.

"No, Papa," she said. "I don't want to hear anything about Mamma. Tonight, I don't care."

Journal, Mariella 1 a.m.,
June 18, 2000

I'm in jail! A prisoner! I'll never be free, and this headache is coming on so strong I'll never get to sleep, but who cares? I don't care what happens anymore. Oh, Matteo! I'm furious with you, and my head is killing me at the same time.

What's the matter with me?

The truth is I feel so guilty, I can't stand the idea of hurting him, of what he'll go through if I call it off. Dio, I can't even say the words to myself: wedding. Marriage. But I do love him, I love going tango dancing with him, and when we make love his eyes pierce, they're so dark. He's taught me so much about the world. About politics. Forget politics. About sex. So why do I want to run away?

I don't know. And why did I take his ring? Of course, pressure, I feel it right now. I didn't think I had a choice. I still don't feel like I have a choice, don't think I have the courage to break it off. Oh, I just can't bear to hurt him. But I'm not going to think about it. It's too upsetting. Maybe something will happen, maybe it'll work itself out and we can put marriage off indefinitely.

My headache is getting worse. If only I could get some sleep. My punishment, Mamma would say, for being such a wicked girl. When I'm not trying to get away from her, or feel like she's my enemy, I do feel sorry for her. Only sometimes. Most of the time I can't stand her. Sometimes I hate her. I think she hates me too. How many times have I heard her stupid sob story: "You don't know what it's like to suffer! I've struggled so hard all my life. Mamma and Papa dead when I was only five . . . blah, blah, blah, the tuberculosis that took them . . . I had to quit school when I was fifteen to clean Auntie's toilets and scrub her floors just for food and a roof over my head—you selfish, spoiled girl!"

So shouldn't she understand my wanting to escape? I mean that's sort of what she did, marrying Papa at seventeen. Escaped Auntie the Witch. Okay, I admit it's kind of sad, but over and over and over?

And it's not just that I don't want to be married. I mean, I don't. It's that I feel so trapped. By Mamma, yes, and all the expectations of how I'm supposed to live my life, and just Sicilian culture in general, although I'm sure my family is more old-fashioned than most. You'd think it was the eighteenth century instead of the twenty-first. But I don't want Mamma's life, I don't want the life of a housewife. Even though I love to cook—I hate to admit it, but I have Mamma to thank for that, the best cook I know next to Nonna. It's just that I want something else and I can't always put my finger on it. I even want to be with someone someday, someone I can be free with, someone I can have my own life with, a career if that's what I want, and I'm pretty sure I do. A life like Nonna had, with her first husband when she went to night classes in London, before he was run down by that taxi.

Matteo says we can have that together, but I know he's wrong—because of Mamma and Papa, but mostly Mamma. And Matteo's family, oh my God! Talk about controlling with a velvet vise. I love them too, but you don't say no to Bruno Gamberini and live to tell about it. I'm sure that's part of why I accepted the ring. You try saying no to Bruno. All that slogan stuff about "You Always Have a Choice"? Well, that's just bullshit.

Chapter Five

She didn't hear her grandmother come into the kitchen in the middle of the night. Didn't see her until Nonna stepped alongside at the counter of matte crème-colored tiles. Old tiles, some of them knife-scarred, backsplash tiles behind the sink interspersed with a few decorative shiny squares, hand-painted with fruits and herbs.

"Nonna, you scared me." They were both in their night-clothes. Her grandmother's nightgown was plain, a pale yellow cotton shift. Her long steel gray hair, which in the daytime she coiled on top of her head, snaked down her back in a banded braid. Mariella wore an oversized white T-shirt—one of Matteo's—over her underpants.

"I haven't been to bed," Mariella said. "But why are you up?"

"I felt you awake, all the way in my room."

Mariella moved to the sink and placed her hands on the rim. She peered into the enameled basin, where she was given her first bath by her mother, before she developed a good brain and a mind of her own. She was born in this apartment on *Via Diodoro Siculo*, both she and her brother, with the help of a trusted neighborhood midwife—Mamma would never have submitted herself to strangers in a hospital—the only home she'd ever known.

She nodded toward the living room, toward the outside balcony, and she and her grandmother went there. They pulled the shuttered doors closed behind them, away from the stucco walls that may have had ears. The night was warm enough to sit outside on the canvas couch, without sweaters or shawls, the moon only beginning its waning phase, still casting enough light that they could see one another.

The balcony garden, thanks to her father's tending, had been there from before Mariella could remember. Red geraniums in hand-painted planters hung from the top railing, spilling their color, luminous in the moonlight, over and through the bars of the festooned wrought iron. Pansies in oblong ceramic planters formed a border at Nonna's and Mariella's feet, and potted palms stood sentry on the rustic terra-cotta tile floor, at either side.

On their third-floor perch, they listened to Papa's buzz saw snores in the distance.

"That's my boy," Nonna said. She shook her head but smiled at her granddaughter, who was staring at her bare thighs, plumped and flattened by the fabric seat. Nonna laid her veiny hand on top of Mariella's smooth olive one, which rested beside her, palm down.

"What are you going to do?" Nonna asked. Her grandmother had been the first she'd told about Matteo's proposal.

"I don't know, Nonna. I guess Mamma just had one of her fits." Mariella's and Olimpio's word for their mother's tantrums.

"Worse than ever. Right there at the table. Yelling and screaming and pretending to pass out. By the time your father and Olimpio helped her out of the restaurant, she was out flat, like she was on a stretcher. You know."

It was always Mamma, center stage.

"Your father and Matteo, they both started to follow you," Nonna said. "Until your mother went crazy. But I told them no." She nudged Mariella's arm. It had been like this between them forever: even from a distance she and Nonna were aware of each other's hearts and minds.

"But listen," Nonna said. "If anything would make Matteo or

his family think twice about him marrying you, all you have to do is trot out your mother to give them a show."

"Oh, I don't think I have to worry about Matteo wanting me anymore." Mariella leaned forward, surveying the empty street below, as if the answer to Nonna's question, "What are you going to do?" would miraculously reveal itself there. Only an orange cat crossed the moonstruck cobblestones.

She nuzzled her aching head against her grandmother's shoulder. "Nonna, what's wrong with me?" She released her pent-up turmoil and sobbed, safe in her grandmother's embrace, wetting her grandmother's nightgown with tears and snot. "My girlfriends, most women my age would kill to marry someone like Matteo."

"Yes, but you're not most women, and so I ask you in another way," Nonna said, smoothing the hair from Mariella's forehead. "Not what will you do, but what do you *want* to do?"

"You're the only one who ever asks me what I want. Except . . . well, at least sometimes he used to, Matteo."

She had been counting the weeks—only three—until she began her internship at the American embassy in Siracusa, sixty-seven kilometers from her parents' apartment. Just an hour away by train, but still, in her mind, it would have been the beginning of her own life, a loosening of the ties that kept her captive, until Matteo delivered his suffocating blow about driving together.

She nestled even closer to her grandmother.

A foghorn moaned in the distance, a signal for those souls braving the Ionian Sea in these predawn hours, each and every morning. Sicilian fishermen had gone out in their small boats for as many centuries as the island had been civilized, their seafaring as ingrained in the landscape as the rocky cliffs and crumbling amphitheaters, residues of the Roman Empire, and of time before. The sound of the sea, like the rhythmical sigh of breathing out and breathing in. Mariella took these wonderments for granted, these everyday backdrops to her life, as regular as her own breath. Except at intervals, like now, when her senses were heightened and her mind open and everything around her cropping up, seeming just born and the sea smelling new: fishy, salty, watery, a little tangy. As if she were taking it all in for the very first time.

"Oh, Nonna, I love you so much. And I haven't changed. I still want to *do* something in the world. At least, somewhere outside of Catania." She sighed—a mournful shudder—resigning herself, as she always did, to her island-bound fate. "Maybe, with the languages, they'll hire me at the American embassy, after my internship. Or maybe I'll do something with the psychology. I've even considered law school, like Matteo." Her lips made a soft, puffing sound as she released her breath. "I think I'm supposed to do something important—help people have a better life." She closed her eyes and cocked her head, as if she were listening to an inner voice. "You know, change the world," she said, with a self-deprecating laugh.

She'd told her parents this much, and they'd pooh-poohed and dismissed her out of hand. "*Ridicolo*," Mamma had said. "What do you think you are? Some kind of miracle worker, like a saint? You only live the life you're born with. Besides, this isn't America. You want to stick out your neck and get yourself killed? You should be on your knees thanking God for Matteo."

Mariella wiped her eyes with the back of her hand.

"Nonna, I know I'm only dreaming right now because I know it can never be," she said, her voice catching on a sob she hadn't been able to swallow. "And I've never told anyone this before, but what I want more than anything is to live in America—in San Francisco."

Nonna laughed, quietly. "I hope I'm still alive to see the fireworks when your mother hears that news. And *bella*, you know I'm the wrong person to say that to, that it can never be, because when I went to England, in those days it was just as revolutionary for a *Siciliana* going by herself as going to America is now. Think of it," she said, peering down into Mariella's face. "How many Sicilian women do you know who've gone to America alone?"

Sicilian *families* had always gone to America to make a bigger life. Mariella knew this. But a Siciliana on her own? America was the place where women spoke out, became doctors and lawyers and some, even heads of corporations. Chiefs of police and senators, important politicians. Maybe a president someday. Of course, there were educated women, doctors and lawyers and college professors in *Sicilia*, and in England too, a queen and even a prime minister there. But America was the land where she could become anything she wanted: graduate school first, if she could get in, then maybe work at an important clinic, or a private practice, maybe a professor at a big university. Or, who knew, the United Nations!

She sat suddenly upright. "I've looked it all up," she said, the excitement of her daydream momentarily supplanting tears and her throbbing head, a residue of moisture still at the corners of her eyes. "I want to go to school in San Francisco, somewhere for literature, like you did in London, to the San Francisco State University or maybe to a place called Professional School of Psychology. Or maybe somewhere for languages."

"Not New York?" Nonna asked. "Isn't that where all the American dreams come true? Why not Hollywood?" Nonna nudged against her. She saw the smile, the teasing in her grandmother's eyes.

"San Francisco is more like a big neighborhood," Mariella said. "Friendly, I think, more inviting than New York, which is very exciting, yes, but too big and impersonal, over eight million people! And even if San Francisco is farther away than New York, it's . . . well, more *Italiano* than other American cities." She'd read about North Beach and the city built on hills, like Catania, and the sea all around, because even if she wanted to be far away from the life she felt stifled by here, she could never be anything but Siciliana. And, like the Ionian tide, going out and coming in, she held to the belief that she would be delivered safely in America, welcomed onto San Francisco's shores.

"You should have seen him, *cara*, my Jeremy," Nonna said, out of the blue, as if they'd just left off talking about her first husband, an English soldier and professor of Economics at London University. Her grandmother stared somewhere into the past, her vision held, Mariella surmised, by the likeness she'd carried inside for over fifty years. "He was handsome, yes, only not like a pretty boy. He was *maschile*, with very kind eyes, as blue as the Mediterranean, and a few lines here . . ." She touched the downward corners of her mouth and around her own eyes. ". . . but that just made him look wise, for one so young."

Mariella remained quiet and still, not wanting to break the spell of her grandmother's remembrances.

"I was only eighteen, working in the communal bakery when he returned to see what it was like here in the aftermath." Nonna had told Mariella about the World War II bakeries where neighbors brought loaves from home to bake in the big brick community ovens, or traded what they could—home grown vegetables or a piece of embroidery—in exchange for a loaf. Nonna's pay was a few lira and daily bread for her family. "It wasn't very pretty here after the War," Nonna said, "with all the rubble and buildings with big artillery holes and chunks missing. I told you he was stationed here in Catania during Operation Husky, when the allies beat back Mussolini? Yes, well, you know even today you can see some of those artillery holes.

"Anyway," she sighed, "Jeremy's blue gaze landed on me— really, on my firm behind—fanny first." Nonna laughed. "I was bent over easing the wooden bread paddle into the big brick oven."

Mariella could picture it: when Nonna turned to face Jeremy

and he looked into her green eyes flecked with gold, framed by long black eyelashes and crescent shaped brows, and that beautiful olive skin, and that raven hair, shiny and naturally wavy, well, he would have been beyond redemption.

And, she determined, as if it were irrefutable, who wouldn't fall in love with her grandmother? Smart, funny, and short like Mariella. Or rather, *she* was like Nonna because her grandmother was born first, except Nonna didn't have her gap tooth in front. And her hair wasn't wiry, like Mariella's. Mariella loved almost everything about her grandmother. She liked the gap between her own front teeth, too, thought it gave her a little character, and besides, Matteo thought it was sexy.

"*O Dio*, what love looks passed between us," Nonna reminisced, a faraway look in her eyes as if she were back there, in those long-ago years, meeting Jeremy for the first time. "When I placed a crusty loaf from my hand into his, the merest touch of his finger set off a roiling in my belly," in her nether parts is what Mariella figured Nonna *really* meant, "such as I never knew existed."

Mariella felt yearning in her own body as her grandmother spoke, the longing that filled and pulsated through her Nonna and Jeremy during those brief, fleeting weeks before he returned to London, making their flat there ready for her, before he returned again to marry her. Desire as thick and as palpable as the honeyed dough with dried fruit and nuts that Nonna kneaded and shaped with her bare, sticky hands.

"We couldn't keep our eyes or our hands away from each other," Nonna said.

Her own grandmother, talking to her like a contemporary! Telling her the sorts of truths no other adults had the courage to reveal.

"Does that shock you *mia*, that your Nonna had so much passion for Jeremy I didn't care what anyone thought?"

Such delight, to imagine her grandmother lusty and maybe even wanton. Fleeing on the night train after their simple private wedding—only Nonna's parents and brothers were present— daring to commit the original Sicilian sin of leaving family and home before anyone knew she was missing. Nonna understood better than anyone why Mariella didn't want a big wedding, let alone marriage. Besides Mariella's closest friends, (the one or two who'd guessed before she told them) Nonna was the only one who knew about sex with Matteo. Well, consciously knew. Mariella suspected her mother knew but pretended she didn't. No, if anything, Mariella was envious of Nonna wanting something— or someone—so much she'd risk everything. That's how *she* felt about getting away. To abandon her family for her own dream was perhaps worth becoming an orphan for or even dying. But would she ever risk as much for a man?

"But I can say with all honesty that I was beloved on this earth and that I loved— twice—including your grandfather," Nonna said. Samuele Russo, twelve years older than Nonna, a gentle man who'd died over ten years ago. He'd adored Giuseppina, and was as kind as their son, Mariella's father, Salvatore.

"My love for Samuele was quieter, more grateful because I was nearly thirty when we met—it took me that long, eleven years, to get over Jeremy—and I never thought I'd care for someone again. Or that anyone would want me at that age." Nonna tilted her head and considered. "But with my Jeremy, I carry him in my heart, my love and mine alone. What more can a human being ask? And no one, not even Samuele seemed to remember I'd been married before, because Mamma and Papa never talked to anyone about him, and when I came home after Jeremy died, we never spoke of him, Mamma and Papa and I. Even in the neighborhood, no one knew for certain why I'd left town. It was as if Jeremy simply vanished, as if he never existed."

She sat quietly for a time.

After a while Nonna leaned into her granddaughter and laughed. She groaned and clapped her palm to her forehead. "Of course, when Jeremy asked me to marry him, I had to introduce him to Mamma and Papa. Oh Madonna, you never saw such wailing and beating of chests."

"Even worse than Mamma?" asked Mariella.

"Even worse—well, at least as bad as your Mamma." Nonna shrugged. "Maybe."

Mariella thought it would be impossible for anyone to be more dramatic than her mother.

"But after Jeremy died, you came back to Catania. Why Nonna, why?" Was that what fate had in store for her? Would she have the courage to stay in San Francisco if she couldn't find work, or she failed graduate school? Or suffered a broken heart? Would she relinquish her dreams and return home, defeated and shamed?

"At first, after he died, I stayed in England for several months, because I wanted my grief to be private. Mamma and Papa never accepted Jeremy, and I didn't want to hear anything they had to say. I didn't want to betray him."

Nonna shook her head. "But I didn't have any means to make a living. I wanted to become a professor, too, or at least a teacher, but I'd only started literature classes at night school, even though I knew enough English. Oh, maybe I could have worked as a maid, or maybe in a shop, but jobs were hard to find even for English people after the war, and I was a foreigner. And Mamma and Papa kept begging me to come home, they'd forgiven me they said. 'We won't tell anyone where you've been. Just come home!' We never spoke of Jeremy again, but inside I was dying; I didn't eat. And I never forgot."

Nonna closed her eyes and watched something in her mind. "I saw a mourning dove once on the olive tree in our backyard, and afterward, whenever I heard its call in the distance, I knew

Jeremy had come back to say hello, because you know, those doves, they mate for life."

Grandmother and granddaughter sat silently and held hands. Then, Nonna reached out and again brushed back Mariella's hair with her fingers, and for a time, they listened to the foghorn and the sounds of the night, the occasional crying out of seagulls calling "Anchovies, over here! This way for sardines!" The backfire of a car's engine, the echo of footsteps on stone, the report of a closing door, perhaps a lover leaving his mistress's bedroom, or a night watchman heading to his lonely post.

Sometimes Mariella worried her small body would break apart from the effort of containment, a yearning almost too keen to endure: America, graduate school, probably in languages, or maybe she *would* become a lawyer there, where the law meant something, at least some of the time. Not like here in *Sicilia*, where the only law was Mafioso, and lawyers were killed for being on the wrong side.

There was a rustling in the living room behind them.

Mariella and Nonna didn't speak for several moments. Mariella sat up and craned her neck around and squinted between the shutter slats into the shadowy, half-dark apartment. No movement, no sound. Probably the apartment settling, as it did from time to time, with Mt. Etna ceaselessly rumbling so close by. She rested her head again on her grandmother's lap. If only she could fall asleep and wake up, and she and Matteo could be happy, without all this worry about something as silly as a wedding.

Nonna held Mariella close and rocked her, swayed with her, as she had when Mariella was little. Jeremy was Nonna's true love, Mariella believed, a love more powerful than her love for Matteo had ever been. A love with a terrible and tragic end. Married for only a year when he was run down by a speeding taxi.

The balcony shutters flew open with a loud crack as if they'd been ripped from their hinges and Mamma appeared before them, staring like a malevolent phantasm. Had she heard what they'd said? No, no. Mariella had never been able to hear more than muffled words when anyone talked out here. Besides, she and Nonna had spoken quietly, and the stucco walls were a mile thick.

"I know for sure you're a *puttana*," Mamma said, waving a miniature wand-like object above her head and riveting Mariella with her hateful scowl. "Because I've seen the proof!"

"You've been snooping in my dresser," Mariella snapped back. "You have no right to go through my things. It proves nothing," she said, raising her chin at the small baton her mother brandished. "You have no clue why that was in my drawer." On the day she'd brought the pregnancy test home, her period had started before she'd had a chance to use it.

"No!" Mamma bellowed. "You think I don't understand about the sex; you think I'm *stupido—stupido* and blind. Well, I've got news for you, puttana. You *will* marry Matteo." She pointed an accusing finger close to Mariella's face, and said, "To keep the honor of this family," and then she dissolved in tears.

"Oh, Mamma," Mariella said, and stood next to her mother. She felt Nonna's strength behind her, her grandmother's admonition to stay firm and true, first of all, to herself.

Mariella brushed her mother's cheek until Mamma turned her head away, but not before Mariella glimpsed the fear in her mother's eyes.

Papa, half-asleep, shuffled onto the balcony in his rumpled, baggy pajamas. "Yolanda," he said, and took her arm. "Come back to bed."

Mamma wrenched her arm away and glared at all of them, her face as furious as Medusa's, her dark eyes flashing, her black hair as wild as if it really were a nest of pulsating, venomous snakes. Then she covered her face with her hands and sobbed again.

"I'm not trying to hurt you, Mamma, but I'm not going to marry him."

Olimpio, who'd hovered just inside the apartment, stepped out of the darkness. "Don't say anymore, Mari. You're just scared," he said. Like their father, he liked to keep the peace.

"Yes, *cara*, you don't mean it," Papa pleaded with Mariella. "You're confused right now."

"Don't you see? It's our only chance, our only chance," Mamma moaned. She doubled over and held her stomach. "Don't you see? Don't you see at all? For our family, we can rise with this marriage. For all of you . . ." She regarded each of them, one by one, granting Nonna a special glare. "For all the work I've done for this family." She gestured to Mariella. "Especially for you, especially for you. You selfish girl! You should be grateful at least you have a family." She hiccuped on a sob. "All I have left of Mamma and Papa is the scent of African violets. Mamma's favorite perfume."

Her weeping was jagged and keening now, like that of an inconsolable, heartbroken child.

After Papa and Olimpio finally coaxed Mamma to bed, Mariella and Nonna lingered on the balcony and watched the morning rise. A thin band of light on the horizon cast a rosy glow on the red tiled roofs and buildings, reflected in windowpanes like flashes of gold. Buildings were crowded together, a patchwork of apartments, houses, baroque monuments, and taller commercial structures, edifices ancient and modern, built of stone and plaster and lava rock from Mount Etna's slopes.

"So now there's only one thing you can do," Nonna said after a time. "You have to move to your San Francisco."

"What? Oh, God, I can't do that!" Mariella started to hyperventilate, as she had earlier in the trattoria. She bent forward and held her head in her hands, trying to catch her breath.

"You can," Nonna said. "And you have it keep it secret because "—she nodded her head toward Mamma and Papa's room—"you know they'll find a way to stop you."

"Look at me," Nonna said. "Look at me." She urged Mariella upright and stroked her granddaughter's aching forehead. "I've got some money," she whispered. "And what else would I do with it? My sweet, beautiful granddaughter, if you want to do big things in the world, then you have to go to a bigger world. And if you remain here, they'll never leave you alone."

Chapter Six

Matteo came to Mariella's door four evenings in a row after graduation night.

The first two days she lay immobilized in bed in her darkened room, suffering the second migraine of her life. Even moving her eyes from side to side felt like a wound probed by the thumb of a giant. The first headache had arrived with the onset of her *mestruazioni*, when she was just eleven: a tidal wave of grown-up hormones flooding her still childlike body.

And now, a tsunami of a different sort: a sea change, a burden too powerful to bear. "A minute's shutdown for rewiring and repair," Nonna had whispered when she'd brought cool cloths for her granddaughter's forehead. For pain she'd brought Naproxen, which had little effect on either the ache in Mariella's head or the hurt deeper inside.

Mamma knew enough to leave her alone.

On the third evening, Mariella ventured out with Matteo for a *caffè* at the bar across the street.

"We have to talk," he said, holding her arm to give support, but she was still too dizzy and nauseated, hungover from the migraine itself, even to speak or to stand with him at the counter for more than a few minutes. The soft recessed café lighting overhead glared at her as if they were 1000-watt stadium lamps.

On the fourth night, she was able to go with him for a slow, longer walk around her neighborhood, old apartment buildings of stone and stucco cheek by jowl with the *panetteria*, the *enoteca*, the *salumeria*, and the newsagent's, the shops interspersed and sheltered with striped blue or red awnings for patrons to sit under at small bistro tables.

Matteo reached for her hand, and she let him tuck it, with his, into the pocket of his light summer jacket. Would he notice she wasn't wearing her engagement ring? A simple diamond solitaire he'd slipped onto her finger the moment he'd detected a possible yes and before she'd had a chance to change her mind. She'd thought of bringing it in its little velvet box and giving it back to him, but she didn't have the courage for that yet.

My Matteo, she called him silently, wondering where the designation would land inside her. She felt nothing, only numb, invoking his name. She stole glances at him, wishing that she could keep *him* while making his proposal disappear.

"I wish you'd kept our engagement just between us. At least for now," she said, finally speaking.

When he'd first asked her to marry him, he'd promised, "We can wait, maybe even a year. Maybe more. Until after your internship at the embassy." But once she'd tentatively said, "I'm not saying no" once he'd mentioned her "sort of" acceptance to his parents, and once his mother had called to rejoice with hers, well, Mamma had practically run through the streets with the news. Like the Lion of Sicilia, with fresh prey in her jaws.

"Didn't you ever want to marry me?" Matteo asked her now. His forehead creased, his eyebrows knitted together owl-like under the streetlamp, as they did when he thought too hard.

"I do, but . . ." the corners of her mouth turned down, a sad attempt at a smile. She didn't want to hurt him, but inside her rose a form of loathing, an emotion she'd hoped would propel her into a new life, far from the constraints of marriage, and from a mother who eyed her with the spirit of a vulture.

She loved him. What was so wrong? The question she'd asked herself daily for the past months, ever since he'd given her the ring.

"We can still wait a year," he said. "We can wait as long as we want. It's our lives, Mariella."

His parents might be satisfied with waiting—but Mamma? Mamma would be inside her eardrum, rasping, whispering urgently every waking and nightmare moment of every night and day.

"Oh, Matteo, I *do* love you," she insisted, as much an affirmation to herself as reassurance for him. "But I can't ask you to wait, it wouldn't be fair, because I don't know . . ." She twisted from him, the pleading in his eyes nearly too much for her to witness. "No, I do know," she said, facing him again. "Maybe the only thing I know for certain besides I love you is that I can't promise you I'll ever want to get married, and I can't—I won't—ask you to wait."

"I *will* wait for you," he protested, grasping her arm. But already, she felt him pulling inside himself, slipping away. Or perhaps it was herself she felt slipping. "My parents still love you," he said. "They say they understand, but I can tell they're disappointed—more than disappointed. I don't think I've ever seen my father so sad."

It was a mystery to Mariella, why his parents thought so highly of her. She of the gapped front teeth and corkscrew hair, and yet they did care for her, and she for them. She'd come to be at ease with, even to take for granted, the good-natured dinners with lively conversation they simply folded her into whenever she visited Matteo at Villa Gamberini, their family home, as if she belonged, as if she really were the third daughter Bruno wanted her to be. Not like at her home, where "strangers" were rarely allowed inside the apartment, let alone at the dinner table. "I don't want anyone snooping around—what goes on here is none of their business!" Mamma insisted, as if there were actually something to hide except her own dramatics. Just as well no one outside the family witnessed much of those. Although Mamma made those special allowances and special dinners when Matteo visited, because *he* was "special," and for Olimpio's friends because he was Olimpio, the Son King.

Mariella hadn't, wouldn't tell Matteo of her intention, her yearning, to flee. Oh, they'd talked about wanting to escape the "provinces," as they often referred to Sicily. But if he understood the imminence of her plans, he'd offer to flee with her, and she'd only wound him all over again.

They walked silently and settled on a bench on a cobblestone sidewalk, on a street with only pedestrians, and held hands—her right one, thankfully—tracing, as if memorizing the texture and lifelines of one another's palms, the knuckles and bones. Her hand, sturdy and small, his tapered fingers, olive and smooth.

"We'll be all right," she said, after a while, her sorrow for his pain matched only by her own. She didn't *want* to let him go.

She studied his face, weary and unshaven yet still with that same keen dark-eyed intelligence she'd gazed into when they'd talked in earnest or made love. Lying awake until dawn these last nights, she'd imagined the ache in his physical heart, echoing the ache in her head, picturing his plans for the future and the hurt she'd caused.

"You've always had a mind of your own," he said with an uncharacteristic coldness, so unlike the Matteo who'd spoken so tenderly only days before.

But had she always known her own mind? Most young Sicilianas, even those who attended the university, craved the title of signora more than any academic degree or diploma. Her friends had witnessed her outburst at the graduation dinner, but if they genuinely understood she'd turned down Matteo some might even have speculated that Mariella preferred women.

"You'd better go see my parents," he said, looking straight ahead and not at her. "It's the least you owe them." This new Matteo, sharper, protecting himself, but piercing, nonetheless.

She knew she was selfish to want him to love her still, and yet she did.

She'd thought about never facing his parents again, but once she'd explained herself to them, her reluctance to marry and her plans for the future, why of course they'd understand, wouldn't they, because hadn't they impressed on her how much they loved her? They'd likely even give their blessings. She was sure of it. Maybe even keep her place open at their dinner table. Why couldn't she remain part of the family, even if she and Matteo weren't getting married? Still, she wouldn't live well with herself if she appeared to be shirking them, especially out of fear.

She bristled at the idea of owing anybody anything, but, she admitted to herself, she did owe his parents, if for no reason other than respect. Besides, her affection for them was genuine, and so she and Matteo agreed, she would come to the Villa Gamberini on Saturday morning.

Chapter Seven

Mariella saw herself as miniature (she was little to begin with) and felt smaller than usual that Saturday as she stepped through the Villa's sculpted ten-foot iron gate, left ajar in anticipation of her visit. A sprawling pink stucco palace, a three-story frosted layer cake with palm trees and succulents on a rise that sloped gently down to the edge of the sea.

Sylvia Gamberini answered the doorbell. Saturday was the maid's morning off. Mariella had never seen Matteo's mother dressed shabbily, and today was no exception: her summer dress of polished cotton with large red peony blossoms, a matching bow at the side of her waist, belted with a sash. Mariella had considered wearing a sleeveless blouse and jeans with espadrilles, and now she was glad she'd kept the beige espadrilles and settled on a light green summer dress.

"Mariella," Sylvia said, taking her hand and guiding her into the cool, shaded foyer. "I'm so glad to see you." Bruno stood a few feet behind his wife, in a tropical print shirt and light slacks. Matteo had said his father was unhappy with her and Bruno's unsmiling face confirmed the warning.

"Thank you," Mariella said, "for letting me come."

"Matteo's not here," his mother said. "We wanted a chance to talk to you by ourselves and . . . well . . ."

"He didn't want to see you," Bruno chimed in. "He says you two are taking some time."

Was it only a week ago that his parents would have exclaimed their welcome? Embraced her, ushered her immediately into the center of their family where the bustle of their lives took place?

Today, only stiffness and forced manners. Bruno motioned her toward the formal room, only steps away, a barely used chamber of floor to ceiling windows, of drapery and brocade.

"What went wrong, *bella?*" Sylvia began. She and Matteo's father faced her, sitting a little apart, on the long, plush sofa, upholstered in a hunting-scene damask. Mariella felt as if she were positioned for an interrogation, in the straight-backed armchair on the other side of the expansive marble coffee table. All that was missing was a spotlight on her face.

"She doesn't think Matteo's good enough for *her* family," Bruno said with a snide curl to his lip, a side of Matteo's father she'd only heard about but had refused to believe. "Is that it?"

"Bruno," his wife admonished. "Please."

"You know that's not true," Mariella said, finding her voice. "I did . . ." she said. ". . . no, I *do* love your son." She lowered her head to conceal the unexpected tears. "I love you too. How can you think I don't? You've been so good to me."

With her eyes, she appealed to them for recognition of all the pleasures they'd enjoyed in one another's company. Sylvia took a breath, then exhaled, as if about to speak, then thought better of it.

When only blank expressions came back to her, Mariella said, "I just didn't have the courage to say I didn't—I don't think I ever want to marry."

"Well, then," Bruno said, standing, and moving toward the door.

An echo of Mamma's long-ago warning: *You never want to get on the wrong side of the rich or the powerful.* Bruno had connections everywhere, perhaps ranging as far as the embassy in Siracusa.

"I can't . . . I don't believe . . ." This couldn't be, there had to be something to convince them they just weren't seeing things clearly, something she could say . . . "You always said you love me—I don't want to lose you!" she blurted.

"You should have thought of that before today," Bruno said, his voice hard as stone. He held the door open, waiting for Mariella to leave.

Sylvia stood and Mariella had no choice but to follow. On trembling legs and fighting back the urge to protest and wail, she went to Sylvia and proffered a tentative embrace. In spite of Bruno's admonition—"Sylvia! Let her be!"—Matteo's mother embraced her in return, and whispered, "You'll always be the one I wanted him to marry."

"Sylvia!" Bruno cautioned.

Mariella walked past Matteo's father, her head bent, eyes on the gravel path in front, leading to the massive iron gate.

As the Gamberinis' door shut behind her, she wondered if Matteo was already seeing someone else, if that's why he hadn't been home. But she no longer had the right to ask. It dawned on her that he'd finally become what she'd named him: an *affair*, and that now, and perhaps always, she would carry the loss as bittersweet.

Chapter Eight

"**M**ariella, take a look at this," Luisa Romano said, peering at her computer screen at the *Agenzia*. She beckoned Mariella to her desk. Luisa was the owner of *Agenzia Turistica*, the travel agency where Mariella worked, and the only one besides Nonna who knew about Mariella's plans for escape.

"This email came through, just this minute," Luisa said.

June 25, 2000
San Francisco Chronicle
Shared Housing under Classified Ads

Ciao! Second-year student at Hastings looking for room-mate, someone close to my age (25), smart, tidy, and thoughtful. 2 bdrm. apt. freshly painted. Safe, family-oriented neighborhood. Near Golden Gate Park and Andronico's. Laundromat nearby; public transportation the best. Your share, $400 per month. If you are remotely interested in finding out more about me or in being my roommate, send references and contact Leslie at leshardy@comcast.net.

"It's perfect!" Mariella declared.

So why the sweating palms, the gasping for breath, the heart beating fast as a racer's, as it had been too often these past weeks, ever since she'd firmed her plans. Partly, it was her fear of being trapped on the plane, the foreboding of her dreaded claustrophobia. But why couldn't she shake off this heavy, guilt-laden vision of herself as a traitor, deserter of the people she loved, the ones who'd been so good to her. People who had given her life, breath, sustenance. People to whom she owed everything, even Mamma, and especially Papa who loved her so dearly and stood by her, whose heart she was sure would break when he discovered her—she thought of it as *profound*—betrayal. Mamma of course would be enraged, but would she take it out on Papa, or even worse, on Nonna?

Her beloved Nonna, who had already given Mariella the money for a plane ticket and her first few months of rent—she offered, insisted on it, and said, "There's nothing and no one besides you I've been saving it for." Still Mariella couldn't shake the guilt, the fear that despite her grandmother's determination to usher her granddaughter out of captivity, like Demeter welcoming Persephone out of the underworld in Spring, that her leaving would sap the remaining life from her grandmother's bones. Oh, maybe she was being overly dramatic, but the tightness in her chest, the tears welling frequently behind her eyes told her otherwise.

Her grief and remorse about Matteo relentless as well, not only for losing him, but for causing him undeserved pain.

And why was Luisa risking, at the very least, Mamma's wrath, the certain threats to ruin Luisa's reputation if Mariella's mother ever discovered Luisa's part in her daughter's escape. Luisa was helping Mariella with all the paperwork—passport, work visa, applications to graduate schools—and the apartment search. And she'd offered to let Mariella store her suitcase there, in a closet at the *Agenzia*, all packed and ready to go once all the arrangements were in place.

"Why?" Mariella had wondered aloud.

"You need an independent woman with connections, like me, as an ally," Luisa had explained. "Besides, you get to do everything

I wanted to do at your age, but I didn't have the means or the people behind me, *and* I get to live vicariously through you. It brings me satisfaction. Understand? Also, I'm not afraid of your mother."

Mariella hoped that when she was Luisa's age, she'd remember and lend a hand to another young woman, like herself, struggling to break free.

June 26, 2000
(sent by email from *Agenzia Turistica*)

Dear Signorina Leslie;

Auguri! Good news, you have found me, your new roommate for your Lincoln Way apartment! I am Mariella Russo, 22 years old. I think you are Italiana, no? Why else would you say *Ciao*? Andronico's is Italiano name, and *Ciao* is our greeting for hello and goodbye in Italia and here in Sicilia, my home. I am just graduating with the very top honors in *Psicologia*, (Psychology, you would say) *Letteratura*, and also Languages, from the university here in Catania (it is the oldest university in Sicilia and one of the oldest in the world—very old, from 1434).

I am a smart and clean person, like you.

I will study for the advanced degree too!—I have sent my application and my diploma papers to your Professional School and your University of the San Francisco for the semester in the fall, or maybe for the next spring, if I am too late. I have money to pay you, and I will get work in the USA very fast, I am sure. I know the economy has been bad there, but as you can see, I know English (and *la Francaise, und ein wenig Deutsch*) and I am a very good worker. I will come in the middle of July.

So please, don't give your apartment away, and would you send to me over email at Agenzia Turistica, (where I

work part time—I also have the part-time work in a trattoria), I will send you my references as you ask, from the
university and from my employment and if you say yes, a
money order now, to reserve the rent.

Ciao, and Grazie Mille.

Signorina Mariella Russo

———

June 27, 2000
To: Mariella Russo
Agenziaturistica@libero.it
via Finnocchiaro Aprile 110–95129
Catania, Sicilia

From: Leslie Harding
leshardy@comcast.net
853 Lincoln Way
San Francisco, Ca., 94122

Dear Signorina Russo. How did you know? I love everything Italian! I thought I could keep managing the rent
on this apartment on my own, but I am finding it impossible to study as much as I need to now and handle a
nearly full-time job at Gypsy Men's, the clothing store
where I work. Against my better judgment (I'm not the
most trusting person on the planet), of all the inquiries I
received, yours intrigued me the most (and believe me, I
heard from a few weirdos and wackos, like the guy who
asked if he could bring his pet boa constrictor and a
cage full of rats to feed it. I mean really!). Your references
are impeccable. I am saving the apartment for you! The
kitchen is fully equipped—a gas stove and a large pantry
closet—a perfect setting for me, some would say.

A little more about me. I'm hooked on style. I faux
painted the second bedroom (yours, coincidentally, to

look like a room in an Italian villa) myself. I am compulsively neat, considerate, intelligent, and reasonably quiet. I have been known to turn up my Queen, Pavarotti, Nancy Wilson, or Robert Cray CDs full blast (an eclectic blend, I know, but that's me!) to help me grasp a particularly difficult tort action brief—only historical and academic cases, of course, because I'm still a student and not yet practicing law. If I want to shake my booty, I'll go with REM, although my favorite song in the whole world is *Take My Breath Away* by Berlin. Anyway, I can be (politely) persuaded to wear ear phones so you won't be disturbed because it's a stationary CD player. And by the way, no animals allowed.

If you send the money order for July, you can pay for your share of the security deposit when you arrive. My intuition is that we will get along famously.

Ciao, Leslie

Chapter Nine

ariella's knife landed swiftly, solidly, *thunk, thunk, thunk,* again and again, on the cutting surface. She diced celery, carrots, and onions with precision borne of fury, her mother's leering face chopped into progressively tinier bits. She was preparing the *soffritto* for tomorrow's ragu. Sunday lunch: for Sicilian families, the big, important meal of the week.

Mamma sat sideways in her chair across the kitchen, at the small wooden table against the wall, thick stucco, like all the walls in the apartment. She'd folded her arms in front of her, a sentry in an apron, standing guard. She'd finished shelling the fava beans at least fifteen minutes earlier, and still, she remained. Mariella could feel her mother's eyes following her, assessing every move she made. Mamma had claimed another of her "heart pains," giving her the excuse, Mariella believed, to bark another of her endless commands: "I'll supervise. *You* make the sauce."

If her mother uttered even one more word about the size of the carrots (*Don't be so clumsy. You're making them too big!*) or anything about her corkscrew hair (*Maybe if you cut your silly curls, they wouldn't fall all over your face and you could actually SEE what you're doing, stupid girl!*) Mariella swore to herself, she *would* take this knife to her.

Forgotten, for the moment, as the knife sounded over and over on the board, was not only her excitement, but also the terror, the remorse, and the sorrow that had plagued her, kept her from sleeping these past weeks. Made her throw up more than once, made her nearly lose her resolve and run to Matteo's big pink palace and plead forgiveness. She'd never been on a plane before, never, in fact, left home, let alone planned an escape more than halfway across the world. And never lived without Nonna's and Papa's soothing, reassuring words when she was frightened and alone.

Tomorrow. Her last day, her last meal with her family. She silently chortled at the sudden image of herself as Christ surrounded by his disciples at the Last Supper. And who else but Mamma would be Judas, the one who would plot against her? The one who would watch her with a fish-eye stare at the same time she would turn away. The one who had always turned away. Or maybe her traitor would be Bruno Gamberini, insinuating himself, posturing as family, like Iscariot in Da Vinci's painting—she'd lingered over a color photo of it one afternoon in a glossy art book at the university library—a Judas audacious enough to look her in the eye.

But wasn't *she* the real traitor? The deviant, turning her back on all of them?

She gathered up the sizable mound of diced vegetables against the back of her knife and lowered them carefully into the olive oil, just this side of smoking, in the ragu pot.

Mamma blurted, "You think you know everything? You make me sick!"

Mariella paused, garlic in one hand, knife in the other. She'd just cut off a bulb from the braid hanging near the stove. She stepped, quickly, toward her mother.

"Then why, Mamma," she said, waving the knife in the air, leaning close to her mother's face. "Why do you invite—no insist—why do you *insist* I come into the kitchen to help you, every single time?" She wasn't thinking about the knife in her hand. It was simply there, as she gestured, and when she realized she was brandishing it, she laughed. She'd never have the courage to deliberately, consciously, threaten her mother this way. She slapped the knife down, hard, along with the garlic, on the wooden table.

Mamma gasped and put her hand to her throat. Her coal black eyes widened and darkened so that Mariella couldn't distinguish the irises from the pupils. Maybe this was another of Mamma's acts. So what if she was afraid? How many times had her mother intimidated *her*, tried to make her feel powerless and unworthy?

"Is it because you like to have someone smaller than you to boss around?" Mariella demanded. "Huh?" She was nearly four inches shorter than her mother. This felt good, this advantage, with her mother sitting down.

"Is it because I remind you of someone you hate?" *Zia* Locasta, the spiteful aunt who'd raised Mamma, now living out her last, lonely, brain-addled days in a government nursing home across town? But would her mother be so mean if she realized this might be the last time she and Mariella would be together, in this kitchen? Mamma was always telling her she was funny-looking, gap-toothed, and calling the smattering of golden brown freckles just under her eyes, along the bony tops of her cheeks, "dirty spots."

"Or is it because you need someone to be mad at because you can't stand your own life?"

"Ohh! Don't you pull that university *psicologico merda* on me," her mother snapped back, rising suddenly, over her daughter. "You think you're so intelligent don't you? Well, I've got news for you."

She had to stop herself from snickering at Mamma standing there, hands on her hips, a caricature of herself. The way she stood when Mariella imitated her to her friends and talked in her mother's loud, raspy voice.

Mamma lowered herself toward her chair, missed the

edge—deliberately, Mariella thought—and landed, first on her knees, and then, bracing herself with her hands, on all fours.

"What's Mamma doing on the floor?" Olimpio asked, backing up and stepping inside the kitchen, on his way past. He had his mother's black hair and dark piercing eyes and his father's (usually) sweet disposition. He blushed when the local girls called after him—"Olimpio, Olimpio!" as he drove his green Vespa through the streets on his way to the university or to his after school job at the *enoteca*. Mariella knew this because of the many rides he'd given her to school or to one of those jobs that had earned her the money to make this journey.

She shook her head and turned down her mouth in disgust, meant for only her brother to see. How many performances like these had they been witness to?

Mamma moaned, as if she'd been poisoned and dying. Too quickly, she sat back on her haunches and raised her agonized face to Heaven. Really, to the kitchen ceiling. Refusing—batting away—Mariella's offer of an arm to help her back to her feet, her mother swayed on her knees and looked as if she might pass out.

"Salvatore!" Mamma yelled, a cross between a bark and a command. "Salvatore!"

"Be careful, *mia*," Papa cautioned his wife, entering moments later. He went to her side, but in no great rush. Mamma was as strong as a mountain goat.

"Salvatore, make her stop," she implored, and reached up to him, managing to grab his pant leg. "Make her stop! She can't talk to me this way, Salvatore."

Papa tried to lift Mamma, carefully, from under her arms, but she collapsed back into herself. He looked twenty years older in an instant, as he always did when Mamma indulged in one of her episodes. Twenty years older. Fragile and torn.

Mariella kept a close watch on her mother as she spoke to her father and brother. "Mamma's acting like I've threatened her, like she's afraid I'll stab her with this knife," she said, picking up the implement and giving it a shake for good measure. "Even though she knows that nothing happened and she's only pretending."

"Madonna!" Mamma wailed, lifting her eyes to the statue of Santa Agatha in the wall niche.

Olimpio brought a dampened cloth and a plastic-lined waste bin from under the sink. He knelt and began, quietly, to pick up the bean hulls Mamma had swept off the table on her way down.

"No!" Mamma cried, seizing Olimpio's hand. "It's her job. Not for you, not for my son!" She sobbed in great gulps, gasping for air. Olimpio dropped the cloth next to the mess on the floor and wrapped his arm around his mother's shoulders.

"It's *your* job," Mamma said, pointing at Mariella. She struggled, with Olimpio's and Papa's help, up off her knees.

"No, her job is to live her life, and you can all stop the silly talk right now," Nonna said, making her appearance in the entryway. "You didn't need to call me; you're making so much noise, I heard you all the way in my room." She wore her everyday costume: the chunky-heeled old-lady shoes, laced-up and black, support hose, and today's floral print rayon dress, purple. Her long gray hair was braided and coiled on top of her head, as always, like a crown.

"Nonna!" Mariella cried. She rushed to her grandmother and threw her arms around her. "Thank you. Thank you for understanding, always."

"You should be ashamed of yourselves," Nonna Giuseppina said to her son and daughter-in-law over Mariella's shoulder. Nonna was once five foot two, same as Mariella, and at seventy-three, her body still testified to its once toned, sturdy frame. She was the only one who could keep Mamma in line.

"Stand up for what you believe, Salvatore," Nonna said. "Trust me, your wife will fall in love with you all over again."

Nonna gave Mamma a slow, warning stare as she passed by

her. Mamma opened and closed her mouth like a fish gasping for oxygen.

"Mari," Olimpio said, catching his sister's eye and looking as stern as he could muster, given his naturally agreeable demeanor. A directive for Mariella to keep silent. She knew her brother disapproved of her rebellious nature, but she also knew he loved her, maybe even envied her for it. "Take me with you," he'd said when she'd confessed to him, only two days earlier, that she and Nonna were conspiring, planning her escape. She needed his help getting to the airport. "Send for me when you get settled. I suffer the island fever just like you."

Mamma clutched her chest, near her heart. "I'm. Going. To. Bed," she said, biting off each word, as if she were trying to keep her teeth from falling out of her mouth. "Go ahead. Have lunch without me."

That afternoon's Saturday meal would be simple: a clear soup, good crusty bread with *caciocavallo* or *pecorino* cheese, perhaps some fruit. Tomorrow's lunch was the important one.

Most of the time her mother's petty vindictiveness rolled off Mariella's back, but sometimes, like now, when the unseasonable late June downpour matched her own gray mood, and she was captive to this claustrophobic apartment, albeit for perhaps the last time, her mother's bitterness pierced too deep.

Her knife hit the board even harder, mincing the garlic, and nearly mashing it into a pulp. She slid the garlic into the pot and let it brown with the *soffritto* a moment or two.

On her own, last week, she'd traveled an hour by train to the hill town of Piazza Armerina as a fitting, final pilgrimage before leaving the island behind. The annual Palio races would be held there, in August, celebrating Sicily's liberation from the Saracens in the 1100s. Her own liberation would take place nearly nine hundred years later, in a single day. She'd stolen those private, secret hours in Piazza Armerina to stretch out under the

Mediterranean sun, and on the brink of breaking the sacred Sicilian code: *la famiglia e tutto*. Family is everything, an unwritten commandment so old and ingrained that anyone who dared go against it risked being regarded as an outcast, or even an outlaw.

She missed Matteo, most times keenly. They'd tried being together casually, once or twice, but it had been too painful for them both. Still, when she'd finally tried to return his ring, he'd refused. "Can't you at least keep something beautiful from me?" he'd lamented. "It was only for you. I would never give it to anyone else."

If only he'd understood, believed, how much beauty she *had* received from him.

There were brief moments she didn't think of him at all. But as she'd sat on the ground that day, she remembered their wanton afternoons, her delight in unabashedly splaying herself on his unmade bed. Would she ever have sex . . . ? Probably. But the bigger question was whether she'd ever again know what it was to make love. Now, in the kitchen on her last Saturday, she built the *ragu* of already seared chunks of pork loin and sweet pork sausages, diced tomatoes, sun-dried tomato paste, a bay leaf or two, oregano, a sprig of rosemary and a pinch of marjoram. She added water and a good dollop of red wine, salt, and a sprinkle of red pepper flakes. She then balanced the wooden cooking spoon on the rim of the pot, under a lid, covering the sauce but allowing for just enough moisture to escape. The sauce would simmer for hours. When it was reheated and simmered longer, again tomorrow, the flavors would be layered and rich. *Sposato*, as chefs liked to say. Something she didn't want to be: married.

Chapter Ten

When Mariella poked her head into the kitchen Sunday morning, Mamma appeared to have recovered from her "fit of the heart." Her mother's expression was self-satisfied, smug, and she was humming to herself—something familiar, a haunting melody—as she stuffed the cannoli shells with ricotta and chocolate bits. Cannoli was Mamma's pièce de résistance, her *cavallo di battaglia*, her unreproducible, secret formula (no one in their neighborhood came close to making it so well), the enterprise that would keep her sequestered all morning in the kitchen. The filling with chocolate bits was Mariella's favorite.

The moment Mamma realized Mariella was there, in the doorway, the moment their eyes met, was the same moment Mariella recognized the melody. Her mother's mouth froze into an "O," her stuffing spoon paused in midair, her humming suspended as Mariella looked from the chocolate bits back to the cannoli shells: the dessert Connie Corleone poisoned her uncle Don Altobello with in the movie *The Godfather*. It was Don Altobello's favorite dessert as well. The tune was the theme from that film.

Mother and daughter stared at each other. And then they both broke out laughing.

Mamma may have been ignorant, and sometimes a fool, but she wasn't stupid. And even if Mamma was vindictive, Mariella couldn't believe her mother capable of genuine evil. Still, she couldn't ignore that crawly feeling at the back of her neck. Was it possible Mamma had gotten wind of her plan to escape?

Later that morning, when everyone else in the household was busy—Papa tugging on his hair as he swore at his computer screen, poring over spreadsheets and client accounts, Mamma fussing over her cannoli, and Olimpio tinkering with his green Vespa down in the street—Mariella and her grandmother again stole moments alone, out on the balcony.

"You must never tell your mother Olimpio knows about your plan," Nonna said as Mariella slouched onto the sun-bleached canvas couch. They watched her brother, three stories below, hunched over the green Vespa's front wheel, tapping at something with what looked like a tiny hammer.

"Why?" Mariella asked. "She won't punish him. She never punishes him." She sat up and tried, futilely, to smooth the wrinkles from her linen pants. "It'll be me she's furious with, probably forever." Maybe Mamma would forgive her someday: for leaving the family, for refusing to marry Matteo, for destroying her dreams for social status, for unknown insurrections and grudges Mariella would never be able, or even want, to make right. Maybe it was better that Mamma didn't forgive her. For now, her mother's anger gave Mariella something to push against, a force to keep her strong.

It was Papa's heart she worried about breaking.

Nonna reached out and touched the back of her hand to Mariella's cheek. "Aren't you just a little afraid, *mia*?"

Terrified was more like it, but simultaneously excited. So full of longing to be in America, to live a life other than the stifling, stove-bound existence of a Sicilian *casalinga*, she worried she might die before she even got there. And yet she couldn't stop thinking about that long flight, and that she was claustrophobic in the extreme.

"I feel two ways, at least," Mariella said, and Nonna nodded as if she understood.

On the sly, Mariella had gone to her trusted family doctor a few days before. Dr. Torrisi had given her a prescription for an antianxiety medication—Xanax, Dr. Torrisi called it—and reassured Mariella that she would not become addicted unless she took it every day for a long time. No worry there. She had never liked being out of control. Had never liked tight, small spaces like elevators or going through long tunnels. And, Dr. Torrisi promised, with the medication, she would not be afraid.

Cold comfort, Mariella thought, for one whose palms sweated and stomach churned every time she even imagined herself hurtling through space in the belly of a metal capsule for which she'd actually paid her hard-earned money to endure. Dr. Torrisi suggested Mariella start taking the Xanax a few days before she left, to get her brain and her body acclimated. She decided to ignore the advice and take her first pill just before she boarded the plane.

"You look so innocent," Nonna said, again stroking the side of her granddaughter's face. "And so eager, like the little girl I remember on your first day of school, with pigtail braids to your waist."

Nonna studied the narrow street, mostly deserted during the late afternoon. She seemed far away, as though remembering Jeremy, who might appear beneath her balcony, as Mariella imagined he must have done so many years before. But no, there was only the old orange neighborhood cat and a wiry street vendor rattling his empty cart across the uneven stones.

The owner of the cheese shop across the way rolled up his maroon awning to open for business after church. On Sundays, hard goods businesses remained closed, but purveyors of food opened briefly in preparation for lunch and again in the late afternoon, in anticipation of the evening's *passeggiata*, when the streets would fill with Catanians in their Sunday best: young couples holding hands, followed several feet behind by their *famiglie*, the ever present chaperones. Married couples leisurely pushing strollers in the balmy evening air and savoring their favorite cones of gelato. The old ones would be there too, either with their husbands or wives, if their spouses were still alive, or perhaps on the arm of a loving granddaughter, as Nonna would be, later that evening, on Mariella's.

Another awning, a blue one, and then a red and another green one, all opened at once. The wife of the wine shop owner stepped from the shop onto the cobblestones. An outgoing woman in her fifties or maybe late forties, with a stocky, fireplug-shaped body. As she glanced up, she saw Mariella and Nonna. They waved and called back and forth, "*Buonasera, buonasera!* See you tonight, on the street!"

How nice it would be if Papa and Olimpio and Nonna would sit outside with me, at one of the little enoteca bistro tables and take a grappa or a Cinzano before bedtime. Mamma would never agree to come. She'd say she was too upset or too embarrassed to be seen in public with her daughter who refused to marry a handsome, rich young man who would someday be mayor. Mamma used to come—she wasn't always that way.

Nonna sighed so deeply it seemed to emanate from the ground, wending its way to the balcony and up through her body. Mariella wondered if her grandmother would cry. But Nonna just smiled, as if silence was her way of paying tribute, of keeping the dignity of her memories sacred and alive, and also, Mariella guessed, because her Nonna didn't want to ruin the gravity of her granddaughter's last hours at home.

"After Jeremy died, and then again, many years later, after your Nonno Samuele died, something inside, something that wouldn't give up made me keep eating and breathing and hanging on. I tell you this," Nonna said, "because if I could be so strong not knowing what my future held, you will be too."

All Mariella wanted was enough determination to leave her family, enough courage to get on that plane.

Nonna brushed her eyelids as if trying to wipe away stray

eyelashes. But Mariella saw her grandmother's wet cheeks and reached for her hand.

"I've told you about the bellowing that went on when Jeremy told Mamma and Papa I'd already left on the train for England," Nonna said. "My father even threatened to shoot him."

"Did *bisnonno* really keep a gun?" Mariella asked. Thank God her own mother didn't have one. She wouldn't put it past Mamma, not to kill her, but she could picture her mother shooting her in the foot or the leg. She shuddered, remembering the song Mamma hummed as she stuffed the cannoli that morning.

Maybe someday, as Nonna said, there would be another man for her, someone she would love as much as she loved Matteo, as much as Nonna had loved Jeremy, but now, the only thoughts she could allow herself were of a more practical nature: had she packed the right kind of clothes for San Francisco fog, her passport and visa, her credit card and traveler's checks, computer and cell phone, the American dollars she'd exchanged lira for, and enough clean underwear for the first week of her new life? At Nonna's urging, she'd accepted Luisa Romano's offer to store her large packed suitcase in a closet at the travel agency, away from snooping eyes. All she'd carry out of the house tomorrow morning was her purse.

Now the street was half in shadow, half in early evening sun.

Nonna reached into a pocket of her dress and dropped a small blue velvet pouch into Mariella's hand. "I want you to take this with you."

Mariella rolled the pouch in her fingers to get a feel for what the "it" might be. A *San Giuseppi di Cupertino* medal, the patron saint of air travel, to keep her safe? A rosary? Not likely. Her Nonna wasn't any more faithful a Catholic than she, and unlike Mariella, who simply found good excuses not to go to Mass anymore ("I have to work . . . to study . . . to help . . .") Nonna flat out refused.

"No *mia*, open it." Nonna pointed at the little velvet bag.

Mariella eased open the strings and felt inside. She knew right away, a simple gold band, her grandmother's wedding ring from Jeremy.

"Are you sure, Nonna?"

"Who else in the world would I want to give it to? Besides, I can't wear it here without everyone asking questions. Of course I could say it was the first ring Sam gave me, before this one." Samuele Rosso, Mariella's grandfather, the second man to make her grandmother a widow, and the only man Mariella had ever called Nonno.

Nonna turned her filigreed wedding band from Samuele around and around, on the ring finger of hands with bones like filament. "But I've always meant Jeremy's ring for you. And what better time than right now?"

You mean in case you die before I come back, Mariella thought. She slipped her grandmother's ring onto the third finger of her right hand. "I don't want to look like I'm married," she said.

"No, no," Nonna said. "*Certo*. But maybe it will help you to remember that I'm always in here." She patted her granddaughter's chest, above her heart. "And maybe, in the new country, it will keep you married to your own soul."

Chapter Eleven

*L*unch was a fraught affair. Although Mariella did her best to keep up a natural, easy front, she was edgy and alert for any clues that Mamma and Papa had found her out. It was guilt making her so squirrely, as she imagined her parents chaining her to her bedpost or putting bars on her bedroom window and locking her in. Olimpio made matters worse by making faces whenever she glanced his way, raising and lowering his eyebrows rapidly, practically all the way to his scalp, like the old-time American comedian she'd seen on TV: Groucho Marks on *You Bet Your Life*.

When Mamma sailed into the dining room bearing her silver platter of cannoli, Mariella fastened her eyes on each plate her mother served. Of course Olimpio got the first cannoli and the one with the most filling. Papa was next, and if it bothered him that Mamma always favored Olimpio, he never let it show. Nonna asked for only a half. When it was Mariella's turn, Mamma made a big display of searching the platter for "Another nice big one for our girl."

"No," Mariella said. "I'll take the other half of Nonna's." She rubbed her stomach to show she was full from Nonna's stuffed artichokes, and from the *mostaccioli* dressed with her own ragu.

"Okay," Mamma said, then shrugged and took a big bite of the cannoli she'd meant for Mariella before placing it on her own plate.

∞

"Oomph!" Olympio grunted as he hefted Mariella's stuffed canvas suitcase into the clown-sized trunk of their parents' blue Fiat the following morning. The suitcase landed with a thump, and he rocked it back and forth to ease in the wheels over the lip.

"Shh, quiet," she whispered, looking up at their apartment. Everyone here, except the very wealthy with mansions and garages, parked their cars and Vespas on the street. It was the hour just before dawn. "You'll wake Mamma and Papa."

"Geez Mariella, you'll never manage this by yourself," he whispered back. "I can barely close the lid." Sweat glistened above his lip and on his forehead.

In the semi-dark, Mariella was frantically rummaging through her tan leather shoulder bag. She pulled out a book, three lipsticks, sunglasses, and a large envelope with her important papers, along with a myriad of other items she laid on the hood of the Fiat: eyedrops, a pair of socks, a hairbrush, a wallet, and a small pouch holding an aqua blue ceramic Tinacria totem for good luck, the symbol of Sicily, the smiling woman with three bent legs circling her face like a windmill. The same pouch in which Nonna had given her Jeremy's ring. Only this morning, in darkness, she'd slipped the ring onto the third finger of her right hand. She wore the Movado watch from Matteo on her left wrist.

"Whew!" she said, holding up her bottle of Xanax. "I thought for a minute I'd left it hidden in my bureau." She shoved everything back into her bag, handling the envelope with special care.

The plan was for Olimpio to be back at the apartment before Mamma and Papa were out of bed. Before they realized neither of their children were home.

On the drive to *Aeroporto di Catania-Fontanarossa Vincenzo Bellini*—named for the great composer and Catania's prized native son, Olimpio kept swiveling his head from the road to her as if, perhaps, he looked at her hard enough, he'd see that this was only a farce, a complicated joke. Mariella felt sorry for him, for leaving him behind. How would he face Mamma down when she understood her daughter had escaped? That he'd *helped* her escape. Or would he face her down?

Or lie, instead, and say he'd witnessed Mariella riding away in a taxi?

She watched the parched, desert-like landscape pass by in the early morning gray, the sun peeking over the horizon on its ascent. She'd been assured by Signora Romano, at the *Agenzia*, that it would be a good, clear day for flying.

"Mamma, she's never felt special, like she belonged to someone, or someone belonged to her, like you and Nonna belong to each other," Olimpio said. He and his grandmother loved each other too, but it was different between Mariella and Nonna. The two women, so alike, yet generations apart. "Sometimes she doesn't even believe that Papa really loves her—she told me so. Just that he's obliged to stay with her, even after all this time. Nonna says she's jealous of Papa's love for you."

"I know," Mariella said. "Nonna told me the same thing." She was too worn out to think about her mother, too tired, really, to worry about her mother's motivations. She had to muster every speck of nonexistent oomph to propel herself forward, to usher herself onto that plane. Fear had kept her from sleep.

All night, she'd trotted from her bed to the bathroom, wiped her bottom so many times she'd rubbed it raw. Her insides in a nervous roil. Applied salve to her sore rear—something Nonna had brought to her room—Italian Balm: mineral oil, olive oil, glycerin, cocoa butter, and rose water to make her *stronzo* smell like flowers.

She'd fly first to *Roma*, and then on to a place called New Jersey, and from there, six hours more to San Francisco. Luisa

Romano had arranged all the flights, with her travel agent's discount.

"It'll be a long journey," Luisa had cautioned her. "Two days, with all the stopovers, and watch your purse, don't set it down, even for a minute, and don't fall asleep at the airport, especially Newark. But sleep as much as you can on the planes. Oh, and drink plenty of water."

At the airport, Olimpio parked the car, heaved Mariella's suitcase out of the trunk, and paused to look up and watch the jets arrive and depart, spiriting passengers to Rome, England, Algiers, and who knew where. Like Mariella, he'd never been on a plane before.

"Oh, wow, I'd give anything to be on one of those big jet planes. Just to be going—anywhere!" he exclaimed. Mariella recognized the excitement in his gaze, for her—she was actually going!—and for the same yearning in him that coursed through her, and she felt both eager for the day her brother might fly away, and fear for herself, along with another pang of remorse. It comforted her only a little to think her leaving might help Olimpio break free.

She grasped his hand and closed her eyes against incipient tears.

Inside the terminal, he kept glancing at his watch, itching to be home before he was missed.

"Oh, hey, Mariella," his farewell almost an afterthought as Mariella readied her ticket for the counter attendant. "Text me," he said, "as soon as you get there. Write me and don't forget to send for me too!"

He hugged Mariella with so much tenderness, and so fiercely he squeezed the breath from her lungs.

"Oh, 'Limpio," she said, not even trying now to hold back tears. "It won't be forever. But I'll miss you and Papa and Nonna"—she could not bring herself to say, "And Mamma too."—"everyday." She tugged on her brother's arm. "Take care of Nonna, please . . .

and Matteo too. His heart is so tender. Explain to him, make him understand."

Her brother stood and waved and watched as she walked toward the security line.

"I promise I'll text and write you!" she turned back and called to him. "I promise."

Inside the gates, she took a Xanax, drank a cappuccino, and wondered if she should eat now—she was so nervous: about flying, about dying, about everything! Did she have enough lira to see her through to Rome? Enough American dollars for Newark and San Francisco airports. She checked and double-checked her wallet for at least the twentieth time. Or should she wait and eat on the plane once she'd calmed down. *Fat chance of calming down*, she thought. *If I'm going to die, I'd at least like to have one last taste of my native land.* She ordered a soft Italian roll with butter and jam. She was so jumpy, the roll turned to cardboard in her mouth, her heart threatened to pound right out of her chest, and the roar of the ocean whooshed in her ears. The unknown, the prospect of being trapped on a plane, leaving home—all of it, awakening and firing up the nerves under her skin, crawly, as if they were insects on the move.

It was all she could do not to turn tail and go home, and beg for indulgence, like a bereft and banished child, sent away for the summer to a family she'd never met.

Dr. Torrisi was wrong. One Xanax was not enough to calm her fears, but when the second kicked in she was able to notice how fashionable some of the international travelers were, mostly Italian and French-speaking women in soft leather ankle boots or strappy sandals, with designer scarves, some with the hand-painted silk Sicilian-style foulard scarf draped over their shoulders, even in jeans. She'd packed two in her suitcase, one with lemons, another of cactus flowers near the sea. And some men in elegant suits or tailored dress shirts or polos; *how cosmopolitan*, she thought. Only a handful of the ones with northern

European and maybe some American accents wore the sort of short pants and jackets one would see at a gym.

On the short Alitalia flight to Rome, Mariella lowered her chin to her chest and grasped the arms of her seat so tight her hands went numb, her palms sweating so profusely they slid off the hard plastic grips. When she raised her head, she met the eyes of her middle seat mate whom she accidentally poked, an old man in a suit that smelled of mothballs, and into whose ear she chattered, nonstop, for the first half-hour. While she was talking, he'd simply fallen asleep. Now, he regarded her as if she were the lady at the circus with three heads.

The old man had already lived a long life, and so it wasn't as big a deal if *he* died in a plane crash. Or went crazy because he was trapped in a metal capsule and couldn't escape. But she still had her whole life ahead of her.

On the ten-hour flight to New Jersey, and after her third Xanax, she fell into a dopey, dreamless sleep, and when she awoke to a night sky somewhere over the Atlantic ocean, she was appalled at the saliva dribbling out of her mouth—some of it dried onto her chin—and onto her prized black cashmere cardigan.

Chapter Twelve

"Welcome to San Francisco!" The flight attendant woman at the front of the plane was so loud. Did she have to shout? Like one of those hearty blonde all-American women with big hair and big smiles, the ones you see on game show TV or beauty pageants. The woman's voice rang in Mariella's ears like a high-pitched steel drum. Her ears hadn't yet cleared from the plane's descent.

This was a really bad idea, the fear was back, worse than ever since she'd been in the United States and she hadn't taken any more Xanax at Newark because that experience had rattled her, shocked her really, and she needed to keep awake, so maybe, she considered, she should just stay on the plane and turn around and fly home.

There had been no "Welcome to the USA!" going through that long customs line at Newark airport yesterday—was it yesterday? She'd lost track of time. Immigration had been okay, the other passengers around her mostly friendly, many from her own flight, several of whom were Italian, and all foreigners like her, perhaps feeling kinship with the same anxiety and anticipation as she of being in a new country. And, the robust immigration lady *had* wished her a "Welcome to the United States!" as she'd stamped her passport.

But the man in a dark blue uniform who'd inspected her luggage in customs hadn't even looked at her, and why had they tagged her suitcase with a yellow strip anyway? She'd felt as much shame as if she'd somehow been discovered as a criminal. That customs officer had plowed through her suitcase and shoulder bag, his hands in plastic gloves as if her clothing carried a disease, insinuating himself into her privacy with sneaky, violating fingers, and when he had finished, he left her belongings in disarray and yelled, "Next!" to the person behind her in line. Mean, with a smug look, like she imagined a prison guard or one of Mussolini's soldiers who'd invaded Catania when Nonna was a girl.

So many people at that Newark airport were in bad clothes, sweatsuits that looked like pajamas, some wearing slippers instead of shoes. *One thing about Italians, we know how to dress.* For some reason that thought had comforted her, helped her to hang onto herself. Lots of fat people there too. Maybe too much bad pizza. Trash on the floor and filthy restrooms. Frayed chairs and seats in the waiting areas. No wonder Luisa Romano had cautioned her to hang onto her purse, "Everywhere, but especially at Newark," she'd said.

Were these the Americans she'd longed to live among? The elegant ones, emanating style and warmth, the friendly ones she'd been certain would greet her with open arms.

That slice of pizza she ate at the Newark airport made her homesick, only two bites, and maybe sick to her stomach too. How long had it been since she'd had a full meal? Sometime yesterday, on the *Alitalia* flight out of Rome. *Another thing about Italians, we know how to cook.*

Exhaustion, without Xanax, exacerbated Mariella's fear. *I really don't think I can do this.* She moved up the plane's aisle toward the exit door that would lead her into the San Francisco Airport. *I can barely move my legs.* But okay, finally she was stepping out of the plane, through the breezeway, and oh, it was so bright inside this San Francisco terminal, glaring and noisy, and she didn't know where to go. At least it was cleaner and more spacious than

Newark and people dressed a little better here. Everyone talking so fast, and even though she had studied English in high school and at university, half of what she heard over the loudspeakers and from people around her didn't make any sense. She didn't know why but it felt like a different kind of bustle from Italy, people didn't look so happy or friendly, nobody saying "*Ciao!*" but *okay, think*, she told herself, *you've got to find the sign for suitcases.* There's the sign, "Baggage claim," with a suitcase, just like Luisa had told her, so just follow the arrows.

"Help you, miss?" the nice man behind the boarding desk asked.

"What? Me? Do I look lost? Baggage claim," she said, and he looked at her funny.

"Valigia?" he said, and she realized she'd just spoken to him in Italian.

"Suitcase . . . baggage," she said.

"Carousel D3. Down two flights, follow the signs and arrows."

Her big green suitcase was so heavy she couldn't lift it off the conveyor, as Olimpio had warned. When it came around the second time, the young athletic-looking man next to her lifted it off like a feather. His dark blue T-shirt said Golden State Warriors, and in a yellow circle was the silhouette of a bridge, the famous Golden Gate Bridge.

"Thank you, thank you."

"No problem," he said, his blue eyes set off against dark skin. Finally someone who smiled at her.

Taxi, where do I find a taxi. There's the sign for outside. She was shaking and sweating so hard she felt it running down her sides, under her clothes. What was she doing here? Okay, that taxi, the one who waved at her from outside the line of taxis was stopping for her. Yellow with "Speedy Taxi," painted on the side. It looked okay, like a regular taxi. Luisa had told her only to take a taxi from the official stand, but she was so tired, and he looked all right and at least now she wouldn't have to wait in that long line. After customs, no thank you, no more lines.

"Where to?"

But she could barely understand him; he wasn't speaking English. Oh, okay English with an accent . . . German? Maybe German, yes, she thought, or Dutch, maybe Scandinavian. Anyway, somewhere from northern Europe. His hair was shaved military-style, close to his sunburnt scalp. His arms, visible to her, rested on the top of the steering wheel and were thick with muscle, the kind one gets from lifting weights.

"San Francisco," she said.

"Bay Bridge?" he said.

"Si, si, yes, San Francisco."

His name with the photo on his dashboard said Armin Hofstader. She couldn't see a license or a meter but told herself it was only because she was too short to see over the back of the seat.

"Here," she said, waving the map she pulled out of her purse, which Armin Hofstader couldn't see from the front seat. "Lincoln Way, San Francisco. Near the oak tree," she said. That's what Leslie wrote in her email. Across the street from the famous park with the oak tree. "How much?"

Armin craned his neck over the back of his seat to look at the map. Mariella leaned forward with it, pointing to Lincoln Way.

Armin waved at the map, as if he could see right where she pointed. "Okay," he said. "Twenty dollars. You relax. I'll get you there. I know."

"Okay, sure," she said. "San Francisco." Twenty dollars was a lot out of her budget, but she supposed that was standard fare. And did he have to play that music so loud? Why was everything here so loud? She couldn't hear what he said next, couldn't understand him. And that really was screeching music, metallic rock.

One thing for sure, even though they both knew English, they were not speaking the same language.

They crossed a long bridge and signs for places like Richmond, Oakland, and other towns, but no San Francisco started looming up outside the smudged and smoky taxi window. "Where are we? Where are we?" she kept asking. He was not taking her to San Francisco. "Help!" She started to yell at him. "San Francisco!" She shouted, but they were still on the bridge, and he kept going and saying "Yes, yes," and now they were across and turning off at the place called Richmond, and he was stopping in the middle of this dirty street with only dark people, a few younger ones with backwards baseball caps on a streetcorner, smoking and staring mean slow looks at their taxi as they drove by. She was at home with black people from Morocco and Tunisia in Catania, and friends at university too, but there was garbage here worse than Newark airport, and falling apart houses with a few people standing or sitting on steps in their raggedy front yards with dirt and weeds, and ugly old cars, some with no wheels but just the metal rod where the wheel fits on.

"You want out here?" he asked.

I am going to die, he is going to kill me, and Mamma will know she was right after all.

"I told you San Francisco! Why you bring me here?"

"It will cost you more to go to San Francisco," he said. She understood. He knew she wouldn't get out of the taxi there, knew she didn't know where to go. Knew she was lost.

"You did this on purpose! You planned this; you are trying to rob me because I don't speak the English so good! Like you don't too!"

Armin laughed at her, but they were turning around and he didn't even care, or seem to, that she was crying, but at least, for the moment, she was still alive. She wouldn't look at him, or even what was outside the window, but just rested her head in her hands, against the window with smears.

"We're here," he said, and it had been at least an hour since they turned around, but it felt like ten, and now it was getting dark outside, nine o'clock and she was supposed to be at Leslie's at six or seven. She was still crying when she opened the taxi door.

"If you want your suitcase you have to pay me," he said with that bad look on his face. Like he really did want to kill her. She thought of telling him he could keep her suitcase.

"A hundred dollars," Armin said.

The door swung open to the apartment building at 853 Lincoln, where she was supposed to live, like the old Victorian houses she'd seen on the computer at the travel agency, and there, at the foot of a gray marble stairway, stood a man. Or was he a boy? Tall, skinny, with bleached blond hair standing straight up. He wore tight black jeans and a black T-shirt that said "Giants" in big orange letters. Did everybody here wear T-shirts with what she assumed were sports team names? The blond man glanced at Mariella and then at her suitcase on the sidewalk.

"Mariella?" he said. "I'm Leslie, I've been watching for you. You were supposed to be here three hours ago." *Madre mia!* Leslie was supposed to be a woman, not a man! This was a crazy place!

"I am Mariella from Sicilia," she said.

"Are you going to pay me?" Armin said.

"You deserve nothing!" she answered, and talked very fast, explaining to Leslie, really to anyone else who might pass by and help her, what had happened, Italian all mixed up with English, and how they ended up in Richmond.

With the exception of a youth in baggy pants who zipped by on his skateboard, there were few passersby. Only a handful of older Chinese women with string shopping bags, hurrying along the sidewalk and keeping their heads down and giving Mariella a wide berth.

At this hour, nearly nine o'clock on a June night in Catania, when streaks of pink and yellow-orange lingered in the sky, the piazza and the sidewalks would be filled with townspeople out for a leisurely stroll, the evening *passeggiata*. Where *were* all the people in this renowned American city? Why were they all hiding behind closed doors?

Cars along the boulevard kept moving.

"She will pay you twenty dollars and nothing more," Leslie said, looking at the taxi license plate and saying it out loud while he punched the number into his phone. "You deliberately tried to swindle her, and if you don't open that trunk and give her suitcase, I'll call the cops," he said. "You don't even deserve that much."

Armin stood on the pavement, staring Leslie down, and refused to move. "Okay, okay," he said after a minute and opened the trunk and threw out her suitcase.

"My *valigia*!" she said.

"Your *valigia*?" Leslie said and watched as Mariella counted out the twenty dollars for Armin. She wanted to spit in Armin Hofstader's face. Armin waited.

"No tip," she said. Brave, now that Leslie was there. Armin did spit, not at her, but on the ground, shook his fist, stuck up a middle finger from a fist, which she knew didn't mean good luck, and sped off.

She reached for her suitcase, muttering to herself, "I should never have left Sicilia. Mamma was right!" She circled frantically in one direction and then the other, dashing only a few feet away before Leslie caught up with her.

"Mistake, sorry, sorry, big mistake," she said. "The Leslie I mean to find is *una ragazza*. You're supposed to be a girl, no? I call for the taxi and then I stay in the cheap hotel, even though I have not much money, but it doesn't matter," she was babbling now, "because *domani*, I go back home!"

"Oh, no, no, no, don't you even dream of going!" Leslie said, snatching up her suitcase, and sounding both pleading and adamant.

"My valigia!"

"Your valigia," he said, echoing her again. He laughed, good-naturedly. "Whatever that means."

She regarded him as benignly as if she were asking for the time of day. "Suitcase," she said. "It means suitcase."

The high-pitched wail of a police siren pierced the hum of the city. Mariella's whole body, even her backbone, trembled. Through her dark jersey and light cardigan sweater, she could feel the sweat under her arms. The air was chilly, but perspiration glistened on the backs of her hands.

Leslie walked away with her suitcase before she could register a protest. He'd propped open the door to the foyer with an umbrella stand and now proceeded to bump her suitcase against the scarred white- and gray-veined marble stairs. She followed close behind, objecting with every step.

Leslie stopped halfway up and turned around and touched her sweater, rubbing it between two fingers. "I'm not trying to touch you, you understand, just the sweater. Italian cashmere," he said. "I knew it. There's nothing like it."

"Of course," she said. "We Italians know how to dress. Even with not enough money, two things we spend money on: clothing and food." Speaking of which, her stomach was eating itself, she was so hungry and so tired. But she would not eat until she was away from Leslie because she was pretty sure she didn't trust him. *I will call a taxi and go somewhere else for one night and then maybe fly back to Sicilia.* She glanced up to see a youngish, sleepy-eyed and scowling man peer over the staircase railing, then retreat, presumably back into his apartment. The man had either shaved his head, or he was prematurely bald.

Mariella stared right back at him and stood an inch taller.

"Papa has sayings for such disagreeable people," she whispered. *"Forse le scarpe sono troppo strette, o, forse il suo fegato che lo disturba."*

"What?" Leslie said.

She shrugged. "Maybe his shoes are too tight, or maybe his liver is bad."

Leslie laughed and patted Mariella's arm. "Oh, that's very good," he said. "Like I said, I think you and I will get along famously."

"Why you care so much if I stay?" Mariella yawned involuntarily. She often did that when she was nervous or scared.

"Why?" Leslie closed his eyes and tilted his head, as if that helped him to better see his thoughts. "Well, I've always felt Italian in my soul, and after I read your email and realized yours was a legitimate response I immediately eliminated all the other applicants—honestly, there were only maybe a dozen—but how exotic . . . well, for me anyway, to have someone straight from Sicily as my roommate. Anyway, wait until you see your room," he remarked over his shoulder, lugging Mariella's suitcase up the last few stairs to his apartment door. "I tried to make it look as Italian as I could so you'd feel right at home."

Chapter Thirteen

*I*nside Leslie's apartment Mariella was greeted by huge red plastic lips outlined in blue neon, lit from inside and mounted on the kitchen wall. Directly below them was a white ceramic clock. The hour and minute hands emanated from an open-mouthed hub of red lips.

Like a sleepwalker, she drifted to a small round wooden table, only a few steps from the clock.

Leslie rushed ahead and pulled out a white, straight-backed chair, then headed toward the hallway, rolling her suitcase behind him.

"Where you taking my *valigia*?" she called.

"Oh." He paused and turned around. "*Valigia*," he echoed again, as if he were memorizing the word. "Well, I thought you'd want to see your room, but"—he opened his hands as a question—"I'll wait, if you want."

"No. No," she said. "*Va bene*."

She watched his skinny backside recede and disappear through a door. Even if he tried to keep her from leaving, she was pretty sure she could overpower him. She was small but strong. Unless, of course, he had a gun and sinister designs.

He returned and said, "My bedroom's the one on the left. And yours is the second door on your right." He took the seat opposite her at the table. "First door's your bathroom. Mine's in my room."

Mariella forced herself to stand. "*Scusi*," she said. "The *gabinetto* I will use."

As she washed her hands, she saw that the mirror's gilt frame matched the brass faucets and toothbrush holder affixed to the wall. Even the soap in the maroon dish was golden yellow.

She peeked into what Leslie had designated "her" room: soft lighting, a double bed with a burgundy comforter, and plush decorative pillows plumped up against a brass headboard. As much as she longed to lie down, she shook her head, ridding ideas of sleep from her mind. She had to stay awake, to stay safe.

Leslie's door was closed.

Passing through the short hallway back to the kitchen, she took in the eccentric décor on the walls, the living room a kaleidoscope of red, white, and black.

"Can I get you anything? Water? Coffee? Tea?" Leslie asked.

"Si, si. Yes, please, the water."

He took two steps from the four-foot square of parquet floor onto the black-and-white checked linoleum, demarking the galley-sized kitchen from the dining area. From the refrigerator, he lifted a glass pitcher of water infused with thin slices of cucumber and lemon.

Mariella gulped the fragrant chilled water and held out her glass for more. She smiled a self-conscious apology. "*Prego*, is what I mean to say. If you please."

Leslie smiled back, and, keeping his eyes on Mariella, he slowly sat down, then suddenly stood again.

"So, do you think you'll be all right?" he asked. "If I slip out for half an hour at the most? I'm sure you'll be fine. Just make yourself completely at home."

He produced a black leather jacket seemingly out of nowhere and pulled it on.

"*Che cosa*?" She flung open her hands, still holding her glass, and sloshed a little of the water onto the table. "Where you going? Why do you leave?"

When he moved to her and touched her shoulder, she jumped up and backed away from him.

"Are you okay?" he asked, halfway shrugging off his jacket and wiping up the water with a paper towel. "It's just that I haven't eaten, and I'm sure you're starving too. I know how awful airplane food is. I ordered a pizza, thought I'd run down the street and pick it up. But I can have it delivered if you prefer." He pulled his cell phone out of his pocket.

"Si, *certo*, I'm okay," she said reflexively before he could punch in the number. "I mean it is okay to pick up food. But only for you. I'm—I have no *appetito*." The memory of that pizza at Newark Airport stifled her hunger.

"Are you sure?" he asked. "It'll take me only five minutes to get there and back. Ten max. Really, I'll be back in a flash." He shut the apartment door behind him. "It's locked," he called from the other side.

She stood speechless, staring at the door, then let out a long, deep breath. "You're safe, you're fine, you're okay," she spoke aloud. "Remember Nonna's words: 'You're a brave, strong girl.'"

Now, slowly, deliberately, she took in everything around her.

The kitchen and dining area opened as one continuous room into the small adjacent living area where a white cotton velvet sofa called to her now, as the bed had earlier. "No," she said, in a round, firm voice. "I will not fall asleep."

Perpendicular to the sofa was a matching white club chair with big throw pillows in the shape of red lips, and in between the sofa and the chair, a black cubed side table with a silvery metallic-based lamp.

She stepped onto the plush black looped area rug that lay in front of the sofa and ran her hand longingly over the soft fabric of the sofa. On the rug was a kidney-shaped coffee table with two staggered black lacquered wood pieces forming its base. A

Noguchi imitation, she decided, assuming an original would be too expensive for Leslie. She had seen the real deal at the Gamberini's, who had purchased it from a fancy design shop in Milan.

On top of the coffee table, a large clear bowl held at least a dozen blown-glass red lips.

What *was* it with the red lips?

Italian café posters and Matisse cutout prints were beautifully framed and hung on the walls along with a pair of pastel drawings that looked like originals, signed by Charles somebody or other, dated 1999.

Yes, an odd but thoughtfully decorated place, well-kept and cared about.

She hesitated, and, as if the walls had ears, tiptoed to the door of Leslie's bedroom. She tested the knob and found it unlocked. What was she expecting? Whips and chains? Photos of men in various poses of *flagrante delicto*? Or even worse, a lover with his hands and feet bound to the four corners of the bed, gagged so she wouldn't hear him?

Clearly, even though he hadn't said so, Leslie was gay. *Uno Finocchio.*

Leslie's room was pale blue and bamboo, with big flower prints on the walls, and yes, a simple line drawing of two male nudes, facing away from each other. The bed was unmade, and on a pillow, a hardbound law book—*Torts and Ethics*—splayed open, spine side up.

She had texted Olimpio at her landing in Rome, and now, back in the kitchen, she pulled her cell phone from her pocket and reread, for the tenth time, the text he'd sent back when she was still in Italy. How many hours ago? Fifteen? Twenty-four? She'd lost track. *6 a.m. and one minute Mamma screams at me to bring you home, the next she goes silent, then curses you and says she never wants to see you again. Papa shocked and sad. Angry too, but mostly relieved you're alive. I suspect he's secretly impressed.*

She'd emailed Olimpio news of her landings at the Newark airport and again when she'd landed in San Francisco. In the next days, she'd have to set up an American account to text or call home. In spite of her defection, at least Papa and Nonna would want to know she was safe. Maybe. At least for now. At least to know she'd arrived.

Her eyes were open and misty, thinking of Papa and missing her grandmother, too. But her stomach, she felt it now, as empty and raw as if it had been twisted into a knot. When she'd still expected Leslie would be a girl, she'd hoped maybe, after a few words—"Hello. Nice to meet you. This is your room."—she could go to bed. She'd wondered if they would speak Italian. After all, Leslie *had* signed her—no *his* email—"Ciao!"

Despite her determination to stay upright, Mariella collapsed onto the hard wooden chair, her head involuntarily lowering to the level of her arm, stretched out in front of her. The watch on her wrist read nearly 10 p.m.

At home it was 7 a.m., and Papa would just be leaving for the office, and Mamma would be imploring Olimpio to eat something—*Mangia! Mangia!*—before he escaped her clutches and the confines of the house into the cloudless blue day. Poor Mamma, Nonna always said, clinging to the last shred of control she wielded over her children.

Before long, everyone in the neighborhood would know Mariella was gone.

She felt a gentle nudge on her shoulder, sniffed the aroma of tomato and garlic and spicy meat. Her hunger announced itself, a loud involuntary gurgle from her stomach.

"You can't sleep all night at the table," a man's voice said.

"Oh." She struggled to raise her head. The white clock on the wall read ten twenty-five.

"*Lo* . . ." she began, but her voice came out in a rasp. "*Sono appena tornado da casa mia.*" Leslie, the man who was supposed to be a woman. His name was Leslie.

"What'd you just say?" he asked, bending to hear her.

She forced herself to find the English words. "I said I have just come from my house."

"Okay," Leslie said. "That does it. You're eating and then going straight to bed."

He stepped—bounded—into the kitchen, dropping the pizza box on the counter as if it were a hot coal.

She propped herself up on one elbow and watched, with one eye closed, as he uncorked and poured red wine for both of them into etched crystal goblets, and placed a slice of the fragrant pizza on a white porcelain plate, in front of her, along with a knife, fork, and cloth napkin. "I think we could both use a glass." He toasted her, "In honor of you and *Italia*!" and set the bottle, a Chianti, on the table.

"It is very nice, but I will drink this," Mariella said, lifting her water glass. Then she cleared her throat and managed, in a harsh whisper, "And after the—how you say—takeout? Yes, I will use your phone and call a taxi."

"Why? Why do you want to go? Is it because I'm gay?"

Mariella abruptly cocked her head, as if she'd been slapped. How could he think that?

"No, no, I don't care about that," she said, moving a hand back and forth, wiping away the sting. She paused for another long drink. "I'm no . . . *innocente*. I only care if you act weird. I think that's the word: weird?"

Leslie regarded her with an expression of half-amusement, half-disbelief. "So," he asked. "What's *weird* to you?"

"Well." She turned down the corners of her mouth and opened her hands. "For example, I know a certain couple. A couple that say tied up is the best and only way to the sexual release." She swallowed more water to clear the scratchiness and sleep from her throat. "No," she said again. "I wouldn't like to know you do that in the next room." She shrugged. "Otherwise, no problem."

"Okay," Leslie said.

"Eh," she said. "Is okay for me too. But what *is* trouble is that you kept from me that you are a man. Why did you not tell to me in your email letters? Why did you not give me the choice?"

"Choice?"

"Si. Choice. So I get to decide if I want to live with a woman or a man."

He thought for a moment. "Okay, what if I'd just said, 'I'm Leslie and I'm a man'?"

She nodded slowly. "Sure, I see what you mean. I think I would not say yes."

"So, why didn't I tell you? I should have," he said. "I realized that after our exchange. But I think I would have felt like I was apologizing or explaining that something was wrong with me." He paused. "Because I'm gay—and, well, also because I was so stoked about getting a roommate from Sicily, I didn't want to take the chance of you slipping away."

"But is nothing wrong with gay!" said Mariella. "In fact, if you tell me you are gay, no problem. Is better than being just a man!"

Leslie rolled his eyes. "That's what I'm saying. I didn't want it to matter to you whether I'm gay—or female—or black or white or red! I just wanted you to come here and meet me, person-to-person."

"Well," she said. "Here we are, person-to-person."

She took a sip of wine on the table in front of her and raised her glass to Leslie and he toasted her back. She held the glass away, underneath the soft, frosted globe hanging above the kitchen table. The wine glowed like rubies in the crystal goblet. The diffused light made her sleepier, made it even harder to keep her eyes open. "This is beautiful color," she said. "And beautiful tasting wine."

She took a bite of the pizza. To her surprise, it was delicious and fresh, not overly cheesy, the oregano and basil just the right amount, the sausage not too heavy but seasoned light, the way she liked it. For a moment she considered that maybe it wouldn't be so bad staying here with Leslie.

He waved an arm toward the window, toward the street outside. "If it's the neighborhood that worries you, this is a wonderful section of town, as safe as anywhere. Well, maybe, except for Pacific Heights or Seacliff or St. Francis Woods or anywhere the really rich people live."

"You say it is safe," Mariella countered. "But how do I know you tell me the truth?"

"What?" His eyes grew large and astonished, his mouth hanging open like a baby bird's. He stopped blinking just in time to catch her smile, to realize she was teasing.

She wagged a finger at him. "I get it," she said. "You tell me is wonderful here. Yes? Right? Just to make me stay."

Leslie's sigh escaped through his teeth, singing like a whistle. "Don't take my word for it. Ask around about the Inner Sunset. You'll find out. But listen," he said. "Of course, it's up to you if you want to leave. So why don't you at least spend the night, and tomorrow we can walk around the neighborhood. I don't have classes until the evening. See how you feel, and if you decide you want to stay, I'll be thrilled. If you still want to go, I'll even help you find a place." He watched her while she mulled over his proposal.

"Deal?" he asked.

"Deal?" she said. "Like in TV program, *Let's Make a Deal?*" She regarded him with her Nonna's hazel green eyes. "Okay. Deal." She shrugged. "I give it one night and see for me how it goes."

Too exhausted even to shower or brush her teeth, she snuggled her head deeper into the feather pillow that Leslie had bought, he said, especially for her, bathed in the citrusy fragrance of the crisp yet smooth pillowcase and cotton sheets with which Leslie had prepared her bed.

Her longing snuck up on her. That sudden, unexpected yearning for the familiar lemony smell of home, the fresh, clean aroma of Mamma's sheets and towels.

Olimpio had texted that her parents were upset, but would Papa hope the best for her? Even if he was angry and hurt? *La mia bambina*, his pet name for her in their sweet connected moments, sometimes kissing the curls on top of her head. Yes, of course, Papa would always be thinking of his only daughter. The feel of his big, comforting embrace, his smell—woody, with a tang of salt—nearly palpable, a sense memory that would stay with Mariella until the end of her life.

Nonna would surely be sending a stay strong prayer. And wishing, "*Buona notte di sonno*" as she'd done every night. A good night's sleep.

She'd simply have to wait until morning to find another place. Tomorrow. She'd send Papa an email explaining every-thing tomorrow. Maybe Matteo, too, even though she had little hope of his absolution.

And what of Matteo? A shock to her, this sudden deep pang of missing him. She fell asleep, too worn out to cry, but with both sorrow and confusion in her heart.

Chapter Fourteen

The smell of freshly brewed coffee and the sound of muffled voices, a man's and a woman's, tugged her from sleep. She stretched and slid deeper under the covers, hugging herself for just another minute.

Mamma and Olimpio must be having *"una poco chat,"* as Mamma liked to call them. Of course, what they really amounted to was Mamma interrogating Olimpio about his personal life, and him doing his put-upon best to answer her without revealing his private business.

It must be Sunday. Weekdays, her mother brewed only one small moka pot for Nonna and for herself after everyone else had left for the day. But even before caffè Mamma ritually imbibed her tonic (Mariella called it her "witches brew") of hot water and lemon juice, claiming it cleansed everything bad from her body. *"Tutto male,"* she declared, moving her hands down the front of her house-coat, and shaking her fingers as if all the evil was falling away.

Maybe Mamma made an extra moka pot this morning.

Mariella stretched again, and her eyes flew open.

"Merda santa!" she said. *"Gesu Cristo!"* And she threw off the covers and sat bolt upright.

She heard laughter. The man's. Leslie's.

Had he heard what she just said? Is that why he was laughing? And who was the woman? Anything was possible in this *pazzo* place where a roommate who was supposed to be a woman turned out to be a man!

She crept out of bed and quietly lifted the slats on the plantation window shutters. Gray and fog cast a haze over the cars driving in opposite directions up and down the busy street. Beyond that, across the way, a lush forest of trees momentarily buoyed her spirits until she reminded herself that she needed to escape this place.

She sat on the edge of the bed. Leslie said he'd help her find another apartment if she wanted to move, but could she trust him? Really? The San Francisco University had offered in its acceptance letter to help her find a roommate or housing. She wondered if it was too late.

What day was it now? She'd left Sicilia on Monday so it had to be Tuesday. No, Wednesday or maybe Thursday, but anyway, a weekday, so the university would be open. Wouldn't it? In the middle of summer? Surely, there was a housing office or student bulletin boards somewhere on campus advertising for roommates.

She exhaled and relaxed, just a little. Last night she hadn't noticed her bedroom surroundings, but now she saw that the walls were textured and painted to look like old earth-toned Italian stucco or marble, the walls that Leslie had mentioned in his letter, walls he'd painted himself. The wooden furniture: the bed frame and slatted headboard, the bureau and night stand, smooth to the touch, but not polished or lacquered, the dark caramel hue of Marsala wine. Bright yellow sunflower faces leaned toward her, as if they were bowing, welcoming her, from a copper-colored pottery jug on top of the low bureau with black wrought iron loops for drawer pulls.

At least in here there were no red lips!

She pulled out a silky, light robe from her suitcase, which lay open on the floor at the foot of the bed. She tied the robe around her and checked in the bureau mirror to make sure she'd covered her ample breasts and cleavage, and that her nipples didn't show through the fabric. Not that her breasts would do anything for

Leslie. Still, she had to enter the hallway to use the bathroom.

"You're up!" Leslie called to her from the kitchen table, the instant she opened the door.

"*Un minuto*," Mariella said, slipping into the bathroom with her cosmetics bag. *Merda!* She didn't want to face him. Not yet. She sat on the toilet a long time, trying to figure out what she'd say: "*Buongiorno*, I'm leaving." Or, "*Buongiorno*, you are very nice, but I'm calling a taxi." Or, "*Buongiorno*, why don't you just tell me everything will be all right so I believe you, and I stay."

Finally, she stood and faced herself in the mirror. Aside from her curly hair, which was always a bit wild, she didn't think she looked insane. She stretched back her lips and examined her teeth before she brushed them. One of these days maybe she would get that small gap closed between the two on the upper front. Or maybe not.

She splashed water on her face and dried it with one of the maroon hand towels that matched the shower curtain.

She took a deep breath and opened the bathroom door.

"Come, come," Leslie said, waving his arm for Mariella to join him. "I have to go," he said into his cell phone.

"Bye," said the woman on speaker at the other end. The woman's voice she'd heard from her room. Leslie hung up. "That was Alice, my coworker at Gypsy Men's." Mariella must have looked confused. "The clothing store where I work, part time, in the Haight," Leslie explained. "She's filling in for me today . . . well . . . so I can be available to you." And before Mariella could protest that she was leaving anyway, that she didn't need Leslie's help, he stood abruptly from his chair, opened his arms, and wished her a resounding, "Good morning!"

"Buongiorno," Mariella said. She glanced longingly around the kitchen for the moka pot she'd imagined in bed. The coffee she'd smelled from her room. At the far end of a kitchen counter she spied a small silver and black espresso machine.

"Coffee?" Leslie offered, as if he'd read her mind. He still sported a Giants T-shirt, only this one was white instead of black, with a ballplayer whose name—Ryan Vogelsong—was written as a signature underneath a stenciled color photograph titled *Vogelsong, 2000*, his leg hiked up, ball in hand, ready to deliver a pitch.

Mariella looked down at herself. "It's okay for me to come to the table this way?" Oversized butterflies and birds fluttered down the sleeves of her robe. A crane took flight across her back.

"Why should it bother me," Leslie said, "if you spend all day in that beautiful gown?" He opened the refrigerator and brought out milk.

"At home, Mamma calls me *una pigra regazza* whenever I stay too long, even on the weekend, in nightclothes." The clock with the red lips showed eleven o'clock. How could she have slept so late? Almost twelve hours. Maybe for the first time in her life, except the rare times she'd been ill.

"*Pigra?*" Leslie poured the milk into a small saucepan and heated it at the stove. "It sounds like she's calling you a pig." He began to spoon coffee grounds into the machine's metal filter basket.

"No." Mariella giggled. "Lazy. But it hurt my feelings. Like she don't see me. And never mind that Mamma herself often stay in her house robe until the midday. She can't stand to see anyone in the family taking it easy unless is Olimpio. Olimpio can lay in the sun and ask Mamma to bring him drinks and umbrella, if he want."

A loud moan outside the apartment door caused them both to simultaneously swivel their heads, on sudden alert, toward the sound.

"Oh," Leslie said, after a moment, breathing out relief. "Nothing to worry about. That's my neighbor, Gardenia. She's still sore from one of her clients beating her up last week. She's just trying to get down the stairs." The moaning continued with each apparent step, and with diminishing volume as the woman descended.

"Your neighbor!" Mariella grabbed the back of a kitchen chair to steady herself. "Clients?" *Was this Gardenia a prostitute? A puttana for real?* "So maybe this *is* bad neighborhood. Not good, like you say, but bad! Maybe the people go around with the guns and beating each other up."

"No, no, no. I promise you, this was just—well, not *just*—but work related."

Work related? A prostitute for certain!

"And it didn't happen in *this* neighborhood. It happened in *his.* But this kind of thing happens everywhere, even in the fancy houses. Besides," he said, "Sicily isn't exactly the crime free Mecca of the universe."

"Anyway," he went on with a sigh, "that's Gardenia, always taking care of everyone else. I've been telling her every time we bump into one another, 'One of these days you're going to get in trouble on one of those home visits you make to the projects. You need to take a cop with you.' She's a social worker," Leslie added, almost as an afterthought.

"Projects?" To Mariella's mind, projects were something you did for school, or a repair or construction, like a shelf, something her father might undertake around their apartment.

"Let's see," Leslie said. "How to explain . . . well, apartment buildings for people who don't have much money, not very pretty, and owned by the government." He paused. "And in the parts of town that aren't so good." Mariella pictured the post–World War II subsidized apartment buildings in Catania, severe and plain concrete and often shabby, with not so much as a balcony to bring in the outdoors.

"Si," she said, "but in Sicilia, unless a woman is the puttana—you know, the prostitute?" Mariella shifted her weight from foot to foot. "So, unless a woman is puttana—or self-destructive, yes?

Okay, she understands better than to go to certain neighborhoods, even if the most likely crime against the woman in Sicilia these days is taking the purse."

"Purse snatching? Are you okay?" Leslie asked, glancing under the table at her moving feet.

"This talk about the beating is what gives me the nerves. But, si, the purse snatching is what I mean, and also the robbing of the wallet." She lifted her shoulders. "Sure, the Mafia does whatever it wants, but not so much on the street anymore. In mostly secret, pulling the government and the strings of the business." She waved her arms around, like her mother. "The Mafia pretty much own *everybody!*" She settled now onto a hip.

Leslie nodded slowly and gestured for her to sit. He set a large cup of strong coffee in front of her, handed her a spoon and pointed to the sugar bowl and the pitcher of heated milk. "Who's Olimpio?"

"My brother," she said. "He is eighteen."

Leslie watched as she tasted the coffee. From the first sip she felt at home, relaxed, and for that moment the safest since arriving on this foreign ground.

"Si grazie, *come Italiano,*" Mariella said, raising her cup. She closed her eyes and inhaled the rich nutty aroma. "Is good. Better than I expect." Like most *Sicilianos,* she drank cappuccino or coffee with milk in the mornings; after noon, the only acceptable caffè was espresso in a tiny cup, concentrated and black, with a sugar cube or a lemon twist alongside.

"I took the liberty of peeking in on you," Leslie said, his voice muffled behind the refrigerator door, which he'd opened between them. "To make sure you were asleep before I went to bed. I didn't wake you up, did I?"

"No." But what would she have done if she'd awakened and found him in the doorway, watching her? "Grazie," she said again, not sure what she was thanking him for.

He retrieved from the refrigerator half a cantaloupe covered in plastic wrap. "I have a job for you," he said. "A good job, work you get paid for. That is," he added, sheepishly, "if you decide to stay."

"Oh, you are very good with the—*come si dice, tangente?*—the bribe, I think?"

"*Tangente*," he muttered to himself, and nodded, as if he was trying to get the word incised in his mind's eye.

He held the melon toward her. "Want some? I bought it just yesterday at the farmer's market."

"Ah," she said. "The *cantalupo*. Yes, grazie, if you please." She watched while he scooped seeds into a wastebasket lined with plastic under the sink. Melons were at the height of ripeness now, in July. She anticipated a sweet and juicy melon, like the ones Mamma brought from the big open-air market in Catania, the *Pescheria*, where she shopped daily for produce, fish, or meat.

"Really? You have the job for me?" she asked. "What job? When you have the time to find me the job?"

Leslie returned to the table with the peeled cantaloupe slices, arranged like a pinwheel, on a green glass plate. "So," he said. "The job is in North Beach."

"Oh, Nord Beach!" Mariella squeezed her hands together in a joyous clasp. "I have heard of that place. I read about it at the *agenzia* for travel where you email me, and I see it in the TV program, *Le Strade de San Francisco*."

"You mean that old cop show, *The Streets of San Francisco*? Michael Douglas, so beautiful back then. I actually saw him . . ."

"*Un minuto*—Nord Beach," Mariella said. "Isn't that the place for the strip dancers where it used to be . . . *quartiere*?" She searched for the equivalent in English. "Like *Italiano* neighbor-hood," she said.

"I've got no clue if North Beach is like Italy anymore," Leslie said, "but the job is hostessing at Basilico Ristorante."

"Hostess?" The image Mariella conjured was one of a nearly naked woman wearing only thong panties, ogled and pawed by sex-hungry men in private booths. "Oh, I read about the old Nord Beach as Italian immigrant settlement. But also about the new Nord Beach with topless and sometimes bottomless dancer clubs. No, grazie!"

Now, for certain, after she'd eaten her cantaloupe, she'd get dressed and call that taxi.

"No, no, no!" Leslie said. "It's not what you think. I can read it all over your face. Basilico is one of the highest end—expensive, one of the best," he explained, anticipating her question. "One of the best Italian restaurants in the city, and the sommelier is a dear friend."

A lover? She bit into a slice of the melon. Delight, along with surprise, registered in her eyes. "Like your caffè this is *deliziosa* too," she said. Aromatic and fresh. Apparently, not only Italians, but some Americans, like Leslie, knew good food.

"I spoke to Pietro this morning. My *friend* ," he said emphatically, "because they're looking to fill the position, part time. The last one just left to have a baby, and the prospect of having someone straight from Sicily with a real Italian accent to greet the customers, and who speaks English too . . ." Leslie waited just long enough for a dramatic pause. "Anyway, Pietro has already talked with the owner, and with your restaurant experience and all . . . well, they'd like to meet you."

"I arranged an interview for you," he said. "Three tomorrow afternoon."

Before she could respond he added, "You worked in a restaurant in Sicily, right? You said so in your letter."

"Si. In the trattoria. But . . ." She opened and kept flipping her hands as she talked. "Sure, I greet the customers and I speak with them too, of course, about the food but . . ." She shrugged. "Is maybe not the same?"

"Listen, girl, there are dozens of qualified young women, men as well, folks who would kill for this job. This is a plum . . ." he paused again, "a very desirable position. Anyone in San Francisco in the restaurant business will tell you." Leslie observed her. "It's up to you, but if you want it, you've got a special 'in.'"

"My head is dizzy with all possibilities," she said. "But okay, I go to Basilico tomorrow. First I send home the email, before I shower and dress in walking clothes, then I pack my suitcase—just in case." Her MacBook Air, a gift beyond Papa's means. Her heart squeezed inside her chest, remembering his pride in presenting it to her on her birthday in her second year at university.

"And," she said, "then I keep my word and we walk together these streets."

"When we go to Basilico, wear the most Italian-looking clothes you brought," Leslie said. "Feminine but not too dressy. But of course, you're Italian, you know how to dress," he said, before she reminded him again. He eyed her robe. "It's a shame you don't have that fabric in a dress. It's perfect. And heels, if you've got them. When you seat the customers, they love to walk behind a woman wearing . . ." He paused. "High heels."

"You mean the 'fuck me' shoes?"

Leslie's eyes widened, and his mouth dropped open.

"Even in Sicilia we know about the sexy shoes." Mariella laughed, raised an eyebrow, and flashed him a warning look.

Mariella shrugged. "Sex," she said. "It is normal. Is part of life."

Leslie waited for her to say more; probably, she thought, to talk about her own sex life, but that was her business.

She dreaded going to bed tonight, when her longing for home and for Matteo would come in the middle of the night, and would, like an incubus, lay claim to her body and purloin any vestige of believing she was safe and on firm ground.

"It's always the booze that seems to amp up the violent ones," Leslie mused. "Oh," he said, apparently catching her expression. "I didn't mean to scare you. I was thinking about Gardenia's client who was probably drunk."

"Amp up?"

"It means get him all excited, in a bad way," Leslie explained. "Back someone into a corner, make him feel like he has to defend himself." He punched his fists into the air. "To fight."

Mariella muttered something to herself in Italian. "Like a frightened *animale*?" she said.

"*Animale*," he echoed back. "Exactly!"

"I understand. We have *animali* in Sicilia too," Mariella said, and for the second time that morning, they laughed together.

"One of my *professori* at the university," she said. "A woman— she counseled prisoners at the penitentiary in Siracusa. She fall in love with one of her dark-skinned prisoners, a man from Morocco. When he's released, they live together and are happy now, for over twenty years. Sometimes, when people are so different, is not always bad."

If she'd learned nothing else from Nonna, it was that love can only be measured by the two people sharing the bond. She looked at Leslie. He was right to be protective of Gardenia, but now, his neighbor needed his compassion, not "I told you so."

"Is not for me," she said. "It is not for anyone else to judge.

Before she took a shower, she emailed Olimpio:

Today is my first morning here after the horrible plane trip and taxi ride I already emailed you about last night. Leslie says he (yes, he's a man, a gay man; don't tell Mamma) will walk with me through this district we live in, the Sunset, he calls it. And he says he has found a job for me, if I want it, at an Italian *ristorante* in North Beach—oh, I have read about North Beach where all the Italian-Americans live, the Italianos with our last name, Russo—the place in San Francisco where I will feel at home. The job is hostess, which I thought at first meant something bad, like a hostess in a place where women strip, but he explained, and now I understand he meant receptionist, and he said the *ristorante Basilico* is one of the best in North Beach and many people would like this job. But he is a friend (a lover?) of the sommelier who says customers will like having a receptionist just arrived from Sicily who speaks with an Italian accent, and who is willing to work for minimum wage, at least to start.

Well, what choice do I have? I suppose I could advertise to tutor in Italian, since I also speak and read English, and maybe I will do that in time, when I am adjusted to being here and know my way around a little. But for today Leslie and I will walk through the Sunset, and then tomorrow I will wear a nice dress—my filmy green and purple one—and then he will take me to this job interview at Basilico.

I am still so tired I think I will sleep for the rest of the day after the walk and the job interview and maybe see how I feel tomorrow about finding another place to live.

Please email me back how Mamma and Papa are reacting to my escape.

Is Papa's heart broken? Does he forgive me? Is Mamma glad I'm gone, or is she hysterical and falling apart and living in her bed? Please kiss Papa and Nonna for me. I will email Papa very soon, I just need a little time to be here before I write him.

Ciao, ciao my dearest little brother, Olimpio. When the time is right, maybe you will come here too.

Olimpio wrote back:

> Papa is sad, but I think he's proud of you too, because even if he doesn't say so, Papa knows inside your heart. He has his hands full, as you can imagine, trying to keep Mamma calm. Well, that's not possible, but at least from ranting and moaning. Maybe Papa would like to escape too. Mamma is pretending to be dying, but she never does that around Nonna for very long because Nonna just gives her that "Stop it, Yolanda!" stare. When I finish university in three years, I will come there too. I'll tell Papa you're going to email him soon.
>
>   Love, O

Chapter Fifteen

"Next time you'll have to take the Muni—if you get the job." Leslie started the ignition of his red Mini Cooper. "And right, you haven't yet decided if you're going to be my roommate. But either way, I'll help you with the bus routes."

He was still in his Giants T-shirt, but now he wore a black leather jacket over it, with black jeans and black-and-white checked Converse high tops that matched the design of the Mini's exterior doors: a wide, black-and-white checkerboard stripe that ran across the bottom. The car's interior was black, with red plush seat covers.

"Eh . . . such style," Mariella said, sweeping her arm toward Leslie and around, inside the car. "And thank you for driving me today, and thank you for setting up . . . ummm . . . the interview—that is right, yes?" Mariella said.

"Yes, interview is correct." Leslie gave Mariella an appreciative once-over. "You look great."

Her dress was filmy and layered, with touches of peach and a shade of green the color of her eyes. Except for little cap sleeves, her arms were bare and tanned from the Sicilian summer; a peach pashmina shawl lay in her lap. She'd been warned that San Francisco could turn cool in an instant, even in June. Peach high-heeled canvas espadrilles adorned her feet, their long laces wound around her ankles.

"Very sexy," Leslie said. "Without trying to be."

"Grazie," she said, intrigued by his admiration. "Thank you,

Mr. Leslie." She surveyed him for a moment as he backed out of his garage onto Lincoln Way. "Will you tell me something?"

"Sure. I think."

They merged onto John F. Kennedy Drive, into the "forest" Mariella had seen from her bedroom window.

"It is famous," she said. "Golden Gate Park, just like Golden Gate Bridge."

"Yep, except there's nothing for people to jump off in the park. Well, maybe if they climbed on top of one of the buildings—the arboretum or one of the museums. But all they'd probably do is break a leg, or maybe their necks. Anyway," Leslie said. "What was it you wanted to ask?"

"Have you ever . . ." She hesitated. "Made the love with a woman?"

Leslie acted as if he hadn't heard. He stared straight ahead as they left the park and turned onto Stanyan and then onto Geary. In spite of a long, awkward silence between them, the city land-scape held her attention. Her head swiveled like a bobble, trying to take in these new surroundings.

This was more like the San Francisco she'd seen in photo-graphs: tall, official-looking buildings, lots of Chinese restaurants, some modern-looking box-shaped apartments, and storefronts, businesses like Subway and OfficeMax interspersed with banks, alongside the Victorians she recognized from pictures on the Internet and in books as the famous San Francisco "Painted Ladies." Buses, trolleys, and cable cars made their way up and down the boulevard. She'd seen cable cars on Sicilian TV, adver-tising Rice-a-Roni, the San Francisco Treat. Drivers honked at one another from cars and vans a lot bigger than Leslie's Mini; a wonder they weren't constantly running into each other or off the road. Of course Siciliano drivers were even crazier, but at home, at least, everyone had a fighting chance, with most all Sicilian cars as small as Leslie's, and Vespa the vehicle of choice.

"It's okay," she said. "You don't have to answer. I didn't meant to be—*scortese*." She searched for the word. "I think rude."

"*Mean* to be." Leslie said.

"*Scusi?*"

"It's not *meant* to be rude. It's, I didn't *mean* to be."

"Oh. Okay. I didn't mean to be."

"Yes," he said. "The answer's yes. I have slept with women once or twice, when I was younger. But not since." They came to a red light on Broadway, just before a tunnel. Her palms started to sweat. She told herself to ignore the warnings, just watch Leslie and she'd be all right. He shifted his gaze to her. "But why do you ask?"

His eyes were gray, and the pupils rimmed in black and full of light, like eyes in the paintings of some old masters. She hadn't noticed them before, Leslie's beautiful eyes that now regarded her with curiosity and, she thought, a flash of anger.

"Because," she said. "I am telling you the truth. When you say . . ." She struggled to stop herself from ducking her head and covering her face as the light changed from red to green, and they entered the tunnel. "When you say you think I look sexy, I see a sparkle in your eyes, so I think you are not liking only the men."

"You don't mince words, do you?" Leslie said.

"What is mince words?" Her heart began to beat faster. *Merda! Oh please, not now, okay?* It hadn't occurred to her, in spite of her dread of being captive on the plane before she left Sicily, that claustrophobia would travel to San Francisco with her. She'd hoped to leave it behind, along with her entrapment, back home.

"You're very direct. You don't hold back." He set his mouth, and she could see the twitch in his jaw.

"Yes," she said. "Everyone says so. They say I'm the same as Nonna—my grandmamma Giuseppina."

"I was simply giving you a compliment on your clothes," he said. "I happen to pay attention to style, and beauty in almost anything or anyone, in all its forms. That's it."

"No. Okay, yes, that is true, because I know you like style, but I think you are afraid now, that I am wanting you to make the love to me." She waggled her finger back and forth. "No, no, no," she said, clucking her tongue. "I am not meaning that." She pointed to her chest, where she was sure her heart was beating loud enough for Leslie to hear it too. "With me, you don't worry," she said.

Concentrate, she told herself. *Think only of the conversation.* "But I like that you like the women too," she said. "In the way that you say, about style, because not all the gay men—not all of those men appreciate the women."

"You're something else," Leslie said, shaking his head and smiling.

Mariella went completely silent as they entered the tunnel. *Breathe slowly*, she admonished herself, trying to keep from hyperventilating. She didn't want Leslie to see her fear. *Breathe and relax. Keep breathing, look straight ahead.* The Broadway tunnel seemed to get narrower and narrower as they drove deeper inside. Her stomach churned and sweat continued to coat her palms. She'd experienced panic in tunnels many times in the Sicilian hill country, driving through long mountain passageways. Why the road builders there hadn't gone around the mountains rather than taking the hard, laborious route of blasting through solid rock had always puzzled her. But not really. Making life out of hardscrabble and a stubborn temperament was in the island's history. She wished she were as dulled on Xanax as she'd been on the plane.

"*Mi dispiace*," she said, exhaling and touching Leslie's arm, feeling the relief slowly seep back into her veins as they emerged from the dark and back onto Broadway. "I have made the insult to you and embarrassed myself."

"Oh, girl, if you can forgive me for surprising you by being a man, I can certainly forgive you for . . . for absolutely nothing!

Oh, maybe for being a little nosy, but I admire that in a person—directness. Anyway, it's true what I said in the email I sent you, that you and I will get along just fine."

Here was North Beach! The familiar aromas of garlic and oregano along with basil and tomato, parmesan and something else it took Mariella a moment to name: fried fish, or perhaps, fish sautéed. The cooked smell of the sea. Was it bream? Sardines? Or another of the vast array of sea food served in Sicilian restaurants and households, rich and poor alike. The scent of something almost like home, but not the same.

"Does it remind you of Catania?" Leslie asked, as if he'd read her thoughts.

"Yes and no," she said. "It smells a little like *Sicilia*, the garlic and the cheese, but the fish here don't smell so good. Not so clean." All the *ristoranti* and most Catanian housewives procured their fish at *La Pescheria*, ". . . the best open-air fish and vegetable market in the whole world," she said. The catches of the day, so fresh they still wiggled when they hit the fry pan, layered in baskets or buckets full of water or displayed on big platters. *Direttamente dalla barca alla tavola*, Sicilians liked to say: straight from the boat to the table.

"Also," she said. "It don't look the same."

"No?"

"No. Here, I think, is more *commerciale*." Sandwich boards with arrows urging people inside stood in front of several restaurants on Columbus, and at some, young men with Italian and some with Spanish-tinged accents were stationed outside, trying to hawk customers in off the street. "Best food in North Beach," each one proclaimed, young, dark-eyed men who reminded her of hoodlums and pickpockets who traveled in groups on the sidewalks of Sicily, some of them beautiful young boys, future Mafiosi perhaps. Bandits born of desperation, but bandits, nonetheless.

Menus were pasted in windows or encased in frames near glass entryway doors.

"Mm-hmm," Leslie muttered, nodding vaguely in agreement. Mariella saw that his eyes flickered up and down the bodies and lingered, for only a moment, on the faces of certain men who passed by. "It's pretty darn commercial."

It was almost too much to take in: the sights, the smells, the bits of conversation from people who walked by, the flashing lights around the gangster on Big Al's sign, and the neon nipples on Carol Doda's breasts at the Condor Club. One of the topless and maybe bottomless clubs Mariella had seen in pictures on the Internet.

Was this all there was to North Beach? Where was the Little Italy she'd read about? Where were her fellow Italians, the streets that held everyday lives, the small leafy parks where neighbors congregated on benches in the shade. She'd imagined retreating to such places when she wanted to feel at home, eavesdropping on heated and lively conversations or surrounding herself in voices of her native tongue.

"There's City Lights Bookstore," Leslie said, gesturing across the avenue at a long, triangular shaped, three-story building with windows for walls and small, diamond-shaped stained glass panes as decoration at the top. The store was well-lighted from within, and a peace sign adorned the broad corner of the triangle on the second floor.

"It's a famous bookstore," Leslie said. "Have you ever heard of Lawrence Ferlinghetti—he's the poet who started it—or beatniks?"

"Oh, *si*, beatniks like Jack Kerouac, yes? And then the hippies came after, no?" She'd read the history of San Francisco over and over when she was still at home and coming to this city was only a daydream.

"Old hippies, now, yes?" she said, nodding across the street at the colorful bookstore where she imagined those hippies and the beatniks before them had congregated. She could make out but couldn't fully see a bright, busy mural that ran along City Light's outside wall on Broadway.

"Are you disappointed?" Leslie asked, pointing to a building with potted miniature cypress trees in front, twenty yards or so ahead. "That North Beach isn't more like Sicily? That's Basilico. We're almost there."

"Disappointed? No," she said. "If I want the same, I should stay home."

Chapter Sixteen

Standing inside Basilico, and perhaps because of its sleek and understated décor, she felt nervous in front of Leslie's friend. A man about thirty, she guessed, with hazel eyes, straight white teeth, and thick, slicked-back black hair, and so suave in his red waistcoat and black pants, a starched white shirt, and black bow tie. A classic sommeliers' tasting cup hung from a burnished chain around his neck. He and Leslie hugged and kissed each other on both cheeks.

So American, those white perfect teeth. She thought again of the gap between her own front teeth, and of the many Catanians who had one or more teeth missing from their smiles.

"I'm Pietro Navona," he said, his accent purely American. He shook her hand. "Welcome to San Francisco."

Navona. Like the Piazza Navona in Rome with the obelisk fountain and the Four Rivers statues surrounding it. She'd visited there only once, as a teenager, when her mother and father took her and Olimpio for a week's vacation.

". . . and I trust Leslie has been giving you the royal treatment," Pietro was saying.

"Oh, si, si," Mariella said and smiled at him. "Si, grazie."

Pietro led them across a floor of tiny mosaic tiles in multiple shades of brown and beige, past gleaming dark oak tables, a few with napkins tossed aside from lunch, others set, simply and elegantly, for dinner. In the center of each, a thin metal vase with a single red or orange gerbera daisy.

Pietro waved Mariella and Leslie toward a leather alcove banquette, where the lowered ceiling and hidden lighting lent an air of mystery.

She hadn't eaten since early that morning. The rich aromas of braised and grilled meats, the *soffritti* simmering for the evening's sauces, made her mouth water and her stomach emit high-pitched groans she hoped Pietro and Leslie wouldn't notice.

A carafe of sparkling water with floating lemon slices sat on the polished table, along with four tumblers, upside down, and four wine glasses, right side up. Mariella and Leslie slid into the seats against the banquette. Two chairs sat opposite them.

"You both like *rosso*, yes?" Pietro asked. And, without waiting for an answer, "I'll bring us a nice bottle."

"Is he your boyfriend?" Mariella asked Leslie after Pietro had gone to fetch the wine.

"You *are* nosy!" Leslie said. He turned over two of the tumblers and poured the water for Mariella and himself.

She sipped her water and wondered if Leslie really was all right with her directness, as he'd proclaimed, or if he merely tolerated her questions.

Floor-to-ceiling windows fronted onto Columbus. Passersby shaded their eyes to get a better view inside the restaurant. Mariella waved at a little blond boy watching her. When he realized she'd seen him, he backed away, ducking into his father's knees.

"See, even children are weakened by beauty," Leslie said.

"You are big charmer," Mariella said. "If Pietro is your boyfriend, I hope he understands this about you."

"Pietro is *not* my boyfriend," Leslie said. "At least not anymore."

"Ohh. Sorry, sorry—again—for two times already, just today." Mariella held up her index and middle finger. "But you are still friends, yes?"

"Much better than we ever were lovers," he said, and downed

half a glass of water in one continuous swallow. "He's happily involved now with a man named Jeffrey."

Pietro reappeared with a bottle of wine in one hand, and four wine glasses, larger than the ones already on the table, upside down by their stems. Mariella had started to say something more to Leslie, but halted, lips parted, when she saw the man accompanying Pietro: a trim, well-built man in sand-colored slacks and a pale green long-sleeved shirt, rolled up at the cuffs.

"That's the owner, Giovanni," Leslie whispered.

Giovanni wasn't handsome like Jeremy Irons, Mariella's belated adolescent heartthrob she'd seen in an old video of *Brideshead Revisited* and reruns of *The French Lieutenant's Woman* or Marcello Mastroianni when he was younger, but good-looking in the way of a man who was really a man, like the deceased actor the Italians called the one with the *viso cesellato*, Burt Lancaster. Giovanni was too old for her, of course, his dark brown hair gray at the temples. The laugh lines around his eyes placed him somewhere in his forties, maybe even as old as her father. He looked at her directly, and she felt the unmistakable flush of desire between her legs.

"No, no, don't get up," Giovanni said, extending his hand to Mariella and then to Leslie before he sat. "Good to see you again." The lunch crowd had thinned out and only a handful of diners lingered over coffee or an unfinished glass of wine.

Pietro set down the new wine glasses, opened the bottle, inspected the cork for disintegration or leaks, and offered it for Giovanni's approval, then placed the cork on the table. He removed the original glasses to an empty table nearby. "A very fine Nebbiolo from Piemontese," he said, as he poured a small amount of the faintly translucent red wine in Giovanni's glass.

Giovanni sniffed deeply into his glass, swirled the wine before he swallowed and with his eyes closed and for a long moment savored his first taste. As the wine settled back into the bottom of his glass it left "legs" or streaks inside the glass, a sign Mariella knew from her days at the trattoria meant that the wine had body.

"*Bene,*" Giovanni said. "A good choice."

Soft track lighting, along with a muted *Nessun Dorma* piping through hidden speakers (she'd recognize Pavarotti at any volume) seduced her for a brief, nostalgic moment into imagining she was back in Catania at the Trattoria Inglese.

"I'm Giovanni Russo," the owner told her as Pietro poured wine for them all.

She laughed, too loud, she thought, and said, "Maybe you are my uncle," though that was the last thing she wanted, for him to think of her as his niece. Or even worse, a silly girl. She found him way too attractive for that. All her life her mother had warned her, "Someday you're going to put your big foot in your mouth, and you won't be able to get it out!"

"What I mean to say, I am Russo, like you," she said, quietly. "Mariella Russo."

"There are probably a hundred thousand of us. Russos, I mean, here in the United States," Giovanni said. When he grinned, the lines crinkled around his brown eyes. He raised his hands from the table. "Probably more. I read it on the Internet, so it must be true." Was he making a joke at her expense? She couldn't tell. "Seriously, there must be at least a couple hundred, at least, in San Francisco alone. Check in the phone book sometime, you'll see."

She could feel her chest tighten. From nerves? Had she overstepped her bounds? Did he think she was claiming to be related? Yes, Giovanni Russo taking her in with his stare made her nervous.

"Well," she said. She couldn't stop herself. "Unless our ancestors were very, very busy—like five thousand rabbits, as my nonna Giuseppina says—I don't think we are *famiglia,* you and I."

Giovanni laughed again, a hearty open-mouthed guffaw. "That's very good," he said. "My nonna was far too straight-laced to utter anything so daring." His voice was calming, confident and deep. She could barely discern an accent. Plus there was something unusual, a refinement, or a remnant perhaps, of growing up Italian but not in *Italia*?

Giovanni raised his glass to his three companions. *"Saluti,"* he said, and to Mariella, "Pietro tells me you've just come from Sicily."

"Si," Mariella said and lifted her glass and inhaled its bouquet. Perhaps breathing deeply would relax her. "But how you did—how did you," she corrected herself. "How *did* you learn to talk English so good?" She swallowed two large mouthfuls of the wine, making her empty stomach swirl and her head feel fuzzy.

"We—my family, that is—moved from Liguria to England when I was nine. *Italiano* was my first language, of course. *La mia prima lingua,*" Giovanni said, with a beautiful lilt and roll of the tongue.

"Si," she said. "Sure, that explains why you talk so good . . ." She caught herself again. She wanted Giovanni—wanted all of them—to see the results of her years of high school and university English. "No," she said. "I mean, speak so *well.*"

She met Giovanni's eyes with her own, over the rim of her glass and tilted her glass toward her lips, but the wine never made it to her lips. Her hand stopped short, and the wine dribbled down the front of her dress.

She grabbed her white linen napkin from the table and dabbed at her chest, then dunked a corner of the cloth into her water glass and rubbed at the purple splotches dead center on her left breast.

Merda! The lace of her rose-colored bra showed clearly through the dampness. She tried to console herself with the thought that she was not herself because she was still exhausted, and maybe the Xanax hadn't completely worn off.

"Such a beautiful dress," Giovanni said. "I hope it's not ruined."

Without meeting anyone's eyes and uttering only a *"Scusi,"* Mariella fled from the table to the restroom, through a rough-hewn wooden door marked *Bagno* in black letters.

Luckily the place was empty, but it wouldn't have stopped her even if it hadn't been. She pulled her dress over her head and ran the tap as hot as it would go, then laid the wine-soiled part in the marble sink inches under the stream and watched the stain bleed away. An old laundry trick passed down from her mother. And maybe her mother was right. Maybe she really was clumsy, though of course Mamma had never seen her dance the tango or the rhumba with Matteo.

When she returned to the table, Giovanni's chair was empty. So he'd given up on her. She didn't blame him. She wouldn't have hired her either, but still, her spirit was bruised. She tried to act nonchalant as she draped herself with the shawl she'd brought in case the restaurant was air-conditioned.

Leslie bounced his leg and tapped his feet under the table.

She searched his face for signs that he'd intended to scold her for making such a mess of things. But no, there was no tension. His toe-tapping, a nervous tick.

Pietro sat silently, watching, then held his glass of Nebbiolo up to the light, slowly turning the glass from side to side, assessing the wine, it appeared, for something unnamed.

Leslie glanced at his watch, began fidgeting with his cell phone.

"We go," she muttered, there being, after all, no reason to stay. *This interview, a disaster, and this man—this Giovanni Russo, he makes me talk too much and say the wrong thing.*

She checked the banquette for her belongings, and when she looked up, there was Giovanni.

"Sorry," he said, sounding out of breath as he sat back down. "I needed to consult with my chef about a last-minute change."

She held still and said nothing. Maybe if she breathed quietly, she could stop time. Maybe she wouldn't make any more mistakes. Even if Giovanni Russo had agreed to the interview just to be polite for Pietro's sake, she didn't want this to be the last time she sat across from him.

"Mariella worked in a trattoria," Leslie announced.

Giovanni raised his eyebrows.

"*Si*," she said. "When I was at university." But why even bother telling him? She *was* sometimes an oaf, and like Leslie said, there were so many other more qualified young women, and maybe men. "I work in the travel agency after classes in the afternoon, and some nights and weekends I serve tables at the trattoria."

Giovanni observed her for a full thirty seconds, but it felt to her like an hour before he asked, "Do you know food?"

"I am *ottimo cuoco*—well, not excellent every time, but very good." She couldn't help herself, she had to say it: "After all, I am Siciliana."

He laughed, that deep, friendly laugh, and held up his hands. "Of course, I should have known. But," he said, "you understand, the reason it's important is that the hostess seats people and is sometimes asked about the food or a particular dish. And if you—if she—doesn't know, then the customers don't think of this as a better . . ." He thought for a moment. "An elegant place."

"I understand," Mariella said.

"Luciano, the maitre d', he's the one who will train you," Pietro said, entering the conversation. "And I will help because, of course, I have to know the food in order to pair it with the right wine."

"There's just one problem," Giovanni said. "I can't legally hire you without a work permit."

"But I have," Mariella said, reaching for her purse.

"You do?" Leslie said. She wanted to erase the amazement from his face.

"Of course." From her oversized purse she extracted an envelope of papers: passport, university diploma, her visa and work permit. Did Leslie think she would work in a travel agency and come to America unprepared? He didn't know her—of course he didn't, but if—*if*—they were going to be roommates, he would learn; he would come to understand. "I received . . . ?"

They all nodded.

". . . when I applied for university here, they folded it in."

"Included?" Giovanni offered.

"Yes, when I applied—when I made the contact for the San Francisco University, your government at the embassy, they included it with my student visa."

"University of San Francisco? So you're attending my alma mater," Giovanni remarked, and nodded, in approval.

"No, no, the San Francisco *State* University. Anyway, I think they let me in. But the university—yes, the *Cattolico* one? No, no," she said. "For me it is too expensive." Even at the state university, the price of admission for international students was at least double the amount for California residents. She'd have to keep working to attend, and she was grateful every day for the money Nonna had given her and for the amount she'd saved from her jobs in Catania.

"Well, anyway, you think ahead," Giovanni said. "I admire an organized mind. Like Teresa's. Did I mention her, Teresa, my sister? She too has an organized mind. You and she would share the job. We own Basilico together, but she doesn't make the restaurant her life the way I do."

On hearing Teresa's name, Pietro rolled his eyes. Or was Mariella only imagining he did?

Leslie drove home avoiding the Broadway tunnel. Did he bypass it deliberately? Had he seen her fear? Her claustrophobia embarrassed her, made her see herself as weak, less than, maybe even a little crazy like her mother. Hysterical, at the least.

Her mind drifted, over and over, back to her interview.

"The customers would be delighted with you," Giovanni had said. "You understand food, you're smart." In spite of her clumsiness and her fumbling with English, he *had* noticed she possessed a brain. "You'll learn quickly, and they'll love the accent."

He'd promised to let her know his decision in a day or two, after he'd finished interviewing other applicants. She had no idea how many.

After several silent moments staring out the passenger-side window, Mariella reached over and touched Leslie's arm. "Thank you," she said. "Thank you for taking this time for me when I am sure you have to do the study."

"Oh," Leslie said. "I think you'll get the job."

"Why you think that?" She clucked her tongue. "No, no. I don't think so. My nervous make me act like I'm *stupido*. Yes? *Goffo*." She flicked her fingers over the bosom of her still damp dress. If she was foolish enough to spill all over herself, Giovanni would never let her near the customers with food or even water, let alone wine.

"First of all, no, that's not true," Leslie said. She couldn't see the smile he fought to conceal, the endearment she created with her mispronunciations. "And secondly, you two should get along fine. He has a reputation for being direct, just like you."

She and Giovanni had stood and faced one another at the interview's end. "Just a word of advice," he'd said, handing her his card. "You're an attractive young woman." His eyes had held onto hers. "Some of the line cooks, and some of the waiters, especially the Italian ones, don't always keep their admiration to themselves."

"I know how to take care of them," she'd said and shrugged.

"Well." Giovanni laughed. "I hope you'd take care of yourself and *not* them."

"It is what I mean." She'd felt her face grow warm, like her mother's old warning slapping her on the cheek: *Only a puttana leaves home without being married!* But she wasn't a prostitute leaving home, she was a career woman! Did Giovanni Russo think she was "bad," as her mother seemed to?

She'd noticed the signet ring on the little finger of his right hand, but no wedding band. Lots of married men didn't wear rings; she'd assumed it was because they wanted to appear free to take a mistress. But she knew nothing about Giovanni Russo other than his name, that he was the owner of Basilico, that he came from Liguria, that he'd lived in London, and that he appeared to be a kind man with a sister named Teresa whom no one seemed to want to talk about.

Giovanni had offered his hand as she and Leslie prepared to leave Basilico, a lingering handshake, warm and reassuring, the gold watch on his wrist against olive skin, an encirclement she'd always found sexy and a conveyance of confidence, a man who belonged to himself. As they'd released one another and he'd smiled and said, "Ciao bella," his voice low and rich, a recollection she'd carried all these years of the Eternal City rose up in her, a sudden remembrance, prompted no doubt by the mention of Piazza Navona earlier and her youthful trip to Rome. How she'd wept at Bernini's sculpture of Pluto abducting Proserpina at the Galleria Borghese. She'd never seen anything so sensual, so sexy, that close up: Pluto's fingers digging into the flesh of Proserpina's thigh, her lips parted as if to appear that she was in ecstasy rather than despair, her hand outstretched in orgasm.

Mariella had been fifteen, a virgin at the time. She'd already discovered the nighttime secret of bringing pleasure to herself.

And even though he was far too old for her, she couldn't push away the thought of Giovanni's warm fingers pressing into the soft flesh of *her* thigh, of lying under him naked and inhaling the smell of his skin, of discovering the taste of his generous mouth.

Chapter Seventeen

She loved the flavors and vibrancy of the Inner Sunset, the chatter, like variations on a melody swirling through the air. The blending of different languages and inflections, predominantly Chinese and Asian, which accounted for the abundance of Thai and Chinese eateries, along with Spanish, Middle Eastern, and, of course, American. The cafés and trattori-style *ristoranti*, with their international menus and aromas, gave her the sensation, as she strolled through these neighborhoods, of being on a side alleyway off the Piazza Duomo, the main square in Catania. There was even a bakery, Arizmendi, a cooperative, like the one where her grandmother had worked over fifty years before.

These streets—Irving, Judah, Kirkham, and the Avenues that intersected—had the feel of long-established communities, exactly as Leslie had described them. People greeted each other on the sidewalks, even stopped to visit neighbors, Mariella guessed, catching each other up on their lives. At least the ones who weren't so engrossed in their cell phones they bothered to notice, or avoid plowing into, other people on the street.

Now, on her Sunday morning stroll, she recalled how fearful she'd been—was it really less than a week ago?—convinced that men who liked to beat up women lurked behind every doorway, ready to leap out and attack.

And now, it was hard to imagine feeling anything but safe.

It had been four days since her disastrous interview. She'd

done her best to struggle with what she was certain would be disappointing news, assuming that Giovanni even bothered to get back to her. And why would he? To pass along a litany of excuses why he hired someone else. Someone more qualified, someone better-looking, someone less clumsy, someone he already knew—someone American? And so she'd been searching the newspaper and Internet ads on her laptop for other employment. A family with two small children in Glen Park wanted a nanny. *No thank you.* She liked children, but she'd never be able to carve out the time for school and be responsible for someone's little ones. Restaurants posted signs in their windows: dishwashers wanted. *No! Absolutely not!* Receptionist for a veterinarian? *Perhaps, if they'd let her work part time.* Even so, her accent and outspoken mouth would no doubt kill her chances there as well.

Maybe tomorrow, when it wasn't so busy, she'd revisit the little Italian restaurants in her neighborhood. Maybe one of them would employ a real *Italiana* waitress, even one who blurted out the wrong thing.

Perhaps the young woman she'd encountered on her first visit to the Beanery would be there again this morning. Mariella and Leslie had stood in line at the popular coffee house that first day, behind a young mother with short spiked hair and nose and lip piercings who'd cooed softly to her baby in a stroller. The woman's arms had been wrapped in metal bracelets, and chains hung from her neck and belt. Mariella had tilted her chin and said, "Ciao," and to her delight the young woman had said, "Ciao" in return. They'd seen each other both times Mariella had been there since.

As she rounded the corner from Irving onto Ninth, she saw the overflow crowd milling on the sidewalk in front of the Beanery. Not today, then. Today she'd pick up a cappuccino and a breakfast roll from a less crowded café and make her way back home.

Home. That word rested surprisingly, peacefully, in her mind. She did feel at home here, and with Leslie as well. And faster than she'd dreamed possible.

Later that morning she sat across from him, perusing various sections of the Sunday *Chronicle* spread out between them on the kitchen table. She'd been concentrating on her English, deciphering a review in the Datebook section of an archived English film, *Enchanted April*, rereleased for a British film festival at the Balboa Theater. *A slow-paced gem*—the critic had written, eight years earlier—*one of '92's best from across the pond, about the civilizing influence of Italy on beleaguered Londoners, both male and female, and it has its own civilizing influence on the viewer* . . .

Yes, the civilizing influence of *Italia*. It would do her homesick heart good to see Italy glorified, without grime or blemish, like a movie actress whose imperfections are camouflaged by the camera's filter.

Images of her own enchanted Sicilian Aprils and Mays arose in her mind's eye, the delight when wildflowers burst forth all at once, all over the island—pink heather, vivid red poppies, wild sweet peas and yellow daisies that blanketed the land like groundcover. Along with those springtime months, this time of year, late June well into July, was the time of year in Catania that Mariella loved most. Plump sweet cherries staining her teeth, the juice of succulent plums running down her chin, summer's suffocating white heat insinuating itself into the flesh of everything that lived and breathed. But now, in the jasmine-tinted evenings it was still sometimes balmy and soft.

She didn't want to *go* home, at least not today. She simply wanted to glimpse the essence of home to soothe her failures, as one would open a jewelry box from time to time, to reminiscence on a treasured keepsake.

That morning's remonstrative, though loving, email from her father had heightened her sense of letting everyone down, including herself. *I didn't realize how unhappy you were*, he'd written. *I'm sorry you didn't believe you could tell me. My dearest girl, if I had known, I might have helped you.*

Leslie's ringing phone jolted her.

"Smokey Joe's Café," Leslie said. He munched on an apple and slurped, she thought, for effect. He'd been singing that old tune—"One day while I was eating beans . . ." (even the denizens of remote Catania knew of the Coasters)—luxuriating, it seemed, in his last moments before readying himself for his afternoon shift at Gypsy Men's out on Haight Street, "The offbeat men's clothing store where I work," he'd explained. Offbeat, she'd thought, like Leslie himself.

"Omigod!" he mouthed at Mariella. "Sorry for the greeting," he said, sitting up straighter and speaking directly into the mouthpiece. "Of course. Yes, she's right here. No, no, I'll put her on." He reached across the table and held out his phone.

"Sorry," he whispered, making a grimace.

"*Pronto?*" she said. Maybe it was Olimpio or Papa. But surely the email she'd just sent back wouldn't have raised any alarms. And, anyway, why would they be calling Leslie? *Oh, please, let there be nothing wrong.* "I mean, 'allo."

"Leslie always did have an odd sense of humor. It's Giovanni Russo," he said, unnecessarily because she'd memorized his voice, its timbre, its roundness and tone. Hearing it, even over the phone, electrified her. "Forgive me for bothering you on a Sunday. I called Leslie because I don't have your new phone number"—*Stupid me, I should have sent it to him!*—"and, I'm calling to offer you the hostess position at Basilico."

"No," she said. "I don't believe . . ." *Dio mio, just keep your big mouth shut!* "*Certo*, yes, grazie, thank you so very much. I am how you say—delighted—and surprised too."

She glanced at Leslie's grin, his thumbs up. "I told you," he mouthed again.

"When? Tomorrow? Si," she said. "Yes, I can be there. Yes, okay, nine o'clock."

Chapter Eighteen

The menu at Basilico? Upscale and seasonal: grilled or roasted whole fish, usually branzino or halibut; braised artichokes and fava beans; sardines and fresh calamari, sautéed or grilled; fennel and broccoli dressed with lemon and olive oil; currants and pine nuts as accoutrements. All familiar staples of the Sicilian table, as well as, Mariella was discovering, the Ligurian.

The heavy red meat sauces she'd been forewarned were hallmarks of Americano/Italian *ristoranti* were absent from Basilico's menu. The pappardelle with wild mushrooms and caramelized onions, the gnocchi with Swiss chard, mascarpone and breadcrumbs: "These specialties," Luciano, the avuncular maitre d', instructed her, "are the dishes that reflect Basilico's northern roots."

The discreet request at the bottom of the menu pleased her: *For the comfort and pleasure of your fellow diners, please silence your mobile phone.* She disapproved of phone conversations in public, how loud and rude and oblivious cell phone talkers often seemed to be. The request helped her regard Basilico as the "better kind of place" Giovanni intended.

As Mariella dispensed the leather bound menus and wine list, she enjoyed regaling the patrons, half in Italian and half in English, describing the day's specials, what dishes she'd sampled and loved best. Occasionally they'd ask her what part of Italy she'd come from ("I am Siciliana!") and what brought her here. And did she have a young man in her life, which flustered her because it made her think of Matteo, and more than once, tear up.

But hostessing came naturally to her. And without any help from Leslie after her first day, she was able to navigate the Muni bus route, even managing the transfer points all the way to North Beach.

Giovanni started her on lunch shifts Tuesdays through Fridays, and one dinner shift on Mondays. "Slowly," he said, though lunch hours were long and fast-paced too. "You do a good job, raises will come quickly," he assured her.

He really *was* too old for her, and besides, he was her boss. But whenever he sought her out, whenever he spoke to her face-to-face ("How are you doing? Everything going all right? By the way, Luciano and Pietro both tell me you're doing a fine job.") she sensed his desire. And when he scanned her body with the slightest flicker of his eyes, she saw something deeper coloring that desire, perhaps the shadow of some old sorrow or hunger—she couldn't tell which—residing in his gaze.

Sicilians had a name for such eyes: *miele occhi.* Honey eyes.

She insisted to herself that she was drawn to Giovanni only because she missed Matteo. And even though he wasn't anything like Matteo—no political rants or raptures about philosophy and poets—there was an intensity about Giovanni that compelled.

He stayed in his office for hours at a stretch, although at least once during most lunch and dinner shifts, he walked through the dining rooms, smiling and saying a few words to the guests. On occasion, he sat for a glass of wine with what she assumed must be old friends. Or perhaps family or long-time patrons.

Without fail, he left the restaurant every day at 2:00 p.m. and returned at 3:30. She asked Pietro, "Where does he go?" She wouldn't ask if he went home to a wife. Wouldn't want anyone to think it mattered.

"Dunno. Why don't you ask Teresa?" Pietro said and shrugged

as he inventoried the floor-to-ceiling wine rack near the hostess station. Bottles were brought up from the cellar and stored there on their sides according to vintner and variety, creating a wall between the spacious entryway and the dining rooms.

"No, I think you know I don't do that," she scolded. Giovanni's sister was cold to everyone except the customers, her brother, and Luciano. But especially to Mariella.

One afternoon during her first week, Teresa entered the staff area and found Mariella enjoying her allowance of one free daily meal and flashed her a sidelong, disapproving look.

Who do you think you are to sit in my family's restaurant and act as if you belong here? She might as well have spoken the words aloud in her clipped English accent, an anomaly in this Italian-speaking enclave, surprising Mariella whenever she heard Teresa's voice. A reminder that Giovanni's sister was raised entirely in London, unlike her brother who lived in London but was born in Italy. Her tweedy skirts and school marm blouses matched her stern demeanor. And, adding to Teresa's perpetual scowl was her unibrow, like the brow of Frida Kahlo, the Mexican painter whose small self-portrait Mariella had once seen in a traveling museum exhibit in *Siracusa*.

"I did something wrong?" Mariella asked Pietro after she'd returned to the hostess desk after her lunch.

"You mean about the old maid?"

"Old maid?"

Pietro thought of how to explain, then snapped a finger and shook it. "Yes, the woman who grows old but never gets married."

Like me, she thought, remembering the words of the angry boy on the Marina in Catania. *Like I could be for the rest of my life.*

"No worries about Teresa," Pietro said. "She's perpetually unhappy. But hey, it was her choice to share hostess duties and a wise one if you ask me. Make her co-manager and half the waitstaff would quit. Rumor has it," he said, leaning closer to

Mariella, "when Teresa turned eighteen she entered a convent in England to become a nun. Apparently, she lasted two years, and then something happened, a love affair gone bad, I think. Anyway, something she never speaks about, but something that made her bitter."

"Well, whatever happened," Mariella said impatiently. "I just wish she wouldn't be mean—what is it you say, *bitter?*—to *me.*"

"Anyway," Pietro said, "after she bolted, she stopped going to Mass. Never had anything more to do with the church."

An assault by a priest? An affair with a fellow novice? Or, as had happened to Mariella, a realization that she could never devote herself to the Catholic Church.

"When I was a young girl," Mariella told Pietro, "I did my best to pray to God the Father. *Dio Padre.* But the face I imagine was my own Papa's, Salvatore's."

She tried to laugh off Teresa's obvious dislike of her, plus both Pietro and Luciano made up for it by complimenting Mariella daily. "You dress just right," they said. "Not too fancy, not too simple. Perfect for Basilico." She mixed and matched so her outfits appeared new and stylish, though day-to-day they were the same pieces she'd worn with a different skirt or pair of pants, or a shawl with a dress.

On her way out the door of the apartment one morning during her first weeks, Leslie glanced up and remarked, "You look really hot today." He was reading the newest legislation on property damages for a professor who had offered him a summer internship in his law practice. For a stipend, as internships go, and, he needed the experience to vie for a decent entry-level position after graduation.

"Hot?" She looked down at herself, then held up the jacket draped over her arm.

"Oh, I don't mean temperature," he said, laughing. "You know, sexy. Like I told you the first time you wore that dress and you asked me if that meant I liked . . . well, slept with women too."

"Oh, yes, okay, I remember," she said. Then, they both laughed at the memory of that early awkward moment in Leslie's car, different from how easy they were now with each other. "I get it, hot means sexy."

She wore the peach and green dress she'd salvaged from the wine debacle the first time she'd met Giovanni.

"I'd wager at least half the waiters are madly in love with you," Leslie said.

Mariella clucked her tongue. "Eh, the waiters. They are nice enough, but most of them still act like boys, even the older ones." Joking and calling to one another as they passed back and forth from the kitchen to the tables. "Making the dirty stories in *Italiano*." Poking fun at one another, also staged as entertainment for the guests. "But the one who makes my skin crawl," she said, "is the sous chef with *pazzo*—no, I think *psicopatico* eyes." Young Mario Bianchi, thin-mouthed and impatient, but who concocted *salse perfetti* and *contorini* side dishes layered with unforgettable, subtle flavors.

Something about him was bound too tight. A man, she believed, who would not be kind to a woman, who would beat her perhaps, or inflict even worse cruelty. Not only rape, but mutilating her female parts, like they do in Somalia or the Sudan, and enslaving her in a locked, soundless room. But then again, she'd always had a wild imagination. The waitstaff sang Mario's culinary praises and included him in their banter, and the other chefs seemed easy and lighthearted around him.

Whenever possible she stood, instead of in front of Mario's station, in front of Cosima's to place her order for her daily allotted meal as part of the staff.

"*Buonasera!*" Cosima sang out, her long, frizzy red hair captured in an orange cowboy bandana. "What you want today, hawney?" Cosima was Mario's assistant and spoke her native Spanish, Italian, and English. She took no nonsense from any of the men: waiters, busboys, line cooks, or chefs.

Yesterday, as she'd handed Mariella her plate of sautéed scallops, Cosima whispered, "I put a little somet'ing extra for you on the side." A glistening, already shelled, fresh lobster claw, and a tidbit of New York steak with black truffle shavings.

It did Mariella's heart good to see Cosima ordering the men around, as if she had a perfect right.

Chapter Nineteen

"Will you come to my office?" Giovanni said, surprising Mariella, looming beside her at the hostess desk. A tall arrangement of orange bird of paradise sat to one side of the desk's lustrous black marble surface. It was August, well into her second month at Basilico, and half an hour before Teresa was scheduled to come in.

Mariella took a reflexive step backwards. *This is it. This is where he tells me I'm fired.*

"Oh, please," Giovanni said, reaching out, barely brushing her arm. "There's nothing to be concerned about. I only want to discuss some thoughts I've had about your work, and," he glanced around the near-empty restaurant, "I would prefer if we could have the conversation in private."

Pietro sidled up to Mariella after Giovanni had gone. "He means in case his sister shows up early and sees the two of you talking," he whispered. He'd been near the hostess station setting up a wine flight. "She gets crazy jealous." He held a wine glass against the soft light of the overheads, checking for water stains.

"Why?"

"I only know what Luciano told me, that she was always left out—the forgotten one in their family."

"You mean like the goat who is scaped?"

"Yes." Pietro smiled. "Like that."

"I hope, again, I have not done something wrong," Mariella said.

"Don't worry, he likes you. I can tell," Pietro said. "We all do." He looked around, conspiratorially, just as Giovanni had done. "It was the same with the woman who worked here before you. She did a fine job, but she definitely butted heads with the old maid."

"Is not right for you to call her that," Mariella said, placing her hands on her hips.

"I'd never call her that to her face," Pietro said. "But that's what she's known by. Except Luciano—and him, of course." He tilted his head toward Giovanni's office. "She hardly ever talks to anyone, aside from the customers. But maybe if she were a little friendlier . . ." He shrugged.

"Well, she know—"

"*Knows*," Pietro said.

"Oh, right. She knows everyone talks about her, I'm certainly."

Pietro raised his eyebrows but didn't correct Mariella again. "Why do you care about her? She's a *bich* to you too," he said, pronouncing the insult the Italian way. He picked up the tray with the flight pours and made off to a table.

Why *did* she care? Everyone had always chided her about caring too much, about feeling too keenly the pain of others, a testament to her big and foolish heart.

She knocked on Giovanni's partly open office door. He sat at his desk, concentrating on something on his computer, although on second glance, it appeared to her he was gazing into space.

"Oh, there you are." He stood to greet her. He opened the door and gestured toward a leather armchair on the other side of his desk. "Sit down, please."

Maschile, was her impression, once again, just as it had been the previous times she'd been inside his office. A masculine room, just right for him: dark wood, beige walls with seascapes in wood and burnished bronze frames, lots of leather, pewter accents here and there. On top of his desk, besides the computer, a brass-framed photograph of a lovely woman with reddish-brown shoulder-length hair. His wife, Mariella had decided on her first summons nearly two months ago. A woman with clever tenderness in her smile, a woman a man might easily cherish.

Giovanni stared at Mariella—through her it seemed—just long enough to make her uncomfortable. He appeared to be searching for how to say her job had been terminated.

"I'd like you to think about temporarily taking over as manager," he said.

"*Che cosa?*" She opened her arms. "You can't mean . . . you are making a joke at me."

"I've given this a lot of thought. George Shelton is moving back to Detroit in a few weeks." The manager, a serious military-looking man with a crew cut. He tended to restaurant business primarily from inside his office, and in collaboration with Giovanni, as well as in the kitchen. Most of the time he left the front to Luciano, Pietro, and Teresa.

"But I am, how you say?—new kid on the block." She was thinking of Giovanni's sister, how Teresa would detest her even more. "Besides, one month from today is not enough time to learn. It is the job for Teresa, no?"

"No."

"No? *Perche no?*"

"It *was* Teresa's. Hers and Luciano's idea to offer you the position."

"No!"

"Yes." He nodded. "She's well aware what people here think about her."

Mariella flushed, recalling Pietro's name for Teresa.

"She knows the waiters and line cooks would never look up to her as manager. That they might mutiny. But you?" He regarded Mariella for another moment. "They all like you. Everyone."

"I like them too," she said. "But how do you know I would do a good job?" It wasn't enough for the waiters and busboys and chefs to *like* her; she would also have to earn their respect. She'd only spoken with George Shelton a few times, but whenever Luciano or Pietro announced, "George says we have to move these two tables to the back," or, "We have to change to Brisco linen, even though Lupton is a long-time friend," it was done, immediately. Only the head chef, Ricardo, or Giovanni held more rank.

"What about the school—the degree for the languages? What about my job as hostess? I like it, I am just getting used to it, and for manager, I would have to work each day more than just a few hours." If he meant for her to give up graduate school, she'd leave the restaurant. But for now, she'd decided to earn some money, take a couple of classes at night, and wait until spring semester, in January, for school full time.

"Of course, I'll pay you a regular salary. Considerably more than the hourly wage you're making now," he said. "And, I've thought about school. That it begins in just a few months."

She didn't like squirming when Giovanni watched her like that, with such intensity.

"That's why I suggested you take the job temporarily," he said. "Until we can find someone full time." He swiveled in his chair and reached into a bottom drawer. He circled back, a manila file in hand. Her name was on the file flap.

"Both George and I will work with you until he leaves. Teresa and Luciano, they'll help too. They know this restaurant inside and out."

"Why me?" Mariella asked. "Why do you want me to take this job?" She tried to imagine working with him, side-by-side, every day. She was a blurter. Would she be able to contain her desire?

"Because you learn fast, and you've got a head for details, and you're smart. Not just school smart, but people smart. Everyone sees that, even Cosima in the kitchen."

"What about Mario Bianchi?" The young chef who frightened her. "What does he say?"

"That you don't order from him," Giovanni said, as if he'd read her mind. "If you're going to be manager, you'll need to work with him."

Was Giovanni checking up on her? Was that what it said in that file? That she avoided Mario Bianchi. "It is wrong to order from Cosima instead?"

"No." Giovanni shrugged. "No, but when Ricardo's not here Mario's in charge of the kitchen."

Could she tell him she thought Mario had *psicopatico* eyes? Could she admit that she kept her distance because there was something about his weird intensity that both repelled and compelled her? That would-be psychologist part of her, the need to comprehend. In truth, that she was afraid Mario would sniff out and exploit her weakness, her desire to help, and pull her in?

"Teresa used to be afraid of him too," Giovanni said. "Ask her. She'll tell you. He's got a chip on his shoulder." Giovanni gestured in the general direction of the kitchen. "He's a marvelous cook, and I assure you, he's harmless."

"How are you so sure?"

"I've known Mario all his life." He hesitated, then said, "He worked with me at Trovatore when I was manager there, before I opened Basilico. He's probably more frightened of you than you are of him. Trust me, you have nothing to worry about. I promise. I give you my word."

She'd seen no more of Mario's body than his ink-free forearms and hands, the sleeves of his chef's coat always rolled up. But in her imagination Mario Bianchi's body was covered with tattoos of knives and dragons and skulls.

Giovanni opened Mariella's folder and pulled out some official-looking forms. "And think about this," he said. "As your employer, I can begin your application for a green card."

He tapped the papers. "You're familiar with what a green card is—a permanent visa?"

"Si. Of course." She hadn't decided yet, hadn't had time to think about staying permanently in America.

"Will you give me one or two days?" she asked.

He stood, indicating that their meeting was over. "Can you let me know by Friday?"

"I think it is possible," Mariella said. "Yes, I will let you know then."

Chapter Twenty

As Mariella stepped into the apartment, Leslie turned down the volume on the CD player. Freddie Mercury's haunting lament, his keen to his Mamma that he'd just killed a man. Leslie had mentioned in his first email to her that Queen was his all-time favorite rock band, and she had to agree; "Bohemian Rhapsody" was one of the best in any genre. He slouched in one of the overstuffed white chairs, his legs propped onto an ottoman, books and papers askew at his feet.

But when she told him of Giovanni's offer, he shouted, "Holy shit, girl!" and sat bolt upright. "You've only been there a few weeks, and he offers you the job of manager? You can't refuse."

"No?"

"Do you know how many restaurant managers and assistant managers in North Beach would kill for the opportunity to manage Basilico?"

"No."

"Take my word. Actually, Pietro's word. They would."

"That is second time today someone give me his word. What does it mean to have someone's word? Is better to say, 'I keep my word,' rather than telling someone to take it, because if you give your word then it is gone and meaning nothing. Yes?" She shook her head. "You *Americanos* indeed have a strange way of speaking, and maybe of thinking, too."

Of late, she and Leslie had managed only minutes together over morning coffee or a glimpse to say goodnight. His being home in the middle of the afternoon, as he was today, was a rarity. Although a few weekends back, he'd taken her for a memorable Sunday afternoon meal to a Thai restaurant out on Clement. She'd swooned over a dish called Pad Ma Kuer: minced chicken and chunks of Japanese eggplant (she loved eggplant) with carrots, green beans, onions, and little toadstool-like mushrooms on long stems, all sautéed in a spicy basil garlic sauce.

She settled into the white armchair kitty corner from Leslie. "Oh, *multo interesante!*" she teased, picking up the book he'd laid, splayed out, spine side up, on the small table: *Wills and Trusts in the Twenty-First Century.* "But you are okay?"

"I'm okay." But something in the tentative way Leslie answered made her believe he wasn't.

Mariella clucked her tongue against her teeth. "Why we don't have a nice dinner here? What you think? Saturday night," she said. "I will cook."

"Sure, dinner would be fine."

"You are for sure?"

He laughed. She was getting used to it now, people smirking or laughing at the way she put words together. But her grammar was improving, incrementally, day-by-day.

"I'm for sure," he said. He chewed on the pencil he'd retrieved from behind his ear. "Actually, I'm a little worried."

"Oh. What it is? Can you say—can you tell me?"

"No, no. It's . . . well . . . I've met someone."

"It is good?" She lifted her hands as a question. "Yes?" She prompted him.

"I met him only a couple of weeks ago." Leslie drifted off, looking past her. "He's at Hastings too, helping out in the law library over the summer. He told me right away he was HIV positive . . ."

The hairs on the back of her neck told Mariella what her housemate was ruminating about, and she hoped she was wrong.

"Mr. Leslie, you think he has the AIDS? I mean your new friend?"

"No . . . probably not. At least I don't think so."

Leslie sucked in his bottom lip and stared at the floor. She leaned forward, waiting for him to say more.

"We had unprotected sex only once." Leslie held up a hand. "I know, I know better. I can't believe I'm even admitting this. His—Darrell's, that's his name, Darrell—his former partner died of AIDS. I mean all he knows for sure is that he's HIV positive—and that he's being treated as part of the new study with antiretroviral drugs through UCSF." Leslie picked at the fabric on the arm of his chair. "We've been very careful since then—and it's more than possible that I'm okay." Without warning, he started to cry.

"Oh, Leslie," Mariella said. She got up and knelt by his side. She patted his hand. "Maybe it will be all right."

Leslie brushed away his tears with his palm, but as fast as he wiped them away they leaked out. "I'm more upset with myself than I am with him, and it's not like he didn't tell me about the HIV, I mean right off the bat. It's the stupidest, oldest story in the world: *We just got carried away!*" He flung open his arms. "But there it is, and sure, I'm upset with him too."

"My friend, I think you have been very foolish, yes, but I have the strong feeling it is going to be okay." She jostled his shoulder. "You want me to go with you for testing tomorrow?"

"No, no," he said. And then, after a moment, he turned to look at her. "I know I should go. Darrell offered to go with me, but I've been afraid . . . well, because we're so new. But really? Would you?"

"Of course." If they went first thing in the morning, she could still make it to work on time. "We can go early?"

"The earlier the better," Leslie said, reaching for a tissue on the side table and blowing his nose. "You know that the virus may not show up right away? I mean even if I'm not infected now, I may have to go back every few months for a new test."

"Well then," Mariella said. "We will go every few months."

At seven thirty the following morning, Leslie eased his Mini into a slot on the Geary campus of Kaiser. At this hour the enormous parking lot was only part full. In another hour, cars would be circling around and around, waiting for someone to leave.

Once inside the hospital, they followed the blue arrows on the linoleum floors and located the testing area. In the examining room Mariella sat in a corner and listened quietly as a sympathetic nurse practitioner—her name tag identified her as Joyce Blevins—confirmed what Leslie had already surmised: if he were recently infected, those results likely wouldn't show for up to three months. The hopeful news was that infection *usually* didn't occur with just one encounter. The initial results would come back within a week.

"I don't like thinking of sex as an 'encounter,'" he told the nurse, watching as she sank the blood-draw needle into the crook of his arm. "I think of it as making love."

"That's good," Joyce said, quickly filling a vial and slipping a Band-Aid over the punctured vein as she withdrew the needle. Leslie was a serial monogamist; one man at a time, he informed her. And, as a sign of good faith, he and all his past loves had gotten tested before their first time.

"That's also good," the nurse said. "And the high probability is that you're clear. But you need to come back in three months to have your blood tested again. That way you'll know for sure." She raised her eyebrows and peered at Leslie over the tops of her glasses. "You hear me?"

She wrote an appointment for three months ahead on one of her cards. "I'll see you then," she said.

"You don't have to tell me twice," Leslie said, taking the

card and slipping his arms into his black jeans jacket. He nodded toward Mariella. "Besides, my housemate won't let me forget."

Later that same morning Mariella caught the N Judah train, one block from her apartment on Irving, as she did every day she went to Basilico.

She stared out the Muni window, not really seeing the traffic or the usual assortment of pedestrians: some well-dressed, some in gym clothes, most in jeans, and some panhandling. Late summer fog had crept in, insinuating itself like a gray dybbuk.

Could she invite Giovanni to the dinner party tomorrow night? Such an odd group already: two gay men, a Sicilian who spoke funny English, and maybe a Latina if she invited Cosima, Mario's assistant from work. No one would think twice about the addition of a middle-aged restaurateur.

Of course Giovanni would never come. He'd be gracious and say he'd love to be there, but especially on a busy Saturday night, he couldn't leave, or some such excuse. Anyway, what was she thinking? He wouldn't come to a dinner party without his wife. Besides, she didn't have the nerve to invite him. But as she watched the buildings and the people on the street pass by, the idea—the desire—lingered in her mind.

He opened his office door at her knock, as if he'd been at attention on the other side, waiting for her. They stood and faced one another.

"Yes," she said. "I will take the temporary job of manager. Just until school. But if I don't do the good job, please, you must find someone else."

"I'm not worried," Giovanni said, smiling and holding her with his steady gaze.

Mai, she thought. *Never will I be comfortable looking him in the eyes.*

"I'm glad," he said, offering his hand. His grasp was firm and dry to the touch, reassuring and warm, like her father's.

That Friday night, by way of a private celebration for them both—he, for getting tested, and she, for her promotion—Leslie squired Mariella to a dance club in the mainly Hispanic Mission District. Murals on brick walls and sides of buildings in vibrant, neon colors—pink, yellow, and aquamarine—depicted the plight of workers in Central and South America, Mexico, and the United States; of Latin musicians jamming with congas and horns; of everyday scenes from neighborhood life. Ethnic clothing and produce shops were brightly lit and restaurants stayed open until midnight. And music: Latino, jazz, and contemporary rock emanating from behind nearly every door, both open and closed.

Club Bahia, where, on a smooth wooden dance floor under soft colored lights, they danced salsa, mambo, and rumba to a live Latin band until one o'clock in the morning.

"Let's do this again!" Leslie declared as they walked to the lot on Guerrero, where he'd parked his Mini. Foot-weary, sore-muscled, sweaty, and exhilarated after three solid hours of syncopated hip-swiveling, they'd discovered, to their mutual surprise and delight, that they were both seasoned Latin dancers.

"Do you know tango—I mean the Argentine way?" she asked Leslie. The dance she'd learned from Matteo, their prelude to becoming lovers.

"Si," he said, executing the signature Argentine catlike walk on the sidewalk. "I took classes for a couple of years. How about you?"

"Of course," she said. "The tango from Argentina is very big in Sicilia. The Milonga parties, you can find one almost any night. In fact, some of the first tango dancers in Argentina were *Italiano immigrati*." She glanced up at Leslie. "Did you know that?"

"Oh, of course," he mimicked her. "If it's beautiful or sexy the Italians must have had something to do with it, right?"

"No, it is true. Oh sure, there were the French *immigrati*, too, and the *Spagnolo*—the Spanish, yes? They were the first from *Europa*. But the Italiani," she said, opening her hands. "Maybe they were the first to tango—maybe not."

Leslie smiled at her. With indulgence. As if they'd always been friends, even though it had been barely two months she'd been sharing his apartment.

Chapter Twenty-One

"*H*ere's to the chef!" Leslie proclaimed, raising his glass of Prosecco as the four of them gathered around the kidney-shaped coffee table. To Mariella's surprise and delight, Cosima had said yes to the Saturday dinner invitation, along with Leslie's new boyfriend, Darrell.

Mariella's appetizer of feta, roasted tomatoes, and pesto rolled and baked in wide strips of eggplant and drizzled with a balsamic reduction drew oohs and aahs.

"Grazie," Mariella said. "What is it you say, *la prova e nel pudding?*"

"Girl, I'm impressed. You're a woman of many talents. And here's to your promotion," Cosima chimed in. Cosima's looking out for Mariella those first weeks at the restaurant, when she'd been leery of Mario, had turned into easy and sometimes revealing conversations between them, and now, a budding friendship. There was no resentment in Cosima's good wishes, no jealousy that the newcomer had a higher position.

"Thank you, Cosima. I am so glad you have agreed to come."

It was hard to distinguish Cosima's sturdy, muscular shape under those loose, earth-mother clothes she wore tonight—a shift from her chef's coat and checkered pants—but her frizzy red curls escaped from one of her signature scarves, a paisley of purple and green.

"This is delicious," Darrell commented, forking in a mouthful of the eggplant roll.

"And you have *la bella acquamarina occhi*," Mariella said, mesmerized by Darrell's turquoise-hued eyes. She'd imagined a typical American: blue-eyed blond or fair-skinned with light brown hair. He was part Asian, perhaps Filipino, a Eurasian whose dusky golden-brown coloring made him resemble a South Sea Islander or a perpetually tanned California surfer.

Darrell ducked his head. "Well," he said, "your boss must think very highly of you."

"Oh, I don't think so," Mariella said. "I think in such a short time he can find no one else."

"You *know* that's not true," Leslie said. "I've already told you, people would kill for that job. And why are you blushing?" He regarded Mariella with a squinty eye. "Do you like Giovanni—I mean *like* him?"

Her cheeks burned. The last person she wanted to suspect she had a crush on Giovanni was Cosima. The woman would think Mariella was a fool. More importantly, Cosima would think she was dishonorable, especially since Cosima had revealed that her former husband left her for another woman.

"You do!" Leslie said. "That's why you talked so fast when we went for your interview. You were nervous around him. It's true isn't it? You *do* like him. I can tell." He looked down his long, outstretched legs encased in black jeans. "Well, I agree with you, Giovanni is one of the sexiest men I know."

Darrell lifted his eyebrows so high, they nearly disappeared under the shiny sweep of black hair falling onto his forehead.

"No offense to you," Leslie said to his new lover. "But believe me, you'd think so too if you met him—so *manly*. You'd agree with me one hundred percent, and," he placed his hand on his chest, "my feelings wouldn't be the least bit hurt."

"I like him, sure, to work for," Mariella said. "But he is my boss, and besides, he wears the wedding ring, and maybe he is old enough to be my father."

They all looked at her as if to say "So?"

"*Merda!* How can I make you stop?"

Cosima looked at her quizzically. "Hasn't anybody told you his wife died?"

Mariella sucked in a loud, shocked breath.

"Giovanni's wife died of breast cancer. At least that's what I remember Pietro saying, but it's been a while so I'm not exactly sure," Cosima said.

Yes, of all people, Pietro, such a gossiper, why hadn't he told her?

"Why did I not know this before tonight?" Mariella asked. As if they'd all deliberately kept this news from her.

"I don't know, I didn't think of it until this minute." Cosima shrugged. "It didn't seem important. After she died everyone just seemed to forget about her. She hardly ever came to the restaurant. I only saw her come through once or twice. According to Pietro, she was such a snob, nobody liked her very much. Nobody cares. Besides," she shrugged, "when I met her, she looked at me like I wasn't even there."

"When? I mean how long ago she died?" Mariella's heart shuddered.

"A couple of years ago, I think. Maybe more."

"She is the woman whose photograph sits on Giovanni's desk." Mariella was embarrassed for herself now, imagining, for even one second, that he'd meant his searching gaze for *her.* "Well," she said, sloughing off any show of interest. "I think for certain he is still looking for his wife."

Would knowing his wife was dead change how she behaved around Giovanni?

"Hey, what's with all the red lips?" Darrell asked, taking in the clock, the throw pillows, and the bowl of blown glass lips on the coffee table.

"The better to kiss you with my dear." Leslie laughed. "I

don't know—I was on a Marilyn Monroe kick for a while." He puckered up like Marilyn had in some of her famous photographs. "You know how we girls are. But we were talking about Giovanni."

"Well, okay, we have the dinner now," Mariella said, quickly rising from her chair. She nodded toward the already set table.

Nobody moved. They all kept watching her.

"What? What you want from me?" Mariella threw up her hands. "It is none of your business!" she blurted.

"Look at us," Leslie said, pursing his mouth in a grimace, as if it pained him to invite too close an inspection. He gestured around the group. "I mean, really—look at us!" He leaned forward. "It's not fair. You know all kinds of stuff, privileged stuff, stuff we'd die if anyone else knew about, every single one of us. Take her," he said, pointing to Cosima.

Cosima opened her arms, the barest hint of a smile teasing her mouth. "Yeah," she said. "Please, somebody, take me."

"I'll bet she's told you a secret or two," Leslie said with a sly wink.

Cosima's head shot up—perhaps in shock, Mariella thought, at the rawness of Leslie's suggestion. Did Cosima think Mariella had broken her confidence about her husband leaving her? Mariella looked directly at Cosima and shook her head. And then Cosima raised two fingers, then, teasingly, three. "Three. I've told her three secrets," she said.

They all waited but Cosima just smiled.

"Oh, well," Leslie said and pointed to himself. "But who did I tell about having unsafe sex? Who did I trust to go with me for testing?"

Mariella looked for Darrell's reaction. It didn't appear to faze him, her knowing he was HIV positive and that his former lover died of AIDS. He went on, seemingly oblivious, draining his glass of its last drop of the Prosecco.

"And we know absolutely nothing about you," Leslie said, folding his arms in front of his chest and staring at Mariella. "No, it's not fair."

It was true. With nosy Yolanda for a mother, Mariella had learned to keep her personal life secret. Otherwise, she and Olimpio used to joke, their father would have had to rent the Catania opera house because it was the only place big enough to contain Mamma's crazy, dramatic outbursts. She was so loud and so good at asking a question and then answering herself, or bringing in an imaginary third or maybe even a fourth person to stir the pot, she needed an opera house stage where she could run back and forth and act out all the parts.

"I don't mean to keep the secrets," Mariella said. "But there is nowhere to go with *la cotta*—the crush, I think—on Mr. Giovanni."

"How do you know?" Cosima asked. "Have you told him?" She sighed and smoothed out the fabric of her long, multicolored skirt. "I'd give anything to feel attracted to someone again. Right now I don't feel much of anything but dead in that department."

"I am sorry you don't feel so good," Mariella said, reaching for Cosima's hand, in the chair next to her.

"My therapist says I have post-traumatic stress," Cosima announced. "PTSD, you know, like the vets who came back from Vietnam."

They didn't call it PTSD in Sicily after WW2, long before Mariella was born, but she thought of conversations with Nonna where her grandmother had told her about the ". . . men, young boys, really, who saw so much horror, fighting Mussolini and Hitler, so many of them shell shocked. Damaged for life." Cosima ran the hand Mariella wasn't holding down her skirt, as if the memory of her husband cheating on her could be wiped away. She sighed and shook her head. "Can you believe it; it's been over a year and I still miss that Black motherfucker?"

Leslie rolled his eyes. Mariella had not understood until now that Cosima's ex-husband was Black.

"It's okay," Mariella said, squeezing Cosima's hand. "We all are *stupido* sometimes."

Cosima brushed away a tear she'd tried to conceal. "Well, thanks a lot."

Madrona! "That is not what I mean," Mariella said. "You know what I try to say, I'm talking of myself, like you say to me when I tell you because Giovanni is first of all married—well, at least I thought he was—and second place, too old. Ehh . . ." She opened her arms and raised her shoulders. "Big deal. It is okay to still miss someone."

Leslie leaned toward Cosima across the low table. "Well, I hope you'll finally meet someone good, someone who knows how to treat a person right. Like him," Leslie said, smiling and nodding at Darrell, who continued to appear perfectly at ease. "And," he said, wagging a finger at Mariella. "Don't think we're finished talking about Giovanni."

"But I am," she said. "Even if you're not."

The *pollo alla cacciatore con fettucine* was proclaimed by all to be "Better than any I've ever tasted in any restaurant, anywhere." Mariella had sautéed wild mushrooms in lieu of everyday white buttons, and those, combined with the white wine and an infusion of smoky tomato paste, made the sauce intense and gave it a flavor of the earth.

Afterward, they remained at the table savoring what was left of the fruity Sangiovese they'd drunk with the meal.

"If you're not careful this Giovanni fellow is going to ask you to cook too," Darrell said.

"No, no," she said, eager to steer the subject somewhere else. "I am everyday cook. *Tipico Siciliano.*"

"I cook every day at the restaurant," Cosima said. "My husband always complained that I never wanted to cook at home."

"Is that why he left you?" Leslie asked.

"Leslie!" both Mariella and Darrell exclaimed in unison.

But Cosima just laughed. "That's it," she said. "Honey, you got that one right!" And off she and Leslie went into peals of laughter that became nearly indistinguishable from sobbing.

"*Vero—Americanos!*" Mariella declared. "Or is that what you mean when you talk about the "Black humor"? A term Mariella had heard the waiters use at Basilico, when they were joking with some of the Latino and dark-skinned kitchen help.

Cosima's mouth fell open, Darrell and Leslie held their breath, and the room went so silent, the only sound was the ticking of the second hand on the white clock.

Without any warning, Cosima leaped out of her chair and, from behind, threw her arms around Mariella's shoulders. Leslie and Darrell appeared startled, as if they were afraid Cosima was about to crush Mariella in a stranglehold. She had the build to do it, too.

"Oh, I like you, girl!" Cosima exclaimed. She rocked Mariella back and forth in her tight hug. "You are *not* afraid to say it the way it is."

"Well, it's good," Mariella said. "I like you too." She patted Cosima's hand as Cosima released her. "So, you want the espresso?" she asked, rising to clear the table.

"Oh no, that limoncello you bought, definitely," Leslie said. "I've never tasted it."

"My first sip of limoncello was with Albert in Sorrento," Darrell said with an expression of dreamy reminiscence. "In a lattice-covered grove. It's what they served us after dinner everywhere we went along the Amalfi Coast—Capri, Positano, Tramonti. They called it sunbeams and lemons in a glass. So romantic." He took a deep breath and began singing "*O Sole Mio*," surprising everyone with his clear, on-key tenor.

"Well," Leslie said testily, rising and snatching away his and

Darrell's wine glasses. "You've had enough. And Albert's not here, so I'm afraid you'll just have to put up with unromantic me."

"Les," Darrell said. He went to Leslie, who stood facing the sink. Darrell touched him lightly on a shoulder. "Don't get your tail in a knot. Weren't you the one who talked about how sexy Giovanni was, and how it wouldn't bother you at all if I thought so too? Hmm? Weren't you?"

Leslie refused to turn around.

"Albert's been dead for over a year," Darrell said. "If you want the truth, I've barely thought of him since I met you."

"Listen, boy, are you really going to be jealous of a dead man?" Cosima piped up. She swirled her wine glass in one hand and rested her head on the other, her arm propped up by an elbow. "That's a losing proposition, I can tell you right now."

Mariella watched the telltale red creep up Leslie's neck; his mark of discomfort. He turned and embraced Darrell so unexpectedly, it caused the other man to flinch and step back.

"You're right," Leslie said, his face pink as he burrowed against Darrell's neck. "I'm so silly sometimes." He looked sheepishly at Darrell. "Just forgive me, okay?"

"Sure," Darrell said. "No big deal."

"You need the caffè anyway," Mariella said.

Minutes later, they gathered again in the living room, sipping the limoncello and dunking biscotti in the espresso Mariella had brewed in Leslie's fancy machine.

"Oh man," Cosima said with a sigh. "Sometimes I wonder if I'll ever even want to *be* with or trust another man."

Chapter Twenty-Two

On Mariella's first Monday in her new position, Teresa marched with her into the kitchen and stood beside her while Mariella informed Mario Bianchi that she would be taking over as temporary manager. A gesture from Giovanni's sister that surprised Mariella, but fitting, she understood, for the smooth functioning of the restaurant. Teresa was nothing, after all, if not invested in Basilico and in her brother.

"I know," the young sous chef said, refusing to look at either woman. "Giovanni told me."

"She knows what she's doing," Teresa told Mario. "Think of her the same as you thought of George," the departing manager, "the same as me. Help her out when she needs it. Work with her."

"I'm always here," Mario said—mumbled actually—lowering his head. Maybe he *was* more afraid of her than she was of him, as Giovanni had suggested.

Mariella worked hard to prove her competence in subsequent days, gradually gaining her coworkers' cooperation and respect. And even though Teresa continued to walk a wide path around her, and even though her unibrow still made her look menacing, she no longer glared at Mariella as if she wished her off the planet.

"Are you very religious?" Giovanni asked her several weeks later. They stood side-by-side in his office; she barely reached his shoulder. They were scanning the employee roster to see who could be moved up to replace a first-rate but temperamental waiter Giovanni had fired the evening before.

The waiter was old-school San Franciscan: efficient, a little haughty, impatient at times to the point of being rude if a customer lingered too long over the menu. "It's not a state decision. Pasta's pasta," he'd been known to snap at a fussy diner dithering over linguine or penne. Then he'd touch his pencil to the menu on what he deemed the correct choice for the sauce, and the customer would be grateful and wouldn't care that the waiter had been abrupt because it was just his "style."

The waiter was fired, not because of his manner, but because he'd been showing up late for his shifts, sometimes drunk.

"Me? Religious?" Mariella caught the scent of Giovanni's Bay Rum aftershave: spicy tobacco and lime. Her eyes involuntarily closed. Her fantasy of smelling his skin as she lay under him appeared unbidden in her mind's eye. "No, not at all," she said, popping open her eyelids. "But why do you ask?"

"Well, I've noticed the ring on your right hand."

"Yes?" Instinctively, Mariella touched Nonna's wedding ring, rubbing it as if it were a talisman. "This was my grandmother's."

"Oh. From your grandfather?"

"No . . . no," she said. "It's from her first husband who died." She looked directly at Giovanni. She'd been practicing that lately—looking right at him—to get past her discomfort. Because still, he stirred her desire. Still, he made her feel as if he was taking her inside of him with his eyes. "Why does my ring make you think of religion?" But she knew that nuns wear their rings on their right hands, the left reserved for secular married women.

Giovanni placed a hand on his desk and pressed down his fingers one-by-one, then glanced at her with a bashful half-smile. "I wondered," he said with some hesitation, "if at some time you'd been married to the Church."

"Like Teresa?" she blurted, then covered her mouth and barked a single piercing laugh. Registering the surprise on Giovanni's face, imagining how he saw her—*like a crazy person who laughs at a funeral*—her body flushed with heat. She told herself it was because of her woolen clothing, her black turtleneck sweater and new tweed blazer. She'd changed up her wardrobe to look more professional, more authoritative, in her new position.

"*Mi dispiace*," she muttered, doing her best not to break out again in nervous giggles.

After a long, uncomfortable moment, he began to laugh too, tentatively at first, and then in round, baritone guffaws. He ran a hand down his face, as if to erase his amusement, but to no avail. His full-throated mirth spurred her on and now she was laughing again, real belly laughs, both of them caught in the hilarity. She was choking and tears were running down her cheeks, not sure what was so funny or why she was laughing, except it felt like relief.

"Ohh," Mariella said, several times over, patting her chest and catching her breath. She reached out and touched the sleeve of Giovanni's rust-colored pullover. Soft, cashmere, a luxurious buffer against the early October fog. In a week or so, another burst of Indian summer would find men once again outdoors in shirtsleeves and women in filmy summer dresses and sandals.

That simple touch of Giovanni's sweater, as intimate as if she'd pressed a hand against his warm, bare skin.

"I'm sorry. That was a ridiculous question," Giovanni said. "And I'm not even going to bother to ask who told you about my sister being in the convent." He nodded toward the office door. "I know they all talk about her out there."

"Well . . ." She opened her hands. "But what makes you think I'm religious?"

He smiled, hesitant again. "I guess I was hoping you weren't."

"Oh." She felt another surge of heat, felt the adrenalin spread through her body. She started talking, babbling really, telling him about praying to God the father and seeing her own father's image instead.

"It wasn't until university," she rattled on, "when I figured out about the Christians—the Catholics, I mean. I took this course, *Religioni del Mondo*. And my *professore*, you know, he was a very young man. Anyway, he explained to us how the Catholics in particular, how the priests say they are the only ones designated to enter 'The Kingdom of Heaven.' 'Are all the others bad people?' the *professore* say. 'All those Buddhists and Jewish and the Muslims, are they all going to Hell?'"

Giovanni watched her with an amused expression as she made loops in the air.

She sighed, letting her arms fall to her sides. "I talk too much when I'm nervous. And I wasn't laughing at Teresa those minutes ago. It was just the surprise—the look on your face." She frowned. "But why did *you* laugh?"

"I don't know," Giovanni answered with that see-right-through-her stare. "Because you did."

He bent to her, and she reached up to meet him as if they had known one another's embraces for a long while. The taste of his mouth warm, like a child's sweet, milky breath.

They held each other, afterward, without speaking.

"Well," he said finally, stepping back.

"Well," she said, surprised by her calm, by how natural it felt to embrace him.

Giovanni sighed and picked up the framed photograph of the woman on his desk.

Mariella had never mentioned the photo but had wanted to ask about it every time she'd been in his office. She hadn't decided if the smile of the woman with the light reddish-brown hair and the mouth curving up at the corners was sly or appealing. Her gray-blue eyes, her softly curled hair fanned across her shoulders.

"Before my wife died, I never thought much about God one way or another, except for Christmas Eve. I mean when everyone goes to Mass." He placed the photograph back on his desk, angling it slightly away. "After she died, I became a realist."

"A realist?" Was that an organized sect, she wondered. Like Zen?

He opened the slats of the wooden window shutters and peered out. An alleyway ran behind Basilico and the businesses adjacent to it; across the alleyway was the back entrance to a Chinese restaurant. "Like that guy," he said. "Every time I look out the window he's there, standing next to the garbage bins, smoking."

Mariella looked outside, past Giovanni. A skinny young Chinese man in a smeared apron and squashed white hat—a cook, judging from his clothes—stood on one leg with the other knee bent so his foot rested against the wall. He held each puff deeply in his lungs and exhaled, luxuriantly, in a slow, steady stream.

"A realist," Giovanni said, turning back to Mariella. "Like that fellow, who probably doesn't expect big happiness, just little pleasures from something simple, like smoking. But I'm glad you're not religious," he said. "I don't know why, but it makes me feel better. Like I'm not the only lapsed Catholic in the bunch."

Still, even as Giovanni spoke, the old pervasive reluctance tugged at her, the refusal to divorce herself completely from her Catholic roots, as one might stay in a marriage simply by dint of having been in it so long. The cellular feel of it, the loyalty of being born Catholic. The lordly priest in his gold or silver threaded vestments swinging pendulous brass censers. Puffs of frankincense and myrrh, perfumed, musty smells. The dreaded confessional, and the Mass, mysterious in Latin. Her rosary, little pink quartz beads her father had to keep her from placing around her neck to wear as jewelry when she was too young to know better. The pain in her knee bones that had to be rubbed back into circulation from almost unbearable time on the kneeler. And that one time, when she was seven or eight, wiggling around and sliding off the kneeler, ending up with her legs caught under the pew, her head wedged onto the back of the hard wood bench in front. When the altar boys rang the bells and the priest indicated for the congregation to sit down again, she couldn't extricate herself. Papa was impatient with her then—one of the few times he had been—embarrassed and apologetic, with everyone watching while he pulled out and set right, his miscreant daughter.

The Church was seductive, like an accomplished first lover. Like Matteo, whose presence she'd felt in Giovanni's kiss, a presence nearly impossible to relinquish.

"You are not happy," Mariella said. She'd meant it to come out as a question, not a statement of fact.

Giovanni watched her and she studied him back. She swore, if she listened carefully, she could detect her cells and molecules rearranging themselves. She knew it wasn't possible, but it seemed as if he was transmitting his thoughts to her in complete sentences, thoughts like, *Being around you gives me hope.* Giovanni was going through the motions of living without feeling alive. Was he simply enduring, with a grief so impossible it had extinguished his spirit?

"Are you?" he asked finally. "Happy, I mean?"

She knew, then, that he had asked her to be manager when others were far better suited for the job because he wanted her close by. He wanted her eagerness for life, wanted whatever allowed her to cross two continents all on her own, to rub off on him.

"I have everything in front of me and that makes me excited and nervous at the same time. But yes," she said, "if doing what I want and looking forward is what you mean by happy, then yes, I think I am."

"Have dinner with me tonight," he said with some urgency.

"You mean here?"

"No." He waved his arm toward the Chinese restaurant across the alleyway. "There. Do you like Chinese food?"

"I thought you never felt okay to leave this restaurant during business."

"Usually I don't."

It took her only a moment to decide. "Yes" seemed like the most natural response in the world.

They sat across from each other in a fake leather booth and drank green tea and the good bottle of Chianti Pietro had sent with them (along with a wink) and ate hot and sour soup, General Tso's chicken, and eggplant in a spicy red pepper sauce.

Giovanni's gaze made her so uncomfortable she looked away and started rummaging in her purse. She had the impression that he was searching for some answer he seemed to think she held inside.

"Sorry," he said. "It's just that, well . . . I'm very glad you said yes."

"I am sorry for the death of your wife." Would he think she was rude, blurting out his loss, too forward? But the desire—no, the *need* to know pressed on her. Was he still in mourning for the woman with the gray-blue eyes?

Giovanni swallowed a large mouthful of the Chianti. "Beth, her name was Beth. She was English," he said. "From the Cotswolds." As if that explained anything.

"English, like my Nonna's first husband," Mariella said. "Oh, I don't know where he was from, only that they lived in London." Without realizing she was doing so, she ran her fingers over her grandmother's ring. She thought of saying more about Nonna's young love, but that felt wrong, a violation of her grandmother's trust.

"But I want to hear about you," Giovanni said. Frown lines etched into vertical furrows between his eyebrows. He reached across, and with an index finger, lightly touched the back of Mariella's hand, the one that encircled the stem of her glass, a touch that set her wanting him again. "About why you decided to go to school here—whatever you have in mind for your future. For your life."

She pulled back her hand. "If it is not so much trouble, I think I would first like to hear more about your Beth." He didn't understand. She *had* to know. Was his heart buried with his wife? Or was the longing in his stare the desire of a man for a woman? For her? She tipped her glass toward him, urging him to say more.

"Mariella." He let his arms fall to the table.

"I'm sorry, again." She shook her head. "I push too hard. Everyone tells me so." If she explained about her life, she'd have to tell him about running away from home, away from her mother. Away from Matteo. And she wasn't ready to do that.

"Are you sure you really want to hear about this?" Giovanni's smile was wistful, melancholy. "I think you'll find my marriage wasn't all that interesting."

"Yes?" And when he didn't speak, but continued to watch her, she said, "Okay, I tell you the truth. I need to know why you look at me the way you do. With so much fierce." She waited for him to react.

"And you don't worry," she continued, not knowing whether to be heartened or concerned by his lack of response. "After you tell to me about your always unhappy eyes—yes, it is the truth, Mr. Giovanni. Sometimes when you think I don't watch, I see the *dolore* in your eyes. No," she said, "after you tell to me about your wife, I promise I tell you about me. So you don't worry."

"You're going to insist, aren't you?" He shook his head, sat back against the booth, and raised his hands in surrender. "I met Beth at university in 1979, at a march against Apartheid." He sighed and gazed beyond, to the side of her, as if it was easier to talk to the booth or into space. "She was nineteen and I was twenty when we married. We had what I believe you would call a stormy relationship, but don't get me wrong. It wasn't her fault. Beth was a lovely woman."

"Yes, I think she is lovely from her photograph. Like teenagers when you married," she said. "And for a very long time?" She was calculating how many years they were together, and if his wife died two years ago how old was Giovanni now? "Wait, you are only five years younger than my father . . ." *Forty-one. Nineteen years older than me!* She groaned and slapped her forehead. "My friends call me *uno blurter* when I say something that hurt their feelings. I did not mean to hurt yours."

"You didn't," he said with a sad shrug. "But I only wish I were younger." Giovanni's expression was solemn, as if being nineteen years older than her was a serious offense.

She thought of her grandfather, her grandmother's second husband, Nonno Samuele, at least ten years older than Nonna. Established in his delicatessen business when he and Nonna married, providing her with a secure and comfortable life from the beginning. A life that helped Papa and Mamma buy their apartment on Diodoro Siculo. She thought of all the neighborhood nonnas and aunties—the *zias*—who had encouraged Nonna to ". . . find someone who's can take care of you right away, someone with a little experience in the world."

Giovanni studied his hands, interlaced in front of him on the scarred Formica table. Competent-looking hands, smooth olive skin and clean, trimmed fingernails. She imagined those hands exploring her, inside of her . . . *Stop!* she commanded herself. *Pay attention!*

He consulted something else, a spot or a scratch on the table, and then, once more, leaned forward and interlaced his fingers as if he were praying. He still avoided Mariella's face. "We didn't think we had a choice," he said. "She was pregnant when we married."

"Oh."

He exhaled as if breathing out would bring to the surface what he'd been holding inside. "Beth's parents were upper class; she was their pride and joy. They had big dreams for her." His worry lines creased together in a deep frown. "They never really forgave me for her pregnancy," he said. "For interrupting her life."

"And . . . well . . . you didn't think about not having the baby—I mean, because you were so young?" Along with languages, Mariella's field of study had been international policy. She knew abortion had been legal in England since 1967. Again, she worried she might have offended Giovanni, being so bold.

He shook his head again, seemingly unfazed. "Because *I* wanted the baby. Because my father died when I was sixteen and I wanted to honor him and be as good a father as he was. She did it for me. Beth never wanted children. But that's why we married so young, because she was pregnant. Maybe it's the reason we married at all." He smiled his lovely, sad smile. "She thought it would have killed her parents to find out she was pregnant, so we moved to the States before she started to show. Both of us had always wanted to come to the States—like you," he said, gesturing across the table toward her, but not touching.

They sat quietly for a time.

"So you had the baby?"

"Yes, we had the baby—a son."

A child, who, if he was still alive, was twenty now, only two years younger than she.

"Where is your son?"

Giovanni's gaze met hers. "He's here in the city. I see him frequently." He sighed again. "Someday I'll tell you more about my son. It's your turn now."

She told him about Nonna and Papa, about Olimpio and her neighborhood. About escaping Sicily, and her envious, dramatic

Mamma. And surprised herself when the mention of Mamma brought tears to her eyes.

She left out the parts about Matteo.

"Will you come home with me?" he asked an hour later, as they stood outside the restaurant. For the second time that evening, his question and her response felt like the most natural invitation in the world.

She took a deep breath and said, "Yes."

Chapter Twenty-Three

There was labored and noisy breathing from the other side of Giovanni's apartment door.

"That's Elmer," he said, inserting a key into the deadbolt lock. "I swear he hears my footsteps a mile away."

Mariella quirked her eyebrows. "Elmer?"

"My English bulldog . . . well, actually it was Beth's English bulldog, but of course he's mine now." The heavy wood door swung inward and there, fixing Giovanni with an expression of adoration, a caricature of Winston Churchill—the embodiment of a dog cartoon: compact body and short legs, breathing through his underbite and depositing slobber on the threshold mat. Brindle and white, wagging his tail stump, setting his low-slung torso swaying side to side.

"Oh, Elmer, you need your evening walk, don't you?" Giovanni said in falsetto, bending and scratching the dog's wrinkled forehead. Mariella swore the bulldog smiled at him.

Giovanni motioned Mariella inside. She followed his gesture, peering into the shadowy room before her. An uncluttered space, from what she could make out, as her eyes adjusted to the dark. Through curved bay windows across the expanse, she could see the San Francisco skyline winking and twinkling in the night.

Giovanni switched on the entryway light. He retrieved a leash from a bent wood coat stand near the door. "I need to take Elmer out," he said. "You're welcome to come with me or just wait here, but he hasn't been out since this afternoon."

"I will come with you," she said. She'd feel like an intruder, and anxious too, if he left her alone in his apartment.

"So this is where you go every day at two o'clock, to walk Elmer, no?" she said as they exited onto the sidewalk through the double glass doors. The gray-uniformed doorman—an older man who reminded Mariella of Luciano, the maitre d' at Basilico—whom Giovanni had greeted as, "Evening, Henry," when they'd entered the building, now watched discreetly from inside as Giovanni checked his coat pockets for plastic bags to collect the dog's poop. On high alert for disapproval from Henry—from anyone who might have seen her going home with Giovanni—Mariella checked Henry's expression. Was he smirking? No, smiling pleasantly at her, appreciatively, it seemed, perhaps glad for Giovanni to have a companion.

Henry nodded at her and looked down, brushing at the two rows of brass buttons on his jacket.

The brick and stucco houses in this neighborhood—Pacific Heights, Giovanni called it—were solid and imposing. Turreted mansions, stately Victorians, interspersed with high-security, palatial apartment buildings, like Giovanni's, made visible through the evening fog by turn-of-the-century streetlamps, glowing and golden. Indoor lighting from fashionably draped or old-moneyed residence windows displayed art deco and Grecian urns turned into lamps.

"You notice when I leave the restaurant?" Giovanni asked, sounding pleased.

"Sure, everybody notice, but no one talks about it. Like some big mystery." She pulled her coat closer as they walked. A surprise to her, still, how chilly the nights. Not like home, where even at midnight in late summer, the sun's warmth lingered in cobblestones beneath one's feet.

"When Beth was alive, she walked Elmer," Giovanni said. "He was her pet project." He laughed. "Even though I've become very fond of him, I would never have brought a dog to live in an apartment." He shrugged. "Still . . ."

Sidewalks here inclined sharply up and then down. Giovanni, she noticed, was slightly out of breath on the uphill parts and per-spiring on his upper lip, while she barely broke stride or a sweat.

The notion that it might be his age cast him, momentarily, in an unromantic light.

Elmer panted and waddled, leading the way for the slow walk around the steep block. Back at the apartment, Mariella watched from her perch on a kitchen stool as Giovanni prepared Elmer's dinner and spoke to the dog in a high, almost childlike voice—"Elmer hungry boy?" Elmer wiggled his body, apparently in anticipation, and when Giovanni lowered his bowl to the floor, Elmer snuffled as he gobbled his food and made short work of his dinner. Then, in the living room, after a bout of rooting around in his fleece bed on the tan leather sofa, he settled himself and snored as he fell asleep.

"A glass of wine—or port?" Mariella had removed her coat, and Giovanni hung it with his on the bent wood coatrack near the front door. She was nervous, and glad of the pause to get her bearings.

"Yes, please, port."

They sat sideways in the window seat at the big window overlooking the city. He pointed out landmarks—Coit Tower, the Transamerica Pyramid, the clock tower at the Embarcadero, and even a glimpse of the Bay, shimmering in the distance with pinpoint reflections from the glow of San Francisco, lit up like a fairyland.

She was comfortable, cocooned in the dimly lit room, the port warming her insides with the heat emanating from Giovan-ni's body near to her, but not oppressively so.

When Giovanni offered his hand, she held it as he guided her down a softly lighted hallway, their footsteps muted by an oriental runner covering the length of the hardwood floor. Water-colors of vineyards and framed photographs of harbored fishing boats hung on the walls. No photo of Beth with the lovely, sly smile suggesting Mariella was invading her domain. This was *his* house, *his* bedroom they entered, its browns and beiges and dark wood echoing the masculinity of his office at Basilico. If the room had at one time showcased the touch of his wife's feminine hand, he'd wiped away those traces. Only one photograph sat on a bedside table, next to a burnished pewter lamp: a baby boy, unsmiling, his chubby legs extended over the edge of an infant seat. The boy wore short blue pants, white lace-up shoes, and a white sweater, a Pooh Bear appliqué in the center. The arm and hand encircling the little boy's chair were clearly those of a man's. Giovanni's, she supposed, supporting his son.

"I didn't bring a toothbrush." Mariella was crazy with lust, trembling with excitement and nerves. *Fool! Is that the best she could come up with?*

Giovanni hesitated only a moment before the laugh lines crinkled around his eyes, then he guffawed, the same kind of belly laugh he'd come out with earlier when she'd blurted out her remark about his sister.

"I have a new one in the guest bathroom," he said and led her back down the hallway to a complete bath suite in bronze, beige, and speckled granite, with a full-size claw-footed tub and over-head shower. "In the drawer just under the sink."

She found and used the toothbrush and toothpaste, but really, she'd wanted another moment to gather herself and to freshen. She stared at herself in the mirror.

She thought of Nonna and wondered what she would say if she knew Mariella was about to have sex with her boss who was old enough to be her father? *Mariella, have you considered this carefully?* Or, *You have that good head on your shoulders, so trust yourself.*

When she returned to Giovanni, she took a tentative step closer, close enough for him to take hold of her, gently, by her upper arms. "It's all right Mariella," he said. "We don't have to do this."

Was he nervous too? She didn't want him to be, wanted him to be masterful, and yet wondered if she'd trust him if he was too sure of himself.

"No," she said. "I want to." If they waited, she'd back out. Her own nagging voice accused her of betraying Matteo. The voice agreed with her mother, calling her puttana! She tugged her sweater over her head and, still wearing her brassiere, crossed her arms in front of her breasts. The only other man she'd ever stood naked in front of was Matteo.

Giovanni stepped to her and searched her face, looking for her permission, and then she saw it in his gaze, his own uncertainty, and she nodded yes. He kissed her forehead, her eyelids, her cheeks, and finally, her mouth. She coaxed his hands to reach around and unhook her lacy black bra. As it fell to the floor, he cupped her breasts, holding them tenderly.

"You're beautiful," he said, traversing her with his eyes and running his fingers over her arms and the contours of her collarbones.

"I'm not," she said. "But thank you. Grazie, Giovanni, just the same."

"Your skin is so soft. Your body *is* beautiful—beautiful to me."

They held each other for a long moment before he eased her down, onto his bed on the cushy quilted spread. She watched him take off his shoes, unbutton his shirt. When he unbuckled his belt, a throb unleashed itself inside her, deep down. She felt herself wet with anticipation. His body was solid and muscular, in a natural way, with olive skin and just enough hair to make him a man. She'd worried that his body would disappoint her.

He slid off her silky panties. Then he explored her with his hands and with his tongue and allowed her to caress all the hardness and all the soft parts of his body. And, as she learned from Matteo, she took Giovanni's maleness into her mouth. And finally, he entered her.

"You weren't worried about birth control?" Giovanni asked as they lay afterward, facing each other in one another's arms.

"It wasn't the fertile time of my cycle," she said. "And you— you didn't say anything either." She'd stopped taking "the pill" after her breakup with Matteo.

"It seems as if we both trusted each other," he said. He ran the back of an index finger along her cheek. "So soft . . . But I need to tell you *why* I wasn't worried," he said, turning serious.

"Okay . . ." Mariella's heart quickened. He certainly wasn't impotent. She could still feel the pleasurable tingling between her legs. And, she knew he would never subject her to any kind of disease, as he must have understood she wouldn't.

"I had a vasectomy."

"When?" *What the hell? Why is he telling me this?* "But no, please, no, you don't need to say." It could have been yesterday, the way he said it. An unexpected and profound sense of loss churned in her belly. He wasn't hers to claim, and yet now that they'd made love, she felt as if something precious belonging to her had been stolen. She would never be able to have a child with this man. That door, and maybe the future: permanently closed. Even if she knew she was being unreasonable, anger and a sense of betrayal flared up inside her. She was wrong to have trusted him! He was no better than those university boys who used her girlfriends for sex and then ditched them. Why didn't he tell her *before* he lured her into his bed? When she'd had a choice. Were all men opportunistic, gay or straight? Like Leslie who'd kept his gender from her until she'd arrived on his doorstep.

At lease with Matteo, I had the chance of having a baby! Even if I didn't want one . . . and why do I keep thinking of Matteo?

"Nearly ten years ago," he said. "When I wanted to believe there was still hope for my marriage." Giovanni let go of Mariella's hand and rolled onto his back. He closed his eyes. "And I won't say anything more if you don't want me to."

"No," she said. She lay, wordlessly, staring up at the textured ceiling. She urged herself to resist him, to hold onto her indignation. But even if it meant choking down bittersweet feelings and hearing about his desire for his wife, she wanted to know. She reached for and squeezed his hand. "No," she said again. "Tell me."

Giovanni turned toward her and propped himself on an elbow. "It's not very pretty, I'm afraid."

"So?" She raised her shoulders as best she could, lying on her back. "Sometimes life isn't pretty." Would it have made a difference if she'd known about the vasectomy beforehand? Would she have wanted him any less? Been any less willing? "Tell me, please."

"Are you sure you want to hear about this?" he asked. "Really? Because I mean it. This is hardly the conversation I had in mind when I asked you to have dinner with me." He searched her face. "I'm afraid you might not like what you hear."

"No," she said. "I mean, yes. I want to know. Please." She was starting to grow impatient. "Please say."

He picked up the photo on the bedside table and looked at it for a long while before setting it back on the glass top.

"Your son," Mariella said. She braced herself against hearing whatever new devastation he was about to deliver.

"I begged her not to get the abortion. The truth is, we hardly knew each other when we found out she was pregnant, and I stupidly thought having a child might bring us closer."

He lay silently for a time. "We hated each other for the rest of her life," he said. "I know she hated me."

"Because you make her have the baby?"

He nodded. "Maybe hate is too strong a word, but I think we stayed together out of misery. To punish each other because we both felt so guilty—I know I did. Maybe she just didn't know what else to do."

She thought of Papa: manipulated by Mamma's dramatics, and Mamma bullying him for no apparent reason, and that gentle and decent man so loyal to her, claiming love for her, tolerating her. Yet Papa was no weakling. Was he? She remembered Nonna's words to her son: "Stand up for what you believe, Salvatore. Your wife will fall in love with you all over again." Maybe Mamma was pushing Papa to stand up for himself. Perhaps that's what she'd been waiting for all along.

"But that's not the hard part," Giovanni said, bringing Mariella back to his own marriage and edging away from her in the bed. "We gave up my son for adoption."

Mariella was struck silent. They gave him up? No wonder Giovanni went around looking miserable. Haunted by his son's *fantasma. And really, why* is *he telling me all this?*

"My son is Mario Bianchi," Giovanni said, turning back and looking directly at her.

"You mean . . ." Mario, the chef with the *psicopatico* eyes?

Giovanni reached again for the photograph on the night table.

Giovanni's eyes glistened with tears. "It's my own lack of courage that tears me apart. That's what I mourn."

Mariella scooted closer and laid her arm across his chest. He rolled to the edge of the bed and launched himself from it so abruptly she thought he might fall and drag her with him. He slammed the bathroom door and turned on the shower, she presumed, to cover the sound of sobbing.

She lay uneasy in his bed, wondering what to do. Leave quietly? Wait to say goodbye?

He emerged from the bathroom with a towel around his waist and wordlessly offered her a large, fluffy towel. He gestured to her that the bathroom was free. He refused to look at her.

She let the warm water wash over her from the jets above and surrounding her in his marble shower, and she judged him. For feeling sorry for himself. For being a coward. For having so much luxury. *He should never have given up his son. How could he?*

Nonna's voice came to her: *But don't you see, it's like the devil and the deep blue sea. He was between them. But,* Mariella questioned, *who was the devil? Beth? Or Giovanni? For making her have the baby in the first place. Oh, I wish he'd never told me.*

She stood under the water for a long while before soaping and rinsing.

She dressed in the bedroom. Giovanni was somewhere else in the apartment, or gone. *On the other hand, he gave the baby away so Beth would be happier because he thought he owed her his life, at least to stay with her, for leaving England and making her have the baby in the first place.*

"I'll call you a taxi right away. I cannot tell you how ashamed I am," Giovanni said as she entered the kitchen. He was fully clothed, likely having dressed while she showered. He stood, cell phone in hand, next to a high leather stool at the granite island that served as both countertop and table.

"Why? Ashamed for your grief?" Mariella asked. "For those natural feelings? No, no, wait," she said as he lowered his head and started to punch in a number. "You should not feel ashamed. It's good you can feel so much, even if it is pain."

But she had many questions: If you gave up Mario, why is he working at the restaurant. Does he know you're his father? And, are you ashamed because you gave him up or because you cried in front of me?

She waited a moment before approaching him. She touched

his arm, encouraged when he didn't shrug her off or keep dialing.

She lightly rubbed her fingers where they lay on the back of his hand. As if by doing so she could keep him tethered.

Giovanni raised his head but said nothing.

Giovanni still wouldn't look at her, but at least he was listening.

"Giovanni," she said softly, "it's true, at first I make a big judgment on you, and maybe I still do, but you did not make this baby all by yourself. Or the decision to come here to America. You were only young man yourself—how you say, a kid, like Beth."

Giovanni raised his eyebrows, as if surprised she'd even want to speak to him after hearing his worst offenses, as if she'd read his worst thoughts.

"But you probably blame yourself for that too . . . yes? And worst of all, for when she gets the bad cancer."

He gazed at her for a long moment. "You're hardly more than a kid yourself."

"I know what it is to feel guilt—to hurt people," she said with a small tilt of her head. "But I'm not meaning to make my *dolore* sound like yours." She tentatively moved into him and after only a brief hesitation, he stepped down from the stool and let her stay there, next to him, close.

Later, around midnight and back in her own bed, she murmured to herself into her pillow, her heart pierced, imagining Giovanni's terrible pain, waking him in the night and seeing his son every day. *On the other hand, how* could *he be such a coward to let his son go?*

Her wish in that moment was that someday Giovanni would come to peace with himself. *But why, why should I care? Would I want to be with him again? Or he with me? And how awkward will it be now at Basilico?*

⌒

When she saw Mario at work the next day, the realization struck her again that she was only two years older than him, close enough in age to be her brother, and both of them young enough to be Giovanni's children.

Giovanni came in late, not until after the lunch hour. He looked weary, yet he was cordial and kind as ever, but definitely all business.

It wasn't until closing time that he requested, "Stay and have a drink with me. There's something I want you to understand."

They sat in his office, he at his desk, Mariella across from him with the door open.

"Luciano and his wife Donatella adopted Mario—because I asked him to," Giovanni explained. "They did it for me, really, such good and kind people, like family—and they couldn't have children, so it was a blessing for them as well. Luciano and I have worked together ever since I moved to San Francisco." Giovanni stared at, then passed her a photograph he'd pulled out of a desk drawer. The same as the cropped one on his bureau, except Luciano (looking much younger) was in this picture, along with a woman, presumably Donatella, and Giovanni with his arm around Mario's shoulders. "This is Mario at six months: Luciano and Donatella had a little party and invited us. Beth wouldn't come, she never went to visit them, so I always went alone." He paused again. "Mario thinks I'm his uncle, or distantly related cousin, so he grew up calling me Uncle Gio."

When she stayed at Giovanni's a few nights later, she took a lingering look at the chunky, somber baby boy in the photograph with inky black hair. Did she really see Giovanni in the boy's features or in the Mario she now said hello to everyday? Or did she only think so because she knew Giovanni was his father?

Chapter Twenty-Four

"*Quel presidente*," her father said. "*E bravo?*" Good, sweet Papa, asking because he wanted his daughter to think he was interested in her new world. She knew her family hadn't called to spend their precious time and money talking about Bill Clinton.

"Clinton is still popular here!" She spoke loud because the connection was bad. They were so far away in Catania: Papa, Nonna, Olimpio, all gathered around her family's landline.

Even Mamma who yelled out in the background, "Nasty man to cheat on his wife with that *puttana* in a blue dress, but who can blame him, married to that ugly Hillary."

"I admire Hillary Clinton," Mariella said. An educated woman, outspoken and a lawyer. "She's strong for health, and girls—women too." A woman whose sense of purpose and self didn't appear to have been absorbed by marriage.

"Of course you'd like her," Mamma snapped, loud and up close now. "A pushy woman who acts like a man and doesn't know her place!" Comforting somehow, to know that her mother hadn't changed. "Talk fast!" Mamma shouted again, "this call is too much money!"

"Mamma!" Olimpio scolded. She could hear whispers, and then Olimpio said, "Here, Papa," apparently wresting the phone from Mamma and handing it back to Papa.

Mariella wanted to tell them something newsworthy, something important from America. *I'm having an affair with my boss!*

176

"Always with politics—like the flea trying to conquer the elephant," Nonna muttered, her voice sounding faint and feathery over the phone. Probably the connection, Mariella decided. Her grandmother was most likely thinking of the citizen organizations and brave individuals in Sicily who publicly dared to stand up against the Mafia. And like the flea trying to defeat the elephant, they suffered a similar fate of being squashed.

"*Pisciare al vento*," Nonna said in that same thready voice.

"Maybe, Nonna, maybe it's the same everywhere." Pissing into the wind, the piss always comes back to hit you in the face. It wasn't like Nonna to be cryptic, but Mariella had the notion that her grandmother was trying to tell her something—send a hidden message in her ominous, shaky words. "But oh," Mariella said, "it's so good to talk to you—to all of you!"

"How is school?" Olimpio chimed in. He'd written her that he too had secret plans to come to America and live with her and make a lot of money after he finished university.

"It's good, the two classes I take now, the *Tranzlazione Inglese*, and the course on Signor Ernesto Hemingway. But I will keep working at Basilico to put as much money in the bank as I can before I start full-time school in January."

"You must be very important," Papa said. "For this Signore Giovanni to make you the manager already."

"Puttana!" Mamma hissed.

Maybe this time her mother wasn't far off base.

After they hung up she wondered what Mamma and Papa would have said if she *had* told them that she was sleeping with her boss. Or that Leslie wasn't female, but a gay man and had a lover named Darrell, and that they'd taken her to the Castro District for a private warehouse party, put on by a wealthy Silicon Valley executive—a friend of Leslie's—a few days before Halloween.

She pictured her mother screeching: "What kind of an idiot

are you, showing yourself off with a *finocchio* and what *kind* of a *puttana?*—*Dio mio!*—even to go to dinner with your boss!?"

Nonna would laugh about the cross-dressers—both she and Olimpio knew that Leslie was gay—the scandalous Halloween costumes, including Leslie's, who'd dolled himself up as Ginger Rogers and wobbled around the dance floor in a glittery fishtail gown and strappy silver high heels. And Darrell who, even though he was half a foot shorter than Leslie, looked almost as debonair as Fred Astaire in his secondhand tuxedo.

And she, who'd emerged ready for the celebration, disguised as a nun. Leslie had instructed her that if she wanted to go with them, she *had* to wear a costume. "Something that flies in the face of tradition," he'd said.

What could be more *contro-cultura* than for a Catholic Siciliana to dress as a nun?

"Well," Leslie remarked. "Everyone will think you're one of the Sisters of Perpetual Indulgence."

"What are you talking about?" And who were the Sisters of Perpetual Indulgence? She'd been so happy to find the nun's habit, and so cheap, too.

"Sister Lost and Found, Sister Anita Blowjob, Pope Dementia the Last, Sister Hellen Wheels—they're sacred clowns in whiteface!"

"What about Sister Homo Celestial?" Darrell piped up. "She's—well, he's—my favorite. But, Les . . ."

"I should take this off?" Mariella had asked. Never mind. She'd stay home. It was *their* party anyway—Darrell's and Leslie's.

"Oh no!" Darrell said. "She looks fabulous! Even if the Sisters notice her—if they even show up—they'll just think of her as support."

Leslie had struggled to his knees, then, as best he was able, wiggled himself down in his Ginger get-up, binding him like a girdle. He'd landed with a thud to the side of Mariella's feet. "Forgive me, forgive me, forgive me!" he'd said. "I'm so sorry."

"Why do you say that?" Mariella looked down at Leslie. "Why are you sorry?"

"Because," he'd said, craning his neck, looking up at her.

"Because he got hooked by his worry about what other people will think," Darrell cut in. "And who cares, but c'mon now, because we'll be late."

The first appearance of the Sisters of Perpetual Indulgence had frightened Mariella until she'd gotten used to seeing beards and dark facial hair under those faces painted white. The Sisters, in shiny nuns' habits the colors of the rainbow, whirled through the warehouse door, worked their way through the crowd, collecting donations with buckets marked AIDS Relief. Everyone donated, or at least cheered loud enough whenever someone dropped money in the buckets, to make it seem as if everyone had.

A hairy arm shot out, grabbing Mariella's hand, pulling her along, away from her companions. A Sister in bright blue danced her through the crowd toward the stage, shouting something inaudible at her, as her panic rose higher.

Leslie was right! They'd taken her for one of them!

"Here! Take my bucket and keep collecting!" the Sister yelled, thrusting it at her, just before he bounded onto the stage.

The Sisters peeled off their habits, revealing spangly formfitting dresses, then performed a drag queen show, just like the show at the nightclub in the French/Italian film, *La Cage Aux Folles*. The revelers, including Mariella—she'd collected over $500 and deposited the bucket on a corner of the stage—drank champagne along with Leslie and Darrell and belted "I Am What I Am" at the top of their lungs.

Fueled by testosterone and alcohol, skinhead and redneck hecklers with military haircuts had burst in during the middle of the show, threatening to dissolve the festivities into violence, attempting to ruin a beautiful celebration.

The worst that happened were a few thrown and broken beer bottles, and no one got hurt—at least not physically.

"Maybe someday we really *will* be free to be what we are," Darrell had said with a Sarah Bernhardt-like gesture, the back of his hand to his forehead. *Pretty melodramatic*, Mariella thought, after the rabble rousers had been banished by security. Darrell's words may have been timely, but he'd appeared preoccupied throughout the evening, as if, even though his body was present, his mind was somewhere else. And not at all the easygoing care-free spirit he'd brought to the dinner table at Leslie and Mariella's apartment only a few weeks before.

She wondered, and then chastised herself for thinking it, if Darrell was putting on a performance. But for whom?

Chapter Twenty-five

Posta Aerea
05 November 2000
c/o Signora Louisa Romano
95128 Agenzia Turistica Finocchiaro Aprile
Catania, Sicilia

Cara *Nonna Giuseppina;*

This letter to you is so soon after the wonderful and surprising phone call last week because you are the only one with an open heart, the one I tell everything to, always.

Also, I have sent an email note to Signora Romano, thanking her for receiving my letter to you at the Agenzia, and for seeing that it goes into your hands, only. I don't know how she will do this, but she is always very clever, so I'm not worried.

I have told you about Mario Bianchi, the young sous chef with the psychopathic eyes, the one who I now understand is more shy than dangerous. I am still not completely at ease around him, but I am no longer afraid. Giovanni Russo, my boss and the owner of Basilico—he was right: Mario is a great cook (almost as good as Mamma, but not as good as you!)

At first I thought Giovanni's sorrow was because of his wife, the one who died of the breast cancer two years ago, but that is not so. Mario Bianchi is the son he gave away when

Mario was a baby, and I am the only one besides Giovanni and our maitre d', Luciano, who knows this, because Luciano and his wife adopted Mario. Giovanni has asked me to tell no one, to keep this secret to myself.

The pain of giving Mario away is great for Giovanni, Nonna. But it's not that so much, or the secret that bothers me. I can carry that now that you know. I don't know what to do about Mr. Giovanni. He's invited me for dinner two or three times every week, and again, for tomorrow night. I think he likes to talk to me—and yes, more—even though he is nineteen years older.

I am sorry if this letter is a burden for you. It is easy to talk to my roommate Leslie, but he is a big gossip and he would tell my concerns to Pietro at the restaurant, and then everyone would know.

I don't think falling in love with Giovanni is possible, because I am still in love with Matteo, and I don't even know if it's all right to have dinner with him again. But I think he's a little bit in love with me. Pietro, the sommelier, says he has never seen Giovanni so happy since we have had our first dinner. Maybe his sister (the one I told you about, with the ferocious expression) will always hate me, but I don't care so much about that either, anymore.

I know I can tell you this because of the story of your great passion with Jeremy. I don't know what is the right thing to do. Please tell me what you think, Cara Nonna. *I trust you with all my heart.*

Con Multo Amore,
Your loving granddaughter, Mariella

P.S. Are you all right, Nonna? You didn't sound so good on the telephone.

Posta Aerea
11 Novembre 2000
29 Lincoln Way
San Francisco, California
94122
USA

Cara *Mariella*, mia bella nipote;

Remember what we talked about on the balcony on your last day when I told you about my Jeremy? Only the two people involved know what is right. It is true, Giovanni is much older than you and if you become serious with him you must think of what it will be like when he is old or maybe sick and you are still young. Or if he will die and you will be alone. Now, at your age, you are not thinking of such things. But it is good he is not married, so you are not guilty of taking someone's husband. If he is honorable and worthy of you, I am happy for you, for whatever time this lasts, my beloved Mariella.

Only please, make certain that his interest in you is caring and real, and not just for pleasure in the bed. And please, think of him in the same way. Even if you're not "in love."

Don't worry that he is your boss. You are both grown-up, no? You won't be manager for long—you wrote to me that he would interview people for the permanent job, for when you go to school full time. Think of all the ristoranti *where the husband is chef and the wife greets the people. Or the other way around.*

He sounds like a very good man, a loyal man to stay with his wife who was never happy with him. And it shows that he has a very big heart to suffer so for his son, and to make the provision that his son is close to him now. Does the young cuoco *know Giovanni is his father?*

And don't worry about the jealous sister, either. It is only her big eyebrows that make her look so mean. She will come to love you, cara, *just like her brother. Younger sisters are always jealous of the women in their brother's lives.*

Mia nipote dolce, *tell me how all this goes for you. I would say I have you always in my prayers, but you know I don't believe in that God, so I will tell you that I have you always in my heart.*

And don't worry. I am all right. I've had a bad cold, but I'm okay now.

Tanti Baci,
Nonna Giuseppina

————

Posta Aerea
23 Novembre 2000

Cara *Nonna;*

This will be a brief letter because we are very busy here at Basilico preparing for the American holiday called Thanksgiving—with il tacchino *and stuffing and pumpkin pies and all the people eat too much and get stuffed themselves, like the turkeys. That is what Cosima (one of the lady chefs and my new friend) and Luciano and Pietro tell me, that it will be a very big day for the* ristoranti.

My last dinner with Giovanni was very nice. At the oldest Italian restaurant in San Francisco called Fior d'Italia. Not as good as the food at Basilico, but everybody there knows Giovanni, and they treated us like the king and queen. It turns out, the waiter there is in my class on Ernesto *Hemingway.*

Mario Bianchi does not know that Giovanni is his father. But I believe he suspects, just from the way he watches Giovanni, every move he makes.

I will write you more, very soon.

Tutto il mio amore,
la tua nipotina, *Mariella*

Chapter Twenty-six

*B*efore the start of her next Hemingway class, she thumped
her books on the floor next to her chair, and hung her bag
over the chair's corner. Without looking, she felt Bernard—their
waiter from Fior d'Italia—watching her, appraising her, with his
amber eyes (Abyssinian cat eyes is how she thought of them) just
as he'd done every week since the semester had begun. She'd
even forgiven him the baseball cap he'd worn backwards when
he'd first walked into the classroom because he'd at least had the
good manners to take it off when he sat in the large circle directly
across from her. An American fetish, those hats. She thought
most men looked ridiculous in them—stupid, even. Oh, sure,
baseball hats had migrated to Sicilia; they'd infiltrated everywhere! Even, no doubt, to barren, volcanic Stromboli. But not so
ubiquitous in everyday Sicilian life as they were here.

Bernard's back was to the windows. Hers, to the door, no
more than two feet behind her. It would be easy to slip out and
never return. When she glanced up, he lowered his gaze.

Had he read her thoughts?

At the break he showed up beside her in the hallway, as if
she'd expected him.

"What are *you* doing here?" they both asked at once.

He laughed and cleared his throat—a more self-conscious
gesture than he'd displayed at Fior, where the face he presented
to the customers, though solicitous, was also confident.

"Don't you think it's time we formally introduced ourselves?"

185

he said, extending his hand. "Especially now that we'll be work-ing together?"

He must have caught her puzzled expression. "Oh," he said. "Giovanni didn't tell you? I'm going to be the new maitre d'."

The following morning, Giovanni knocked and opened her office door—her very own office!—before she had a chance to let him in.

"How are you?" he asked. His body filled the frame of her doorway. He stepped through and closed the door behind him. "You didn't check in." That was their routine now, her stopping by his office first thing on arrival.

"I was just on my way." In fact, she'd been stalling, studying the list of mostly Italian wines, wines she already knew by heart.

He looked good in a crisp white shirt under a maroon V-neck pullover and charcoal gray slacks. His shoes—probably Italian—soft black leather, the lace-up kind.

"Are you all right?" Giovanni asked. He was more relaxed than she'd ever seen him. *Of course he's relieved. Besides the sex, he's passed his secret burden along to me.*

"No. Well . . . yes and no," she said, standing and touching his arm, receiving his kisses on both of her cheeks. "I need to speak with you."

He cocked his head to one side and raised his brows. "Sounds serious."

"Giovanni." Mariella took a deep breath. "It is almost Decem-ber, yes? I start the full-time school in January, and I don't believe you have made one phone call or made one advertisement in the paper for the new manager." Why hadn't Giovanni told her he'd hired Bernard? Did he think she was a child? Or an insignificant woman? How could he treat her with such little respect?

She faced him, with her hands on her hips. Her "mighty mite" stance, her brother used to call it, making fun of her when he'd wanted to deflect scolding. Her lipstick and dangly earrings the same shade of fire-engine red as her blouse.

"Well," he said, a smile tugging at the corners of his mouth. "I'll have you know it's taken care of."

"Really?"

"Of course. Really. Why would you think otherwise?"

"Because. I don't know. I think maybe you are reluctant to let me go."

He laughed, but abruptly stopped. His pupils dilated so wide his irises appeared almost entirely black, ringed by only a thin border of light brown. "You don't mean *go*, as in go away completely?" he said. "I thought you were staying on as hostess part time, even while you're in school."

"Si. *Certo*. Of course, that is the plan." It made her glad that he didn't want her to leave. But not in the way that Mamma had wanted to keep her. Not suffocating. It wasn't Giovanni's temperament to be selfish. She knew that from how he tended to her when they made love. Still, she regarded him with a suspicious eye. "Why did you not tell me you have hired a new manager? And besides, who is this person?"

"Ah ha, you're jealous," he said, laughing again.

Was she? "Maybe," she said. "Yes. A little, I am jealous. Actually, I will miss the managing a lot."

He bent to caress her soft curly hair with the side of his cheek, her head barely reaching his chin. "Don't worry *bella*," he said, enfolding her. "Luciano will take over in January when you're ready."

"Luciano?" she mumbled into his chest. "But who will be the maitre d'?" she persisted.

"The night we went to Fior d'Italia? Remember I told you everyone in this business knows everyone else—at least here in North Beach?" The staff there had gone out of their way to welcome and to speak to Giovanni. Treated them like a king and queen, as she'd written in her letter to Nonna. The old maitre d' there had nearly fallen all over himself, as if the Godfather incarnate had graced them with his presence. And Bernard, who'd moved with a loose-limbed dancer's grace, anticipating their every little comfort and need with just the right measure of attention and distance, speaking mainly, and, as if they were long-time comrades, to Giovanni. In fact, barely looking at Mariella. And was it the manager or the owner, the one in the dark blue suit, clapping Giovanni on the back and pumping his arm so hard Giovanni had to shake it out when the man turned away?

"Mmm hmm," Mariella sighed, relaxing now, nuzzling into Giovanni's smell, redolent of nutmeg and lime. Even through his sweater and the shirt underneath, her body remembered the firmness of his arms, the solid yet yielding muscles of his torso.

"Well, our excellent waiter—Bernard? We've known each other from way back—from Trovatore, where he had his first waiting job, and I was manager."

A closed network, she thought: Giovanni, Luciano, Mario, when he was just a boy, and now Bernard. Who else at Basilico had migrated with Giovanni from Trovatore? Maybe Pietro. Their own little North Beach *famiglia del uomo*. An honored profession for a selected handful of men in San Francisco. A tradition.

"He's a bit younger than me," Giovanni said. "Somewhere in his thirties, but we've always liked each other—I guess you could say we're friends. Anyway, he's been assistant to the maitre d' at Fior for a few years now, just waiting to move into the head waiter position, which will never happen until Angelo drops dead or retires."

"So," she said, looking up at Giovanni, still in his arms. "You have hired him, this Bernard?"

"Yes, because even though I would keep you managing for all the days and all the nights you wanted, *mia cara* Mariella, you have promised yourself to become a translator, an ambassador, or who knows," Giovanni said, kissing the top of her head. "Maybe a big important diplomat."

Why hadn't she told Giovanni, right away, that Bernard was in her Hemingway class? Why was she keeping it from him now? And why, that night at Fior, had Bernard barely acknowledged her? And why hadn't she spoken up then and told Bernard that she recognized him?

"Giovanni! Giovanni!" Cosima banged on Mariella's door, the rasp in her voice unmistakable.

"Giovanni!" Pounding now, a demand.

He broke from Mariella's embrace and flung open the door. "What's wrong?"

It wasn't like Cosima to panic. Mario's assistant was strong and sensible, a feisty one of whom Pietro once remarked to Mariella, "If that woman were in a wrestling match with almost any man I know, I'd bet on her, two out of three takedowns." Right now the flush-faced redhead looked anything but sturdy or victorious.

"One of the dishwashers, he cut off a finger!" Cosima shouted, her eyes wild and urgent. "I've already called the ambulance, but you have to come!" She pulled Giovanni by the arm, but he was out the door and running in front of her before she'd finished speaking. The two women hurried on his heels.

The young Hispanic lay groaning at the far end of the kitchen floor. His hand wrapped in a towel soaked through with blood. Mario Bianchi knelt in front of the boy, his hand on the fellow's good arm, speaking softly, murmuring reassuring words. In the small plastic bag next to Mario was the severed finger, packed with ice and fastened with a rubber band.

"How the hell did this happen?" Giovanni demanded. "What was a dishwasher doing handling sharp knives?" Good knives were always washed by hand, never in the dishwasher, and, aside from the cooks, only by assistants who knew how to care for them and keep them sharp and safely stored.

"Pablo was playing like a Benihana chef when no one was paying attention," Cosima said. "We were all busy prepping when he screamed and fell down. Mario knew to do that," she told Giovanni, pointing at the iced finger. "He says the finger can be reattached if they can get the boy to the hospital right away. The finger next to it was sliced, but it probably only needs stitches."

Distant ambulance wails came nearer from outside, then suddenly whooped to a stop. Within seconds two uninformed paramedics in dark blue shouldered their way through the swinging kitchen doors and went to work on the injured boy.

"Whoever did this . . ." One of the paramedics held up the bag with the finger in it. "Good job. It'll probably save his hand."

"Mario," Cosima announced, loud enough for everyone to hear. "The sous chef. Mario did that."

Mario had stepped away from the injured dishwasher when the paramedics took over. Standing, now, behind the long stainless steel counter with its line of gas burners, sinks, and granite chopping surfaces, he ducked his head and shrugged, as if to say, "It's nothing."

"That's my boy," Giovanni murmured, only for Mariella's ears. After the paramedics wheeled Pablo out on a stretcher, he went to Mario and put his arm around the young chef's shoulders. Mariella couldn't make out what he said to his son, but whatever it was, at first Mario frowned and tried to pull away. Giovanni patted him on the back, and when Mario lowered his head this time, it was with a smile.

Chapter Twenty-Seven

Before she walked away from Basilico's hostess desk on Wednesday, Mariella observed that lunch was in full, voluble swing, most every table occupied, appetites and noses piqued by the aromas of garlic, onions, the braised or grilled meats and fish, savory sauces and, of course, wine. Conversations purred along in crescendos of rise and fall, pierced now and again by a shrill laugh, or the voice of someone hard of hearing—or just plain obnoxious—barking above the din.

In the sanctity of her office, she clicked her tongue in disapproval as she perused that evening's reservation schedule, thinking of rude people who never bothered to show, nor bothered calling to free up their table. For the twenty minutes it would take her to make the calls to remind people of their reservations, Luciano or Pietro would direct the occasional walk-in to the bar, or invite them to put their names on the waiting list.

The still new status of having her own office, on the other side of the wall from Giovanni's, suffused her with pleasure.

"*Americano* entitlement," she muttered to herself as she systematically dialed down the list.

On her way back to the reservation desk, she happened to glance up.

"*Che cazzo!*" Nearby conversations slowed to a standstill. Surely, she was mistaken—the woman was only a resemblance—an apparition.

Mamma bore down on her, a harpy in full sail, a banshee as

alarming as if she were, indeed, a shrieker of death and doom.

"*Che cazzo!*" Mariella exclaimed again.

Mamma smacked her daughter across the face. "You don't use those bad words!" she shouted in Italian, her caftan-like dress billowing around her like a dervish skirt. She raised her hand to strike again.

Someone gasped.

"What'd she say?" a woman customer asked.

"'What the fuck!'" an Italian-speaking waiter cheerfully obliged in a mock whisper.

All eyes, even those on the periphery, turned toward the commotion.

Giovanni rushed up alongside. "What's going on?" he demanded, placing his arm protectively, around Mariella's shoulders. "Are you all right? Who's this woman?" He signaled to Luciano at the front desk, "She's disturbing the customers. Get her out of here!"

"This woman," Mariella said in a low voice, "is my mother." She rubbed her face where Mamma's hand left her cheek smarting.

"Si," Mamma spat at Giovanni's feet. "*Sono la Mamma!*" She pointed to herself. "You," she pointed to Giovanni. "*Il* pimp! Child molester!" Mamma knew that much, in English.

"I am neither a pimp nor a child molester, Signora Russo," Giovanni said in Italian and as quietly and with as much dignity as he could muster with everyone watching. He swept his arm, gesturing for Mamma to follow its direction. "Can we step into my office and continue this conversation?"

Mamma stood with her arms folded, against the background of the curious diners. Giovanni shook his head as Pietro and Luciano approached.

"Mamma," Mariella said, struggling to absorb the reality of her mother, standing before her. If only she could blink her eyes and open them to find her mother had magically disappeared.

"You'd better do as he asks, because if you don't, the *polizia* will come and take you away."

"*Puttana!*" Mamma snarled. "Of course, you'd sacrifice your own mother to the pimp. And why do you look like your eyes are about to fall out of your face? Eh? Did you think I wouldn't find you?" Still, she took Giovanni's arm, and with the bearing of a queen, allowed him to escort her, with Mariella trailing, into his office.

"What are you *doing* here?" Mariella demanded as she shut the office door behind them. Superstitiously, she raised her hands to her ears. If Nonna or Papa were dead, or if Mamma had come to live with her, she didn't want to hear.

"I come all this way, I risk my life on a piece of tin flying through the sky, and all you ask is why am I here?" Mamma cried. "Is very nice, this room," she said, looking around Giovanni's office. She spotted Beth's photo on Giovanni's desk. "Your wife?" she asked, a cunning accusation.

"Yes," Giovanni said. "She died two years ago."

"Why are you here, Mamma?" Mariella asked again.

"To take you home, you stupid girl."

"Don't call her stupid—or puttana," Giovanni cautioned.

Mamma started to answer back, but stopped herself, as if Giovanni might actually have some power. She looked him over, saw the cut of his expensive trousers and the lushness of his cashmere sweater, his aura of confidence and command and was, apparently, impressed.

"I've come to take my daughter home," she said more sweetly. "Where she belongs—with us, and with Matteo, her fiancé, the man who waits for her. The man who loves her. The man she promised to marry." Mamma flung her arm toward the door, as if Matteo might be waiting just outside.

"Matteo?" Giovanni said. "Who's Matteo?" He cocked his head and looked at Mariella. "*Are* you engaged?"

"No," Mariella said. "Yes . . . I was, but he . . . oh, never mind. I'll explain later."

A wince crossed Giovanni's brow. "Yes," he said. "You will."

"You didn't know she ran away?" Mamma said. "She lied to you too?"

"I'm not going home," Mariella said. "And I haven't lied to anyone." She was certain her thumping heart would betray her attempt at a calm veneer. Betray the longing for Matteo that the mention of him stirred in her, the longing that lay continuously beneath the surface of her skin

Could Mamma really force her back to Sicily?

"Roberto's waiting in the car, outside," Mamma said. "We have the plane tickets." She hesitated. "For tonight!"

"Roberto?" Mariella and Giovanni said in unison. But of course, Mamma never would have—never could have—made the journey alone.

"Matteo's friend, from that university where you learned to be a fool. The place that made you think you know everything," Mamma said, eyeing Mariella with displeasure.

"Matteo sent you?" Mariella asked. Now, rivulets of sweat trickled down between her breasts. *Why did Mamma make me say his name? I've tried so hard to forget him.*

"Naturally," Mamma said, edging closer to the bookshelf. She picked up and inspected a small teardrop-shaped pewter vase, then opened a mahogany box, inlaid with mother-of-pearl. She sniffed inside, as if some suspect substance might have been stored there. "It was Matteo's idea. How else would we pay for tickets?"

"Mamma!" Mariella said. She didn't believe for a minute—didn't want to believe—that the expedition was Matteo's idea. Or that they actually had tickets for that night. "Put that down. You're being nosy!"

"It's okay," Giovanni said.

Mariella gave him a warning look. *Is he taking Mamma's side over mine?* Death to their connection, choosing Mamma over her.

Giovanni gave Mariella a small nod. "On second thought, please put it down. It's very precious and old."

"Old?" Mamma said, hesitating, holding the box above the floor in drop position. When neither Mariella nor Giovanni reacted, she coyly placed it back on the shelf. "Like you, eh?" She raised her chin at Giovanni. "Too old for her." She braced her hands onto her hips. "I'm not leaving until you come with me," she declared, spitting the words at Mariella.

"Then you'll have to wait a lifetime," Mariella said, mimicking her mother's posture. She leaned toward Mamma across Giovanni's desk. "Besides, why do you want me home? You don't even like me."

"Who cares if I like you?" Mamma said. "That's not the point."

Giovanni swiveled his head back and forth between them, following their rapid-fire Italian.

"What *is* the point, Mamma? What does Papa say?"

"That doesn't matter you stu—" Mamma glanced at Giovanni and caught herself. "Of course," she said. "I have his blessing."

Luciano knocked softly and poked in his head. "Sorry to disturb," he said. "But do you want me to call Teresa to come in and take over?"

"No," Mariella said. "I'm coming now." She glared at her mother. "Mamma was just leaving."

"No," Giovanni said. "Absolutely not." He lifted his head to a bullish, I'll-brook-no-argument position. Mariella had seen it before, with recalcitrant employees, and she knew better than to argue.

"Do you mean no, I can't go to work? Or no, my mother isn't leaving?"

"Both." He fixed her with a stern eye.

"What about their tickets?" she asked, throwing Mamma a triumphant sneer. Now her mother would have to confess they didn't have them.

"We can change those," Giovanni said. "After you've talked."

"See!" Mamma crowed.

"Oh, don't assume anything," Giovanni instructed Mamma. "I'm not getting in the middle. I'm only saying you need a place to talk. I can put up you and Roberto, Signora Russo," he nodded in the general direction of the street, "in my spare rooms, at least for tonight, and you can talk there with Mariella and figure out what you want to do."

"Puhh," Mamma and Mariella both mouthed.

"I'll stay with you at your apartment!" Mamma protested, pointing at Mariella. "I prefer to talk there."

"No!" Mariella said. "I mean . . . no, my roommate will be there, studying. Besides, there's nowhere for you to sleep. And besides, I have nothing to say to you."

"Yes," Mamma insisted. "I stay with you. All girls. You and your Leslie can sleep together, and I'll sleep in your bed. And Roberto can stay with Giovanni. All boys."

Mamma looked as smug as the canary cat. She knew. Olimpio, most likely, thoughtlessly let slip, "Oh yeah, her gay roommate . . ."

"Okay, so you know he's a man," Mariella said.

"Si, *uno finocchio*," Mamma said, her mouth turning down in distaste. "But at least this way, he doesn't get into your pants." She slid her eyes toward Giovanni. Mariella could see her mother struggling to hold back her favorite invective.

With surprisingly mild complaint, Mamma agreed to talk at Giovanni's. Probably, Mariella figured, because Giovanni was commanding and handsome. And to challenge her daughter. Mariella would look like a brat if she refused.

Giovanni held Mamma's elbow and walked her to the taxi

where Roberto waited—or rather, slept. Giovanni gave the driver his address on Leavenworth. He and Mariella followed in his gray Volvo sedan: fifteen years old, and, like its owner, well maintained.

"I'll walk you up and then leave," he said, pulling away from the curb. "There's a good lasagna in the freezer." He sounded distant, aloof, and she knew it was because of Mamma's mention of Matteo. But she was angry with him too, for taking over, and for backing her into a corner.

They rode in silence. She questioned herself: *was keeping Matteo secret a betrayal?* She refused to think so. No. Revealing him—revealing *them*—would be the betrayal. Because even if it was fair and right to disclose their intimacy to anyone who came after—to Giovanni—her *impassionata* with Matteo was a seminal part of who she had become, a sequestered first love belonging only to them, shaping her womanhood, giving voice to her ambitions. And keeping her awake at night. She wouldn't discuss him with Giovanni—with anyone. Only Nonna.

Mariella sighed. "I didn't tell you about my engagement because I haven't told anybody here. I never wanted to get married and . . . I wanted to leave the past in the past."

"You're not still promised to this Matteo?" Giovanni said. He briefly took his eyes from the road to look at her.

She remembered Matteo's intensity, his intelligence, his passion for life and for her; she remembered the sex.

"No. I broke our engagement. We—I said my goodbyes." She didn't speak for a moment. Wouldn't tell him she loved Matteo, still. "But my mother was right," she said. "I did run away."

Giovanni didn't respond at first. And then, he laughed uproariously. "Oh," he said, catching his breath. "That's wonderful! That spirit of yours." He glanced at her again. "Don't take this wrong," he said, wiping his eyes. "But you get that fight from your mother."

Chapter Twenty-Eight

Well into the night, Mamma harangued, pleaded, cursed, condemned her daughter to Hell, even got down on her knees. One for the books, Mamma begging for anything.

"He waits for you," Mamma said, giving her campaign one last gasp before she collapsed in one of Giovanni's leather club chairs. "We both thought by now you'd come to your right mind."

"I don't believe Matteo waits for me, Mamma." The image of Matteo pining—passively enduring—didn't fit. Even if he missed her, as she missed him in the alone, quiet hours, he had too much pride. No, too much self-respect. She couldn't even imagine him speaking of her to Mamma.

Elmer snored on the sofa under the bay windows, a third incessant voice, interspersed with slobbery snorts. He whimpered intermittently, his underbite chattering along with his chin, perhaps dreaming of chasing butterflies. His legs stuck out, straight and stiff, and twitched when he whimpered. The two women ignored him.

"But why, Mamma, why?" Mariella asked, for the hundredth time. "Why *do* you want me to come home?" Useless question. Yolanda Russo would never admit she was desperate to win.

"To save your soul," Mamma said. Her words, her whole body, lifeless now, slumped in the chair like an old cloth doll, its joints hung together only by a string. Her caftan dress draped over her feet onto the floor, in deflated folds.

Mariella knew her soul had nothing to do with it. She was the lightning rod, the grounding, protecting the Russo household from burning down, the centrifuge that prevented Mamma and Papa from looking each other too closely in the eye. Not that she saw her parents' marriage dissolving, but without her as focal point—with Mamma on one side and Papa on the other—what would their relationship revolve around?

There was more to it, a mystery Mariella only vaguely glimpsed about her family. And she wondered, not for the first time, how Olimpio was faring now that she was gone. And what, if anything, he'd had to do with Mamma showing up.

She was worn out, too, from holding *her* ground. And sad, for what she imagined was Papa's disappointment with himself, his failure to corral Mamma. And sad, as well, for Mamma's disappointment, and for herself, for once again, letting everyone down.

It was just past midnight when Giovanni's key turned in the lock. Roberto staggered in behind him. Even from across the room, Mariella could smell alcohol seeping from Roberto's pores, reminding her of too much partying in Catania. He'd gone out hours ago. "To see the city," he'd declared on arrival at Giovanni's apartment.

"I found him outside, walking up and down the block," Giovanni said. "Well, lurching up and down the hill is more like it. Good thing I spotted him, if the cops had picked him up, he'd be in jail."

Oh, thank God. Imagining the delay, the complications, and how long Mamma might be in town if Roberto *had* gone to jail set Mariella's empty stomach roiling again. Mamma had had two helpings of the lasagna, but Mariella had been too upset to eat more than a bite. And she had no idea what happened to foreigners incarcerated here.

"*Ciao*," Roberto slurred, making it sound like "schow." He waved a hand and staggered off down the hallway behind Giovanni.

Giovanni returned and took one look at the two women. "Roberto's passed out and I'm taking you home," he told Mariella. And to Mamma, in spite of her gaping protest, "I'll be right back. It's a locked building. You're safe. Everyone needs to get some sleep."

Mariella fell into an unconscious slumber for exactly one hour until the tango ringtone of her cell awakened her. No one would call in the middle of the night except for an emergency. Her father knew the time difference between San Francisco and *Sicilia*. She reached blindly for the phone on her bedside table. When she could focus, she saw it was Giovanni. She answered with a pounding heart.

"I'm at your door," he said, his voice urgent and strained. "Let me in. Now."

She pulled on her silky robe and buzzed him in. He was unshaven, uncombed, with a coat thrown over pajamas. No socks, only moccasin slippers.

Leslie was overnight at Darrell's, so there was no danger of waking him.

"She'll be all right," Giovanni said, without preamble. He stood in the living room, his arms hanging loose at his sides. "She's in the hospital. But . . . oh shit, I hate to tell you this. She took pills," he patted his coat pocket, "and left you a note."

"The hospital?" It took her a second to understand. He meant Mamma.

"Read it to me," Mariella said, shivering. Cold. She was so cold.

"Are you sure?"

"Read it," she said.

Giovanni pulled out a crumpled sheet:

Puttana! *Ruining the name of Russo, forever—at least in Catania, and now San Francisco too. Taking up with a man old enough to be your father, who only cares what's between your legs. Thinking only of your own pleasure, like always. Since you will make no sacrifice for the family, then I, Yolanda Russo, must sacrifice my very soul—yes, you know in the Church it is a mortal sin to kill oneself. But I have no choice. And so I condemn myself forever to* Il Diavolo. *But this is what I must do to make you understand how much misery you have caused. Besides, I know you like your father better than me. I think your father likes you better too. I don't know for sure if he has ever really loved me. Ask him. Maybe you have both wanted me out of the way. I know for certain your grandmother doesn't like me. Well, I don't like her either. So now, you don't have to worry. You all get your wish. I hope your life is as miserable as mine.*

Arrivederci, *(Because I cannot bring myself to call myself your mother)*
Yolanda Russo

"Get dressed. I'll take you to her," Giovanni said.

"No," Mariella said, her voice a monotone. "Tell me. Tell me how it happened." She couldn't have despised her mother more than she did at that moment.

Giovanni sank into one of Leslie's white chairs and gripped his head in his hands. His shoulders began to shake.

"Oh, Giovanni," Mariella said, squeezing in next to him and placing her arm across his back. "I'm so embarrassed, so sorry you have been dragged into this." Mamma's debacle must have reminded him of his wife's death. Hadn't he said she died, being cared for by hospice, at home?

No! He was laughing. Laughing! Not crying. What was the matter with him? He'd laughed like a lunatic last night when she'd told him she'd run away from home and now this? Was *he* slipping over the edge?

"Your mother's a real character," he wheezed.

"Just tell me," she said. Even to her own ears she sounded heartless. She searched for fear, for any emotion, and couldn't find it.

"Well," he finally managed between breaths. "When I got back to the apartment, your mother's and Roberto's doors were both closed, so I figured they were asleep. I took Elmer out—his routine got disrupted, you know. So anyway, when we came back, I went into my room, and there's a knock on my door."

"My mother? In a long white nightgown? Looking like a phantom of Lady Macbeth?"

"How'd you guess?" Giovanni observed Mariella *come un ucello*, like a bird, with a sideways glance. "Of course. How would you *not* know?"

"So?"

"So your mother hands me the note and says, very formally, 'I'm going to die now. I just took the pills,' and shows me the empty bottle. I didn't know whether or not to believe her, but to be on the safe side, I called 911 right away."

"*Did* she take the pills?" It would be more like Mamma to make a big drama without any action.

"Before I could grab her, she ran to her room and locked the door. But," Giovanni said, holding up a finger. "Of course, I have a key to that room, so I broke in."

Mariella snorted. "Trust me, she was counting on it. She wouldn't have done it if she hadn't known you'd find a way." So predictable. "At the least, she was testing to see if you were man enough." She would never have risked it with Papa. Mamma had threatened him, but never followed through.

"Anyway," Giovanni said, "there she was, lying on the bed like a corpse, except she was breathing and her eyes were wide open. So I pulled her up off the bed. But man, is she determined." Giovanni turned his cheek to show a scab of blood from one of Mamma's long nails. "She even tried to bite me."

"How'd you stop her?" If only Papa would act half so powerful.

Giovanni shrugged. "I guess just because I'm bigger and stronger. Anyway, I got her into the bathroom, but what a fighter! You should have seen her." He blew through his lips. "I got her arms behind her back—by then Roberto was helping me hold onto her. I must have called for him. I remember yelling and banging on his door on the way to the bathroom. That's what he told me later. Between the two of us, we made her throw up. At least three times. Stuck our fingers down her throat."

"But did she take the pills?" Mariella asked again.

"Yes. We counted at least twenty."

Papa answered on the first ring, as if he was standing by, waiting for her call. It was lunchtime in Catania, and Papa always took his afternoon meal at home.

"Why did you let her come?" Mariella demanded.

"When have I ever been able to stop your mother?" Even over the thousands of miles, the defeat in his voice as palpable as Mariella's anger. He mumbled something that sounded like, "Maybe I'll explain it someday."

"She took pills," Mariella said.

The only sound was Papa's silence. Not bothering to ask if she was alive. He didn't need to.

"What do you want me to do?" she asked.

"Where are you now? Are you with her?"

"No. I'm at my apartment. I'm not ready to see Mamma yet." At that moment, she didn't care whether she ever saw her mother again. "Papa, why *did* you let her come?" If her father were more like Giovanni, he'd have persuaded Mamma in the first place.

"It's not a matter of *let*," Papa said. "It's . . . I owe your mother a great debt," he said miserably. "But I don't want to—I can't— talk about it right now."

A great debt? Wouldn't it be more the other way around?

One heartbeat . . . two heartbeats . . . three . . .

"I want you to get your mother on the plane with that moron Roberto, and I forbid you to come with her," Papa said, more forcefully than she'd ever heard him. "I forbid you to sacrifice your life."

Like you have, she thought.

Only breathing, on both ends of the line.

"I guess her plans backfired," Papa said. She swore she could hear her father's smile. "And I promise," he said. "Someday I will explain about the debt. But don't you dare come home. I'll never forgive you—forgive myself—and neither will Nonna."

Chapter Twenty-Nine

Mariella got to the hospital a little later that same morning. Mamma was placed on a seventy-two-hour hold at California Pacific Medical Center. In the ER, they pumped her stomach and admitted her onto the psychiatric ward. Before entering the room, she studied her mother from the hallway through the transparent thick glass divider. Mamma looked shrunken and terribly alone. Silent and still, all the fight seemingly drained out of her. She was in a single room, belted down so she couldn't get out of the bed. Sedated, but not unconscious. Chicken wire was embedded in the sealed windows on the far wall.

"Mamma," Mariella said softly, bearing African violets in a ceramic pot. Mamma's favorite, but they wouldn't let Mariella bring the plant into the room. Mamma could use the pot as a weapon. Part of Mariella wanted to clobber her mother over the head with it. Instead, she gave it to a nurse who placed it on the counter at the nurses' station.

Inside her mother's room, a box of tissues and a paper cup of water with a flexible straw sat on the bedside cabinet.

"Look what kind of trouble you got yourself into now," Mariella said.

Her mother's eyes, huge and dark in her pale, frightened face. "No one here understands me," she said and turned her head from Mariella. "And no! It's not my fault, you idiot girl; it's your fault I'm in this trouble." Her sedation made her sound sibilant and slurry. "I'm going home and you're coming with me," she hissed. "Even if I have to kill myself ten more times!" She lay like a sphinx, refusing to look at her daughter.

"I'm not going home, Mamma, and you can't leave yet. It's the law here. It's what happens when you do something so stupid." Possibly, this was the first time in her mother's life she'd endured any kind of consequence for her antics.

"Stupid?" Mamma yelled, with alarming vigor. She strained against the straps, unsuccessfully, to sit up in the bed. "Ha! You think it's stupid because I want to die?"

"No, because I don't think you want to die at all," Mariella said, struggling to contain her own anger. "But you can't control me, Mamma. Not anymore. Not even with such a threat."

"You think this is a threat?" Mamma demanded, her fury bringing spittle to the corners of her mouth. "It's not the end, I promise you that!"

Mariella had searched herself before coming to the hospital, asking herself what she would have done if her mother had died. She'd been pierced with a sorrow she wouldn't have imagined, as much for the mother she never had as for the mother she would have lost. Knowing Mamma would recoil, she touched her mother's hand anyway.

"They won't let you out of here until they know you're safe," Mariella said, sounding far more neutral than she felt. Having her mother restrained brought freedom from responsibility, a guilty sense of relief. "Until they know you're all right, at least for a couple more days."

"Safe?" Mamma echoed. "Safe? You think I can be safe among vipers? *Americanos*?" She paused. "Okay, fine, I'll act all right and then kill myself the minute they turn their back." She clamped her jaw and didn't speak.

Over the next three days Mariella watched her mother give every attendant and nurse who came into her purview a tongue lashing in Italian none could comprehend but understood, through the translator, (provided by law) wasn't complimentary. With doctors, but only the male ones, she was meek and compliant. She wouldn't ever admit that any woman could be a doctor. She insisted they were only nurses.

"*O, dottore*, I am fine," she purred to the bespectacled young psychiatrist with stringy light hair and flashed her most engaging smile. It was the morning of the fourth day. "My daughter will take care of me. I'm ready to go home, yes?"

This day, Mariella stood by and translated.

"Yes, but only when all the papers are signed," the young doctor cautioned. His nameplate identified him as Dr. Howard Butler.

"Papers?"

"Yes, signora. Your daughter will sign for you on this end, and you will be released into her care only long enough for her and . . ." Dr. Butler looked to Mariella for verification.

"Giovanni Russo and Roberto Polti," Mariella said.

". . . for Giovanni Russo and Roberto Polti, and your daughter here, to escort you to the airport. And your husband, Salvatore Russo, will be there to meet you at the other end." The doctor waved a sheet of paper at Mamma. "We faxed him papers, and he sent them back. Signing you into his care."

Mamma huffed so hard she sounded like Giovanni's dog, Elmer.

"And," Dr. Butler went on. "We've arranged with the airports and the airline for a medical officer to meet you and Mr. Polti and escort you onto the planes, both here and in Rome. And, the flight attendants will know what to do, once you're in the air. Otherwise," he explained, "we'd have to keep you here indefinitely."

Giovanni, with Roberto's feeble assistance, booked return flights for Mamma and Roberto for that evening. Roberto was hung over again, but he had the tickets, visas, and passports in his possession. Mariella hung onto the signed hospital paperwork. After an early dinner, Giovanni would drive them to the airport, with Mamma between her daughter and Roberto in the back. Roberto may have been ineffectual, but he was bullish and strong.

Papa, it turned out, with Nonna's help, had paid for two round-trip tickets, with an open return. And an open one-way ticket home for Mariella, at Mamma's hysterical behest, no doubt. Mariella had known, instinctively, that Matteo had nothing to do with the tickets. And it had been Olimpio's idea to enlist Roberto, who had been one of Matteo's university pals.

Giovanni, somehow, managed to have the Alitalia ticket held for Mariella, on future account.

Mariella, Giovanni, and Roberto retrieved Mamma from the hospital in the late afternoon, Mamma declaiming to no avail, "Keep your hands off me!" Roberto and Giovanni whisked her from the car into Giovanni's building as if she were a child swung along between two parents.

They assembled, once again, in Giovanni's living room, Mamma, Mariella, and this time, Giovanni and Roberto. Mamma holding center seat in Giovanni's big armchair. They ate Chinese takeout on their laps, the boxes of kung pao chicken, Mongolian beef, fried rice, and pot stickers open before them on the enormous dark wood coffee table, large enough for all four of them to gather around. Elmer wriggled in and nestled between Mariella and his dog bed on the couch. He rested his head on her thigh and drooled on her woolen pants, hoping for a morsel to land nearby.

"What's this?" Mamma raised the containers of food, her entire face a scowl. She pushed aside her chopsticks as if Chinese food was an affront. "I'm not hungry."

Mariella shrugged. She knew her mother was panicked and furious even after all those days in the hospital. And that she kept herself from putting up a physical fight only for fear of going back into the hospital. Defiance was Mamma's way of staying strong.

Eschewing her plate, Mariella plucked a mound of the chicken and vegetables onto chopsticks and popped it directly into her mouth. It had dawned on her: even if she longed for Mamma to love her, she no longer feared her mother's cruel tongue, her seemingly deliberate withholding of tenderness, her quest for revenge.

"You need to eat, Mamma," she said. "It's a long flight."

Mamma pursed her mouth and shook her head.

In all fairness, her mother looked terrible. Worse than Mariella had ever seen her: dark sunken eyes, her face swollen yet pale, seemingly new lines making her appear far beyond her forty-two years. Her red lipstick, a gash across her mouth. Still, even if she wore the same caftan, at least she was free of straps and out of hospital clothes.

"You know that Papa will meet you at the airport," Mariella said. "He'll be there right when you're escorted off the plane." She turned to Giovanni. "This is good Chinese," she managed between mouthfuls of the vegetable pot stickers.

"I'll never forgive you!" Mamma blurted. "You didn't have to tell your father; he didn't have to know."

"Oh, Mamma," Mariella said calmly, belying both the annoyance—nay, the rage—and the tenderness bubbling beneath the surface, along with her impatience to see her mother onto that plane. "Of course he did. Papa knows anyway. He always knows. Besides, how else would you be able to go home?" She thought of Papa, secretly fretting about Mamma but acting steady. And her brother, Olimpio, biding his time until he finished university, itching to earn money and move out.

Mariella sighed. "You don't have to worry, Mamma," she said. "Papa will always take care of you." She hesitated, thought of telling her mother she could live without her forgiveness now, but thought better of saying more and stayed silent.

Chapter Thirty

"**C**'mon," Bernard said at class break the following week. He wore a dark brown leather bomber-style jacket, with a green wool scarf tucked and zippered inside it in front. And no baseball cap. "The coffee machine's around the corner. I'm the last of the big spenders—my treat."

Mariella had come to class still anxious that evening, still reeling from her mother's tempestuous arrival and departure only four days earlier. And she was nervous about facing Bernard. But she was relieved to be back in her own life, at least back in her routine.

What harm could there be in saying yes to coffee?

When he turned his head to glance at something or someone going by, the curly fringe along the nape of his neck set off a small shiver of desire down Mariella's body.

"I'm always in school," he said as if she'd asked. They walked toward the coffee machine. Part of his charm, she realized, was the incongruence between his self-effacing demeanor and his grace of body and voice. Beautiful, but without vanity. "Actually, I've been taking classes toward my degree for three years now, part time, you know—when I'm not working."

"Your degree?"

"Yeah. Creative writing." He ducked his head as if he was embarrassed to admit it. His thick blond hair wound of its own accord behind and around each ear. "You?" he asked, tilting his chin toward the dispenser. "Cream—rather, whatever they use that passes for cream—sugar?"

"Only black, grazie." She watched as he inserted dollar bills into the slots and pushed the buttons; he had sensitive hands, like a pianist's or a surgeon's. What would those finely shaped fingers feel like on her body . . .

Christo! Was she such a loose woman that every man's decent-looking hands made her think of sex?

Bernard's expression was not condescending, exactly, but amused, as if he could see what she was thinking. As she spoke of her ambitions, he kept his gaze—eyes that were variously gold, green, or blue—on the institutional beige linoleum flooring and nodded thoughtfully, as if he were carefully considering each of her bits of information.

Nearly choking on the mouthful of tepid black bitterness she held in her mouth, and wavering between spitting it back into the cup and swallowing, she chose the latter. "Sorry, it's not your fault, but it is terrible stuff, this *caffè.*"

He laughed but said nothing.

"You've known Giovanni and Luciano a long time?" she asked. "Giovanni says you all worked together at Trovatore."

"Oh, fifteen years ago, at least, maybe more. He appeared to be considering what more to say. "You're with Giovanni?"

"What do you mean, '*With* Giovanni?'" She struck half of her "mighty mite" pose: only one hand, her free one, on a hip. How dare he insinuate that Giovanni—that anyone—had a claim on her.

"Oh, hey," he said. "I don't mean any offense. I'm just curious, that's all . . . You know, you seem like a couple." He paused and glanced down the hallway, away from her. "Okay, the truth is I was curious for selfish reasons. I know you've seen me looking at you in class."

"Well . . ." She searched around for a garbage bin, securing her purse strap firmly on her shoulder, preparing to step away.

"I promise you, I'm not a stalker," he said, moving alongside her again. "I've been watching . . . you know, trying to figure out how to approach you. I was really thrown, that night you and Giovanni showed up at Fior. You didn't say anything—I mean about us being in class together, so that's why I didn't either. Well, that and wanting to show Giovanni respect." He nearly blushed. "I think a lot—I mean highly—of Giovanni."

"Oh," she said. "Well, that's good, the part about respect." As if prompted by a collective, silent signal, students began drifting away from the machines, back toward class.

What a relief, this course would be over in just one week and she wouldn't have to face Bernard here anymore. She *would* tell Giovanni, first thing tomorrow, about already meeting him.

"So what made you take Hemingway?" he asked, as they headed back to class, as if the prior conversation hadn't happened. He held the classroom door open for her.

"Oh, for the simple English," she said, passing in front of him. Her English had improved steadily, almost daily. Yet, even if her mispronunciations were less frequent, her accent would remain for a lifetime. "And also because Hemingway doesn't try to make everything different. Like in *The Sun Also Rises*, where everybody goes to Spain to make big changes in their lives." She raised her shoulders. "Eh, they get drunk, they fight, but in the end, everybody stays who they are."

Like Mamma. Her nerves were more frayed than she wanted to admit from her mother's calamitous visit. The memory of her mother strapped down and enfeebled haunted Mariella daily. Now she couldn't help but envision Mamma, stubborn and unchanging like the characters in Hemingway's novel, set in her ways until what would eventually be her dying breath. And wondered if she, herself, wasn't just as stubborn.

"Hemingway is honest," she said. "Like in real life."

The next day, when she told Giovanni she'd met Bernard in class—recognized him from Fior, and he'd finally introduced himself—Giovanni said, "Hmm. I know he's been working toward a degree, taking classes at night when he's not at the restaurant. I admire him for that. Says he wants to be a writer." And then, "Did I tell you, he'll begin training with Luciano on Monday?"

Chapter Thirty-One

Leslie held up the Thursday morning *Chronicle* in front of his face. He wore sweatpants and a gray sweatshirt with a hood that all but covered his eyes, nose, and mouth, making him appear like the Unabomber, or a hollow-eyed ghoul left over from Halloween. It was two days after her Hemingway class with Bernard, two weeks before Christmas, and four days before Bernard would come on board at Basilico.

Mariella sat across from Leslie at their small dining table. She'd slept here, at the apartment the night before rather than at Giovanni's, and Leslie hadn't stayed at Darrell's, nor Darrell with him. Even though she missed Giovanni the nights they were apart, missed the drowsy, musky smell of him, the sex, she liked the freedom of waking up in her own bed on her days off.

Mostly, she wanted time alone because sex with Giovanni brought up her longing for Matteo, which was always there, just under the surface. And she needed time to grieve him in private.

"What's the matter with you?" she asked Leslie. She'd been watching him for a full five minutes. Not once had he glanced her way.

"What? Why do you ask?" Evasive, still not lowering the paper.

He'd been rather sheepish these days. Withdrawn, and not at all his usual flamboyant, sardonic self. It seemed to her he crept around the apartment, ducking past or casting a sideways smile on the rare occasions when they were both home.

"You going to pretend with me there's nothing going on?" she persisted.

"Nothing I really want to talk about." He spoke at the newspaper rather than to her.

"Are you mad at me, Mr. Leslie?" Maybe he didn't like her spending time away from the apartment. Or maybe he wanted her to move out. Maybe . . .

"No." He rose up suddenly from his chair and threw back the sweatshirt hood. "Do you always have to keep at me!" He spat out the accusation. The rims around his gray eyes were swollen and red. Either he'd been crying, or he was hung over—or maybe he was ill.

"Mr. Leslie, is it the AIDS?" She did a quick mental calculation. It hadn't been quite three months since his first round of testing at Kaiser, which had come up negative, as she'd predicted. His next appointment would be in a few weeks, right after Christmas.

"Nooo." He sounded disgusted, impatient. He stomped into the kitchen. "Jeez, Mariella," he said, whirling on her. "You could try being a little diplomatic once in a while!"

"*Scusi.* Sorry," she said softly. "I am worried about you."

Leslie stared at her for a moment, then rushed out of the kitchen and fled down the hallway. Mariella watched him, wide-eyed and mouth agape.

"If you must know," he shouted from the end of the hall. "Darrell broke up with me!"

"No." She got up and hurried after him. "I don't believe it," she said, catching up as he entered his bedroom.

"Believe what you want!" he yelled and slammed the door in her face.

Around noon, Leslie called her on his break from Gypsy Men's, the clothing store in the Haight where he worked.

"I'm sorry," he mumbled into the phone. "I didn't mean to

take my upset out on you—and really, I would like to talk. I mean when you have the time."

"It's okay," she said. "I'll stay home again tonight." Two nights in a row she'd be away from Giovanni. Even though her body wanted to be with him, and to nestle into sleep against his solid warmth, she had no choice. Her roommate needed her more.

She missed Papa, Nonna, Olimpio—and Matteo—sometimes profoundly, sometimes not at all. But this would be her first Christmas without them, her first Christmas ever, away from home.

She puttered around the apartment, catching up on laundry, and, in spite of her mother's "surprise" arrival and monstrous manipulation just two weeks earlier, she wrote letters to her family telling them how much she loved them—something she'd done from childhood, something almost all Italian children did at Christmas. And even though some young ones these days also wrote letters to *Babbo Natale*, asking for worldly goods, it was *La Befana*, the old woman who delivers gifts on Epiphany, who still embodied the most traditional and revered figure of Christmas. Almost everyone in every household left stockings for *La Befana* on Epiphany Eve, no matter the age.

When she'd told Leslie all this, he'd realized how much she missed home and had taken her to Union Square to cheer up her homesickness. Mariella found the dazzling, sometimes garish department store lights and the lavish, ostentatious decorations in and around Union Square overwhelming and even a bit shocking.

"I think *Americans* are maybe what they call greedy in English—*molto avido*," she wrote to her family of the hectic pace, the crowds of people pawing through merchandise, sometimes pushing and shoving each other in their frantic searches for just the right "thing" to buy and to give.

Perhaps because Sicilians were poorer, or perhaps because they were islanders and more isolated from such gross consumerism, Christmas in Sicily and most all of Italy had always been to celebrate the *Natale*, to light candles and prepare traditional, sumptuous food. Even if crèches or nativities were displayed in shops, or a tall, lighted tree was installed in the Piazza, gifts were generally simpler and meant to honor the season of darkness and the coming of light—blessings for continuance into the coming new year. Even if most Sicilians were Catholic only in name, almost everyone went to midnight Mass on Christmas Eve.

To her and Leslie's tabletop Christmas tree, she added her own homegrown touches—miniature pinecones and tiny Italian *Buon Natale* flags. She'd propped her present to Leslie against the tree: a gift certificate in a silvery envelope. Dinner for two, at Basilco. And from Leslie for her, a slim rectangular package in Macy's wrap.

Later that afternoon, a large box arrived for her from Catania. She was almost reluctant to open it after the trauma of Mamma's visit, afraid of what she might find. Gingerly, she cut the twine and tape securing the box and peered inside. On top was Mamma's home-baked Christmas *buccellato*—Mariella's favorite holiday treat, the fig and almond-filled Sicilian cake ring no one here seemed to have heard of. She'd scoured the Italian *grocerias* in North Beach. She'd found *pan forte*, *pannettone*, cannoli, and of course, the ubiquitous oblong-shaped almond scented biscotti, but no *buccellato*.

She cried when she lifted the *buccelato* from the box and peeled back the layers of pale green tissue in which it was so carefully wrapped.

Maybe this was Mamma's way of saying she was sorry. No. Mamma as penitent? Not credible. Not even close. More likely, she feared Christ's all-seeing presence at this sacred time of year, seeing as how she'd brought herself so close to eternal damnation. After all, her mother was nothing if not superstitious.

There were also Mamma's little brown biscotti balls Mariella loved, the ones laced with rum, cinnamon, and ginger, and rolled in powdered sugar. There was no note, only Mamma's food.

Nonna had tucked in a jar of rich, red sauce made from her succulent home-dried tomatoes. Mariella didn't understand why people here in San Francisco made such a big deal of sun-dried tomatoes, or why they were so expensive—in some specialty grocery stores, like Molinari's Italian Delicatessen in North Beach, (the closest food store like home she'd found in this city, filled with the aromas of salami and cheeses and the wood floor darkened and musky from years of olive oil stains) up to twelve dollars a pound! At home, in summer, almost every householder laid out trays of tomatoes and fruits on rooftops, or on balconies and courtyards, to intensify and to sweeten under the white-hot Sicilian sun.

Olimpio's gift was a small album of photographs, taken with Papa's old-fashioned Brownie Instamatic. The photographs were laid on stiff sticky pages under cellophane covers: one of Olimpio himself grinning into the camera, leaning against his Vespa with his long legs stretched out. Another of Mamma, Papa, and Nonna on the apartment balcony, their hands atop Nonna's shoulders. Nonna, sweet Nonna, with her gray hair coiled on top of her head, looking like a child standing between Papa and Mariella's mother, Papa nearly a foot higher than his mother. Had Nonna shrunk? Shriveled since Mariella's departure? Or perhaps, hopefully, her stature was only a trick of the eye because Mamma and Papa were taller.

Papa smiled tenderly into the camera, and Mamma couldn't help herself from looking fierce. Even so, Mariella thought her mother was striking—beautiful in her defiance, with her still mostly black shoulder-length hair interspersed now with gray, and a figure she'd kept from turning to fat. She wore her usual crisp white blouse and black full skirt, which would have looked like a uniform without the red belt and red sandals.

In other photos, shopkeepers and acquaintances she'd known all her life waved at her, and she could see they were mouthing, "Ciao, Mariella!"

From Papa there was a check for one hundred euros. Her heart turned over, thinking of the sacrifice he'd made to send her that money: only taking shirts once-a-week to the cleaners, perhaps no dinners out with Mamma for several weeks. Enduring her complaints.

Mariella would go to her American bank for the exchange.

From Nonna, a book of love poems by an American poet, E. E. Cummings. Nonna had slipped a note inside the front cover:

Cara *Mariella. Because, I believe, you are full of love (maybe new or maybe still for Matteo or maybe just for life itself) and also a young woman who is a little unconventional, I think you will like the unusual way—especially for the time in which he wrote—this man arranges his lines. The one Jeremy used to say reminded him of me is the one beginning, "I carry your heart with me . . ." As I,* mia bella *Mariella, carry your heart with me,* ogni giorno.

Con molto amore, *Nonna Giuseppina*

Nonna's letter made her cry even harder, especially when she discovered the book had been a gift from Jeremy.

She sent them computer printed photos (taken by Cosima) of Leslie and of her beside their little Christmas tree; of Luciano and Pietro standing and grinning under the awning in front of Basilico; even one of Teresa Russo and Mario Bianchi; and finally one of Pietro on one side of her and Giovanni on the other, each with an arm around her waist and hers around theirs. Nonna would recognize Giovanni as "him."

Her special gift to her family would be a telephone call on Christmas Day. She had never taken to social media, chafed at the notion of broadcasting her thoughts, tidbits from her life, or, especially, the self-important custom of photographing a restaurant meal. In that case, why not a photo of brushing your teeth? But now she wished for a way to check on Matteo. To see if he really waited for her, as Mamma had told her, or if he even mentioned her at all. He'd loved Facebook, used it as a political forum, posting slogans, far left meeting notices, cartoons about corruption, and slamming what he considered the dangerous stupidity of the far right from any country. She made a mental note to email Olimpio, asking if he'd heard any news about Matteo. Surely by now, she reckoned, he'd found someone to take her place, and disliked the part of her that hoped he hadn't.

When she returned from grocery shopping at six that evening, she didn't expect to find Darrell squashed up against Leslie on the white velvet sofa. She'd had to deposit the two bags of groceries on the hall floor outside the apartment and jiggle the key in the old lock, twisting and turning it this way and that before the door had finally swung open. Surely, if they'd heard her, they wouldn't have just sat there and listened to her fumble! The sympathy she'd felt for Leslie, the compassion that had prompted her to walk the several blocks to Petrini's and carry home the heavy bags for the dinner she planned to cook for him to soothe his spirits, gave way to anger.

"Why didn't you open the door?" she asked, staring down the both of them.

"It's my fault," Darrell said, his voice raspy and low. He huddled himself into the side of Leslie's body. "I asked him to stay here with me on the couch."

"It's rude anyway," she said. The bags still sat on the floor outside the door. She stood next to them with her hands on her hips. Leslie disentangled himself from Darrell as if his body weighed five hundred pounds rather than the one hundred and sixty it did. He hauled himself up from the sofa to help her with the bags, grunting and moaning like an overburdened old washerwoman carrying a load of a thousand peoples' dirty laundry.

As Leslie approached Mariella, she saw the dark pouches under his eyes, the rims so red she had the impulse to call him "Mr. Christmas Eyes."

She put away the groceries, then took a seat across from them in one of the white club chairs. She restrained herself from telling Darrell, "I think you have AIDS." Instead, she said, "Okay, now you tell me what's wrong."

"It's me." Darrell spoke in a whispery croak. "I'm not doing so well." He looked fine to Mariella. Yet again, as at the Halloween party, that whisper down her spine told her something was off. *He's lying.*

"That's why he broke up with me," Leslie said, tears spilling over his raw, scarlet rims. "He didn't want me to go through the same agony he went through with Albert."

They resumed their huddle on the sofa. Leslie petted Darrell's hair, as if his lover were a cat or a dog.

"What are you going to do?" she asked. She found herself wondering if she'd be safe here anymore, drinking out of glasses or cups Darrell had drunk from, putting into her mouth the same spoons and forks he'd put into his. Was he covering up purple blisters with his long-sleeved jerseys? Was it too late for treatment? In spite of knowing better, she felt queasy about picking up the virus from her toilet seat, the one Darrell sometimes used.

"AZT, amongst other drugs," Leslie said. "His doc's getting him started on HAART."

"Okay," she said. "That's good." An antiretroviral cocktail she'd read about, with the potential to prolong life. "And what about you?" she asked Leslie. "Yes? Isn't it time for you to get the retests?"

"After Christmas," he said. "I haven't forgotten. I still have my appointment card."

Side-by-side, looking like haunted twin ghosts, they both regarded her with big round Orphan Annie stares.

"What is it?" she asked, looking from one to the other.

"I've asked Darrell to move in with me so I can take care of him," Leslie said, speaking so quickly the sentence tumbled out like one long word.

"I won't if you don't want me to," Darrell rasped. "I don't want to be a burden."

She liked Darrell—a lot: his intelligence, his sense of humor, his easygoing manner that often kept Leslie from going into dramatics or veering toward the deep emotional end. There was no way she could tell a man who could be dying that he couldn't live with the man he loved.

Chapter Thirty-Two

Teresa stood with Luciano at Basilico's front door and waved Giovanni and Mariella on their way, like proud parents seeing their children off on their first day of school. And assuring Giovanni, "Don't hurry back, we'll take care of everything here." Teresa had gifted her brother with two Sunday matinee tickets to *A Christmas Carol* at the American Conservatory Theater, better known to locals, Giovanni informed Mariella, as ACT.

It was rare to see Teresa with a smile, even if it had the look of a painted-on grimace.

"Your sister, maybe she doesn't hate me so much anymore?" Mariella said as she and Giovanni stepped onto Columbus Street into the chilly December afternoon. "She seemed happy just now for us to go out together." She pulled out soft brown leather gloves, her Christmas present from Leslie—one from each of her coat pockets—and fit them finger-by-finger onto her hands.

"Oh, I don't think she ever hated you," Giovanni said. "She's just territorial, protective of me."

"You sure she meant the ticket for *me*? Maybe it's really for her?" Mariella was excited, feeling elegant and cosmopolitan, in her new soft wool winter coat—a gift to herself—and her Italian leather boots with dainty heels. And glad for the escape from Leslie, Darrell, and her apartment.

"Silly," Giovanni called her, shaking his head. "She specifically said they were for me *and* for you."

"Anyway, why do you need protection?"

Giovanni offered his arm, and she hooked hers through it. With his free hand, he hailed a taxi from amongst the many that cruised along.

"Well, she never liked Beth, for one thing—more accurately, she never liked the way Beth treated me." He held the cab door open for Mariella and smiled down at her. Once they were settled in the back seat, Giovanni said, "My sister thinks every woman would be lucky just to be in my presence." His cheeks flushed. Mariella couldn't tell if it was from embarrassment—bragging on himself— or from the cold they'd just escaped. "That they should treat me like the prince she thinks I am," he said. "Besides that, she believes most women are just looking for a man to take care of them."

"Teresa's right," Mariella said. "In Sicilia most of the women in university go to find a husband—oh, not everyone of course." She shrugged. "Some of the women . . ."

"Like you," Giovanni said. "Some of the women like you want more out of life than just marriage—or children. Isn't that right?"

"Yes, sure, I want more," Mariella said. "Of course, marriage—family—they are important too, for some people, I realize this." She turned to the window, away from Giovanni so he wouldn't see the glisten of tears. She hadn't meant to think of Matteo, but there he was, in her mind's eye, the two of them holding hands last Christmas (he'd brought her hand to his lips) in a taxi on the way to the Teatro Massimo Bellini, Catania's Opera House, for a sing-a-along concert of Handel's Messiah. Oh, she had loved—still did love him so. In the midnight hours, it was Matteo's face and body she imagined making love to her, not Giovanni's. A whiff of his scent—sandalwood mixed with fresh air—from a man passing on the street would make her turn and hope, for a moment, it might be him.

They rode in silence, and after a while, Giovanni interlaced his fingers with the fingers of her gloved hand.

Finally, she said, "Yes, you're right. Maybe someday, marriage for me. But not this day." In her deepest self, the only one she even could imagine marrying—but far, far off on some unnamable day—was Matteo.

When the play ended at five o' clock, nightfall had dropped its curtain outside the theater on Geary, along with the rain.

"Did you like it?" Giovanni asked. He helped Mariella with her coat.

"Oh, very much." She shrugged her arms into the sleeves. "We read the Dickens at university, you know, in classes for the English literature."

She'd fretted about Darrell's possibly dying presence at her apartment, and about Bernard's arrival at Basilico tomorrow. About whether she'd act natural and casual, which is, after all, how she felt about Bernard. Casual. Annoyed, even, that *he* cropped up in her thoughts.

Whenever she'd stolen glances at Giovanni during the play, she'd caught him looking at her. They'd both laughed and reached for one another's hands.

"I have an idea," he said now, pulling on his coat and tucking a rust-colored scarf inside the lapels. He peered through the lobby doors onto the dark, wet street.

"*Que?*" she asked. He hesitated long enough to pique her impatience. "What is it?"

"Okay, instead of going out, how about if we pick up some cracked crab and French bread and go to my place? What d'you say?"

They hailed an empty taxi, cruising slowly past.

At Fisherman's Wharf, she stayed inside the cab, keeping warm and dry, while Giovanni disappeared into a crab stand. Despite the old and uncomfortable fake leather upholstery, and the frenetic Middle Eastern music the driver kept at full volume, she drifted into her own thoughts. So many people on the streets, most in some combination of shapeless sweatshirts, windbreakers and jeans, and many carrying umbrellas. She'd been here to Fisherman's Wharf once before, with Leslie and Darrell. "You haven't really been to San Francisco until you've had a crab Louie at Scoma's," they'd insisted. A salad as big as a watermelon, and piled so high with fresh, snowy crabmeat, one would have been enough for all three. She'd found the tourist trade repellant, shops packed with cheap souvenirs, shelves and walls overflowing with those ball caps she detested, along with T-shirts, key chains, and snow globes with Coit Tower and the Golden Gate Bridge trapped inside. Hairy stuffed animals wearing miniature replicas of the same T-shirts and caps proclaiming either San Francisco, Alcatraz, or of course, Fisherman's Wharf.

Even from inside the taxi she caught the mingled, nauseating smells of sweet caramel corn, brine, and deep-fry.

Commercial boats bobbing at the waterfront pierced her with a sudden longing for the tangy, salt aroma of the Ionian Sea and the fishermen that docked and delivered their daily catches to the restaurants along rustic Catanian piers.

Giovanni emerged from the crab stand with a large parcel wrapped in butcher paper and a crusty round loaf tucked under his elbow. "All set," he said, reentering the taxi, his black coat beaded with rain. "The only place in town to buy Dungeness when it's in season." He nodded toward the crab stand. "That's my guy—Peppini—the one we buy from for the restaurant. You know, the truck that makes the deliveries nearly every day."

He gave the driver his address on Leavenworth Street.

A new moss-green sculpture, a suggestion of two heads nestled together, perched on a dark polished wood pedestal in a corner of Giovanni's living room, near the bay window. "It's marbled serpentine," he said. "Shona sculpture, from Zimbabwe." Chiseled straight noses and linear mouths, one of the heads tilted at a right angle. "I brought it home yesterday."

Elmer sniffed her calves, warm in maroon tights, and circled her ankle boots, his breathing labored, as it always was, angling for her to scratch his head and sweet talk him the way she did. He waddled along behind them into the kitchen, a sleek, simple affair with granite counters, stainless steel appliances, and floor tiles of rosy beige.

Giovanni stored the crab parcel in the refrigerator and pulled out a bottle of Veuve Clicquot. "A toast?" he asked, retrieving two flutes from a frosted glass cupboard.

Had he chilled the bottle earlier, anticipating the evening here?

Her first taste of the crisp, prickly bubbles puckered her mouth. Giovanni's expression: intense, serious, and unsmiling.

Now the hairs on the back of her neck *did* stand up. She was sure of it. He'd had something in his mind all along.

"Move in with me," he said.

She gazed at the Victorian mansion next door, a distracting, glowing presence through the stained glass kitchen window, reflected from a streetlamp's yellow light.

She'd told Giovanni about Darrell's HIV, about Leslie asking him to move in. She *hadn't* told him the part about feeling like she didn't belong anywhere: not at home in Catania, not here, and not in her Lincoln Way apartment with Darrell moving in soon.

"Move in with me," he said again, smoothing back her rain-damp curls from her forehead.

"You like to make jokes," she said. "It's not funny, Giovanni." She hadn't given him the remotest inkling of wanting to leave her apartment. She liked her arrangement with Giovanni just the way it was: spending two or three nights a week at his elegant apartment; the sex that was both earthy and satisfying; the exquisite food and wine; the theater; and then, on the nights they weren't together, the sanctuary of her own room. When Darrell moved in, that sense of sanctuary would be destroyed.

"No," she said with a shrug, hoping to lighten the intensity. "I'll give it more time, see what happens with Darrell. See how it goes."

Giovanni threw back his champagne and banged his glass on the counter so abruptly it sheared off clean at the base. A gesture that left Mariella feeling frightened. *Do I really know this man?*

Giovanni appeared to have surprised himself. "Sorry," he said, looking both chagrined and posturing to stay indignant. Comical, she thought.

He ignored her then, turned his body away. She reached out and tugged on his sleeve to bring him back to her. Elmer whimpered, and still, Giovanni wouldn't look at her. Here, finally, their first rift. And didn't that prove her fear—that it wasn't all right, even with Giovanni, for her to be independent?

"Have you thought about what it will be like when you start school?" he asked, still not facing her, his voice hollow, as if he were restraining himself from sounding too angry or too hurt. "Will you have enough privacy to study? What if Darrell gets really bad and doesn't sleep at night?"

She felt sick to her stomach. Now, even staying overnight with Giovanni would be fraught, burdened with entrapment. And she'd looked so forward to the holiday week she'd planned to be here with him, over Christmas and the New Year.

"Look," he said, more gently, as if he'd realized his mistake. He laid his arm over hers and bade her sit next to him at the little cushioned bench in the breakfast alcove. "I know you need your independence and freedom. And God knows, I would never want to rob you or even try to take those away from you." He held back from touching her, allowing her the privilege of separateness. "You know I care deeply for you, Mariella. And if you can make it work at Leslie's, more power to you. But I want you to understand, if you do decide to live here—even if it's just until things are resolved with Darrell—your life is your own. You come and go as you please."

She sat with her eyes closed. Too much, this was all too much for her to take in. They'd never spoken of love. She hadn't allowed herself to consider it.

He watched her, waiting for her response.

"You wouldn't have to pay rent—think about it."

Still, she said nothing.

"The only thing I'd ask," he said, "is that you wouldn't see other men."

He needs someone to take care of. Something he'd done all his life: first, his mother, after his father died; then his wife, and now her, a presence to fill the void. *Is that it? Is that why he wants me to move in? So I can be a replacement for Beth, or more likely Mario, the child he was never allowed to raise? Or does he simply love me and want me near?*

Others were always the ones offering: first, Matteo, to marry her; Leslie, to be her roommate; Giovanni, to hire her as hostess, then as manager, and now, to share not only his bed, but his home. And she, always the one to say, as she did now, "Still, I will try it first with Darrell and Leslie. And Giovanni, thank you." She grasped his hand and brought it to her lips. "Really, I thank you so much. I promise, I will think about it, and I will let you know."

After their repair—"No pressure," Giovanni swore, raising his right hand. "Scout's honor. No strings attached. If you decide to stay on at your apartment, I'll help you any way I can."—they laughed and drank the champagne and attacked the cracked crab as if they were starving, melted butter and lemon dripping down their chins and onto the big cloth napkins they'd tied around their necks.

Even so, after Giovanni's declaration of love, and in spite of their "repair," she felt that she was leaving him already, even as they remained together. She could no more reverse that inevitability than she could stop the waves at Ocean Beach from crashing onto the shore.

But the sucking of crab meat from claws, the dripping juices and the butter, along with champagne relaxing their tensions, led easily to kissing and licking of faces, and then surprising, the desperate reaching for buttons and zippers, and hands touching each other everywhere. Clothes were hastily discrded and left on the kitchen floor, and completely naked they barely made it down the hallway before they disrobed and made love.

Afterward, Giovanni sat at the end away from the faucets in the oversized, old-fashioned claw-footed bathtub; he'd made a hollow for Mariella between his legs, and she reclined there, her back up against him. He seemed to delight in washing and inspecting every inch of her, down to her feet, and including her hair, as if she were his erstwhile child, the one he'd longed for all these years. She almost expected him to produce a flashlight and check inside her mouth for cavities and the condition of her gums.

"You look okay to me." He grinned. "Inside and out."

Too intimate, suddenly, this bath.

"Giovanni, we both have to work tomorrow," Mariella said, easing herself around to face him. It was nearly midnight. "We either go to bed, or I go home."

Oh, *dio*—home. For a moment, she'd indulged herself in forgetting. Darrell would likely be there, as he'd been for the past week, almost every night and every day. The two of them keeping to Leslie's room as much as possible, staying out of her way, giving her the run of the house. But she could hear Darrell whimpering behind Leslie's closed door, and he and Leslie up 'til all hours, talking, talking, talking.

"Stay the night," Giovanni said. "And don't worry," he laughed as she watched the water with their comingled bath water circling the drain. "I won't say another word about moving in, and I promise not to shackle you to the wall."

The question that had nagged at Mariella ever since he'd first told her about it burst out of her now. "Giovanni, why did you *really* get the vasectomy?"

"I told you. I hoped it would bring Beth and me closer."

She thought for a moment. "No—I don't think so. Well, maybe a little. But I think with the operation you punished yourself for Beth's unhappiness. So you can never become a father with someone else to a new child you can love—a child who can live with you—a child of your own who can love you back."

Chapter Thirty-Three

*B*ernard started the following Monday, and conducted himself just as gentlemanly and discreetly as he had when he'd waited on Giovanni and Mariella at Fior. Friendly, but with professional distance, engaging Mariella when necessary and otherwise reserved. Anyway, it wasn't him, but her own attraction that worried her. She sloughed it off, chalked it up to his being a writer, his seriousness about reading, his quiet manner that made him seem troubled and deep. Whenever she glimpsed him on break, he was immersed in a novel or a treatise on literary theory. And that containment: the way it kept him just there, slightly out of reach, making him seem all the more mysterious and profound. Reminding her of Matteo in intensity and in intellect.

And, even though she had misgivings about spending Christmas week with Giovanni after his declaration of love, the prospect of being in hibernation with Leslie and Darrell loomed as even more stifling, depressing, really.

Besides, Giovanni had been true to his word and hadn't pressured her further. Still, a small niggling voice inside questioned: *am I using Giovanni when it's convenient for me?* She tried to console herself, but not very convincingly, that they were using each other. *Haven't we been doing that all along? Isn't he using me for bringing pleasure into his life? Oh, there's too much going on, I can't think about that right now.*

But the small voice wouldn't be silenced.

∾

Staying at Giovanni's did bring her a reprieve from her apartment and her attendant ambivalence, from feeling the intruder, the third wheel, to Leslie's and Darrell's twosome. And a deep sense of contentment she hadn't anticipated.

It wasn't the presents she and Giovanni gave one another that made the holiday so special: he to her, a necklace of irregular freshwater pearls and a pale green silk blouse to match her eyes. And she to him, cashmere socks and a stunning photograph book of Sicilian sea ports, including several of Catania. Knowing it was time proscribed—a mere week—made the interlude all the more delicious. A vacation, even with long, pre-Christmas shifts at the restaurant.

The pleasure of falling, exhausted, into bed together, the discovery that they both liked to read, or at least open a book, before drifting into sleep. Henry, the doorman, now greeting her, "Morning, miss," or "Evening, miss, hope you had a good day," as if she were a regular. As if she belonged.

They walked Elmer in the morning and again at night, with Giovanni's daily walk by himself at two o'clock sandwiched in between, Giovanni more breathless and perspiring than the walk around the inclined block warranted. Probably, she decided, even though he was trim and sturdy, he simply didn't exercise enough.

And lovemaking. Most evenings after work, and occasionally arousing each other again in the night. The claiming of one another's bodies at random moments: a proprietary cupping of a breast or a pat on the bottom as they stood and talked in the kitchen or passed in the hallway. Or dozing, at one end of the long, wide sofa, with Elmer snoozing in his dog bed at the other, her hand resting unselfconsciously on Giovanni's thigh, as if they no longer belonged simply to themselves, but now, if only for the moment, to each other. Passing thoughts of an ending drifted through her mind with no more significance than clouds.

But still, the small voice wasn't altogether silenced.

She made a visit to her apartment during that week to leave off and pick up clothing, check mail, and spend a little time with Leslie before the New Year, even if it meant persuading him to go out with her for coffee. Alone.

He was on his computer at the kitchen table when she came in. He was on break from law school, but still had work for his classes. Darrell was in the bedroom, she assumed, asleep or resting.

"How's it going?" she asked.

"S'okay." Leslie shrugged. "He's gone to his place for a couple of days. His parents are flying in tonight from Maryland. They're trying to persuade him to go home with them so he can be treated at Johns Hopkins."

She'd fleetingly heard of Johns Hopkins but hadn't given it a thought other than imagining it as a hotel or event center run by someone named John. "I used to think it was a spa or maybe a hotel," she laughed, "but now I know it's a hospital."

"They're doing great HIV/AIDS research there, but honestly, we want him to stay here," Leslie said.

"Oh, too bad!" she blurted before she could take it back. "Well, I don't mean *here*," she backpedaled, gesturing around the apartment. "What I mean is I am concerned for you sacrificing your own life."

Leslie gave her a look, ignored her, and read whatever it was he'd just written.

"What are you doing?"

"Making a will."

Merda! "Whose will?"

"Mine."

"Why?" *Jesu Cristo!* Was Leslie now sick and dying as well?

"Just in case," Leslie said. "And for your information, we plan on him pulling through, and . . ." His neck flushed, as it did when he was about to say something difficult or embarrassing. "Darrell doesn't know it, but while his parents are here, I'm knocking on his door with a ring. I'm asking him to marry me—in front of them!

"Oh, I know we can't legally marry, not yet." He looked wistful, as if he was gazing into an impossible future where he could marry the man he loved. "But we *can* pledge ourselves to each other—and don't look so shocked," Leslie continued. "I've met his parents once over the phone, and they're very nice people." He sniffed. "For your information, they told me I'm welcome any time!" He turned back to his computer and pretended to be engrossed.

"I don't disapprove, Mr. Leslie," Mariella said. Yes, something was definitely off here, not right. The crawl of her skin told her so. "But I worry about you." Leslie was gullible, generous, and would give away everything, perhaps even himself if he thought it would help someone he loved. She'd received his tender shepherding firsthand when she'd arrived here, months ago, on his doorstep.

He glanced at Mariella. "You look radiant. I think staying at Giovanni's agrees with you."

Was Leslie trying to get rid of her?

"What do you mean, you're making the will just for practice?" She knew that Leslie had inherited money when his mother died—young, in her forties, from a congenital heart condition. That his mother had come from wealth, that she'd loved him and he'd loved her, and that when he was a young boy, he'd longed for approval from his father, who only tolerated him. A military man who lived somewhere in the Midwest, distant and dismissive, and most important, disapproving of Leslie's being gay.

"Oh," Leslie said with a wave of his hand. "I've already done Darrell's—you know, one of those do-it-yourselfers from Nolo Press. Just in case, but really, we're counting on the HAART treatments." University of California Medical Center—locally known as UCSF—had apparently accepted Darrell as part of a trial program: AZT in low doses combined with other, newer antiretroviral drugs.

Leslie shrugged. "Not that he has a pot to piss in, but he says he's leaving everything to me." He dabbed at the corners of his eyes with a tissue from a box on the table. "So I thought the least I could do is practice making my own will and see who I would leave what to if *I* were to die."

He tilted his head and gazed at Mariella. "You're in it," he said. "I've decided that the Mini and all the furniture, even the dishes, go to you."

"I don't care about your things, Mr. Leslie."

His mouth took the shape of an O.

"I mean grazie, you are very generous because I know how much you love the Mini and your beautiful glasses, but it is *you* I want to keep."

She was pierced by sudden grief at the prospect of leaving Leslie. Her housemate and friend. And yet. Would he be relieved or upset if she told him that if Darrell moved in, she wanted a place of her own?

"I have something to tell you," she said, drawing up a chair next to him and holding his hand.

"You've gotten married," he said. "No, wait, you're moving in with Giovanni."

"Well, he did ask me—I mean to live with him, but I'm not ready to do that."

Leslie breathed a sigh of relief. "Oh, thank God. I don't think I could stand it if you left. I mean, I love Darrell with all my heart and soul, but," he swept his arm around the apartment, "you hear how quiet it is. I mean *all* the time, like a tomb—no pun intended. But that's a lie. He loves opera so when he's up and around we listen. The Italians: Puccini, Verdi—*Carmen*'s all right, and *La Boheme*, but you know how I feel about that music." He pulled down the corners of his mouth.

"*Carmen* is French," she said. "Bizet—but it's very beautiful, I agree."

"Forgive me," he said. "I forgot. You love opera."

"Only some." She shrugged. "*Como tutti Siciliani.*" *Norma*, the most famous opera from Sicily's beloved native son, Vincenzo Bellini. And even though Maria Callas wasn't Sicilian or even Italian by birth, her magnificent rendition of the "Casta Diva" aria from *Norma* was the one regularly played in the Russo's and nearly every other Sicilian household. After all, the natives reasoned, Callas was trained in Italy, and didn't that make her almost Siciliana?

But who cared about opera or Maria Callas when one's autonomy was at stake? How could she stay in this apartment alongside Leslie and Darrell and his miserable disease, ingesting the smell—real or imagined—of lifelessness and decay? Of death.

And why *was* she always saying to the people she cared about, "I have to go." Why not "Yes, I'll stay here. Yes, yes, I won't go anywhere." Isn't that how commitment was supposed to sound? And if she were to make such a commitment, who would be the right person to make it to? Leslie? Giovanni? Or herself?

Chapter Thirty-Four

At the end of her stay at Giovanni's, on the last night when their lovemaking was especially intense and verging on desperate, Mariella wept. As if she'd already left him, as if all her ungrieved grief had waited for that moment to unleash.

"What's wrong?" Giovanni said, holding her to him. "What's the matter, *mia poco* Mariella?" he murmured, stroking her hair as best he could through her mop of curls.

"I don't want to go home," she said, the ache in her voice heartbreaking.

"Well, you don't have to," he said. "You know that." He arched away to look at her, frowning, trying to make sense. Then, after a moment, "So you're staying with me?"

"No," she said. "I mean *home* home, to Sicilia."

"Sicily?"

"Si. Olimpio sent me an email and a photograph last night."

"Yes?"

"Well, he told me my Nonna is very sick, and from the photograph, she looks it."

The image on her cell phone of Nonna—a different one, more recent than the one Olimpio had mailed for Christmas— had nearly sent Mariella to the airport right on the spot, back onto the plane to New Jersey, back to Rome, and finally onto the tarmac at *Aeroporto Catania-Fontanarossa* Vincenzo Bellini. Nonna looked as if she had shrunk at least four inches. Her long gray hair, normally braided and coiled into a crown, stuck out in short, wild frizzles, framing her face like fine-gauge wire. She appeared as if she'd poked her finger into a live electrical socket and had come away in permanent shock.

She's had a couple of bad weeks, Olimpio had written. *Kidney stones.*

In another photo, Papa pointedly observed his wizened mother beneath lowered brows, blaming her it seemed, for making her kidneys produce the offending crystals.

Big ones—a whole week in the hospital, Olimpio wrote. *You know she's never liked to drink water. She wasn't getting enough fluids. Nearly died of dehydration.* He was leaving something out. Mariella read it in the evasion between the lines.

But Nonna's okay now, Olimpio declared. *She wanted to make sure you understand she's not in danger anymore. She's okay.*

Of course Nonna would say she was fine. She wouldn't want her granddaughter worrying. Not like Mamma, whose life was one big scheme to get her family's attention.

Mariella pictured her grandmother, drinking only caffè in the morning and wine with meals, keeping her distance from the kitchen—from Mamma—or wondering what Mamma might put in her food. She didn't like to think of Nonna suffering, of her body (and maybe her life) going dry. She didn't like to think of Nonna missing her so much she was losing the will to live, as she had when Jeremy died. "I mourned like a dove who'd lost her mate," Nonna had said of Jeremy. "You know doves only mate once. They mate for life."

Mariella called Catania the moment she got out of bed, at six thirty the next morning. In *Sicilia*, three thirty in the afternoon.

In a stroke of luck, her grandmother answered.

"Your mother," Nonna rasped. "She's gone completely over the edge this time."

"Nonna, forget about Mamma. How are *you*? Tell me the truth."

"I hear them walking around," Nonna whispered. Mariella's mother and father were just stirring from siesta. "But I do tell you the truth, *bella nipote*, I'm still weak but much better. Really, I think a bug got a hold of me too, but now I drink at least two liters of water, every day—okay, okay," she said, "here comes your Papa. And don't forget, *cara*, I send you love for the New Year and all the days and nights."

Mariella could hear footsteps and Papa's booming voice as he came near. "Why didn't she tell us she was calling?"

"Here," Nonna said, her voice faint and faraway as she handed over the phone—her parents still using a landline—her once fearless grandmother fading into the distance.

"Is everything okay?" Papa asked as he came on. "Is something wrong?"

"I'm fine, Papa, Merry Christmas to you too, and thanks for asking." No *Buon Natale*, no, *How are you? I'm so glad you called.* Her father's anxiety, unusual and confusing.

"Oh *mia*, forgive me. Of course I want to know how you are."

"Papa," she blurted. "How can you let Mamma make Nonna sick?"

A strained silence—a rare event—between father and daughter. She couldn't shake her suspicion that Mamma was trying to get rid of Nonna. Make her too weak to cause trouble.

Except for the sound of breathing, Papa remained silent.

"Why haven't you put stop to it, Papa?"

"Here's the thing," he said, his sigh a sound of defeat. "You, Olimpio—even Nonna. You'll all be gone one day. *You* are already—and Nonna . . ." In her mind's eye, she could see her father raising his shoulders as if to say, "We all know she won't live forever."

A bleak outlook, the prospect of life without her grandmother. But she felt it in her bones: like Olimpio, Papa was keeping something from her.

"And," her father went on. "I have to live with your mother all the way to our last days. No, let me say it another way: I love your mother. She and I are the ones together after everyone else is gone. We've made a vow, she stands with me to the end, and I with her."

"Yes, well, about *your* mother," Mariella said, unfazed by her father's declaration of loyalty to Mamma. "Nonna could live another twenty years." She stared at Giovanni's leaded glass window toward San Francisco Bay, toward the Golden Gate Bridge, neither of which were visible through the fog and rain, or the rippled pane.

"You promised me, Papa," she said. "When I called you while Mamma was here you promised to tell me about the debt. The one you owe Mamma."

"Nonna's moving into her own place," Papa said, as if that answered anything.

"Good for Nonna!" Maybe her grandmother would be all right. At least she'd be safe, away from Mamma, living on her own, as she'd always wanted in the years since Nonno Sam died. It had been Papa who'd insisted Nonna live with them, against Mamma's protestations of, "Not enough room! You should never have two women under one roof!" If anyone put a cramp in her mother's dramatics, it was Nonna. Still.

"She'll be just next door," Papa said. "The young couple who lived there went to the country." The couple whose wife had always kept her head down when she passed Mariella in the hallway.

"Tell me about the debt," Mariella insisted. "About why . . ." she searched for the right words, "why you always give in to Mamma."

Papa was so quiet, she wondered if he'd hung up. Then, she realized he was probably listening to make certain her mother was still in the bedroom.

"Papa?"

"I made a terrible mistake," he said, his tone somber and low.

"You mean marrying Mamma?"

"No! Wash out your mouth, *mia figlia!*"

"Sorry, Papa. I thought that's what you meant."

"I'm lucky to have your mother," he said. "Lucky she'd still have me . . ." His voice broke.

Papa? Having an affair?

". . . after the shame."

Mariella didn't realize she was holding her breath until she let it go. It was Mamma, the lunatic, who should be ashamed of herself, not Papa.

"When you were little and Olimpio was just born, I stole from my employer," Papa said, sounding emotionless and detached, as if he were reciting from a script. "I had a plan to pay it back, but we needed money. I was the apprentice accountant, and I stole from him, even though I told myself I was only borrowing. And your mother saved us."

"Mamma?" How could Mamma save anyone? She couldn't save herself.

"Her cousin Antonio," Papa said. "The one in Palermo—the insurance salesman?" The one who was too good for his relatives in Catania. Mariella had met him once: rich, doughy-skinned Antonio who sweated. With a spoiled wife in expensive, gaudy clothes and two girls in the best private schools. The "business-man" with connections.

"Antonio paid off my boss and paid him even more not to press charges. Blackmailed him never to tell. Otherwise . . ." Papa hesitated, "otherwise, I would have gone to prison." He made no attempt to hide his sob. "Or worse."

"Oh, Papa! You were only trying to help your family."

"I owe him—I owe your mother my life—*our* lives. I paid Antonio back, every penny, and still, I can never forget," Papa said.

She wanted to say, "Of course not, because Mamma will never let you."

"But I didn't forget you *bella*," he said, attempting a happier note. "I remember, you start full-time school in the next weeks."

"Oh, Papa," she said. "You were so young—ask Nonna if you don't believe me. I think you were brave to risk your life, to take that money." Yet, even as she said so, she knew she would have to search her soul, adjusting to this new, tainted aspect of her saintly father. But weren't saints often rendered into sainthood by obstacles they overcame? Demons conquered and dramatic conversions from heinous deeds, like Saint Paul, or living loose, like young womanizer, Augustine.

After she and Papa said goodbye, she recalled, once more, her grandmother's words from her last days in Catania: *Stand up for yourself, Salvatore. Trust me, your wife will fall in love with you all over again.*

Later that last day, after the rain subsided into a soft drizzle, Mariella and Giovanni boarded the Hyde Street cable car to Union Square for a walk and late lunch at Scala's Bistro on Powell Street. Her first venture onto one of those clanging San Francisco legends, wheels clicking, straining, groaning upward on narrow rails. Then down, down, gaining speed, like a carnival ride, only not nearly so fast or hair raising, but scary, nonetheless. Mariella didn't trust such hulking, fast-moving machinery to come to a halt at the bottom.

"Best salmon in San Francisco at Scala's," Giovanni proclaimed as they hopped onto the glistening, still wet mica-flecked sidewalk, the air earthy and rain fresh. "I hate to admit it, but I like it better than Basilico's. Wait 'til you taste it—pan-seared, crispy on the outside, tender, underdone in the middle."

"Maybe just because it's different," Mariella suggested as they entered the restaurant, adjacent to the Sir Francis Drake Hotel.

"Something you're not used to that makes you think it's better." Like she did? Always believing the world is better somewhere else, or the next big thing is just ahead, somewhere out of sight, around the corner.

Afterward they strolled by the Christmas windows at Macy's and Saks, the same window dressings she'd written her family about only weeks before, decrying them as what was over-whelming and garish about *consumismo Americano*, appearing to her now as clever and whimsical. A diorama of elf shoemakers, mechanical limbs moving up and down as their little hammers hit leather on the anvil; another, an intricate forest scene with snow-covered pines and a cabin in the woods, the ice queen in her jeweled hooded robes, pointing claw-like fingernails— like Mamma's—at her minions. Even the giant Christmas tree in Union Square, with ornaments the size of melons, seemed bright and brand new, as if it had materialized just that moment. She'd walked by the tree a dozen times, only now really noticing for the first time: magical, winking lights as big as Giovanni's hands. All that was missing was the fragrance of pine. The Christmas tree, a fake.

Why then, the sudden sorrow? Once, again, like in bed that morning. The overflow that trickled down her cheeks and bowed her head, her surreptitious attempt at wiping it away.

"*Cara*, Mariella." Giovanni's voice thick with concern. He bent to her, encircling her shoulders. "Whatever *is* the matter my darling girl?"

"Nothing." She hiccuped, her sobs jagged, like a child's. "It's a Sicilian thing," she joked, her voice creaking. "We cry when we're happy." She wouldn't tell him, didn't want to make the mis-take of letting him know how much at odds, how neither here nor there she felt—so homesick and displaced, how much she missed Matteo and wished it was his arm around her. Because Giovanni would rally even harder for her to live with him. "I don't know," she said. "Maybe I'm just a little frightened because right now everything is too good."

Her phone pinged a text message from inside her purse. Leslie. *Sorry to bother. When are you coming home? I need you here, ASAP.*

Chapter Thirty-Five

"He's a lying sack of shit!" Leslie wailed before Mariella had barely squeezed through the door with her overnight bags. He paced between the kitchen and the living room, pounding on every available surface—walls, countertops, tables—as he went. She was more concerned about him hurting his hand than she was about him breaking dishes or damaging walls.

She wondered how long he'd been wearing the beige terry cloth robe, stain splotched down the front, as if everything he'd ingested—mostly red wine from the look of it—had missed his mouth and dribbled down. The ties hung open to reveal an equally stained T-shirt, wrinkled blue boxers and bony white legs.

"A lying sack of shit!" With a bare foot, he kicked the rungs of a wooden kitchen chair and hopped in pain.

Mariella came up beside him and laid a hand on his shoulder. The smell of him, sour and unwashed. "What happened?"

More pounding, more pacing, sobs rising and falling with a crescendo, then convulsions before a new torrent. It was a good half hour before she could get words beyond "I'm an idiot!" or "Fucking stupid fool!" assuming he meant himself, but he could have meant Darrell.

Finally, he slumped into one of the plush living room chairs and managed, between moans, "He lied to me—about everything!"

Not now, but later, was the time to say, "I knew something

was fishy." She sat on the ottoman, facing him, and reached for his hand. Leslie's eyes pleaded with her, as if she could banish his misery.

She waited.

He inhaled deeply and closed his eyes. "He never had AIDS. The sick and dying routine was a big act. He may never even have been HIV positive." Leslie curled into himself with a fresh wave of waterworks. "It was all staged to break up with me—'Letting you down gently' was the bullshit way he put it."

"But what about his lover?" Mariella protested. "The one who died? I thought that's how he got the HIV."

"Albert? Albert died of AIDS all right, but he was never a lover. They did go to Sorrento, but only as friends. Or so he says." A wry smirk twisted Leslie's mouth. "I'm sure Darrell agreed to go because Albert paid his way."

"Oh, Leslie, he seemed like such a good man," Mariella said, wistfully. "So kind."

Leslie's sigh seemed to come from the ether, an otherworldly lament. "That was all part of the charm." He stared into the distance, seeing something not in the room, then threw up his hands and let them flop onto his thighs.

"I'll never know if he really was HIV positive. He wanted me to think he was brave when we first met—you know, stalwart in the face of the danger or some crap. And why would he lie about that?" Leslie's gaze bore into Mariella as if he might extract the answer. "Why would he lie about anything?"

Mariella shook her head. "*I* can't believe it—he was such a good actor." She hated Darrell. Hated him! She'd find a way to make the punishment fit the crime: Inject him with AIDS. Tell everyone he was a fraud, a fake, a liar. A manipulator, even worse than her mother! Get him thrown out of school.

She hated him most of all for hurting her beloved Leslie.

"Did he really think he'd get away with it—that I wouldn't

find out? God, I can't believe I'm such a fool." Tears slid down Leslie's chin onto his robe.

She climbed into the chair next to Leslie and held him and let him cry himself to exhaustion.

He mumbled into her shoulder, as if what he was about to reveal was so shameful he didn't want her to listen. "Last week when he said his parents were visiting?—they were never even here. Made up excuse." Leslie hiccupped. "He was there with a new lover."

When Leslie raised his head, his expression was so bereft she could hardly bear to look at him. "The new guy was in the bedroom—I saw him, stark naked—oh, I can't stand it!" he broke off, burying his face in his hands. Finally, through ragged breaths, "He was on the bed and calling Darrell to come back, and there I was, such a jerk, champagne in one hand and a fucking ring in my pocket!"

Her sweet, giving, naive friend, Leslie.

"I didn't even have the sense to leave," he said. "I just stood there like a big dumb animal and listened to all his stupid fucking explanations." He moaned. "I didn't want to accept it. I didn't *want* to leave."

If she could have, she would have enfolded Leslie into her center, not only in her arms, keeping him tucked away and safe while he mended. While some other part of her wanted to shake him silly. Knock some sense into him. Yell at him, "Wake up! Protect yourself!" The same part that wanted Papa to protect himself from Mamma.

"I haven't told anyone else," Leslie said. He regarded her, beseechingly. "He told me he knew I was a man with money, and he figured I'd be a good lay. But he was never in love with me. Those were his exact words. That's when I couldn't take it anymore—I ran away—and he shouted them at me: 'You were always just a meal ticket and a good piece of ass.'"

"You're the best person I know," she said, kissing him on top of his smelly, unwashed head.

"I'm so ashamed. Please don't tell anyone. Not even Giovanni." He paused. "Especially Giovanni."

"Not even Cosima?" Mariella had become progressively closser and closer to the fiery line cook at Basilico. Sharing comments and gossip about fellow workers, mostly Teresa and the waiters, but also revealing more about themselves.

"Only you," he said. "I know Cosima's a solid friend, but I'm not ready for anyone else to know." He paused. "Besides, I think it would just make her even more suspicious of men." Mariella was gratified that Leslie held her as trustworthy, someone he could depend on. And even with that reluctant part of her whispering in her ear, *Careful! He might want too much!* she promised herself she would be there for him.

"You're always giving away too much of yourself," she said, rocking him as Nonna had rocked her the night of her graduation dinner. "And *I'm* always afraid I won't keep anything of myself. We make a fine pair, don't you think?"

"We're really the same," he said after a while. "But for different reasons."

"Hmm?"

"Well, think about it. Your mother pretends not to like you but she really wants you right next to her, inside her skin. So she manipulates you, or tries to, and you're afraid everyone else will too. And me, I've got a father who really doesn't want me, and I want to be wanted so badly I let myself be manipulated by the first sexy boy who comes along. Don't you see how we're both the same—just at different ends of the spectrum."

Chapter Thirty-Six

Undeclared graduate. That's what she was: officially unde-clared. She hadn't been able to make up her mind between humanities or comparative and world literature, both of which involved languages, philosophy, the arts, and history, as well as fiction, fables, classics, and myths. And, with her degree in inter-national relations, all potentially leading to a diplomatic career at an embassy, or maybe nowhere.

"Take courses that overlap in both programs," an academic advisor had suggested before the end of last semester. A Ms. Ber-nice Cohen, a fifty-something woman with a fireplug body and magnifying lenses so thick it was hard to discern the direction she was looking.

"And throw in a couple from the Communications depart-ment," Ms. Cohen had added. Mariella liked Ms. Cohen's direct manner, and trusted her advice. "Give yourself some time. You have at least a semester before you have to declare yourself."

Declaring herself. Ms. Cohen couldn't possibly have realized the implications.

But spring semester was starting mid-January, and Leslie wasn't bouncing back. At least not as rapidly as Mariella had hoped. In truth, she needed to know that he would be safe with-out her watching over him as she had the first days, like a broody hen. She needed to know she'd be unencumbered when her courses began.

Every day, she ordered him out of the bathrobe (which she'd

laundered) and into the shower. She made excuses to Gypsy Men's for the days he missed work. And often she cooked for him—pastas with all manner of sauces: *amatriciana, pesto, aglio et olio*, with a generous grating of *parmigiana*. And of course her favorite, *pasta alla norma*. All with Giovanni's blessing for not staying over; she told him that Darrell had decided not to move in but not why, and that Leslie had injured his ankle from a fall in the kitchen. She brought home half-drunk bottles of good wine and parcels of food from Basilico.

On Mariella's days off, they walked in Golden Gate Park or around the neighborhood. And rented or watched old movies on TCM: *Citizen Kane, La Dolce Vita*, and *La Strada*, and for Leslie, *Casablanca*, over and over, which worried her because every time Ingrid Bergman walked onto that plane at the end, he dissolved into a keening puddle.

"It's good for me," Leslie insisted. "I don't know why, but it's comforting." He laughed, a spark of hope rising from the ashes. "Like that old song says, 'It hurts so good.'"

Caring for Leslie gave her pleasure because she did care—she loved him—in some ways even more freely than she'd been able to love Matteo. Because Leslie didn't want anything from her except friendship. Oh, yes, rent, of course, and her share of the utilities, but those didn't count. Leslie wouldn't try to control her or hold her back. She held fast to that belief, because she wouldn't have been able to live here with him if he needed too much. Just as she held to the beginning of school in only a few days as the weaning of around-the-clock devotion to Leslie's healing.

Because school was hers, it belonged to her. Relinquishing it, unthinkable.

And because time contained, like a shipboard romance or the Christmas week she'd spent at Giovanni's, made it possible for her to surrender, completely, for that interlude of taking care of Leslie.

When Leslie hauled himself out of bed, the first day he was due back in class at Hastings, she held her breath and quietly rejoiced when she heard him turn on his shower and, afterward, rummage for clothes through his closet and dresser drawers.

He shuffled into the kitchen. A contrast in color, his jaunty, red-and-blue-striped vest and the pale skin under his eyes, tender with delicate blue veins, bruised from so much grief.

"I have to face him someday," Leslie said, absentmindedly powering up the cappuccino machine. Darrell would be in at least one of his classes this semester. "It won't get any easier if I put it off."

She was so proud of him, she really did feel like a mother hen. But not without a twinge of guilt at being set free.

Once her classes started, she still spent nights at Giovanni's, though less frequently, only once or twice a week, now that school was full time. Giovanni said he understood she had to study. But at the restaurant she often caught him watching her with a haunted, lonely expression.

Bernard watched her as well, but discreetly, from under his brows. It alarmed her when occasional glimpses were simultaneous and mutually charged. More than once, she spied Cosima watching Bernard through the round window on the swinging kitchen door.

Chapter Thirty-Seven

On a Monday evening in January, Mariella stood outside that swinging door of Basilico's kitchen and watched Mario through the porthole window as, with concentration, he diced carrots, celery, and onions, preparing the *soffritto* for an array of sauces and soups. Tonight, in addition to the regular menu, there would be Spezzatino di Manzo, an Italian beef stew.

He took up a small spoonful of sauce from a pan on the stove, and stuck a little finger into the spoon and then into his mouth. Satisfied, apparently, that the sauce was correct, he placed the spoon in the stainless steel sink next to the burners. Even with no one watching, he wouldn't contaminate the sauce with a licked-on utensil.

Mario had been giving her the cold shoulder lately—more frigid than usual, considering that a few terse words were his normal response. From him, even a flicker of a smile was akin to the sun bursting through a gray, rain-swollen cloud cover. Too bad, because she needed him as an ally.

Mariella had considered approaching Giovanni's sister, but Teresa would never be more than a *pragmatico* colleague. She was as taciturn as Mario, and except for the customers with whom she conducted herself professionally (which substituted for polite) and the regulars with whom she was welcoming, almost friendly, most of the staff at Basilico cut a wide swath around Teresa. Maybe it was the big eyebrow. Maybe it was the bitterness she leaked into the ether. Whatever the reason, Luciano was the only fellow Basilican, besides her brother, who treated her with any semblance of affection.

But in Mario, Mariella recognized her own aching sense of displacement, and, she knew, despite his practiced aloofness, his vulnerability. And, like her, he carried the aura of someone who harbored secrets from the past. She wondered if he understood in some atavistic way the mystery about his childhood.

It puzzled her, the way the other cooks and waiters—even Bernard—took to Mario, often clustering around and kidding with him, and he sending them back swift parries. She'd recently overheard one of the waiters hurrying into the kitchen through the swinging doors to pick up an order. "Mario!" the waiter called out. "There's a rich woman out there who wants to meet the chef. I told her how handsome you are. She's a devil of a looker. She wants to shake your hand, and maybe something else too."

Mario, unfazed, had continued to plate orders, that hint of a smile just there, but not deigning to look up. "Yeah, well, people in Hell want ice water."

Mariella waited until he laid down the big chef's knife and wiped his brow with the back of his white coat sleeve. He pulled off the black hair covering—that all the young male chefs wore when they were working—a piece of black cloth tied in the back, a "doo-rag," they called it. Ridiculous name. He fished his cell phone from his pocket, his hair, black and wavy, shining under the bright kitchen lights.

She pushed her way through the doors. "Hello, Mario," she said, trying to sound nonchalant, as if the farthest thing from her mind was talking to him. Her outfit today, all brown and black, a flared skirt and black turtleneck sweater covering her hips, the severity softened only by a small silver dragonfly pin. Her stockings were black, her shoes brown and laced up. Clothing only a step away from a nun's.

"Hmp," Mario grunted back, keeping his gaze on his phone.

She went to the oversized stainless steel refrigerator at the far end of the kitchen and peered in, as if she was looking for something in particular.

"What'cho want?" he asked in a monotone. This was *his* territory, even if she was Giovanni's special friend, and briefly, manager of the restaurant.

"Actually," she said, closing the refrigerator door and walking toward him. She could feel him wanting to move away from her, even as he stood still. "If you have a minute, I'd like to talk to you about something."

Mario looked around, as if he were searching for an escape route. "Yeah," he said. "I still gotta lotta prep before dinner." Except for the head chef, Ricardo, Mario was always first at work, at least half an hour before the rest of the crew. Today, Ricardo's day off, Mario was in charge.

"Well, it's about Giovanni," Mariella said, edging closer.

"What about him?" Mario's head snapped up, dark eyes flashing.

"I'm worried about him," she said. What else was she going to say? *I want you to get close to him so I don't feel guilty for pulling away.*

The other chefs had begun to file in.

"Hey, Mario! What's cookin'?" as they passed in and out through the swinging doors at the back of the kitchen, exchanging street clothes for chef's whites and head coverings.

Cosima wrapped an arm around Mariella's shoulder and punched Mario gently, good-naturedly on the arm. "Hey, how you guys doin'?" she said, glancing back and forth between them. "You two look preoccupied." Today, her frizzy red hair was captured in a bandana of purple and green paisley.

Mario quirked his mouth and shook his head. "I'm okay," he said. "You?"

Cosima rewarded him with a nod and a raised eyebrow. In her parlance, "Good" or "Good enough."

Mario cocked his head toward the rear exit door. Mariella assumed she was meant to follow.

Outside, in the alleyway across from the Chinese restaurant, he pulled out a pack of Marlboros from the pocket of his chef's coat, offered her one, which she refused, then shook out one for himself. He struck a small wooden match with his thumbnail, took his time inhaling, and turned his head to exhale.

"So what about Giovanni?" he asked.

"Well, I know you are very important to him."

"Look," he said, dropping the cigarette and grinding it on the cement under his heavy Doc Martens. He leaned forward, ready to flee back into the kitchen. "Before you even begin, lady, let's cut the crap. If he's sent you to tell me he's my father because he doesn't have the balls, forget it. I've known all along."

"So, why don't you tell him you know?" she asked, simultaneously caught off guard, yet not surprised.

"Because. It's *his* job. Get it? It was his job from the minute he gave me to Luciano—his job along with that snotty bitch Beth I have the misfortune of knowing is my mother!"

"He wanted to tell you. He told me that . . ." She released a big puff of frustration. "That he never wanted to give you up!"

"Right, he tells *you*. And what? He thinks he can make it up by having me work with him, paying me a good wage? And I'm supposed to be grateful that he was my "benefactor"? Mario made quotation marks with his fingers, in the air. "*Uncle Giovanni?* Fuck that shit! The reason I'm here is because of Luciano, the only father who's real to me."

"Yes," Mariella said. "He does try to make it up to you because he wants you closer to him, but he doesn't know how."

"Yeah? And he didn't imagine that I'd hear Luciano and Donatella talk about who he really is over the years when they didn't think I could hear? Oh, don't get me wrong, I loved—love—Luciano and Donatella. Mario thumped his chest near his heart, "the best mother and father anyone could have. But when they'd tell me how generous Uncle Giovanni was to send me to the Cordon fucking Bleu." He spat on the ground. "You expect me to believe he's so wonderful?" he said, stepping away. "No, try guilt, that's what motivated him—guilt. And if he wants to make up for being such a pussy by paying my way, I'm sure as hell not gonna stop him."

"*Aspetta*." She grabbed the sleeve of Mario's coat. "Wait, please. At least let me tell you why I want to talk."

"You think I care?"

"Yes," she said softly. "I think you care."

Mario's nostrils flared like those of horses she'd seen in Palio races at home, after they'd run their hearts out, adrenalin still coursing, trying to catch breath. She couldn't tell if he was frightened or enraged.

"Giovanni's very lonely," she said.

Mario snorted. "Really? You think I give a shit?" His eyes, hard and bright. "And isn't that your job, keeping him company? Isn't that what you do every night in his bed? And don't tell me you don't realize everybody knows. It's no secret you're Giovanni's piece."

"Piece?" She had an idea what he meant, and it didn't make her happy. "Well," she said, attempting to slough off the insult. "Then you also know I don't have so much time now because of school, and I think it's time for you to be brave and tell him you know he's your papa—because he's lonely and ashamed, and he needs you to forgive him." She shrugged. "Maybe," she said. "Someday."

He glared at her. "You really are something," he said, shaking his head. "You really have a lot of nerve."

"Yes," she said. "That is what they say about me." She opened her arms. "And it's true, as you say, it would be best for Giovanni to come to you. But he cannot. So, what do you want them to say about you? That you are brave, like the day you saved the dish-washer's finger?" She recalled how pleased Mario had been that day, accepting praise from his father. "Or that you're afraid to be the first one to speak?"

Mario stomped off and returned to his cooking. And again, Mariella watched outside the double doors. It had been a dreadful mistake, engaging him. If anything, she'd alienated him further from Giovanni. And honestly, wasn't it her own guilt she'd wanted to assuage, trying to persuade Mario to fill a hole in Giovanni's heart? A vacuum already in place before she'd come along, and made larger now by her squeezing into his hollow place. How selfish she'd been, entering his bed and leaving it empty, a gaping, pulsing wound.

Mario melted butter in the big soup pot, and as it began to foam, he layered in a quantity of the *soffritto*. He added in the herbs he'd chopped earlier, letting them sizzle for several minutes, along with the vegetables. Then he added, large ladleful by ladleful, the right amount of broth from the chicken parts he'd already seasoned and boiled down.

Chapter Thirty-Eight

"What are *you* doing here?" Mariella asked, as, from seemingly nowhere, Leslie scooted in beside her at the hostess desk. She was still agitated from her encounter with Mario. Leslie proceeded to welcome dinner guests right along with her, as if he and she shared the job. He was nicely dressed, eccentric as always but well put together: purple and green argyle vest over a purple checked long-sleeved shirt and dark green jeans. Clearly, he'd just come from work at Gypsy Men's. He was better, overall, but sometimes in the night when she got up to go to the bathroom, she could hear his heartbroken whimpers.

"Well," he said, lining up papers and pencils on a waist-high shelf hidden from patrons, beneath the black granite counter. "I figured the only way I'd see you is here. Now that you're never home." His old teasing humor was returning.

She rolled her eyes. "*Buona sera*," she said before Leslie could interfere, addressing the stately older couple standing before her. "Do you 'ave the *prenotazione?*"

"Excuse me?" the gray-haired woman said. Her boucle pink suit and pearls reminded Mariella of Sylvia Gamberini's pink silk sheath, startling her as if she were back in Sicily, the night of her and Matteo's graduation.

"Oh, scusi, of course, I mean the reservation." When she was rattled, she lapsed, unconsciously, into Italian. She found the couple's name on her list, marked it off, and, menus in hand, bade them follow her to their table, throwing Leslie a glare as she went. As if it was his fault she'd forgotten her English.

On return, her pulse quickened at the sight of Pietro, the sommelier, and Bernard huddled at the desk with Leslie, and the three of them chattering away like it was a reunion. Why was Bernard there? She'd avoided almost everything except essential contact with him.

"Ciao," she said, attempting nonchalance. "What's up?"

"If you must know," Leslie said, hands on his hips. "We were discussing your birthday."

"My birthday?"

"Yes, and don't pretend you've forgotten because every time I *have* seen you, you've reminded me of it, *and*, that there's nothing you'd rather do on your birthday than salsa dancing. So . . ."

"So?" She nodded at Leslie. "Dancing with you again . . . okay." She greeted the next customers, "*Buona sera*," checked off their names, and followed Bernard with her eyes as he escorted the trio to their table.

"He is one pretty boy," Leslie said, tracking Bernard along with her.

"No party," she said. "Please." She shook her clasped hands in front of Leslie's face, forcing herself into his line of vision. "*Prego*, I beg of you, no party." Her last party, that graduation one, had been a disaster. Since then she'd avoided being the center of attention, even if it had gotten her out of Italy.

But this, her birthday, was different. If felt important to her, and a little melancholy. On January 27th, she'd be twenty-three years old.

"I love Latin dancing," Bernard chimed in, returning just at the end of Mariella's plea. "What I mean," he said, color rising in his cheeks, "is that I was looking forward to a party because there would probably be music and you know—we could all dance?"

"So, we'll go dancing," Leslie declared. "You," he said, pointing at Bernard, unaware of the frisson between Mariella and the new maitre d'. "Not you," he told Pietro. "I remember, it's definitely not your strong suit—plus Giovanni and Cosima; she told me she loves to dance too. And you, of course," he said, indicating Mariella. "And me!"

"Giovanni, no," Mariella said.

"Giovanni, no what?" Giovanni said, coming up beside her, nodding at her companions and the next patrons whose name Mariella called from the list and whose table was ready: a beleaguered, pretty mother and stoic father with two young sons who poked each other in the ribs and could barely stand still without rough housing.

"Oh, dancing," she said to Giovanni offhandedly, checking off the family's name and walking away to seat them on the far side of the restaurant, where the boys wouldn't be too disruptive to others.

"They," she said on return, waving her hand at Leslie and Bernard, "want to take me dancing for my birthday."

"I know. It's a wonderful idea!" Giovanni said.

"Yes, but you don't dance," she said. "It wouldn't be any fun for you."

"I want you to go," he said. "As a matter of fact, I insist."

"But why?" What was the matter with Giovanni? Why was he relinquishing her, possibly sending her into Bernard's arms?

"Because, I *don't* dance, and I know how hard you work." He regarded her fondly, gesturing somewhere outside the window. "Between this place and school, " he said, "you need to have some fun." He must have caught her bemused expression because he hastily added, "But we'll celebrate, no question." There was a pause. "Your birthday's on a Sunday, right?"

"Si."

"So why don't you all," he said, sweeping his arm at the other three, "go dancing the Saturday night before, and you and I," he addressed Mariella, "will do something special on Sunday."

"Yes, that's a wonderful idea!" Leslie enthused. "Saturday night it is!" She understood that Leslie needed something to look forward to, and her birthday was it.

"Sorry, Mariella, count me out," Pietro said, sounding contrite. "I really *don't* dance."

Giovanni assured her over and over later, "I'm fine, just fine about your going dancing—delighted in fact, because you'll get your fun, and I'll have you all to myself on your actual day."

She'd noticed that women patrons of every age fell all over themselves while simultaneously falling prey to Bernard's charm. She saw it when they seductively nicknamed him "Bernardo," drawing out the "o" at the end. saw it in the coquettish tilt of their heads, the surprised smiles in their eyes ("Oh! There's more to this man than his quiet professionalism) as they accepted the chairs he held for them, their glances as he placed a white cloth napkin across their laps, their touches on his jacket sleeve lingering just a moment too long. "Please stay," inherent in their gazes. "Come back—find a reason to attend to me—to me alone, and I'll take care of you." Yes, that was it. He made women and girls alike want to take care of him.

After only a few words of suggestion—"The grilled calamari is particularly good tonight, it was just delivered fresh, two hours ago."—or a glimpse of his crooked boyish smile, his demeanor both vulnerable and masculine, female customers were charmed into believing that *they* were the ones who could soothe what they perceived as Bernard's aching spirit, bring peace to his unsettled heart, smooth out his troubled brow. Whether he was aware of his effect or consciously tried for it, Mariella couldn't tell.

When Cosima learned she'd been invited to Mariella's dancing birthday evening, she did a dreamy, slow dance around, closing her eyes and pretending to be held in someone's arms. "Bernard's such a nice man," Cosima said, revealing a first inkling of an attraction. "Maybe one of the few. He seems trustworthy enough, like he is who he seems to be." Mariella was glad her friend felt drawn to a man, even if it was only a daydream, especially in light of the distant but crushing aftermath of her husband leaving her.

Bernard seemed easiest with Luciano, now serving as manager and doing a sterling job of it, but then they—Bernard and Luciano—had the experience of maitre d' in common, and, as Mariella had suspected, as waiters during the time even before Trovatore, where they all worked along with Giovanni a few years before he opened Basilico.

During the week before Mariella's birthday, Bernard cautiously approached her. "I wanted to tell you," he said slowly, "that Giovanni is happier now—at least he acts that way—than any of us have ever seen him. We're all glad for him, and . . . well . . . it's pretty obvious that it's because of you."

"Oh." He'd meant it as a compliment, she supposed, or perhaps a bit of flattery. Taking a moment to calm herself, she breathed before she spoke. "When you put it that way, I have to thank you—I think. And," she said, raising her shoulders, "forgive me, at the school last semester, for thinking you meant I am only a stupid woman belonging to a man."

"I would never see you that way," Bernard said with an expression so earnest that she too, like all those women customers, wanted nothing more than to take care of him, to hold him in her arms (and maybe in her bed) and reassure him that everything would be all right.

Chapter Thirty-Nine

At Club Estilo, they stepped from the arcade of neon and side-walk revelry on Mission Street into a darkness deeper than the January night. And where a doorman instantly demanded payment. Mariella couldn't quite see his face, except where a pinpoint of light crossed his high cheekbones and deep eye sockets.

"Should we knock three times and whisper?" she blurted, the lyrics from "Hernando's Hideaway" springing up in her mind, her voice metallic in the silence. She was nervous, being here with Bernard. The image of them knocking and whispering a password struck her as funny, and she laughed, too loud.

In the narrow beam of the doorman's flashlight Leslie snapped her a look, and Cosima leaned into her and said, "Shush!"

Mariella wriggled her shoulder away. She had never liked being told what to do—who would, with Yolanda Russo for a mother? She rooted around in her small evening purse, but before she could produce the cash, Bernard told her to put her money away, which she was hoping someone—*he*—would do. It was, after all, if not her actual birthday, her birthday treat.

Just ahead of her, single file in the dark, Bernard searched behind him for her hand. Bumping up against him, she took hold and followed him to the end of the partition and around to the other side where small multicolored globes were strung from the ceiling like a perpetual Christmas. When he released his grip, she was surprised by how much she didn't want to let go.

She told herself Giovanni was right not to have come. She'd danced with him only once, at Basilico, at the wedding reception of a long-time customer and his Brazilian bride. He'd been clumsy and wooden, too self-conscious to feel how the samba music begged his body to move. So unlike his suppleness, his willingness to relinquish his body to the give and take of making love. He'd been magnanimous about tonight, urging her to "Dance so hard you wear a hole in your shoes." Was he only pretending not to notice the pull, the exaggerated avoidance, between her and Bernard?

As she stood with Bernard for a moment, her eyes adjusted to the nightclub dim. This was the kind of club where she'd danced in Sicilia with Matteo. Where she'd first surrendered herself to the dance and fallen in love: with him and with the mambo, with the rhumba, and the one that really spoke to her, the Argentine tango. Especially the tango. Elemental and lush.

The crowd drifted in, the band already warming up. Mariella relaxed, let herself exhale. On the wall in black script, in both Spanish and English: "Dance is a perpendicular expression of a horizontal desire."

"Do you know who first said that?" Bernard murmured, and, without waiting for an answer, he said, "Oscar Wilde, or George Bernard Shaw. No one knows for sure."

What interested her was him standing so close. And his black silk shirt and beige slacks and soft black leather shoes. He was supposed to be paying attention to Cosima, not to her.

The other men—mostly Latino—appeared handsome and dangerous, with their slicked-back hair and slim suits, the dark and light-skinned women seductive in tight-fitting skirts and dresses and heels so tall they could break their ankles with one wrong step.

As the resident Latina, Cosima's counsel had been to wear something easy to dance in but not pants. "Dance moves look better in tight dresses," she'd said, as if Mariella were a novice. "It's all in the knees and hips. Besides, it's not the custom. Latinas don't often dress up in pants. And they never go to nightclubs alone or with just one other woman. Three or four together is okay, but better still to come with a man. Otherwise . . . well, you get the idea."

It was now the twenty-first century, but apparently in Cosima's mind, the Latino world was still old-fashioned. Mariella, in ankle-strap heels and snug, straight skirt flared at the bottom, her sheer, silvery blouse frilly and low-cut.

"See, it's good you trusted me," Cosima said, coming up beside her, the reflection of lights a kaleidoscope in her light brown eyes. Her curly red hair hung below her shoulders and was held back from her face by French braids woven below the crown of her head. Occasional long strands were highlighted with extensions of shiny colored tinsel. An electric blue jersey dress molded itself to her curvy body, belted just below the waist with a rope of red braided leather, and red open-toed heels and even her toenails matched. Dressed to kill.

On the prowl, came immediately to Mariella's mind. *A caccia.* She wondered if Cosima's allure would have its hoped-for effect on Bernard.

They settled at a tiny table alongside the polished wood dance floor. The cocktail waitress, an earnest-looking young Latina in a white shirt and blue jeans, took their drink orders: rum and soda for Mariella, and rum and Coke for Cosima and Leslie. Bernard ordered Scotch.

"I haven't had one of these in ages," Cosima said, draping an arm across Leslie's shoulders. More than once, she recounted to Mariella how much she and her former husband liked dancing together and drinking rum and Coke.

"Uh-huh," Leslie mumbled. He'd been the one excited about tonight, though he seemed only half-present, preoccupied, as he'd been ever since they'd left the apartment hours ago.

On the Estilo stage, four men in short-sleeved shirts were blowing on horns or tuning guitars and one band member with a black pencil-thin moustache struck keys on the piano with his left hand while he tapped on a conga with his right. Other instruments—triangles, drums, a trombone, a set of brightly colored maracas and a long gourd with indentations—lay on top of speakers.

"It's a Cuban band," Bernard said. Then, as if on cue, half a dozen more musicians, including a woman, mounted the stage, took up their instruments, and within seconds the place was alive. Dancers were on their feet, the walls and floor vibrating, and the rhythmic, hip-swiveling tempos pulsed in time to the beat of Mariella's heart.

Leslie pulled Mariella out of her chair, and he hustled her on to the floor, and then, into the rhythm of the mambo.

"Why the rush?" she asked.

"Cosima wants to put the moves on Bernard—so cute, that Bernardo—or so she told me after dinner. I figure with us out of the way . . ."

Mariella glanced back at the table. Cosima looked put out. Bernard was watching *her*, and when he realized she'd noticed, he quickly reached out for Cosima to dance. Mariella tried not to be too obvious, observing how easily, how naturally, Bernard and Cosima fit together on the floor. Cosima's dream come true.

Leslie's dancing was labored, deliberate, as if he was thinking ahead to every next move. So unlike his easy, loose-limbed abandon the last time they'd danced. Even his slender hands paddled stiffly at the air. She understood: it was Darrell he wanted to be with on the dance floor.

When they all converged back at the table, and before Mariella even had a chance to sit, Bernard held out his hand to her and said, "May I?"

An invitation that spelled danger, an invisible line of desire one crossed, or didn't. She stood and smoothed her skirt.

She wondered if he knew it too, the peril of moving close, though she liked that he admired how her hips and knees moved together as they danced, liked that she was letting it show.

She closed her eyes and let the music take her. Closed her eyes against her desire for Bernard. When she opened them, Bernard was smiling, the other women snaking their torsos as if they had no bones in their bodies, the dance floor their domain.

Bernard nodded slowly, as if he found her deflection both innocent and seductive. His potency, the seriousness of his stare . . . she could barely hold herself from reaching out and smoothing back the wave of dark blond hair that had fallen across his forehead.

Moments after they sat—she, deliberately next to Leslie, away from Bernard—the band started playing "Happy Birthday" with a Latin beat. Before Mariella could swallow her mouthful of rum and soda, Bernard grinned, stood before her again and offered his hand.

"Yes," he said. "Dance with me." Alone? In front of all those people who *really* knew how?

This time he held her closer, under his chin.

"You did this," she said. "You told them it's my birthday." Even on display she felt safe with him now, as if no one else were in the room. After all, "Happy Birthday" was such an innocuous song. Before long, other couples drifted back onto the floor, Cosima and Leslie among them, and the birthday song morphed into a different tune, back to the present.

During Cosima's next turn with Bernard, Mariella sat and watched the easy, natural sway of the dancers' hips and attempted to appear absorbed. Leslie had vanished, to the men's room, she supposed. Or perhaps to have a private cry.

A voice above her said, "Dance?" She glanced up into a dark

face—Indian—Mexican, she assumed. Baby-blue polyester suit, tight pants, a gold cross hanging against the hairless chest in the "V" of his black polyester shirt. And then she saw the gold front tooth. When he asked again, "Dance?" she was afraid of making an unnecessary scene, of jumping to her mother's foolish conclusion: "Stay away from gypsies, the ones with the shiny teeth. They'll cut off your fingers for the gold." She took for granted that she hadn't the right to say no.

"*Mi nombre*," he said right away, pointing to himself. He smiled and flashed his gold tooth. "*Es* . . . Juan." When she told him "Mariella," he said it back.

Juan held her so close she could scarcely breathe. She kept backing away to talk, as if that were even possible, hoping he'd get the message, as uncertain of herself as if she were seventeen. He smelled of the same floral hair pomade as the Moroccan boys back in high school.

Juan nodded and grinned and pulled her up against him again. She chided herself for feeling panic and anger. She was, after all, a twenty-three-year-old woman—at least she would be tomorrow—who ought to have been able to tell him, "Back off!"

She spied Leslie, back at the table, alone and looking forlorn. And Bernard on the floor with Cosima, watching her with Juan. If only he or Leslie would break in.

"Your *marido*?" Juan asked, nodding at Bernard.

"Si," Mariella answered, too fast. She still wore Nonna's wedding ring, though on the wrong hand. "Yes, he is."

When the music stopped, she broke from Juan and nearly sprinted back to the table, knocking all their drinks onto the floor and onto the chair that held their coats. A sliver of broken glass pierced her leg.

"Well," Leslie said, leaping to his feet to avoid the carnage. "If I'd known one drink would affect you this way . . . oh God, you're bleeding!" He wrested napkins from under the drinks at the nearest table, startling its occupants, and gingerly patted the paper squares onto the back of Mariella's calf where a streak of blood seeped from a small cut.

"I'm so sorry," she said, ignoring Leslie's ministrations. She tried to mop the table with a cocktail napkin, alcohol dripping onto their coats and onto the floor.

The waitress appeared as if out of thin air with a mop and a sponge.

"You're bleeding!" Bernard proclaimed, coming up behind Mariella, and leaving Cosima in his wake. He whipped a cotton handkerchief from his pants pocket, crouched to Mariella's leg, and gently probed her wound with his thumbs.

His fingers were cool and soothing to her bare, warm skin, and his touch caught her breath. She gripped a chair for support. More disturbing was her desire for him to probe her thighs, and higher still . . . "No glass," he said, searching for any trace of shard, then wrapping and tying the handkerchief around her calf. "Pressure to stop the bleeding," he explained. "Give it a couple of minutes."

"It's nothing," she said, "no big deal, just a scratch."

"And yes," Bernard said, coming to his feet. "We'll have another round," he told the waitress, pointing above Mariella's head. "All except this one."

The waitress looked at Bernard, then at Mariella.

"He's kidding," Mariella protested, willing herself to calm down and breathe normally. Although she wondered, did they really think she was a drunk?

"Listen," Mariella said now, turning to Bernard. "You know that fellow I danced with?"

"You mean the Indian?"

"Whatever. I didn't ask."

"I think he's Guatemalan," Bernard insisted. "Cosima, don't you think he's Guatemalan?"

"I don't know," Cosima snapped. "And I don't really care. Anyway, what are you? Some kind of racist?"

"Juan asked me if . . . if . . ." Mariella groaned. "Oh, *Dio*, this is so embarrassing."

"Yes? Juan asked you if . . . ?" Bernard kept smiling, as if he'd anticipated what was coming.

"If you are my husband," Mariella said.

"Ah. And what did you tell him?"

"I said yes."

"Okay," Bernard said. "The only problem is," and he addressed Mariella. "If you really were my wife, you wouldn't have danced with him in the first place. Not unless you meant to cause a whole lot of trouble, because now I'm obligated to beat the shit out of him."

"Oh."

Bernard gave Mariella's arm a pat "It's all right," he said. "I think it's cute.

Leslie clucked his tongue, disgusted with them both.

"That fellow knows better," Bernard said. "He won't believe me, but I'll see if I can make a, remediar, man-to-man."

Then Juan was there, inviting Cosima, who simply stood and followed him onto the dance floor.

So that's how you do it without making a fuss, Mariella observed. She untied Bernard's handkerchief from her calf. "I'll wash and give it back," she said, and despite Bernard's protestations, stuffed it into her small purse. She replaced the handkerchief with a Band-Aid the waitress had delivered, along with their drinks.

"You two go ahead," Bernard said, taking a long pull on his drink, and urging Mariella and Leslie to dance. "I need to sit this one out."

"I'm sorry if I've made a mess," she told Leslie as they moved together around the floor.

"You have," Leslie teased. "And if you're going to hang out with Latinos, you'll have to learn how to behave. Look around," he said, sweeping his arm toward the other dancers. "Do you see anyone out there dancing ten feet apart?" She couldn't tell if the band was playing a cumbia or a salsa, but whatever faster-paced tempo, they moved against each other, body to body.

During her next dance with Bernard, how comforted she felt when he moved against her in a kind of soft undulation, and which she accepted as part of the dance. How reluctant for the sensuous, haunting melody to end.

When they were all back at the table, Leslie ordered yet another round of drinks. She'd barely touched her second. When the band took a break, club music pumped through the speakers in its place.

"I have to use the restroom," Mariella said. She'd noticed the sign for it, pointing up a stairway to a balcony, where several men congregated and smoked.

Cosima harrumphed.

"Want to come?" Mariella asked her. Cosima shook her head but didn't answer.

When she came out of the bathroom, she was surprised Bernard was there, waitning for her. Had she said something wrong? Had she again broken some cultural code?

"Well, I fixed up things with old Juan," Bernard said.

"What?"

For one terrible moment, Mariella imagined he was going to tell her he'd cold-cocked Juan and left him stretched out senseless. Juan was nowhere in sight. She leaned over the balcony to see if perhaps Bernard had thrown him onto the dance floor. Nothing but hip-churning bodies.

"Yeah," Bernard said. "He came by to go to the men's room while you were in there." He nodded toward the women's bathroom. "So I stopped him and shook his hand. He asked if it was okay to dance with you and I said, 'Juan, old buddy, it's my wife's birthday, and I told her before we arrived that she had my permission. So I guess she can if she wants to. '*Con permisso*,' I told him."

"You didn't!" Mariella inhaled a short, sharp breath. This garrulous man before her was nothing like the reserved Bernard she'd encountered at class or at Basilico. "I don't believe you." Bernard was laughing so hard he didn't notice Mariella wasn't. Not like Olimpio, when he was a little boy and used to laugh at his own jokes and watch her, wanting her to laugh with him. "You are really silly," she would tell her young brother, then give him a hug. She could never tell if her embarrassment was for herself or for him.

"I'm not kidding," Bernard said and raised his right hand, cracking himself up, a big nerdy, ha, ha, ha. He wiped his eyes. "I did tell him to wait a while because we'd like to dance first. But you wait and see—he'll ask you, guaranteed."

"I will kill you," Mariella said. Up there on the balcony with all the men, she felt sleazy, as if everyone thought she was fair game. "But first let's go downstairs."

Bernard repeated to Cosima and Leslie what he'd said to Juan and broke up all over again. Mariella rolled her eyes in Cosima's direction, who still faked nonchalance.

The trombone player, a woman, came over and leaned her hip against Bernard's arm. Like the rest of the band she wore trousers and a vest.

"Hey," the woman said to Bernard. "Long time no see. You given up the congas?"

He'd never mentioned that he played. Mariella imagined Latin musicians (even though Bernard clearly wasn't Latino) more soulful, more passionate, more understanding of women than other men. She pictured Bernard's fingertips tapping out rhythms on those stretched, taut drum skins.

Juan appeared during the lull and asked her to dance. And with permission now, she said yes. Besides, with club music, they didn't have to touch. She saw Bernard watching their every move with a proprietary eye.

The idea that Bernard was rightfully hers had taken hold inside her, in spite of Cosima's claim, in spite of Giovanni. She felt as territorial about him as she had about the boys she'd liked when she was an adolescent, as if the mere act of having a crush on one of them staked him as hers. Back then it hardly mattered if the crush went only one way. The dream and the excitement, that was the point.

Her next dance with Bernard was a rhumba, and he guided her into the sway of its slow, sensual rhythm, then back into the syncopations of the salsa and the cumbia, and for Mariella, back into what she'd been wanting: the feel of them together, the soft silkiness of his shirt, not too tight or polyester like Juan's. When she murmured into his shoulder, "I like the way you dress," he stepped back and danced with her from arm's length, watching her, as if searching her face for a clue.

"You know I like you," he said finally.

"I like you too."

"No. I mean . . . really like you. Ever since that first night in class."

"Oh, right," she laughed. "I don't remember of course . . ."

"No kidding?" He smiled, all the while keeping perfect time and a perfect lead to the salsa beat. "You expect me to believe that?"

"What do you mean?"

"That you don't remember. I saw you looking back."

"Oh," Mariella said and shrugged. "Maybe . . . some."

She tried to relax, which was difficult with Bernard's body so close and with him observing her that way, straight on.

"If my old girlfriend walked in here," Bernard said, abruptly dropping Mariella's right hand, which he'd cradled in his left, against his chest. He made a chopping motion in the air. "No kidding, she'd be so jealous she'd kill us both. Thank God I don't have to worry about her anymore . . . well, almost."

Mariella glanced around, as if the wild-eyed ex-girlfriend with Medusa crazy hair might be lurking behind a post in one of the dark corners, a knife between her teeth, ready to pounce.

"It's complicated," Bernard said. He sighed. "But I guess it means neither one of us is free."

A sudden blow, Bernard's news of entanglement.

And I'm twenty-three and only free to dance . . .

Her musings were pierced by one strong, clear note from the singers, a man and a woman, huddled on either side of the microphone, harmonizing in a solitary, mournful voice. They wore matching pink and blue ruffled shirts and pants.

"Do you know what they're saying?" Bernard asked.

"Trust me, I only speak *Italiano*, and a little German, not so good with Spanish."

"They're saying, 'I've wasted my life in one sad love affair after another . . . how many bitter pills does a man have to swallow before he dies?'"

"No!" She didn't know whether to believe him or not.

"Anyway," he went on, "I was happy when Leslie said you wanted to go dancing. I couldn't believe you'd go through with it."

"I didn't expect . . . well, to dance with you. At all," she said. "I mean, Cosima's the one you should dance with."

"Naww." Bernard waved across the room. "She's got Leslie. Look at them." She followed the arc of Bernard's arm to the far side of the floor, where Cosima and Leslie were clowning a salsa-style bump and grind. "See, they're like family, she doesn't care."

Mariella and Bernard released one another slowly, reluctantly, as the salsa wound down and the band took a brief retuning break.

"I want to go," Cosima announced as soon as they converged at the table, her face all ill temper and pout.

"You're kidding!" Bernard protested. "The night is young—have another drink!"

"I don't want another drink," she complained. "I have a lot to do tomorrow."

Leslie shrugged, turned down his mouth, and consulted his watch, but said nothing.

"Wait a minute!" Mariella said. "It's my birthday—It's only twenty more minutes until midnight."

Cosima sat, unrelenting and mute.

"And then we can go," Mariella said. "Whenever you like."

"Okay," Cosima said. "But only because it's your birthday."

Mariella silently cursed her new friend.

As the band resumed and Bernard drew Cosima onto the dance floor, she mumbled, sarcastically, loud enough for Mariella to hear, "If *you* don't mind."

Leslie and Mariella sat and drank. Until Bernard reclaimed her.

When they danced their last dance, all of her resistance vanished. He brushed the back of her neck with his hand, and she touched his face and his neck as if they were lovers. She wasn't surprised when he kissed her, though it was a deeper kiss than she'd imagined.

"I forgot myself," he said. "I forgot where we were. I've never done that before."

"Well," she said, pushing him back, resisting her desire to kiss him again, to tell him she wanted more.

They moved to the far side of the floor, putting the other dancers between them and Cosima.

"When can I see you?" He moved his thigh into her skirt, and she let it stay. "Can you get away from those two? Can I take you home?"

"No," she said. "I came with them, and it's not . . . it wouldn't be right. And what about your girlfriend?"

"We're not together," Bernard said. He looked away and then

at the floor. "As I said, it's complicated. I've broken it off, but she won't let go . . . she makes threats."

How manipulated we all are.

"It doesn't make sense, but you're right." He sighed. "And I wish you weren't." He explored her face for a long moment. And touched her cheek. "That's one of the things I like about you, the way you know about things."

The only thing that made sense to Mariella was that she needed to think.

As Leslie drove the two women home, Cosima remarked over her shoulder to Mariella in the back, "I don't think you should see him."

"Oh?" *None of your business, witch!*

"No, because then you'd be a cheat, wouldn't you?" Cosima may as well have called her *puttana*! Like her mother did.

"But I wouldn't want to know if you did," Cosima said. "Just don't tell me. Of course, if you do get involved, I suppose we'll have to work it out. I mean the part about being unfaithful."

Like Cosima's faithless husband. Mariella knew, as well, of Cosima's alcoholic father cheating on her mother one too many times, and her mother shooting him in the leg. And how Cosima had been in years of therapy to redeem herself, but she'd still succumbed to a husband who was just like her father.

Hours later, and still awake, Mariella stared into predawn shadows, tossing in a welter of sheets and sweat, and wondering how she would tell Giovanni about dancing with—no, about kissing—Bernard.

On the other hand, why tell Giovanni? He didn't *own* her. They hadn't promised to be exclusive, although, if she was honest with herself, monogamy was tacitly implied. He'd certainly made it clear when he'd asked her to move in with him. "The one thing

I'd ask of you is that you wouldn't see other men," he'd said. And he and Bernard, such longtime friends.

So did that mean if she *didn't* move in with him (thank God she hadn't!) what she did with other men was her business? Anyway, why was she worrying about monogamy? She and Bernard hadn't ended up in bed, and one kiss didn't amount to infidelity. But would Giovanni see it that way?

Chapter Forty

"You've certainly got yourself in a pickle!" Leslie declared, gleefully, before Mariella even had a chance to mumble, "*Buon giorno.*" He bustled around the kitchen in checked pajama bottoms and a white T-shirt with "WE GIRLS RULE!" emblazoned across his chest in Day-Glo green. He stirred something thick and pink-tinged in a mixing bowl. Her stomach turned over on itself.

"Thanks for the reminder," Mariella groused, still half asleep, hoping the evil eye she was aiming at him hit its mark. "What are you making?" she asked, waving her hand at the bowl and turning her head so she didn't have to look at it.

"Pancakes with fresh raspberries."

"I'm sure it's delicious." She patted her stomach. "But I'm a little upset."

"Well, I should think so," he went on in that annoying chatty tone, as if he were commenting on the correct way to hold one's fork or prune roses.

"You're lively this morning." She tried to ignore Leslie's chirpy scolding. She already felt edgy, jumpy, and out of her skin. Confused was more like it, an ominous confusion, something momentous and unknown struggling to burst free. She checked her cell phone for the tenth time. Why hadn't anyone called from home to wish her *buon compleanno*? She remembered how distant, how anxious and unfatherly Papa sounded when she'd called home at Christmas.

"Well, never mind," Leslie said, aiming for breezy. He continued stirring his pancake batter. "I'll just take this over to Gardenia's." His social worker neighbor. "I'm sure she'll appreciate a good breakfast."

"Oh, Leslie, you know I appreciate it. I just really can't eat right now—maybe later?" He didn't say anything.

She surveyed him for a moment. "Excuse me for saying so, but . . ." she inhaled sharply, "you don't look so unhappy anymore." He had a determined cheerfulness about him, almost bordering on manic. As if he'd decided, *I'm over him*, and sloughed off his mourning cloak by sheer will, and stepped into a new skin.

"*Buon giorno!*" Both Mariella and Leslie startled and jumped back. "*Buon compleanno, cara Mariella!*" Giovanni's bass voice boomed through the speaker.

"*Che . . . ?*" She looked inquisitively at Leslie, then down at herself in her flannel nightgown. Had she forgotten what time they were meeting? She knew Giovanni was taking her somewhere for dinner. But had they set a time?

Leslie buzzed in Giovanni, and he and Mariella stood, immobilized, listening to Giovanni's quick footsteps on the marble stairs, resounding louder the closer he came. Almost as an afterthought, she moved to unlock and unbolt the apartment door.

Giovanni kissed her, chastely but joyfully, rain hat in hand. If he had any judgment about either of their appearances, his face registered only radiance at being in Mariella's presence.

"You have half an hour to get ready," he told her, catching his breath and shrugging off his raincoat and scarf. "No questions—oh, and bring a bathing suit."

"A bathing suit? In the rain?" She hadn't brought one with her from Sicily.

"Never mind," he said, "we'll buy one along the way. And just wear regular clothes, the kind you always wear, simple but nice."

Her feet seemed rooted, interwoven with the loops of the black living room rug.

"Go ahead," he said, checking his watch, and waving her toward her room. "It'll take us a couple of hours, and we have a one o'clock appointment."

An appointment? She was too bewildered, too drained to resist.

"Oh, and bring whatever cosmetics you need after a shower," he called to her as she retreated down the hallway. "Makeup too."

"Pancakes? Coffee?" she heard Leslie offer Giovanni, as she closed her bedroom door. And Giovanni asking Leslie, "How was the dancing?"

They traveled north on 101 in Giovanni's new Subaru hatchback, in the latest shade called "Toast," across the Golden Gate Bridge over San Francisco Bay. A panorama of piers and charter boats, and, like a Renoir at the shore, blurred edges through the fog and drizzle. Hornblower and the Red and White Fleets docked by the Embarcadero clock tower, the high-rise financial district beyond, a Golden Gate ferry making a leisurely excursion into Marin County.

She'd been out of San Francisco once before, late one September evening, when Giovanni had taken her to the Horizon, a waterfront restaurant in Sausalito. Formerly an artists' enclave and hotbed of ill-repute establishments in the early 1900s, he'd informed her. In the seventies, a former prostitute and madam— Sally Stanford—was even elected Sausalito's mayor. A colorful town of sailing boats, fancy shops, houseboats and fishing vessels, hillside homes reminding her of Taormina, a Sicilian seaside resort frequented by film stars, tourists, and artists-in-residence.

On that earlier Indian summer evening, they'd been in the bloom of new lust.

Now they wound north through Marin, a wealthy bedroom community—"One of the wealthiest suburban counties in the country," Giovanni said—contiguous small cities and towns, past turnoffs for Tiburon, Belvedere, and Mill Valley, Mt. Tamalpais and the silhouetted "Sleeping Lady" rising above.

Patches of sunlight poked through overcast the more northern they drove, unlike San Francisco, where gray and dampness seemed to lay continuously over the city, like a blanket for a long winter's sleep. Her birthday, even in Sicily, almost always marked by rain.

"Mmmm," she murmured occasionally, letting him know she was taking it all in.

At the county's northernmost, more industrial end, Giovanni turned off on Rowland Boulevard into a giant shopping complex. Mariella knew of Costco and "big box" stores, but in Sicily, they didn't exist.

She'd never seen so much "stuff" gathered in such quantities, and in a warehouse larger than a soccer field. TVs, luggage, even sofas and patio furniture. She found the sheer volume dizzying and oppressive. No such thing as a pint or a small bottle of olive oil. Quarts hooked together so one had to buy two, or the other option, a gallon.

"Look at this!" she exclaimed, holding up six loaves of whole wheat bread encased in plastic wrap. Back home, one purchased bread from the neighborhood *panetteria*, one loaf at a time, baked daily and fresh.

Women—mostly older or overweight—in hairnets and red aprons, offering food samples in little paper cups.

In one of the aisles, she spotted a four-pack of enormous bath towels.

It took Mariella less than five minutes—she had to get out of there—to grab a dark brown bathing suit with orange and white flowers. Style hardly mattered, and she paused only a moment to double check for size small from a stack in a shallow bin the size of two walk-in refrigerators.

Back on the road, Giovanni crossed an overpass, turning off on Highway 37, an overhead freeway sign indicating "Vallejo, Napa."

"Napa!" she said. "Of course, I have heard of it—the famous *Americano* wine country."

"How do you know we're not going to Vallejo?"

She threw him an unhappy look.

"I thought you might like to be reminded of home your first birthday away." Giovanni reached for her hand, across the center console. "They say the wine country here is very like *Italia*."

When she didn't answer, he said, "You're quiet. And you haven't said a word about last night. Is something wrong?"

"No. No," she said. "I think I am still coming awake. And everything here," she waved her arm, indicating outside the car, "it's all so new." What was there to say? *I am afraid for the next time I see Bernard?*

"Leslie said you're a very good dancer." Giovanni laughed. "He said his only regret was that Bernard didn't dance with *him*." There was a pause. "He also said Bernard was a real gentleman, taking turns dancing with you and Cosima."

She shrugged. "Everyone was good." Bless Leslie for covering her. If she closed her eyes she would recapture the feel of Bernard's body moving, rhythmically, sensually, close to hers. But she wouldn't do that. She'd made up her mind: the dancing, kissing Bernard, they meant nothing. An evening's titillation, and no more. Just get on with it—school, work, and today, she would be completely present for her birthday with this most wonderful of men, Giovanni, who'd arranged it, especially for her.

At Indian Springs Resort in Calistoga, a historic, rustic town with tourist shops at the far end of Napa Valley, Mariella peered into a tub brimming with steaming black sulfuric smelling ooze. Tiny twiglike bits—from peat and ash, she discovered—making it appear rough.

"I will sink in!" she protested, standing alongside the tub, her nakedness in front of the female attendant forgotten, touching the mud, finding it surprisingly fine-grained and soft. "I have claustrophobia!" Not to mention the thought of that slime entering her crevices.

But after observing that the muck held a woman buoyant in the next tub over, and that it was carefully layered on by the attendant—a young Mexican woman who barely spoke English—Mariella relented. She was soothed by the warm enveloping mud, and surrendered to the mindlessness of suspension, even to rivulets of sweat where, immobilized like a mummy, she couldn't reach. Floating free.

She and Giovanni swam in the Olympic size mineral pool, naturally heated by on-site geysers, then afterward, took massages side-by-side in the "couples" room.

"I know we always go to Italian restaurants," Giovanni said, heading back down 29, the two-lane highway out of Calistoga, toward St. Helena. "But this one—Tra Vigne—is special."

"Among the vines," she said. "That's what it means."

Vines indeed, field after field of vineyards, stretching out in groomed, evenly spaced trellised rows, covering flatland and rolling hillsides on either side of the road, everywhere, as far as she could see, even on acreage of elegant private homes. Stately, Mediterranean-like or modern wineries, gates open for visitors; one, gleaming white, like a Greek island church on the crest of a hill, offered a gondola ride to the top. And on a slope near the outskirts of St. Helena, a sprawling stone monastery turned world-famous restaurant and cooking school, Culinary Institute of America.

It was at Tra Vigne that she finally broke down.

It wasn't the Liquore Strega poster of the woman in a backless green dress or the one of the ape wearing a bellhop hat, leaping out of the frame and brandishing a bottle of banana liqueur. Not the gleaming dark wood bar with the Doric column spacers, nor the Italianate stucco walls, or the high ceilings, or the long, granite waiters' counter, so reminiscent of home, pizza ovens fired up, and the kitchen behind them, open and exposed.

It was the lights twinkling through the canopy of mulberry trees on the rainy brick patio, visible through mullioned windows that swung out on heavy iron hinges. And the round black metal table with the forged iron fountain tableau: a bird perched on the edge; a sun hat, as if flung and forgotten there; a pitcher on its side, the wine drunk and ceaselessly pouring out, a small tumbler close by, as if the *patron* were off in another part of the villa for an afternoon, wine-soaked siesta.

She was home again at Trattoria Inglese, at graduation dinner with the rough marble banquet table, like the one outside here, long enough to seat twenty, surrounded by smaller, round and square tables topped with the same, unpolished marble. The fronded leaf motif—like a pineapple crown—scattered on outside railings.

Never mind that it had been summer in Sicilia, then, or that the twinkling lights there had been strung through a lattice of grapevines. Her sudden grief, even for Mamma, unspeakable. But no. Not for any one person, rather for belonging, for knowing the terrain, however bumpy. For knowing who to count on and what to expect. For family. And for Matteo too, because Bernard's love of language and ideas, his animal nature barely tamed by intellect, had momentarily reminded her, last night, and made her regret, yet again, renouncing her first and fiercest love.

Even the dainty loaf of warm, crusty bread placed directly on the white cloth at their window table overlooking the patio made her homesick, the dish of fragrant green olive oil, the tiny bowls, rather than shakers, of pepper and salt.

"I need to go home," she said.

"Okay," Giovanni said, his expression unsettled, rising to pull out her chair.

"No, Giovanni." She motioned him to sit down. Words swimming on her bound, folio menu, like images glimpsed through a rain-streaked windshield. "I mean *home*. Where I have family. Where I'm wanted, even loved . . ." She thought of Nonna and of Papa too. "No matter how bad."

"*Buona sera!*" Their waiter appeared, his accent more Spanish than Italian. His uniform snappy: white shirt, bow tie, and gold and black brocade vest over black pants. "Welcome to Tra Vigne."

"It's okay," Mariella said, intercepting Giovanni's intent to send the waiter away. "Go ahead. You know what's good here. Surprise me. *Prego*, go ahead."

As much as she longed to spill her heart to Nonna, and unburden herself in Papa's big embrace, going home was only a pipe dream. It would be a step back, and she needed to move forward, or at least hold steady. But she couldn't fault herself for the daydream, or the yearning.

"Is the *mozzarella al minuti* really to the minute?" Giovanni asked, keeping a concerned eye on Mariella. He'd told her about Michael Chiarello, the celebrated chef/proprietor who'd opened the restaurant at twenty-five, nearly fifteen years ago, in the late eighties. A hot-tempered perfectionist—it was rumored he'd hit his first wife—who'd also made his mark with high-end cooking store entrepreneurship, TV cooking shows, and bestselling cookbooks.

"Si," the waiter said, feigning an imperious demeanor, the contrast of his clear porcelain skin against coal-black hair a study in opposites. "*Ogni notte.*"

Ordering complete, Giovanni immediately homed in on her. "What are you talking about, Mariella? What . . . what do you mean, 'no matter how bad'? And the part about being loved—you *do* know I love you?"

She stared at her lap.

"Don't you?" he said.

"It's not that." The reluctance in her voice close to complaint.

"So?" Giovanni said, opening his hands.

"I don't know," she said. Stalling.

"Did something happen?" And when she didn't answer, "Do *you* love me?" he asked, leaning toward her.

He sat back, as if needing the support to steady himself.

She raised her eyes halfway, but with a penitent and stubbornly bowed head.

Giovanni slumped in his chair. "I'm sorry," he said. "I've ruined your birthday. I shouldn't have asked."

"I care very much about you Giovanni," she said, lifting her gaze. "I'm . . . it's just that . . . we've never talked about love." He'd said it that once, before Christmas. She'd never said it in return.

He inhaled lightly, quickly. "Is there someone else?"

"No. No," she said. "There's no one else." She wasn't lying. And, she swore to herself, there wouldn't be. She was toxic, hurtful and destructive. Only taking, incapable of returning devotion from two remarkable men—Matteo and now, Giovanni—so inexplicably devoted to her. Yes, going forward, she would keep her head down. From now on, only what she'd pledged to herself earlier: school and, assuming Giovanni didn't fire her, work. Her devotion would be to accomplishment. And, of course, Nonna. Always to Nonna. Forever.

The arrival of wine, Valpolicella from the Italian north, providing relief and a reason for silence, as they watched the waiter uncork and pour for Giovanni to taste and then for them both.

"Giovanni," Mariella said, raising her glass. "I want to enjoy this. It's so special, what you have done today. Please, for this moment, be happy with me."

His smile, melancholic and wan. She did love him, in the way of gratitude. For his spirit and for the way he made love to her. But she was not in love. Her infatuation with Bernard had proven that.

The antipasto suddenly before them: buttery yet firm, creamy, cheesy discs of mozzarella with roasted wild mushrooms and a balsamic reduction ragu. The toast rounds both chewy and crisp. Ambrosia, paradisiacal: the words that came to her mind.

"One of Tra Vigne's specialties," Giovanni said. They were in accord for an instant, reunited over the food and the wine.

The braised short ribs, reminiscent of Sicily, with sun-dried tomatoes, arugula, and pine nuts.

They drove home in a silence both companionable and strained. Giovanni, wistful, attempting to hide his disappointment, not inquiring if she wanted to stay the night with him, but delivering her, instead, to her door. Their parting embrace so tender, so still, they could hear one another's hearts.

Leslie had left a note on her bed, alongside her cell phone: "Your family called me, about half an hour after you left." She'd given Papa Leslie's cell number, for emergencies. "In your rush, you left your phone behind, and they wanted to wish you Happy Birthday. There's a message for you, I'm sure. Your dad sounds like a really nice man."

Chapter Forty-One

Giovanni's door was closed when she came to work the next evening, before the dinner shift. She chose to let him be. She heard muffled male voices from inside his office—all the more reason not to intrude now that she was no longer manager. No longer *his*.

Probably one of the waiters, she decided, or a vendor. Always, someone wanting a meeting with the boss.

"Sit with me," Bernard said, passing her at the swinging kitchen doors, she going in, he coming out with a plate of steaming, buttered gnocchi in hand. He indicated the table nearest the kitchen, set aside for employees between lunch and dinner, when there weren't any customers.

She hesitated, holding open her side of the kitchen door with her body, watching as he grated *parmigiano* and ground a liberal amount of black pepper over the gnocchi.

She'd wrestled with herself in the night, ricocheting between feeling sorry for herself and hating herself for hurting everyone she'd ever cared for: Matteo, Papa, even Mamma, and now Giovanni. For damaging everyone who'd ever loved her. Except Nonna. Perhaps. Perhaps Nonna's kidney stones were her fault as well. Yet, simultaneously hoping she and Giovanni might keep going for dinners and plays. She'd never afford those luxuries on her own. And making love? Was she ready to give that up?

How could she even think of her own sexual pleasure when she'd just sliced a hole in the heart of that superior man?

She excoriated herself. *Mamma was right. I am a puttana! Bad, and selfish too.*

She secured her own evening meal from Cosima, who'd refused to meet Mariella's gaze. Mariella had reached over the counter and grasped her friend's hand. "Don't worry," she'd said. "I'm not interested. I'm not going anywhere with him. Your friendship is far more important," at which point Cosima had graced her with a thin but promising smile.

Mariella slid opposite Bernard into the booth with her plate of grilled fish and broccoli. Something simple after yesterday's riches.

How to tell him their Saturday sizzle was nothing more than that: a flash in the pan, a lapse in judgment, a quickening of the blood brought on by the driving Latin beat.

"Are you okay?" Bernard asked, a pillow of gnocchi speared on his fork, halfway to his mouth.

She nodded and shrugged. "You?"

"Listen," he said, laying the fork on his plate. "About Saturday." He sucked in his breath. "I meant every bit of . . . my attraction. But the problem is, I just got out—well, mostly out—of a difficult relationship."

"You mean the woman who would kill us both?" She laughed, recalling her image of his ex, a crazed Carmen with a knife between her teeth.

"That one," Bernard said, twisting his mouth into a wry grimace. "It's not an auspicious time for me." He leaned forward, his expression at once both pained and earnest. "I got carried away Saturday night. But everything I told you is true."

"Whew!" she said, skipping over the part about feeling let down and cast aside. More disappointed than she expected, more than she wanted to acknowledge just then, even to herself. Still, her instincts about people were generally sound. And now, in spite of Bernard's rejection, they told her she could trust him. He spoke ingenuously and outright, and, because of that, his motives, whatever they were, struck her as innocent and unsullied.

"You have no idea the relief," she said, a little too enthusiastically. "Me too. I mean, I also loved dancing with you and the . . . you know . . . the flirting?" Afraid of conjuring up the sensation, and not mentioning the kiss. "But," she said, waggling an index finger back and forth, "I am not ready." She shook her head. "No, I am not interested in anything serious." She looked at him straight on. "With anyone." What she didn't say was that Bernard had shown her the possibility of falling in love again. That somehow, just glimpsing that possibility gave her courage, now, to stay strong. Even with the tug of regret.

"Including Giovanni?" Bernard looked puzzled.

"Yes," she said. "Including Giovanni."

"Well," he said after a pause. "I would never do anything to jeopardize my friendship with Giovanni. So," he said, shrugging, "it all works out."

"Yes," she said. *Poof! Just like that.* Perhaps if she said it enough to herself, the attraction would vanish.

"What I want," he said after a pause. "What I want is a friend."

"Why are you telling me this?" She eyed him now with suspicion, waving her arm around the restaurant. "You have lots of friends. I see you laughing and talking with Luciano, with the waiters. Even a little bit with Teresa."

"It's not the same." He sighed. "Look, it's just that I really enjoy talking to you . . ." He held up a hand. "Okay, okay, I know how that 'friends thing' sounds," he added, making quotation marks in the air. "Corny, like a way of letting someone down easy or some kind of come on. But I really *do* want to be your friend. I mean, how profound—how much do you think I have in common with any of them?"

Leslie was her friend. Cosima had been, and she would be

again, once she realized Mariella *was* only having lunch, here at the restaurant, with Bernard. But there was no one to talk with openly, not really, outside of Leslie. No one who wasn't listening for her plans to include *them*, no one who wondered what she was reading, or thinking, or envisioning becoming, as she had once daydreamed with Nonna, and with Matteo, before the marriage nonsense.

"You think we can be only friends?" she asked, appraising Bernard with her gaze. Beautiful. There wasn't another word to describe his classic, David-like head. He was beautiful. The dark blond curls cradling the sun-bronzed, smooth curvature of his neck, his demeanor, both self-effacing and strong. And so what? She'd been around beautiful men before—her own brother. She was already more outspoken, more herself with Bernard than she'd ever been with Giovanni. More equal. Not worrying if every word she uttered would be taken as an indicator of whether or not they'd be together. She needed friendship. But would it be possible with Bernard?

Yelling, now, from Giovanni's office, a ruckus so loud the waiters setting up for dinner froze mid-task, cutlery and glass-ware held in suspension.

Mario crashed through Giovanni's door—had he punched his way out?—his rage rendering his face purple, a stretched skin about to explode.

"Mario! Wait!" yelled Giovanni, on his heels, reaching out. "Mario, please come back."

"Fuck your apology!" Mario roared, fists in the air, stumbling, turning this way and that. The waitstaff, immobilized and stunned. Luciano rushed forward; Pietro cautiously followed.

"Oh, hey people!" Mario shouted, gesturing to the room at large, his voice cracking, and waving Luciano to stay back. "You want to know what's going on? Well, I'll fuckin' tell you!"

Deadly quiet, slowing his breath, and, like a laser, he surveyed the servers, one at a time—*Who's with me or against me?* Mariella's and Bernard's mouths agape as his scowl grazed them—lingering on her in particular.

"That prick is my father!" he shouted, gesturing toward Giovanni, whose expression had sagged, making his face appear deflated and old. "Asshole married to the bitch who gave me away, the both of them!"

Mario snorted, noisily gathering a wad of mucous in the back of this throat.

"Just look at the guilt all over his chickenshit face. Thinks I didn't know—figured he could make it up to me by springing for the fancy-assed Cordon fucking Bleu."

He spat the wad on the floor.

"Tells me *he* never wanted to give me up," he went on. "You think I believe that? Ha, ha!" His mouth a vicious sneer, Mario leaned in closer to his father. "So where were your balls, *d-a-d* . . ." he stretched out the words, "when that snotty bitch, Beth— excuse me, my *m-o-t-h-e-r*—gave me the heave-ho? Huh? Why couldn't you have been honest with me from the beginning?"

"Please," Giovanni said. He'd crumpled inside his shirt, as if he were a scarecrow in garments too large, held up only by clothespins. He raised a hand, then let it drop, and took a step back. "Enough, Mario," he said, his voice weary with defeat.

"Enough?" Mario said, moving forward. "Enough? Oh no, I'm just getting started." He strutted back and forth in front of Giovanni, taunting him, slowly, deliberately lighting up from a pack of Marlboros he pulled from his pocket. Like all San Francisco restaurants, Basilico was smoke-free. He inhaled, threw the match on the floor alongside the spittle, and blew smoke in Giovanni's face.

"Don't get me wrong," Mario said. "I'm glad you gave me away because you could never have been the father that Luciano is— and oh crap, imagine Beth as my mother? She wasn't fit to lick

Donatella's shoes. But you think I forgive you?" he said. "You think I don't remember the times you brought Beth here and . . . and . . ." Mario's breathing came loud and heavy, his chest heaving as if his lungs wouldn't hold. "And yeah, the way she looked at me like I was scum, like something that might infect her. Fat fucking chance!" he said, landing a spray of saliva on Giovanni's cheek. "Like she was so much better than me even though half my blood was hers."

He ground the cigarette under his boot heel. "Shit! I bet I've read more books in the last ten years than she ever read in her whole fucked-up life!" he bellowed. "That prissy cunt, she got the big 'C' anyway, didn't she?"

"I was right, *psicopatico* eyes," Mariella muttered. Giovanni seemed to shrink right in front of her.

"So, ask me," Mario ranted, "am I sorry she's dead? Not one fucking bit. I'm *glad* she got the cancer. I'm glad as shit the bitch is dead!"

Luciano hustled now, into the fray, the man who raised him, his father, come to intervene. "That *is* enough," he spoke sternly, grasping Mario's arm.

Mario jerked his arm away from Luciano, stopping short of a backhand, whirling toward Mariella. "Even before our shitty little 'talk,'" he said, snarling at her, "I could read it all over you, that dog-faced look, all sympathetic and soft." He pointed to Giovanni. "The same as him. Guilty as hell!"

Then, the quiet, as sudden as the outburst. The young chef methodically gave everyone the finger, and walked through the swinging doors into the kitchen.

"You talked to him about me?" Giovanni asked Mariella, either not mindful or not caring that others heard.

"Giovanni," she said. She rose and went to him, pulling him into his office and shutting the door behind.

"You betrayed me," he said, collapsing into his desk chair as if there were no place lower he could sink.

Mariella remained standing. Not sure enough of her welcome to sit. "I didn't want you to be lonely after I started school," she said. "I wanted someone else for you to love. *Mi dispiace*, Giovanni. I shouldn't have interfered," she murmured, dropping her chin to her chest. She heard herself repent as if she were making a confession. "I was trying to take care of you."

Giovanni stared at his desk, not seeing her, not seeing at all. "Who else did you tell?" he asked after a while. "Pah!" He lifted his hands. "As if that makes any difference." He swept his arm toward the door. "Everyone knows now, anyway."

"Giovanni," she said, willing him to look her in the eye. "Giovanni, I swear on my Nonna's life, I did not tell anyone—and Mario . . ." She hesitated. "He already knew."

He nodded, refusing to look at her, closing his eyes. "I know," he said. "I was fooling myself to think he hadn't figured it out. And thank you. I do know you wouldn't betray me—at least not about that."

"Giovanni, I haven't . . ."

He held up a hand. "Don't," he said, facing her now. "You don't owe me anything. You never promised yourself to me. And I had no right to ask."

"Oh, that's not true! You *had* the right." She talked with her hands, flipping them in emphatic circles as she spoke. "I have so much respect for you—and caring, yes, deep caring too." Penitent, once again, lowering her head. She couldn't bring herself to utter the word she didn't feel.

"I know," Giovanni said sadly. "You loved me for a minute, but you didn't fall in love."

"But," she said, suddenly animated. Willing herself to sound hopeful, to bring Giovanni hope. "I think you can have a repair now, with Mario. Believe me, even though he's very angry, he will come around, and you two will be like father and son." She shrugged. "Or at least friends—who knows, maybe nephew and uncle?"

"Pawning off the old man, hey?" Giovanni said, shaking his head, his laugh sardonic. "You're something, you know. No matter what's going on, you cut right to the chase." Reminding her of Leslie's pronouncement that day he'd brought her to meet Giovanni several months back: "You don't mince words, do you?"

Would she ever understand the customs of *Americanos*? In this country, some things were okay to talk about, like money and sex and possessions, which were considered bad taste to bring up in Italy. But in America religion was not okay to bring up, and, sometimes, people got in serious trouble, even friendships sometimes ended, she'd noticed, over politics. In *Italia*, and especially in *Sicilia*, if you couldn't speak your mind and have a big argument, what was the point?

"I need to be alone," Giovanni said, not unkindly. He swiveled his chair sideways, away from her, and reached for some papers in a drawer.

Chapter Forty-Two

She found Leslie's phone on the kitchen counter and thrust it at him, along with the outdated appointment reminder card she'd kept in her room after it had fallen out of one of his textbooks. "It's time—over time—for you to make the follow-up with Kaiser." She waited, hands on her hips, while he punched in the number and got through to the HIV/AIDS center.

"Today?" he said, speaking into the mouthpiece. "Four-thirty?"

Mariella nodded her head, mouthing, "I'll come with you," even though she was scheduled for Basilico in just half an hour.

She called the restaurant, securing Teresa's agreement to stay until she could get there. In the last weeks, ever since Mariella and Giovanni had taken a step back, his sister had become, if not engaging, at least cordial. Even to the extent of asking Mariella about school, inquiring about her family at home. Reclaiming her ascendancy was how Mariella saw it. Her rightful place, alongside her brother.

"I'll order a rapid read test as well as the standard one," the nurse practitioner announced, preparing to draw Leslie's blood, the same all-business nurse, Joyce Blevins, who'd tested him before. "The rapid reads are new and expensive, and we don't like to use them if we don't have to," she said. "But since you're not sure if your partner was HIV positive, we need to know right away if you're carrying antibodies."

"*Former* partner," Leslie corrected her. "How long?"

"Only takes a second," Joyce said, expertly tying off his forearm with a rubber tourniquet, locating a vein in the crook. And, if the calm of Leslie's expression was any indication, inserting the needle with only a whisper of pain.

"No," Leslie said. "I mean how long for the results?"

She withdrew the syringe and released the rubber tie.

"Twenty minutes," she said. "Thirty at most." She peered at him over the tops of her half-glasses as she'd done on his previous visit. "But that's not what you were asking, is it?"

"If you know," he said, "how come *you're* asking?" He closed his mouth in a grim line.

"You want to know how long before you die?"

From her chair in the corner of the exam room, Mariella unsuccessfully stifled a gasp. She'd ordered herself to sit there and not make a peep.

"How about if we take it one step at a time?" Joyce suggested, placing the vials of Leslie's blood on a small rectangular shelf and pushing it through, the wall magically closing up behind it.

"Wait here a minute," she told Leslie, gently rubbing his shoulder, and nodding at Mariella. "Okay?"

"*Gesu Cristo!*" Mariella said when she and Leslie were alone. "What are you trying to do? Make me have a heart attack?"

"I may as well face it head on," Leslie said, his lip quivering despite his best efforts to appear stoic. "No point in beating around the bush. Besides, it's the least I deserve."

"For what? What are you talking about?" She thought for a moment. "Wait. After that first time, you used condoms. Didn't you? Isn't that true?"

Leslie could be as dramatic as Mamma, but now, he was genuinely scared.

"I'm such an ass," he murmured, turning his face to the wall so she had to lean closer to hear. "I trusted him when he said he always used a condom, but there were a couple of times . . . you know, I wasn't sure." His spine twitched in a shiver. "And I was stupid enough to go along." Gone was the pretense of being jolly or tough. "If I hadn't been such a wimp, he wouldn't have treated me so bad—he probably wanted me to die!"

"You don't think like that," Mariella ordered, truly alarmed now. "You didn't make him leave you—he wasn't a good person. He was never a good person. And . . . and . . . you don't talk that way about dying because I need you to live. You stop thinking that way, Mr. Leslie." She shook his arm. "Do you hear me, you stop it now!"

He didn't answer.

"Well, I'm . . ." she started to say *certain*. But his dread was beginning to infect her too. "I cross my fingers you are fine."

Joyce bustled back into the room. "Why don't you go get a cup of coffee or walk around the block? You'll be too nervous sitting in the waiting room. Go on," she urged when neither of them moved. "By the time you get back, we'll have the initial results."

On the drive home, Leslie pulled off to the side of the road, allowing himself, finally, to breathe and to laugh while he cried, released from fear, and perhaps, at least for a moment, from self-loathing. She called him "Lucky Leslie." She patted his knee and held his hand.

The rapid read results, negative. Not even a carrier, so far.

She hadn't lied when she told him she needed him to live. They were family now, as much a part of each other's lives as Papa, Olimpio, Nonna, and Mamma were hers. For better and worse. They were the roof over one another's heads, the food on the table, the abiding love even when they annoyed one another and, as she had today, stuck her nose in his business.

No sign of Giovanni at Basilico that evening. Rather, Luciano was ensconced behind Giovanni's desk, waving Mariella in as she passed his open door. Which was normally closed, and, without framing, appearing as a seamless extension of the tan, textured wall, a bronze levered door handle the only giveaway.

"Oh, sorry I'm late," she said, assuming that was the reason Luciano had summoned her. "I'll go now to relieve Teresa." The photo of Beth, conspicuously absent atop the desk. "Where is Giovanni?" Perhaps he'd missed Elmer's afternoon walk and was making up for it now.

"That's what I wanted to tell you," Luciano said. He was no longer maitre d', and his uniform tonight was a brown tweed jacket, white shirt, and dark slacks.

"What about Giovanni?" A sudden panic took hold. Giovanni had never missed a day of work since she'd known him. Was he ill? In an accident? Sweat coated her palms and blood rushed from her head. She lowered herself into the chair across from Luciano.

"He's on vacation," Luciano said.

"Vacation?" Giovanni didn't take vacation.

"Yes. At my insistence—and Teresa's. We've been concerned about him ever since . . . well, the altercation with Mario."

No. Because of me. Her guilt was as insidious as a stranger's fingers slipping inside her purse.

"Where did he go?"

"On a cruise to Mexico," Luciano said. "Where it's warm. We—Teresa really—made the arrangements, bought the tickets, and I drove him to the pier."

Giovanni on a cruise? A private, self-contained man in a crowded setting where twenty-four seven socializing was the prescription? She couldn't imagine him agreeing to such an excursion. But, perhaps he'd have a large room with a view, a balcony, where he would read, or muse, or—and this thought troubled her most—drink too much, eat too little, and nurse a broken heart.

Or, and more the possibility, Giovanni would be pursued by attractive single women. Of course. Someone as appealing, as refined as Giovanni—ha! Every woman on board, married or single, would scheme to meet him.

Luciano's graying eyebrows raised above kind eyes. "Only a week—just for now. We thought he needed to get away from Mario."

He refrained from adding, "And maybe from you."

Chapter Forty-Three

"Your brother's in big trouble," Papa revealed over the phone. She heard the catch in her father's voice. "I didn't mean to tell you, but when you asked for him, I couldn't . . ."

"None of your business!" Mamma shouted so loud a shot of pain pierced Mariella's eardrum, leaving a ringing in her ear. "The wedding's in two weeks, and you can't come. You're not the only one who can marry someone fancy."

"Yolanda . . ." Papa pleaded.

"Wedding?" Mariella said, holding her cell phone away from her and switching it to speaker as if the screen might give her the answer. "What wedding?"

Papa whispered something aside to Mamma who, for once in her life, apparently, did as she was asked and backed off.

"Your brother's marrying Isabella Gamberini," Papa said, his words heavy with foreboding. "In the Duomo." Catania's cathedral of Saint Agatha, where Mariella's wedding to Matteo was to have taken place last year. "In March, on the twenty-sixth, the Sunday after the first day of spring."

"They're babies!" Mariella said. "Olimpio's nineteen, and Isabella's, what, not even eighteen? You can't be serious."

Her father's protracted silence told her everything. She didn't ask why the Gamberinis hadn't insisted on abortion. Or why they hadn't sent Olimpio to jail for child molestation. This was *vendetta*. Revenge for her not marrying their son.

"She just turned eighteen," Papa said. "She'll graduate early from high school—before the wedding." No, it wouldn't do for Isabella to be seen in a June procession, her stomach protruding under her gown as if preceding her.

Oh, how miserable Olimpio must be, completely out of his mind. Her once happy-go-lucky brother with the sunny disposition, wretched now, any chance for a full life or finishing his college education vanished—swallowed in one foolish stroke.

And, curious as well, that Isabella's parents hadn't chosen the cathedral in *Siracusa* or quiet nuptials to avoid wagging tongues.

But of course! *Her* family had to pay for Mariella's insurrection. Cough up, literally, their pound of flesh. Rather, Olimpio's. Isabella wouldn't be showing yet; only family and a few insiders would know she was pregnant. And, of course, the wedding had to be public. Neither the Gamberinis nor Mamma, who surely saw the impending marriage as a victory, would have it remarked any other way.

"Mamma sounds happy about it," Mariella said.

"Yes," Papa said. "Mamma's overjoyed."

There was a pause. She watched the rain gush down in sheets outside the kitchen window. She'd heard on the news that streets throughout the city were flooded, backed up because of clogged sewer drains, and some busses weren't running. Even though she loved her class—the Twentieth Century British Novel—a good excuse to snuggle in bed and feel sorry for her brother, and maybe for herself.

"What your mother meant," Papa said, "is that no one expects you to leave work or school and come home for the wedding."

"No, Papa. I understand, Mamma doesn't *want* me at the wedding. I'm sure Bruno wouldn't like to see me, either." Mamma wouldn't want the chaos, the scandal Mariella's appearance might unearth. Or the chance of Mariella stealing her thunder. She hesitated. "Will Matteo be attending?"

"He's in the wedding," Papa said. Even harder to grasp: she

and Matteo would, in a twist of fate, become family, just as Bruno wanted. Her brother-in-law.

After a long moment, her father asked, "Mariella, are you still there?"

"I'm here, Papa," she said. She'd placed her hand over the receiver so he couldn't hear the sobs she struggled to stifle. If Matteo despised her, she didn't want to know. If he was in love with another woman, she didn't want to see.

Yes, this wedding would be Mamma's coup, albeit at the sacrifice of her son, the victory Mariella had denied her mother. She could see it now: Yolanda Russo all aflutter, cheek by jowl with dignitaries, politicians, high-powered (likely underworld) and wealthy friends of the Gamberinis. Her mother, too loud, flushed with excitement, not considering that such fancy people might ignore her, not think her important enough for more than a cursory congratulation or hello. Might see her as intrusive, coarse. Mamma, elbowing her way into discreet conversations, and Papa trying futilely to hold her at bay. And the ache that would follow, even now squeezing Mariella's heart with empathy, the imagined wound to Mamma's pride.

"But your brother wants you there. You have to go!" Leslie said when Mariella informed him that Olimpio had called on the sly and insisted that she come to the wedding. In fact, Olimpio had protested, he wouldn't marry at all if she wasn't there. Not likely, she thought, considering how persuasive Bruno could be. But her brother's plea had been so raw, so real.

"I can't go," she told Leslie. "They'll eat me alive. Besides, I haven't got the money for plane fare home . . ." She hesitated. "I mean, back here." She smiled at the irony, the unlikelihood that "here," this American city, would ever have come to mean "home." The Alitalia ticket her family had purchased for her for a one-way flight to *Roma* and on to Sicilia was still on reserve. "It's all right," she said, her voice dejected, her head bowed. "It's my brother's big moment—Mamma's too. I'd only spoil it for them."

A cunning look came into Leslie's eyes.

"We're going!" he declared. "Yes, that's right, you and I. Both of us. No. No argument. Close your mouth. Not a word," he said, holding up a hand. "Just leave it to me, I've got it all figured out."

Chapter Forty-Four

*H*ere, then, was Olimpio, on a dreary March afternoon, waving hello as Leslie and Mariella approached the exit at *Aeroporto di Catania-Fontanarossa Vincenzo Bellini*, just as he'd waved her goodbye last summer. Angry purple clouds were a shroud overhead, visible through floor to ceiling windows and rolling like thunder.

And Papa? She looked past Olimpio, hoping for a glimpse of her father hurrying in from the car park. She knew better, understood his unwillingness to prevail over Mamma's wrath, but felt let down nonetheless. *"You have to choose, Salvatore! It's your daughter or me!"*

"Your brother's gorgeous," Leslie said under his breath, smiling and waving at Olimpio as if they were long-lost familiars. "Oh, how delicious, why didn't you tell me?"

So tiny, not first seen: Nonna alongside, a dark coat over her floral print housedress, holding out both arms as if hers was an ample bosom, a sturdy sanctuary for her travel and spirit-weary granddaughter. Mariella didn't realize how deep was her longing for that bosom until she bent over and buried herself in it, unable to stanch the flow, not even trying, letting it all pour forth, heedless and uncaring of onlookers until she'd cried herself clean.

After the outpouring, she embraced her brother. Leslie stood by at first, waiting to be introduced, then circled an arm around Nonna's and Olimpio's shoulders. "Group hug!" he proclaimed, all the while surreptitiously checking out Olimpio's clothed body.

"Oh, my beautiful brother," Mariella keened, her head nestled on his chest. "Have they made you sell your soul to *il diavolo*?"

"Look at me," Olimpio said, easing her far enough away so she could take him in. "Do I look like an unhappy man?"

"You look fantastic," Leslie said, simultaneously catching Mariella's warning glare.

But a man now, was he? Her brother, at nineteen, already claiming the title. Was it impending fatherhood that made him so? Where was the fretting, the dark circles under the eyes, the body gone slack and slim with despair?

Rather, he was grinning. Beaming, slicked and polished in a brown silk shirt and tan, tailored pullover. Seeming happier in fact, than she'd ever remembered him.

"You don't have to pretend with me," she said. On the periphery now, Nonna shook her head and closed her eyes. "Okay, so . . . ?" Mariella urged.

"C'mon," Olimpio said, shouldering the carry-on bag she'd dropped on the floor and snapping up the long handle of her large suitcase and rolling it behind him. "Let's get in the car. We can talk about everything on the way home."

Home. An ominous, heart-pounding prospect.

"Will Mamma let me in the house?" Mariella asked once they were in the car. She'd hopped in first, saving the front for her grandmother before Nonna could protest and intercepting Leslie from climbing in with Olimpio. "Does she really know we're coming?"

"You're both staying with me," Nonna said, craning her neck as best she could and speaking to Leslie and Mariella in the back.

"Oh, thank God," Mariella said. She translated Nonna's words for Leslie, although Olimpio knew some English from university and Nonna had learned it from Jeremy and when she lived in England.

"But does Mamma even know we're coming?" she asked again.

"Papa told her," Olimpio said, speaking half in English, half in Italian. "Last night. And even though she knows better, of course, it proves once and for all that you're a *puttana*, living with a man."

"Did you tell her I'm just one of the girls?" Leslie piped up. Olimpio laughed and Mariella rolled her eyes.

"I'll bet she's locked herself in the bedroom," Mariella said. Her brother's silence told her she was right. She could hear Mamma now: "What choice did I have but to let my daughter come home!" Olimpio's ultimatum, enough of a threat to allow Mamma saving face.

She patted the brushed twill seat beside her. The same old blue Fiat that had delivered her to the beginning of her quest last June.

But *had* she found any of what she was searching for? Her own Holy Grail? Blessedly, she was here, in Catania, and Nonna was here, and they would sort it all out on Nonna's balcony, as they always did.

"We had to promise Mamma you'd stay in the background," Olimpio said. "Wear a veil over your head, if that would make her happy." A bag would please Mamma more. "But I told her I wouldn't go through with the marriage if you weren't here." An empty threat, of course: she knew her brother was trapped, even if he didn't like to believe it. Owned by Bruno, lock, stock, and down to the designer clothes he'd taken a shine to.

He glanced at his sister in the rearview mirror. "But how did you manage the plane ticket? You said on the phone you didn't have the money."

"Miles," Leslie said. "My father's miles. Military. One of the perks of being his son, even though he completely disapproves of me." He paused. "You know I'm gay, right? *Uno finocchio.*"

Both Nonna and Olimpio shrugged. "Anyway, my father keeps me signed onto his Delta miles, thousands of them because he flies everywhere—except to see me, of course. Always makes excuses. He lives in Ohio—that's a state in the USA almost three thousand miles from San Francisco. Anyway," he said, flipping a hand, apparently realizing that no one cared about his geography lesson. "Delta's partnered with Alitalia, so hey, presto! We're using the miles before they expire."

Mariella had worked extra shifts to pay for the short, Alitalia flight back from Catania to Rome. Leslie wouldn't hear of her paying for him. They'd used the bulk of his miles for her one-way ticket back to San Francisco and Leslie's round-trip ticket to and from Rome. "The one good thing my father's given me," Leslie declared. He snickered. "He can afford to be generous—as long as he knows I won't use them to come see him." But Mariella hadn't missed the shadow cross Leslie's eyes, the glimpse of sorrow that his father would never want him to come home.

She'd arranged with her professors, as had Leslie, for time away—ten days, if she could bear being here that long, although they'd left return flights open, just in case. And brought books: *The Gothic Cathedral* for humanities and Ian McEwan's *Amsterdam* for modern British lit.

Giovanni had returned from his trip several weeks ago, looking tanned and healthy, except for the sadness lingering in his eyes, and in ample time to send her off from work with his good wishes.

At her tentative knock, Papa flung open the apartment door as if he'd been waiting for her on the other side. She walked into his arms, inhaling his woodsy citrus smell, and lingered there under his chin, her disappointment in him all but forgotten.

Mamma, as Mariella predicted, was locked in her bedroom, one of her multitudinous ailments the excuse, refusing to greet her daughter.

She poked her head into her childhood room, converted now to her mother's sewing lair. A late-model Necchi sat on Mariclla's scarred school days desk, and swatches of brightly colored fabric were strewn across a daybed, taking the place of her old single one, alongside the levered window. A bust in the corner where her *armadio* once stood—her wardrobe closet with nursery rhyme painted drawers—the bust, Mamma's dummy no doubt, a model for the formfitting wrap dresses her mother liked to wear.

No homecoming aromas from Mamma's kitchen. No longer a place for Mariella, even if she'd wanted to stay.

Chapter Forty-Five

*L*eslie stood with arms wide open at Nonna's balcony railing, as if he were a king, embracing the city and his subjects: the Duomo's round cap rising above, the aromas of the Ionian sea, the landscape of red tiled roofs. Olimpio, as armchair guide, pointed out the awnings and bustle of Catania's open-air market, *La Pescheria*, and the university, Mariella's alma mater and where he now attended. "Oldest in Sicily," he said, "from 1434."

The ancient Roman amphitheater, barely discernible as other than a horseshoe of crumbling rock.

"You see that tiny pink speck, that villa off in the distance by the shore?" Mariella overheard her brother remark. Then proudly, "That's where my fiancée's family lives—that's where *I'm* going to live."

"You're living with your in-laws?" Leslie said. "Oh, no, no, my dear, you do *not* want to do that. Believe me, you do not."

"Oh, not in the main house," Olimpio said. "A separate house built for carriages, a long time ago."

"Oh, well," Leslie said. "Still . . ." He shook a finger. "Don't say I didn't warn you."

"Your room is the second one," Nonna told Mariella, gesturing down the stuccoed hallway. Her grandmother's apartment: small, uncluttered, and full of light. Shutters thrown open, a welcome to the faint breeze drifting in, a lush ficus standing sentinel just inside the balcony doors and thriving in the salty, pungent sea air. The ocean's rhythms as fundamental to Catanian life as wine and food.

Nonna's favorite flowered easy chair—had Papa wrested it for her from Mamma's grasp?—perpendicular to a sofa in eggshell green. A plain pine coffee table fronted the sofa (where Leslie would sleep) sanded smooth and fragrant from lemon oil. To the side, an oversized anthurium on a small glass-topped table, its leaves glossy and salmon pink. And on the coffee table, today's *Corriere della Sera* tossed to one corner, a large, colorful, hand-painted ceramic plate in the bold Sicilian style occupying another.

A palpable calm.

"No saints in the wall niches," Mariella said, laughing at the memory of Mamma's ritual prayers to Agatha. Rather, small polished wood sculptures, paired but dissimilar, round and open in the center, and reminiscent of one of the large Henry Moore marbles in the garden at the Legion of Honor in San Francisco. Mariella and Leslie had made a field trip there, ostensibly for her Humanities class, but really, because Leslie wanted to flirt with the Latin *baristo* in the museum café. His preference in men as dark as he was light.

"You didn't let Mamma give me—I mean my things—you didn't let her give them away," Mariella said, peering through the doorway of the bedroom designated as hers. Nonna stood silently behind her granddaughter, letting her enter at her own pace.

Mariella rediscovered favorite clothes she'd left behind in the *armadio*, treasured sweaters and pullovers she hadn't been able to take on her escape, dresses she'd regretted not having in San Francisco.

"Oh, and the paper lamp!" A folded floor lamp Matteo bought for her one rainy afternoon when they'd wandered through the maze of Catania's backstreets and come upon a Chinese mom-and-pop hole-in-the-wall, Chang's General Store. She'd loved the soft, diffused lighting inside the lopsided spiral shade, thick paper imbedded with bits of what looked to her like straw and seeds and scattered petals. So inexpensive she'd worried how the proprietors survived.

Matteo had paid more than twice the amount on the price tag and hustled Mariella out of the store before Mr. Chang had time to count out the change.

At home in her room, when she'd lifted the lamp from its flat cardboard container and watched it unfold and spring to life, like a jack-in-the box, Mariella had believed that the light inside was the love that would always burn inside her heart for Matteo.

Later, when they were alone, Mariella and her grandmother held hands, relaxing on Nonna's sofa with a glass of native *Corvo Rosso*. The balcony too risky for conversation, so close to Mamma's and Papa's.

"Your Leslie is good for you," Nonna said. "He makes you light-hearted." Mariella smiled, recalling Leslie's ploy for Olimpio to take him on the Vespa. "But you must be too tired for a long ride," Olimpio had suggested. "Maybe a short walk instead?"

"Oh, no, a good long ride on the Vespa," Leslie had countered. "I'll buy the gas." Aside to Mariella he'd muttered, "And miss the chance to wrap my arms around him? I may have been born at night, but it wasn't last night!"

"So what about your Giovanni?" Nonna asked. Mariella understood: without words, her grandmother knew, intuitively, that theirs had been a transitory liaison. "A kind of insurance," Nonna offered, "that you were still desirable?"

"You mean after Matteo? What the Americans would call a security blanket." "Sugar daddy" crossed her mind, but Giovanni was too elegant, her esteem for him too fine to name him that.

He hadn't avoided her after his return from the cruise. In fact, he'd invited her to dinner, "For old times' sake," he'd said. And told her he *had* met someone on the ship: a real estate broker living in San Francisco. A woman closer to his age. But Mariella hadn't detected delight in his voice as he'd described his new companion. A neutrality, rather, more a sense of liking, a commonsense friend. "She's a nice woman," Giovanni had said.

Mariella had hoped for him to fall in love and puzzled over the yearning for him that still remained. It was only a matter of time, she believed, before she'd have to leave Basilico.

Later, she'd cried herself to sleep, aching for the goodness in Giovanni, for the loss and for the generosity of his soul.

"Olimpio tells me Matteo goes out with many young women," Mariella said, watching Nonna for her reaction. "Some of them not so savory. The ones his parents don't know about." Her grandmother seemed herself, again. Not the wizened, alarming old woman in the Christmas photos, but sturdy, even if she had shrunk a bit, her demeanor and her bearing, upright and steady. The relief of being out from under Mamma's roof visible in the relaxed contours of her face.

"Apparently, your name isn't allowed in the Gamberini household," Nonna said.

"No? What about next door?" Mariella tilted her head in the direction of her parents' apartment. "Does Mamma ever ask about me?"

Her grandmother closed her eyes, barely nodding her head. "Your mother slept in your bed the whole first week you were gone," Nonna said. "We could hear her crying in the night, but of course, we weren't allowed to say a word, because . . ." Nonna lifted her shoulders. "Because she'd say *we* were all crazy, or that it must have been the cry of a wounded animal in the street."

"Mamma? Crying for me? I don't believe it!"

"*Cara*, your mother loves you. Maybe *needs* you is the better word—more than she can ever admit. That's why she wanted to get rid of all your things, because it was too painful to see them every day." Her grandmother leaned toward her. "But if she hates you a little too, it's because you get to be everything she could never be, and when you left, it just rubbed the salt in deeper."

Red splotches bloomed on Mariella's cheeks. "So what are you saying?" she asked, springing up from the sofa, startling her grandmother. "That I'm supposed to forgive her?" She paced back and forth in front of the coffee table, the hem of her loose-fitting peasant blouse billowing out at each turn. "That because she's jealous she has the right to be mean to me?"

Was Nonna implying she'd been selfish, that she should have stayed home? How would she be able to leave again if the one person she counted on thought she was wrong? She'd never had a rupture with her grandmother, and that possibility, now, set her heart pounding and her breathing gasping and shallow.

"Sit down, *mia*," Nonna said. "Sit down. I can't talk to you with all that walking around."

Mariella sat, not meeting her grandmother's eyes, but keeping her gaze below the hem of her denim skirt, on her trim, bare knees.

"If *I* don't want to live with your mother," Nonna said. "Why would you ever believe I think you should?"

Caught off guard, Mariella brought up her head.

"*Mia*, you *want* to know your mother loves you. I know you do. I've seen you turn yourself inside out for her approval, even before you could walk. I've seen her try to break your spirit over and over again. And it would be the worst thing in the world for her—for both of you—if you stayed home. Do you understand? Because you carry the hope for her life too, even though she can never admit it, and she doesn't even realize it herself. But she *feels* it"—Nonna clenched her fist and thumped it near her heart—"I see it every time she brags to someone how brave you are. '*Mia coraggiosa intelligente figlia*,' she tells anyone who will listen. 'Crossing the world, working in the best restaurant in San Francisco, going to a big important American university . . .'"

"It's not important," Mariella said. "It's a state university—I mean it's really good, famous writers have gone to school there or come to teach—but not a big important school." Nonna wouldn't have heard of the renowned writers, and neither would Mariella if Bernard hadn't enlightened her. About former celebrity student, Peter Coyote, or alumna poet, Kim Addonizio. Nor James Dickey, a deceased faculty legend who authored *Deliverance*, made into a big movie starring Burt Reynolds and Jon Voight.

"No matter," Nonna said. "Your mother thinks it's Harvard."

"Mamma only brags because she thinks it makes her look good," Mariella said, but not without a tug, the pull that had always been there between her and her mother, the magnetic force of repulsion and attraction. And she, always hoping, just a little, that even if Mamma couldn't confess it, she *did* love her and was proud of her daughter.

Cooking smells wafted in from next door: a roasted chicken, the scent of rosemary. Olimpio's last meal at home as a bachelor, and as his mother's treasured son. Hours later his groomsmen and pals would take him for a final "boys only" night out. *Un addio al celibato*, even if, in time, it would become obvious that he and Isabella had not been celibate.

As dusk swallowed the last orange streak of day, the two women remained, joined now by Leslie, lingering over conversation, crusty bread, *caponata*, and wine. Papa knocked on Nonna's door, bearing a large platter of the succulent chicken, roasted potatoes, braised chard, and a bouquet of purple tulips.

"I'm sorry," he said, "because your mother is too nervous to see you tonight—I mean nervous about the wedding," he said, speaking rapidly. "You know how she gets, but she sends her wishes for *buon appetito*. She cooked two chickens, one especially for you—for all of you." Papa set the platter and the flowers on the coffee table, then without hesitation, scooted between Mariella and Leslie on the sofa, embracing her shoulders and pulling her close. "It's so wonderful to see you, *cara mia*." He gave a little sniff. "So wonderful to have you home."

Here was her true home, her sanctuary, in the comfort of her father's arms and her grandmother's grace.

She and Leslie offered the gifts they'd brought from San Francisco: for Nonna a silk scarf from Saks Fifth Avenue, floral of course; and for Papa a blue-patterned silk tie.

"We have something for Mamma," Mariella said. "But we'll wait until she's ready to say hello." A red silk clutch with a rosette latch, and for Olimpio's wedding, a tan cashmere/cotton throw he and Isabella could use on their sofa, or for the baby.

"I suspect Yolanda will be too nervous tomorrow, as well," Nonna said from her flowered chair, a smirk pulling up a corner of her mouth.

"You think?" Leslie remarked, stealing a crispy potato off the platter.

"Tch," Nonna said but couldn't stifle her smile.

"It's all right," Mariella said. "I want to walk in the city, maybe look up one or two old friends."

"I'll come with you!" Leslie said. Mariella frowned but didn't say anything. She wanted to visit her old haunts on her own, wanted to see Chef Angelo in particular, her employer at Trattoria Inglese—hardly a boss, more like a mentor—all through her high school and university years. Her last glimpse of him: when she'd fled that disastrous graduation dinner. Not her best moment, and with no thought for farewell. And she wanted to thank Luisa Romano, her conspirator at *Agenzia Turistica*, for helping to set her free. In truth, she wanted to see no one her own age, no one from university days, didn't want their judgmental, gossipy inter-rogations. She hadn't said goodbye to any girlfriends last June, nor explained anything to them of her breakup with Matteo.

Chapter Forty-Six

Next morning, Olimpio, barely able to contain his excitement (or, Mariella speculated, was it masking fear? Or was too much alcohol from the night before fueling his nerves?) insisted, even as the sun barely warmed the sky, that his sister and grandmother dress, "*Immediatamente!*" and accompany him for caffè at the neighborhood bar.

"You can't sleep?" Nonna asked, tying the sash of her pale yellow cotton robe as her grandson shot through the doorway. "You don't look to me like you need more *caffeina.*"

He was so jittery he danced in place like a frenetic puppet.

Leslie groaned from his bed on the sofa, his head buried under the covers. The other three turned to the sound, seemingly surprised, as if they'd only just remembered he was there.

"When else am I going to see my sister?" Olimpio said, taking in Mariella's sleepwear as she emerged from her room—a soft jersey T-shirt hanging below her knees with the silvery inscription: Silicon Valley, Take a Byte. A gift from Leslie. His executive friend, the one who'd staged the Halloween party, had given him two.

"You mean this is it?" Mariella said. "This is our only time?"

"Bruno is sending us for a week's honeymoon in Taormina—a suite in the best hotel," Olimpio bragged, puffing out his chest. "Belmond Grand Hotel Timeo."

The best indeed. She'd seen computer photos of the luxurious Belmond Grand suites when she'd worked at *Agenzia Turistica*:

classical European mahogany furnishings, silk throw pillows, plush carpeting, Carrera marble tubs with polished brass fittings in two bathrooms, a living room, sitting area, and patio balcony as large as Nonna's whole apartment.

"Bruno's gift, eh?" Mariella said. The head to toe cosseting, the discreet indulgence for the newlyweds from the service staff, instructions that would no doubt be commandeered by Bruno. One of countless bestowals dazzling Olimpio, including the lavish wedding, that he wouldn't, for the time being, have the wisdom to refuse. "You two go on," Nonna said, heading toward her room. "I want to go back to sleep. I see you every day," she waved at Olimpio over her shoulder.

Leslie threw back the covers and sat up, ready, it appeared, to leap off the sofa, get dressed, and go with them.

"It may be years before you see your sister again," Nonna said, signaling Leslie to stay put. She gave him a sly wink. "I have something better in mind for you and me today."

The difference between Nonna and Mamma epitomized in that one gesture: if Mamma knew Olimpio was going out with Mariella alone on this, his final day, she'd be demanding he stay and have caffè with her.

"After all," Mamma would say, "I make it better than the bar."

Between sips of cappuccino and swooning over bites of her firm yet crumbly-in-the-mouth breakfast roll—unreproducible, she was certain, not found anywhere in the world but here—Mariella watched Olimpio's dark eyes lighten as he described all the wonderful opportunities ahead of him as Bruno's future son-in-law.

"I'll be rich," he said. "I'll be a famous lawyer, someday, maybe even as successful as Matteo. He's a star in law school— did I tell you? No surprise there. But I'll be Bruno's business partner and right-hand man." Matteo had sworn he'd never work for his father, not with Bruno's mysterious connections. "And,

I can help out Mamma and Papa, so he doesn't have to work until he's so old he can't see the numbers—and Nonna—Nonna as well, for the rest of her life."

What about love? She wanted to ask, but kept her tongue quiet, despite a nearly irrepressible urge to warn him of the backlash to Bruno's benevolence, a smiting she knew only too well. If these were to be her ultimate moments with her brother, let them be uneventful and tender.

After caffè, he drove her on the back of his lime-green Vespa, as he'd done so many times before, down to the marina, to the stand of palm trees surrounding the little elephant statue watching the sea. The site of her hiding place the night she'd run from Matteo. The night forever emblazoned in her memory, the night she and Nonna first schemed.

They walked the marina pathway arm-in-arm, she, grieving silently, an intermittent, unremarked trickle sliding down her face: for her brother's ill-fated future; for all she'd relinquished by abandoning her home, in spite of all she'd gained; for losing Matteo; for Giovanni's kindness; for the yearning she'd felt briefly for Bernard; and for the bittersweet state of being in love without loving anyone in particular. Or so she told herself. Perhaps being on her birth soil brought on her melancholy. A pang, even, for her mother's unlived life. She let the breeze dry her face, leaving salty traces, like the journey of a snail, moving slowly through the sand.

"You'll be there tonight?" Olimpio said, swinging their now intertwined hands. The rehearsal dinner at an informal trattoria, which Mamma arranged and Papa was to have paid for—a celebration traditionally falling to the parents of the groom. But which Bruno surreptitiously covered, Nonna revealed, telling Papa afterward, "We can settle it later.' Bruno refused to discuss the amount or accept your father's reimbursement." Mariella wouldn't ask Papa if he felt grateful or diminished.

"Of course I'll be there," she said, smiling up at Olimpio, having no intention of exposing herself to the Gamberinis under such intimate circumstances, let alone to her mother.

She wasn't worried about Leslie: Nonna had promised— volunteered—to keep him occupied. He'd accompany Nonna on her daily eight-kilometer walk, then she'd prepare the best lunch he'd ever eaten, and later, he'd escort her grandmother to the rehearsal dinner. And, if Mariella knew her roommate as she believed she did, by the end of the evening he'd have charmed Mamma into calling him, "My second son. You come and stay here any time!"

Mariella and Olimpio lunched at an "art café," currently featuring pastel cityscapes by a local woman artist. A café near *La Pescheria* and the Piazza del Duomo in the shadow of the Cathedral, where tomorrow, Olimpio's fate would be sealed. A simple shared meal: pizza margherita of fresh, hand-pulled mozzarella, fragrant basil leaves, and a light, sweet tomato sauce from whole, garden-picked fruit.

After the *insalata verde* and a glass or two of white wine, a *Corinto*, Mariella wanted nothing more than sleep. Even *espresso* didn't revive her. She was jet-lagged and spirit worn. But she would stay away from her family until she was certain the rehearsal dinner was in full swing.

For siesta, she'd find a place to rest in the shelter of a park, or possibly sneak into her grandmother's apartment, without anyone except Nonna and Leslie the wiser. Perhaps she wouldn't be missed tonight, but if she were, Olimpio would surely forgive her, and maybe even understand.

He let her off at *Agenzia Turistica*, only to find it closed. Signora Romano always did keep uneven hours.

"I'll walk from here," she told her brother, motioning him on. "I'll come back later in the week." As he drove away, his thick dark hair blew back and shone under the sun, and the back of his white shirt rippled like a ship's sail. She wondered if she'd ever again witness him so carefree.

At Trattoria Inglese, Chef Angelo couldn't get over her showing up, "*Proprio come una fantasma!*" he exclaimed, slapping his portly midsection. "*Una apparizione!*" Everyone in her family along with Leslie had left for the rehearsal dinner at a different trattoria, and Mariella was blessedly on her own. Angelo insisted she stay at *Inglese* for her dinner, pulled off his chef's hat, and sat with her in a secluded corner table, treating her as an honored guest.

"Your favorite," he said when his assistant placed before her a plate of *pasta alla norma*. "I didn't forget."

"No," she said. "Neither did I." Maybe it was the salt air that seeped into everything in Catania, even the semolina. Or, perhaps it was her imagination. But nowhere she'd eaten in San Francisco was that dish—like the crumbly breakfast rolls—comparable to here. The ricotta *salata* clung to the ribbed penne just so; the eggplant was smoky; the simple sauce barely coated the pasta, yet was layered and rich, like Nonna's sun-dried tomatoes.

And because she knew Angelo would keep her confidence so there was no danger of Mamma's prying, and also because Angelo asked her so sincerely, "Tell me how you are, bella," she found herself revealing to him, as she had last night to Nonna, what she'd lived through in San Francisco, including her night of sensual dancing and subsequent failed "friendship" with Bernard.

"So now you are alone and it's okay?" he asked, his bushy gray eyebrows knitting together, like an aging caterpillar traversing his forehead.

"Sometimes I think I'm one of those people who will never be able to surrender," she said, gazing out at the vine-trellised courtyard, recalling images, there, of her infamous escape. "Not in the traditional way."

"So, who knows? Maybe you'll end up with someone who's

also independent and nontraditional, and you'll have a nontraditional life, with nontraditional children and rules that aren't really rules," Angelo said, making wavy hand gestures, echoing his eyebrows. "But, instead, a way of living you carve out for yourselves."

"I can't imagine it," she said. "I only see people swallowed by other people." She thought of Mamma's manipulations and Papa's loyalty; Giovanni's sad marriage to Beth; and now, her brother's inevitable engulfment by the Gamberinis. Even Bernard's struggle to free himself from Carmen, an unwarranted sense of responsibility and guilt keeping him in place. Even though she understood: the charge between her and Bernard would rekindle if they tried to be friends. She'd been saddened by the finality of their connection. They'd hardly spoken since their night at Club Estilo, as though mutually, silently, they'd agreed to behave as if they'd barely met.

"But that's it, isn't it," she said now. "The impossible task of being connected and living a full, separate existence at the same time—of being able to be wholly oneself."

"Especially in marriage." Angelo nodded, tapping his own worn, gold band.

Mariella had always admired the partnership between Angelo and his wife of thirty years, Bianca. Bianca handled the bookkeeping, and sometimes substituted for the hostess on the latter's days off. But what impressed Mariella was, they *were* partners: friends, affectionate allies, two adults who listened to one another, and even when they didn't agree, spoke to one another respectfully. Mariella knew this because she'd overheard them at times when they weren't aware anyone was listening.

"But give it time," he said, echoing her family's urging when she'd announced her refusal to wed Matteo. "Right now," he said, "of course you can't see it. Now, you only need to live in your present life."

Chapter Forty-Seven

When Papa stopped by the apartment to collect Mariella, Leslie, and Nonna for their ride to the wedding—he would return for Mamma, he said, claiming there wasn't room for them all in the car—he reported that the "boys," the ones in the wedding party, teased Olimpio all morning while he'd attempted to dress: "'Oh, you'll see, your Isabella,' they taunted. 'She'll be the bride that runs away, like Julia Roberts in that *cinema Americano*. Besides, why would she ever want to marry someone so ugly as you?'"

"I wish you'd called me over," Leslie chimed in. "I love to help men dress. Oh," he said at Papa's raised brow. "Of course, I haven't explained. I work at a men's clothing store."

Mariella silently cringed, but not because of Leslie's remark. The "runaway bride" prediction pierced her too close to home.

She lingered with Nonna and Leslie in the early spring sunshine, off to one side of *Il Duomo di Catania*, the imposing baroque *Cattedrale di Sant'Agata*. They would wait until all the attendees, the fancy ones on the Gamberini side—even the well-dressed underworld ones—and, the smaller, more eclectic Russo crowd on the right, had been escorted to their seats by Olimpio's groomsmen: his four best university mates and Matteo. And until Mamma, appearing both to clutch on to Papa and simultaneously drag him along, had assumed her rightful place on the left of the Russo front-row pew.

Mamma's lovely new dress, flowing and lavender, was a contrast in dramatics like Mamma herself, against her still black hair. No hat, but a dark lace head covering draped like a flag over her extended left wrist, an ostentatious gesture to make her appear pious, or at least prepared to be. Papa's neck strained red above a too-tight shirt collar, and Olimpio's groomsmen wore pale gray tuxedoes with bow ties and pastel green vests, jollying the guests, doing their utmost to keep the mood light.

Mariella's plan was to sneak into the back pew at the last moment. Her grandmother was adamant: she would wait with her, wouldn't allow her granddaughter banished, alone. Nonna's outfit today was a step up from a housedress, though floral as always. She wore some sort of slippery rayon-like fabric and a plastic visor, matching the bright pink hibiscus flowers in her dress.

"You go ahead," Mariella and Nonna simultaneously urged Leslie. "Go on in." He couldn't resist popping forward to get a better look at the ushers, including Matteo, escorting female guests and the more unsteady elderly men.

"No," Leslie said, impatiently. "I'll wait with you. But you've been holding out on me." He shook a finger at Mariella. "You didn't tell me how gorgeous all these Sicilian boys are. And you deliberately kept Matteo secret, didn't you? Even from me."

"It was nobody's business," she said. Leslie looked hurt, and she tried to sound casual. "No big deal, I just wanted to keep the past in the past." She supposed someone at the rehearsal dinner—probably Mamma, or maybe Matteo's older sister, Leonora—had given Leslie an earful about her antic escape, her broken engagement, her selfish abandonment of them all.

"Well," Leslie said. "Matteo's very special—I had a chance to talk with him last night." He sniffed, flicking imaginary lint from the lapel of his sand-colored jacket. "I told him we're roommates. He didn't say so, but apparently he's drinking far too much these days—ever since you walked out on him. You've broken his heart."

"Thanks, pal," Mariella said. "I really needed that." She turned her attention back to the incoming wedding guests, attempting to ignore the pulse pounding through her veins.

She'd had only glimpses of Matteo inside the massive, open wooden doorways as he made his round-trip journeys, offering his arm to approaching female attendees. Seeing him from her vantage point, off to the side, had kept him—until Leslie's scolding—on her emotional fringe, like watching a small figure, impersonal but recognizable from a distance, as in a photograph or on TV.

Invitees on the Russo side were indeed a heterogeneous bunch: out-of-town relatives, including doughy, perspiring Antonio from Palermo, the one who'd rescued Papa from infamy nearly twenty years before; other cousins as well as long-time neighbors who were also good friends; local vendors including the fishmonger; the husband of the duo who owned the *enoteca*; the baker and his brood of six, who were akin to family; and Papa's accounting associates. Olimpio's numerous university pals made their way in, in staggered succession, some of whom, if the plethora of dark glasses was any indication, were likely suffering hangovers from absconding with Olimpio after last night's rehearsal dinner for a second night of revelry. Also, their girlfriends, those who had them. And even some of Mariella's university friends she hadn't anticipated—in fact, dreaded—facing.

She stared at the bigger than life frontage statue of Saint Agatha ensconced in the cathedral's niche, as she was in Mamma's and Papa's apartment, only here Agatha was haloed and surrounded by cherubs against background rays of heavenly sunshine. Such a strange and contradictory lot, she thought, her fellow *Sicilianos*. As superstitious as gypsies and children, when it came to bowing before stone effigies, yet fierce to the core, their reputation for independent contrariness well deserved. *We never wanted to be part of greater Italia. We do things our own way!* Immovable and unyielding as that statuary rock.

While Mariella was still looking up and musing over Saint Agatha, a male arm enclosed in a pale gray suit sleeve—a chronographic gold-toned watch encasing the wrist—swooped around the waist of her filmy green and peach dress, the same one she'd worn for her first meeting with Giovanni. Then, after inserting himself between the two women and encircling Nonna with his other arm, came the clear, confident voice, as familiar to her as her own: "Ladies, and Leslie, Olimpio sent me as his emissary. He wants you in the front row, next to your mother and father." And to Nonna, "Excuse me, *Donna Russo*. I mean, of course, next to your son."

No time to protest, to take stock of her reaction to his sudden appearance, or to drape herself in her own black lace head covering—part of her plan to enter incognito. It would be unseemly to resist and make herself the center of attention. Matteo moved them along, with just enough arm pressure to let her know that escape, this time, wasn't an option.

Every head in the Cathedral turned, every eye followed their progress to the front. Nonna still wore her plastic visor, and Leslie inclined and raised his blond head, smiling, practically bowing at the guests as he went, as if this were his party and he was the benevolent host. And not only did Matteo escort them up the center aisle, past the alcove housing Bellini's tomb, past St. Agatha's side chapel: he paraded them in front of Mamma's and Papa's pew, and, sweeping his arm at the intended spot, bade them sit at her parents' right, albeit a foot or two away. He then assumed his place at the altar, alongside Olimpio and the other groomsmen.

Nonna yanked off her visor, Mariella lowered her head, but not before catching her brother's wink. Leslie waved and winked back. Olimpio waited until his grandmother and sister were settled in before signaling someone in the back of the long church—Bruno? The father and escort of the bride—to begin the procession.

Papa closed his eyes, nodding in what appeared to be gratitude. Perhaps thankful because his daughter was close to him, where she belonged. Or perhaps in approval of his son's assertion against Bruno.

Mamma stared straight ahead, ignoring her daughter harder than before.

Even in the limousine afterwards on the way to the reception, when Mariella remarked, "You look beautiful, Mamma. Are you ever going to say hello?" Mamma's only response: "Hmpf."

She hadn't reckoned on ever again entering the massive Villa Gamberini gates, the expansive curving drive flanked by towering cypress trees. But there were only so many festivities she could avoid without being downright rude or without ruining the day for her brother. Leslie had promised to be her front man, her dogsbody, when she needed one, her protector and shield. Which was only possible, she realized, if he could contain himself from sashaying past every good-looking male, like a hummingbird sampling nectar, flitting from flower to flower. She'd stay at the reception long enough for congratulations, the wedding photos, and a toast, then slip away. No one aside from Papa and Olimpio wanted her there anyway.

Sylvia Gamberini greeted guests at the villa foyer, elegant as always, in a silvery sheened coatdress reflecting the silver in her groomed, swept-back short hair. She held Mamma and Papa by the shoulders as they entered, bestowing her warm smile on first one and then the other, welcoming them as if they were now, indeed, *famiglia*. "Yolanda! Salvatore! You know your way around. *La mia casa 'e casa tua*," she said, motioning them inside. Her expression of intimacy so sympathetic, its authenticity doubtless.

Mamma lifted her chin higher and strode in as if she owned the place.

Nonna accepted a kiss on each cheek from Matteo's mother, who kept her eye on Mariella, in line behind Nonna, even as she greeted guests in line before the Russos.

When Mariella stepped up, Sylvia grasped Mariella's hands, gazing at her for what seemed like an hour. Mariella's eyelids blinked in overdrive, like a doll's whose batteries had gone haywire. She struggled not to look past Sylvia or at the ground, commanding herself to keep her eyes directly on Sylvia's, forcing herself not to run, concentrating instead on the vertical lines above the bridge of Sylvia's nose.

Leslie's arm shot out, like the quick tongue of a chameleon. He moved past Mariella in an instant, seizing Sylvia in a tight hug, leaving her gasping for breath. "Oh, I'm so glad to see you," he declared, addressing no one in particular, over the top of Sylvia's head. "We didn't have a chance to speak at the dinner last night."

"And I'm so glad to see you," Sylvia said, attempting to extricate herself from Leslie's clutches. Recovering, like a plumed bird shaking its feathers back into place, she reached around Leslie for Mariella's hand, and pulled her close, leaving Mariella little choice but to accept her embrace.

"I'm so very glad to see you, most of all," Matteo's mother murmured into Mariella's ear.

"I think you're the only one," Mariella managed, her lips mashed against the large standup collar of Sylvia's dress. Everyone was taller than she.

"I told you I would always wish you'd be Matteo's wife," Sylvia whispered. "I still wish it was you two who were married today, but," she sighed, "if it can't be you, at least now . . ." She released Mariella to stare at her again from crystalline blue eyes, one of those throwbacks to the Normans cropping up now and again. ". . . we have your brother."

Oh yes, the Gamberinis *had* her brother, all right.

"Sylvia!" Bruno's booming voice rising above the assembled hum, commanding from across the Great Room.

"Come," Sylvia said, her reception duties apparently inconsequential now. "Come, say hello to Bruno. It'll be all right," she urged, leading Mariella by the hand and giving Leslie a nod. "He's forgiven you, especially today."

Mariella didn't care whether or not Bruno had forgiven her, didn't give a damn, anymore, about the Gamberinis. At least not Bruno. She reached behind her for Leslie, assuming, hoping, he'd follow.

The steady crescendo and fall of chattering guests softened against floor-length antique leaded windows, draped in maroon velvet and held back on either side by gold-tasseled swags and draped again, now, with garlands of fragrant white blossoms echoing Isabella's bridal bouquet: gardenias, lilies, jasmine, and Hawaiian ginger. The walls festooned for the occasion, with oversized beribboned gold wreaths.

A fountain of sparkling wine—Prosecco—held center stage, surrounded by a pyramid of upright, overflowing champagne glasses. Male servers in black waistcoats and young women in black dresses with straight skirts and low-heeled shoes passed trays of the Prosecco, red and white wines, and an assortment of cocktails, along with fancy hors d'oeuvres: caviar on petite potato pancakes, *involtini* of swordfish and ricotta, a *caponata* of marinated olives, red peppers and eggplant on crostini, and the delicate bright-red raw shrimp from the Gulf of Catania. Maroon shrouded long tables skirted the room, replete with ice sculptures in the form of a swan, a dolphin, and two intertwined hearts engraved with *Isabella and Olimpio*, ready for the silver chafing dishes that would magically appear, later, when circular tables and straight-backed upholstered chairs would transform the room into a banquet hall. Now, a string trio played soft chamber music in a far corner.

Where was Leslie? Mariella glanced back as she and Sylvia made their way across the room. In search of one of those handsome men, she supposed. She didn't blame him, but she should have known better than to trust his steadfast promise. And God knows where Mamma had got off to.

She spotted Nonna, standing with Papa, sampling an *involtini*, tilting her head in skepticism and then nodding approval, listening to whatever it was their good neighbor, Alfredo the proprietor of the *enoteca*, was saying.

Mariella approached Bruno, her spine as upright and hard as forged steel. Neither of them extended a hand to the other but kept a five-foot distance between them, as if by mutual agreement. Bruno's demeanor cool and impassive, his black suit making him appear as if he were attending a funeral rather than his youngest daughter's wedding, and perhaps, like Mariella, he made the comparison.

"You look well," Bruno said, his tone neutral.

"And you," she said, equally bland. Out of the corner of her eye, she saw the wedding party, including her brother and Isabella, on the back terrace, posing for photos in front of dwarf palms in giant terra-cotta urns atop large marble pedestals. Matteo was there, with them, looking intense and out of place amongst Olimpio's jokey pals. Most of the shots were formal, but some playful, like the one of Isabella raising the skirt of her gown, revealing her green garter, with Olimpio pretending to peer under her petticoat, and the groomsmen looking lasciviously on.

And in the distance, as backdrop, beyond the sand-colored concrete balustrade and carved benches, the Ionian Sea.

Silently, Leslie sidled up to her, a glass of Prosecco in each hand, one for her and one for him. "You thought I'd given you the slip, didn't you. Well, surprise," he whispered. "I figured you needed reinforcements." He smiled and bowed ever so slightly as Mariella made the introductions to Bruno.

"Ah, yes, you were at the dinner," Bruno said. And no mistaking the expression in his eye: distaste and revulsion, contemptuous of anyone who didn't reflect his own, perhaps even fragile, sense of masculinity.

In minutes, family members would be called for the second round of photos, and shortly after, when all the party was assembled inside, Mariella would get lost in the crowd and leave.

She watched as Matteo reached behind him for a bottle of whiskey concealed by his body, on one of the marble pedestals. Scotch, she guessed, probably the peaty single malt Bruno and he preferred. He poured himself a glass, downed that, plus two more quick shots before returning the glass and the bottle to the pedestal. This wasn't the Matteo she remembered; he'd always sipped his Scotch, savoring the "mouthfeel," so he'd instructed her, allowing the earthy aromas to infuse his nostrils and settle over his tongue. An astute disciple of his father's princely tastes.

And where was the bevy of women Matteo was reputedly squiring? Why weren't any of them hanging on his arm? Or, at least gazing at him adoringly from inside while he was being photographed.

From out of nowhere Mamma appeared on the terrace. Was she staggering? Mamma hardly drank, but she faltered, looking disoriented and befuddled. Dark streaks ran under her eyes. She hurled herself at Olimpio, latching onto her son as if he were a life buoy, gesturing frantically, talking fast, words Mariella couldn't hear through the thick glass doors.

Olimpio peered inside, shielding his eyes with his hand, beckoning, mouthing, "Papa! Papa, come quickly!"

Mariella tugged Leslie away from Matteo's parents and whatever it was Sylvia was proclaiming—something about "One big extended family"—and hurried with him to her father, who was still conversing with Alfredo, in between receiving handshakes and congratulatory hugs. She pointed at Mamma on the terrace.

"Oh no," Nonna muttered, shaking her head. "She can't even let her son have his wedding day."

Two bright red spots colored Papa's cheeks. Anger? Embarrassment? But for whom? He lowered his head, took a deep breath, murmured an apology to Alfredo, and plunged onto the terrace through the glass doorway, held open by one of the male servers. Conversation hushed to a standstill as everyone, it seemed, watched Papa place his arm around Mamma's shoulders, and speak low, no doubt soothing words, and lead her off the terrace, like players in a Shakespearean tragedy, exiting stage left.

After a moment or two, both wedding party and guests heaved a collective sigh, shaking themselves into the present, and resumed where they'd left off, as if they'd been frozen in time and brought back to life.

Three of Mariella's female schoolmates spotted her from across the room, waving and moving through the crowd, toward her.

"Oh, please," she said, groaning. "I don't want to see them. I don't want to talk to them at all."

"Leave it to me," Leslie said, plucking three glasses of Prosecco from the tray of a passing server—a young woman, as it happened, so he wasn't tempted to linger—and making a beeline for the three young women.

"Enjoy!" Bruno declared suddenly, raising his glass to the crowd as he elbowed his way to where Mariella and Nonna stood with Alfredo.

"Time for family photos," he growled at Mariella. "You two go on out there, and I'll find your father and *mother*," he practically spat the word, "so we adults can give our children an album to remember."

Mariella and Nonna both stared at Bruno, steely eyed, in unison. Little Alfredo—not much taller than either of those two diminutive women—dipped and fidgeted, not knowing, it seemed, whether to stay still or flee.

"It's okay," Nonna said, patting Alfredo on the back. "This won't take long. Don't go away. There's Giacinto and Maria, why don't you go say hello." The fishmonger and his wife, along with other Russo neighborhood merchants, engaged in lively conversation yet kept to themselves on the fringes. Nonna glared at Bruno. "You're as welcome here," she said to Alfredo, "as any of the other important guests."

Nonna and Mariella slipped through the glass doors and hovered at the periphery of the combined Gamberini and Russo clans on the terrace. The only ones missing were Mamma and Papa.

Olimpio broke from Isabella to embrace his grandmother and sister. "Mamma's okay," Olimpio assured them. "She overheard some women talking about her—uncomplimentary things—in the powder room. Her feelings were hurt." Mariella's sad prediction come true.

She imagined what her mother had overheard: *Putting on airs . . . low-class . . . crude . . . such a devoted husband; what does he see in her?*

The wound to her mother was a compression, a tightening of sorrow in her own chest, and, as if compelled to find comfort, Mariella scanned the group for Matteo and caught him scowling at her from under lowered brows. He manned his station at the pedestal, drinking steadily, refilling his glass, one pour after the other.

Momentarily, Papa escorted a subdued Mamma on his arm onto the terrace from the same archway through which they'd made their exit, and once again, everyone watched from inside. Mamma stared straight ahead, acknowledging no one and fighting, it appeared, to act composed. At least the black streaks were gone from under her eyes.

The photographer made quick, efficient work of the fifty or so family photos he snapped, moving people around according to height and sex. He kept the mood alternatively light and serious, flirting with and cajoling the more somber oldsters. Particularly

Matteo's, Isabella's, and Leonora's upper-class grandparents, both maternal and paternal. Papa refused to leave Mamma's side, and Nonna, the shortest of them all, placed squarely in front next to Leonora's stuffy banker husband, at least twenty years older than his wife. He looked Nonna's age, even though he was twenty years younger.

As the families disassembled and milled around, the glower Mariella once again caught from Matteo sent a shiver across her scalp. He frightened her now, this new aspect, morose and dark.

She looked away, then turned and nodded, thinking a friendlier greeting might dilute his menacing aura. After all, hadn't they once loved each other so very much? Unconsciously, she reached for Nonna, who'd apparently seen what transpired, and squeezed her granddaughter's hand.

Matteo's bared teeth appeared more like a grimace than a smile.

Papa sidled up to them with Mamma still clinging, fighting back tears. She did her best to ignore Mariella but only succeeding in looking pitiful, sliding her eyes between Papa and Mariella, like a child wondering what fate the grownups will decide for her.

Leslie stepped onto the terrace, next to Mariella. "No worries about your girlfriends," he whispered. "I redirected them, snagged a couple of good-looking young men and introduced them." He sighed. "Just about everyone here's straight," he said. "Unfortunately."

"Since when did you become a matchmaker?" she whispered back.

"I'm taking your mother home," Papa said, his voice doleful and low.

"Oh, Mamma," Mariella said. "Such a shame. I'm so sorry you heard those silly women." She touched her mother's hand, and Mamma jerked it away.

Mariella dropped her arm to her side, her breath, a moan. "Aren't you ever going to forgive me Mamma? And I don't mean just for leaving, but for whatever it is I've done wrong—apparently my whole life."

Her mother inhaled sharply but said nothing.

"Salvatore, one of you has to stay. It's your son's wedding," Nonna said, addressing her own son, reaching up and giving him a light smack on his shoulder. "One of his parents has to be here, you have to give him this day."

"You stay out of it!" Mamma barked. "You've never taken my side—you hate me, just like everyone else!" Her outburst halted surrounding chatter and shined the spotlight, once again, her way.

"No, Yolanda, I don't hate you," Nonna said, softly. "I never have. But I have wished for you to see beyond yourself. And here comes Olimpio," she remarked. "Do you think for this one minute you can do that, Yolanda? Do you think you can see beyond yourself?"

"The hell with all of you!" Mamma shouted, gesturing at the gawking assembled families. "You all think you're so much better than me! Well, guess what? I've got news for you—your fancy shit stinks too!"

Olimpio stopped midtrack, shook his head, and lowered it to his chest. Then he turned and walked away, back to Isabella and his new parents-in-law.

"Time to join the party!" Bruno commanded. And Mamma, Papa, Nonna, Leslie, and Mariella watched as the others on the terrace, including Olimpio and Isabella, filed into the main hall and mingled with guests.

"Good for Olimpio," Nonna said.

"I'll go," Mariella volunteered. "I'll go with Mamma."

"No!" her mother exclaimed. "Salvatore, you have to come with me . . . because she . . . because I . . ."

"I'll go too," Leslie said, using broken Italian and hand gestures—pointing to himself and then to Mamma. "But only if your daughter comes along." He exchanged confirming glances with Mariella. "Will you come with me, Signora Russo?" And he held his arm as if he were offering to squire her to the grand ball.

Papa breathed a barely audible sigh of relief.

"Salvatore, you think it's okay?" Her mother was meeker now, more unsure of herself than Mariella had ever seen.

"I think it's just right," Papa murmured, patting Mamma's free hand.

Mamma stood a little taller yet braced herself on Leslie's arm.

"You wait here for a minute with Leslie and Nonna," Papa instructed her, "and I'll go tell one of the drivers to take you home. I'll be right back."

"I need to use the restroom before we go," Mariella said, heading into the main hall and toward the mahogany spiral staircase to the second floor, where all six bedrooms had their own bathrooms, all in marble or stone and polished brass, and each as big as her bedroom in San Francisco. She knew the Gamberini house top to bottom, its secret crevices and crannies. More than once, when no one else was home or at a large gathering here when they wouldn't be missed, she and Matteo had escaped to the third floor, to one of the unfrequented hideaways and made love.

She could have used one of the downstairs powder rooms, but she wanted a private moment to collect her thoughts. And, perhaps, to remember.

Chapter Forty-Eight

"What're you doing up here?" Matteo demanded as Mariella emerged from the bathroom. He stood in the doorway, blocking her exit. She startled and stumbled back and caught her elbow on the corner of the stone basin.

"Were you hoping I'd follow, like old times?" he said. He must have been waiting, listening in the hallway, until she opened the bathroom door. The set of his mouth, his scowl, meant to convey meanness, though his eyes were impossibly sad.

"What's the matter with you?" she said, rubbing her elbow where it smarted. "What's happened to you?"

He shouldered his way inside the bathroom and slammed the door behind him with his foot.

"Why are you doing this, Matteo?"

"Go ahead, scream, no one will hear you."

"I don't want to scream," she said. "I just want to talk." Mamma was waiting downstairs. Oh, God. But Leslie and Papa would figure it out, they'd get Mamma home.

"Talk? You want to talk?" Matteo said, trying for bravado, thrusting his face to hers. His breath stank of whiskey, both recent and stale. "Why didn't you think of that last June, when it mattered?" He combed nervous fingers through his straight black hair, a thick swath falling onto his forehead. A gesture so familiar, for a moment the Matteo of old stood before her, determined and focused, gearing up for a student demonstration against Mafia corruption or preparing a speech advocating rights for women, gays, or the working poor.

"I didn't know how to explain myself," Mariella said. She could see his pulse jumping at his temples. "I was afraid you would try to make me stay."

"We could have worked it out," he said, landing spittle on her cheek, his voice raspy with pain. He seized the frill of her low neckline and pulled her to him so abruptly he ripped her dress.

"Matteo!"

"Oh God," he moaned. "I didn't mean to do that." He held her face in his hands, his tears pooling at the rims of his eyes. "I'm sorry," he said. "I'm so sorry." She wondered if he was apologizing for only the dress, or was it for everything that had gone wrong between them. For his family, for hers, for an ancient way of life they could escape, but never really leave behind.

She tried to mutter his name, but her words were buried in the crush of his mouth. She could taste his sour breath. She tried pushing him back, to no avail, and she realized she didn't want to push him away. She wanted to stay with him, to *be* with him.

Matteo moved his mouth away but held her to him, clumsily pawing at her dress, ripping it further. "Why did you leave me? Why *did* you?"

"If you stop I'll tell you," she said. "But you have to let go." She wasn't afraid, and she questioned herself: why not? And she understood. Even in his drunken, animal state, she trusted him. He would never hurt her. He ached for her, loved her still—and she, did she love him? So much pain, there was just so much pain.

"Say it now," Mariella urged him. "It wasn't you—it was our families—the pressure. Please, tell me goodbye." She nuzzled her face into his neck, the oils of his clean, warm skin, a smell so much a part of her she'd once told him, "Even if I were blind I'd always know you by the smell of your skin." Like the aroma of a lighted, unscented candle.

"We don't have to get married," he said, kissing her face, her hair. "We can leave together, move to another part of Sicily, somewhere else in Italy—I can finish law school anywhere—I have connections."

The past came rushing over her, the sensations of feeling trapped and bound, the nausea of too little room, of being crowded in. And yet . . .

"I've never stopped loving you, Matteo."

She wiped his cheek, the tears that slid down even as she brushed them away.

He touched her tattered peach and green dress, rubbing the filmy fabric between his thumb and forefinger. "I'm so sorry," he said. "I didn't mean to tear your dress." The one she'd spilled wine on and nearly ruined when she'd first met Giovanni. A dress meant for beginnings, and apparently for endings too. "I'll find you one of Isabella's."

"I can't stay here," she said, gently. "I mean here, in Catania. It would be the same all over again. I need time . . . I can't explain. Matteo, you have to understand."

They ignored the insistent knocking at the door. Not caring, wishing whoever it was would go away.

"Mariella?" Leslie's voice, urgent and concerned. "Are you all right?"

Neither she nor Matteo answered. Leslie tried to push open the door, but their stretched-out legs blocked him.

"I'm okay," she called out. "I just need a minute."

"Uh . . . your mother's in the limo," Leslie said, "and . . . well . . . she's raring to go to put it mildly. And mad as hell at you." Mariella could imagine Mamma, cursing her out loud, calling her all the names she could drum up in rapid succession, and the limo driver lamenting his unlucky fate.

"I can't come now," Mariella said. She wouldn't let Leslie see her ripped dress, nor Matteo's wretched state. "But how did you know where to find me?"

"I watched," Leslie said. "I saw Matteo follow you up. I got worried because you took so long." There was a pause. "Is Matteo in there with you? Are you sure you're all right?"

"*Sì*," Matteo answered. "Don't worry *paisan*, your friend is just fine." He stroked Mariella's hand and managed a weak smile.

"What do you want me to do?" Leslie asked.

"Go, go home with my mother."

"You mean stay there with her—alone!" he protested.

Mariella laughed. "Don't be silly," she said. "Just until I get there, maybe half an hour." She intertwined her fingers with Matteo's and held on.

"Really?" Leslie groaned. "Achh . . . it's not that I don't like your mother, I actually think she's a kick, but I don't know, with the mood she's in now . . ." The harder he pushed on the door, the harder they held it closed.

"Are you sure you'll be there in half an hour?" he asked.

"What is it you say—scout's honor!"

They listened as Leslie's footsteps tapped a retreat down the hardwood stairs. When they could no longer hear him, Matteo locked the door and made cushions for Mariella's head and under her hips, with large, fluffy bath towels. He attempted to carefully remove what was left of her pretty dress. She laughed and ripped it off, like a child tearing the wrapping off a present. He undressed himself, draping his groomsman clothes on the counter so he could wear them later at dinner.

For times past, or perhaps because they'd never stopped loving each other, or because this was always how she'd meant to say goodbye, they made love. At moments desperate, even ferocious, but mostly tender and bittersweet.

"I wish . . . I'll always wish we'd met at a different time," she said afterward, curled up next to him, naked, on the floor.

"If I come to find you in two or three years," Matteo murmured, "who knows."

Chapter Forty-Nine

"Where were you? Why are you wearing that dress?" Mamma demanded from her position on the sofa, half on her back and half on her side, like a reclining odalisque. *Just waiting for me*, Mariella thought as she entered her parents' apartment. Not "Thank you for seeing that Leslie brought me home today" or "Thank you for leaving the wedding and coming now." Rather, "Why did you take so long—what happened to your dress?"

"I didn't think you even noticed what I was wearing," Mariella said. *Matteo ripped it off and I threw it away.* "But since you asked," she said, "I spilled wine all over it, so Sylvia gave me one of Isabella's."

In fact, Matteo had chosen the dress for her from his sister's closet: a blue-green polished cotton with spaghetti straps and a big bow in the back, like a bustle, over a straight skirt. "Isabella won't be wearing this for a while," he'd remarked.

"I should return it," Mariella said with a sly smile. "Or maybe you can do that for me—take it to Sylvia after I leave."

"Return it to Sylvia!" Mamma hissed, rising up slightly, then collapsing again. "You know I don't ever want to see that—that vicious woman—that place again!" Never mind that it wasn't Matteo's mother, but a handful of Sylvia's snootier pals Mamma had overheard.

Then, as if it had just registered, "When are you leaving?" Mamma asked.

Leslie emerged from the kitchen, carrying a metal tray with

two big glasses of lemonade and a plate of Mamma's round, spicy biscotti. "Leaving?" he said, rapidly nodding his head from behind the sofa. "Did I hear you say we're leaving?"

"I was thinking day after tomorrow," Mariella said. "Monday or Tuesday if we can get a flight. But look," she told Leslie, "the driver's downstairs, waiting to take you back to the reception. You don't want to miss the luncheon, do you?" At Matteo's urging, she'd considered staying at the banquet herself, and being held again in his arms and feeling his body so close dancing the tango, the love dance they'd mastered together.

"We can ignore my parents—and everyone else," he'd said. "We can pretend it's only you and me." But in the end, they'd kept their farewell private. With the party in full swing, Mariella had slipped, unnoticed, out the back villa stairs and into one of the waiting limousines.

And she'd already said her goodbyes to Olimpio—he understood, though regrettably, he'd said, about her leaving the reception to be with Mamma—and her chest was too full to stay, too bursting with homesickness to be in company, even if she didn't know where home was, anymore. Already, she pined for Matteo, as she never did before, when escape had been foremost, and attachment got pushed aside. More, she realized, with every new parting from Papa and Nonna in the years to come—even from Mamma—her grief, each time, would be more poignant than the last.

"You go too," Mamma said, waving her hand at Mariella as Leslie deposited the tray on the coffee table and hurried toward the door. She brought the back of her hand to her forehead, as theatric as Camille. "It's all right, I'll just stay here alone."

Mariella laughed. "Oh, Mamma," she said. "You'll never change. You don't even mean it." She sank into the easy chair on the other side of the coffee table. "You know very well I won't leave you alone—but it is a shame for you to miss your only son's wedding reception, don't you think?"

Mamma sat up and thought for a moment, tilting her head back and forth as if she were weighing the decision: Yes, to the left. The right side, No. Then she leaped up and ran to the balcony. As she opened her mouth to call down to the driver, she whirled toward Mariella. "You," she said, pointing a finger at her daughter. "You tried to trick me. You want me to go so they can make fun of me again!"

"No, Mamma," Mariella said. She sighed. "I'm just worried you'll feel bad later on." But honestly, wasn't there, perhaps, a touch of getting back her own? It surprised her, how little her mother's accusations affected her, how calm she felt in the face of Mamma's dramatics.

"I already feel bad," Mamma said, jutting out her chin. "Isn't that what you really want?" Her mother would be miscrable either way, and Papa would have to hear her recriminations, for at least the next month: "It's your fault! You didn't protect me! You should never have let him marry that tramp!"

Mariella didn't answer. "What shall we do?" she asked instead. She couldn't recall the last time she and her mother were home alone together.

"Do?" Mamma said. As if this were the first time she'd heard the word.

"Do," Mariella said. "Like go for a walk—or shop. Go for lunch." Had she ever done those things with her mother? Not since she was a little girl and Mamma held her hand when they'd walked nearly every day to *La Pescheria* to select the fish or meat and vegetables for the evening meal.

"I'll go to bed," Mamma said.

"No," Mariella said, with an authority that startled even her. "Not today. I came home from the wedding just to be with you and the least you can do is keep me company." Never mind that she'd left the reception primarily for her dignity, for herself.

Her mother glared at her and didn't speak. But she didn't leave the room.

"Tomorrow's Sunday, and we've always cooked the ragu together," Mariella said. She looked down at her borrowed dress and at Mamma's lavender wedding outfit. "Let's change and get started. C'mon, Mamma. What do you say?"

Mariella was already in the kitchen, scrubbing carrots at the sink, when Mamma entered. Her mother had changed into a house-dress, belted to highlight her slim waist, probably one she'd sewn herself on her new Necchi.

Mariella cleaned the carrots and listened, without fear, for the first onslaught of Mamma's orders and fault finding. Instead, not meeting Mariella's gaze, her mother cast a sidelong glance at the scrub brush in her daughter's hands, now poised above the sink.

"I haven't forgotten," Mariella said before her mother could comment. "Don't peel them, because all the goodness lives in the skin."

Mamma's cheeks flamed. She inhaled and exhaled, noisily, a display of what it cost to hold her tongue. She stepped into the pantry and fumbled with pulling aprons off a hook. With her back turned, her mother tied an apron around herself, then, seemingly on second thought, held another out to Mariella.

"Oh, no thanks, that's why I wore these jeans," Mariella said, rubbing her wet hands down her denim clad thighs. On top she wore a faded gray T-shirt from college days, one she'd discovered in her *armadio*.

Again, that blush in her mother's cheeks, and Mariella watched, with a mixture of detachment and curiosity as Mamma rehooked the proffered apron with a rough tug, her mouth clamped in a grim line, as if it took all her will to contain herself.

"You chop the vegetables and I'll brown the sausages and meat," Mamma blurted, her self-control apparently only stretching so far.

"You sure?" Mariella said as she reached for the big chef's knife from the wooden storage block. Thinking it would dispel the ghost of knife brandishing on that Saturday last June, when they'd prepared the final ragu together, she waved the knife in the air, several feet from where Mamma stood. "You know how I am with knives, Mamma." She laughed. "You sure you can trust me?"

Mamma's eyes grew wide, and at first she made a gasping sound, then, "Tch," she said, and flapped a hand at Mariella, dismissing her. "Just cut your vegetables." She opened the refrigerator and retrieved the sizeable parcel of paper-wrapped meats.

Perhaps it was only wishful thinking, but Mariella thought she detected the hint of a smile playing at the corner of Mamma's lips.

Sometime during their mostly wordless collaboration, Mariella pondered why she no longer dreaded the lash of her mother's sharp tongue, no longer steeled her nerves against a barrage of vitriol and belittlement. Still, Mamma's restraint bewildered her. Was it she, her newly found independence that rendered Mamma's bitterness silent? An internal, unspoken boundary entering the ether, understood between them. Or had something changed for Mamma, as well?

Even more surprising, Mamma remarking, out of the blue, "Your Giovanni, why do you like him?"

"Well," Mariella said cautiously, not sure yet of where her mother meant to lead. "He's not 'my Giovanni,' Mamma. We're only friends. You met him, so you should know, he's a very good man."

A moment's pause.

"Maybe," Mamma said.

"*And*, he's got a lady friend in his life. A real estate woman—someone close to his age."

"Ha!"

Another long silence ensued. Finally broken, again, by Mamma's question, "Are you staying there—in San Francisco—forever?" Leaving Mariella even more confused, and, on the verge of tears. Mamma had always *told* her daughter what her plans should be. Never before, not once, had her mother *asked* about intentions.

"It's not right," Mamma declared. As if it were fact.

"I don't know about forever," Mariella said softly. "But it's the right place for now."

Still, the two women worked with their backs to each other on opposite sides of the kitchen.

When Mariella began to lower the chopped *soffritto* vegetables into the pot with the shimmering hot oil and Mamma started to instruct, Mariella interrupted. "Don't, Mamma," she said. "I know what I'm doing. I learned from the best—I learned from you."

Before they left the kitchen, Mariella touched her mother, gently, on her arm, before Mamma had a chance to recoil.

And later, when Mamma finally retired to her room for siesta—more likely, Mariella thought, to nurse her hurt feelings and fret about what the fancy people at the reception thought of her—Mariella slipped out, donning a sweater against the March afternoon chill, hoping that today, she'd find Luisa Romano at *Agenzia Turistica*. A three kilometer jaunt to clear her head, and to pass by some of her favorite old haunts along the way: the caffè bar at the end of her street; the hole-in-the-wall used bookstore—Pirandello—two cobblestone blocks over, where, if one was lucky enough to arrive early, you could claim the worn easy chair and be visited by the resident gray cat, curled in your lap, while you read. And, closer to the *Agenzia*, the club, Buenos Aires, where she'd fallen in love with Matteo, dancing to Astor Piazzolla's "Vuelvo Al Sur," the same melancholy, sensual bandoneon melody she treasured, still, as the ringtone on her cell.

She'd brought a token for Luisa Romano from San Francisco, a gratitude for the woman who'd conspired with her and Nonna in her escape, and through whom Mariella had sent her private letters to Nonna. The present, one of those kitschy snow globes of Golden Gate Bridge and Coit Tower, with San Francisco Bay rippling underneath.

"Perfect for the *Agenzia!*" Luisa said, shaking the globe and watching the "snow" brush the tops of the Tower and the Bridge's girders and spans and slowly settle on the blue plastic Bay. As delighted as a young girl, she threw her arms around Mariella, and planted a kiss on her cheek, leaving an imprint of her signature firecracker-red lipstick. She then closed up shop, in spite of Saturday being her busiest and most lucrative day, and insisted they go for *antipasti* and wine.

Chapter Fifty

Sunday dawned clear and cold. And lethargic. At least for Leslie, who'd apparently indulged plenty in the liquor and the dancing and the general merrymaking at the reception.

"I was the last to leave," he said proudly, accepting Nonna's offer of his third *caffè* from her moka pot and adding a good quantity of heated milk. "Making friends," he said, raising his cup. "Up to the very end. I even danced with the bride—and with her mother!" Mariella pictured him, much to Bruno's disapproval and chagrin, pulling Sylvia onto the dance floor, as if refusal wasn't an option. Leslie's hair, still spiky on top from the gel he used, but now disheveled and sticking out at the sides, giving him the appearance of a mad scientist or someone just plain unhinged. Mariella wanted to ask him if Matteo danced, and with whom, and how close, but she held herself back.

They lingered around Nonna's small pine table in their nightclothes: Leslie in pajama bottoms and his Silicon Valley T-shirt, Nonna and Mariella in robes.

"I hope we have a little less excitement today," Nonna said, tearing off a corner of a breakfast roll and popping it into her mouth. She nodded toward Mamma's and Papa's apartment next door.

"I think she'll be all right," Mariella said. And she recounted how she and her mother had managed yesterday afternoon together mostly peaceably.

"You're not so afraid of her anymore," Nonna commented. Mariella nodded. And while she was thankful, especially on the

verge of this leaving, that something impossible and imperme-
able was silently dissolved between her and Mamma, it was with
a sense of nostalgia—a deeper sorrow—for all that might have
been, for all those lost and early years.

Someone in one of her lit classes had quipped, after a sober-
ing discussion of *What Maisie Knew*, "Well, it's never too late to
have a happy childhood." Mariella knew better. Tender, sensitive
young Maisie would never harbor carefree memories, shuttled
as Henry James wrote her, between two irresponsible, egoistic
parents. And Mariella and Mamma would never reflect on the
mother-daughter closeness she'd heard women friends describe:
"My mother's my best friend."

Indeed, the day unfolded leisurely and without eruption. At least
none visible, though Mount Etna continued to chuff away, in the
distance, but always nearby. Mamma was present for most of the
time, albeit subdued. Late morning, long before the afternoon and
evening *passeggiata*, when the streets would be thronged with Catanians of all ages, and singles of both sexes would dress extra sharp
to catch someone's eye, Papa and Mariella set out, arm-in-arm, for
a quiet walk through the neighborhood. Most of the apartment
buildings on *Via Diodoro Siculo* were like theirs: limestone or concrete, with carved stone arches above balconies and wide columns
of rosy beige granite brick columns, in relief, as adornment between
apartments. Granite blocks wrapped the corners, with rougher trav-
ertine pavers adding texture at the bottom. Businesses were closed,
metal shop doors rolled down, or iron gates pulled shut, but it was
one another's company father and daughter sought, not goods.

"Mamma didn't try to stop us," Mariella observed. "And you
didn't ask if it was all right and, she didn't say a word."

"No," Papa said. "These last months—since her return from
San Francisco, she's been different." He considered. "At least
some of the time."

She smiled up at her father, grayer now, yet leaner in the middle than the year before. The buttons on his favorite black-and-red-checked flannel shirt—his weekend shirt, he'd always called it, now frayed at the cuffs—no longer pulled apart above his belt. And also, he seemed less worried, stronger with Mamma, less on watch.

"Maybe it's you who's different," she said. Perhaps his confession to her at Christmastime had helped release him, she mused, but kept her thoughts to herself.

"Are you happy?" he asked after a while, as they headed toward the sea down a narrow cobblestone *calle*, free of cars, three- and four-story apartment buildings—historic rather than modern—all but blocking out the sun. The same question Giovanni had asked her on their first dinner together.

"I'm not *unhappy*," she said. She reached for her father's hand. She wouldn't tell him about feeling displaced, or lonely, or homesick.

He waited for her to say more.

"I just haven't figured it out yet, Papa."

"And you feel like you have to move halfway around the world to do that?" he said. "Figure it out?" Then he squeezed her hand.

"I know it's hard to understand, Papa, but I don't think I can live here again until I have my own little piece of ground to stand on."

She hooked her arm through his, and they walked in companionable silence.

"What about you, Papa?" she asked. "Are you happy?

"Hmm . . . funny you should mention a 'little piece of ground.'" He tilted his head side to side and raised his eyebrows. She tugged gently on his arm, urging him on.

"Well, I was thinking of the size of a postage stamp—you know I've always been interested in stamps?" Whenever he'd managed time from Mamma's demands or needed quiet and relaxation, her father's favorite pastime was to pore over stamp books, often remarking how he'd love to buy this one or that special stamp, if only he had the money. The Penny Red and the Penny Black were two he'd frequently commented on, entirely out of his reach. Only for millionaires. He had stamp books and a sizable collection but had never joined a philatelist club or managed time away to attend a trade show or collector's convention.

"I'm going to my first trade show," he said. "Next month, in *Siracusa*. And I'm staying over." She couldn't decide if he looked sheepish or proud.

"Without Mamma?" She couldn't imagine her mother allowing him out of range, even if *Siracusa* was only an hour away.

"Without Mamma," he said.

She waited for him to explain, and when he didn't, she squeezed his hand back, and giving it a shake, said, "Good for you, Papa. Good for you."

Throughout the afternoon, Olimpio's essence hovered in the Russo apartment like a *fantasma*. Mariella caught her mother standing in the doorway of her son's room, staring through the dust motes that tumbled though the shaft of light from the many-paned window, as if her concentration would make Olimpio appear. Mamma lifted the hem of her apron and wiped her eyes. And once or twice, she beckoned Papa into their bedroom for a whispered conference, but other than that, nothing remarkable occurred.

The ragu, rich and layered as always. Leslie declared it "The best I've ever eaten my whole life. I swear!" They ate penne, al dente, and afterward, Mamma's almond cake, moist and crumbly, with powdered sugar on top and Nonna's preserved peaches spooned over.

Mariella and Leslie's plane would leave early tomorrow, and this time, no subterfuge, no sneaking away at dawn, no adrenalin masking regret. Papa would drive them to the airport before he went to work.

Before she and Leslie retired with Nonna to her apartment, Mariella cleared the dishes and followed her mother into the kitchen. Leslie started to assist, but Mariella signaled him to stay at the table.

Mamma tried to ignore her, but Mariella stood beside her mother at the old, scarred, enameled sink. As Mamma turned to reach for a pot on the stove behind her, Mariella wedged herself in so the two women faced each other.

Mamma pursed her lips and acted as if she would back away, but she held steady.

"You take care of yourself, Mamma," Mariella said, carefully placing her hands on her mother's shoulders. "And please, take good care of Papa. You have no idea how much he loves you."

Mamma even stood still for Mariella's light embrace, and though she closed her eyes, she received her daughter's kisses on both cheeks.

Eschewing the *passeggiata* for a last few, companionable hours, Nonna, Leslie, and Mariella sat on Nonna's balcony and listened to the murmur of the nightly parade from the Duomo *piazza* close by and watched the purple dusk go dark. The lights of Catania came up, shimmering like bobbing lanterns at a perpetual party, and the stars brightened in the chilly night, like pinpricks against a background of velvet.

"You're welcome any time," Nonna told Leslie, lifting her glass of Vin Santo to him. She nudged Mariella, next to her on the canvas sofa swing. "Even without this one." Leslie straddled a blue metal chair; a tiny, low, bistro table between them sported the Vin Santo bottle and a dish of oily, salted Marcona almonds.

"Maybe I'll come back again when I fall in love," he said. He sounded mournful, a bit daydreamy, but mostly wistful. "When I find the right one."

"Are you thinking about Darrell?" Mariella asked. He'd told her he missed the initial head-over-heels but hadn't known Darrell long enough before the lies and the AIDS drama to fall deeply in love. Like a malignant third presence, betrayal had inserted itself between Leslie and Darrell, and now finally, Leslie admitted, he was relieved to have the both of them gone.

"Here's to decency," Leslie said, raising his glass, staring into the night, and sinking deeper into pensiveness.

"To decency," Nonna and Mariella said.

After a silence, Leslie rose and kissed both women on top of their heads, excused himself, went inside, and buried himself under the blankets on the living room sofa.

"All those beautiful boys at the wedding—all those couples— got to him," Mariella murmured.

"Yes, and what about you?" Nonna asked. If her grandmother had an inkling about Matteo, she didn't let on. And neither did Mariella. She wondered again about the possibility of pregnancy. But no matter. Her treasure, their lovemaking—held in her pocket, like a polished stone, to carry home.

They remained awhile on the balcony, then went to Mariella's room and kept company as she packed and snuggled together in Mariella's bed well into the night.

Before Nonna retreated to her own room, Mariella said, "It's all right if you don't get up in the morning, Nonna. I don't know if I can stand saying goodbye to you more than once."

Chapter Fifty-One

*A*t five thirty the next morning, Mariella opened Nonna's front door at Papa's soft knock. She blew a kiss toward Nonna's bedroom and took a long, last look around her grandmother's apartment. Then she and Leslie slipped noiselessly, with their suitcases, into the carpeted hallway.

Papa offered a white square box tied with string. "From Mamma," he said. "For the plane—her ginger biscotti." The spicy brown balls Mariella had loved from childhood. "She baked them last night."

So like Mamma. Unable to give to her daughter in person.

As Papa drove them away from the building, Mariella glanced up at her parents' balcony. She discerned a twitch of the shutters, a shadow behind the slats, as Mamma pulled them closed.

She insisted on saying goodbye to Papa outside the terminal. She lingered as long as possible without breaking down in her father's big, comforting embrace, tucked under his chin and breathing in his clean woodsy smell. As if the memory would become more imbedded with each inhale.

Papa shook Leslie's hand, man-to-man, but Leslie came in for a hug. "You're a wonderful father," Leslie murmured into the brushed wool of Salvatore Russo's jacket. "I wish my own father had been like you." Still mournful, still melancholy, Mariella observed, as he'd been the evening before.

As the plane sliced upward into the mottled blue Catanian sky, Mariella gripped Leslie's hand, rather than the arm of her chair as she'd done the year before. This time, as well, she'd taken a Xanax, but only one.

They watched, Leslie in the window seat, she, leaning over him in the middle, as the dark center of Mount Etna receded further and further from view.

"So?" Leslie said once they were safely airborne and the plane leveled off.

"So," she said. "I can never thank you enough, my whole life, for coming with me."

"You owe me big-time," he said.

"What do you mean?" Leslie's words alarmed her. He hadn't paid money for her ticket; he'd used his father's miles. She earned barely enough to pay rent, books, and her share of food. Then she saw him struggling to hold back a smile.

"You have to be my roommate until we both finish school."

She leaned back in her seat and closed her eyes. "Right now," she said, "I don't believe that's a problem."

Was she a crazy woman? Leaving behind the man who was most likely the love of her life. Leaving, for who knew how long—maybe even for good—the people she loved most in the world. Leaving the taste, the salty, earthy, sharp smell of the land she would forever seek—or attempt to detect—in a glass of good red wine or a curl of pasta in a sauce made just so. Back to a city where she was still a stranger and not even settled within herself.

She thought, fleetingly, of Bernard. Bound, at least for now, to his Carmen. And Giovanni? A man nearly as good as Papa.

How long would he let her remain at Basilico? How long would it feel right to stay?

And still . . . and yet . . . drifting into a light sleep, she suspected the possibility of joy.

Acknowledgments

Thanks to my brilliant advisors at Pacific University: Jack Driscoll, Frank Gaspar, Carolyn Coman, and Mary Helen Stefaniak. Without you, Mariella would have indeed remained, if not a shaggy beast, at least scattered.

And to my fellow "Gasparians:" our enduring friendship was born there in the Northwest; David Smith, James LaLonde, and Marti Mattia, your keen eyes held me to the heart of the book.

To my Sonoma collaborators: my dearest Sue Salenger, Kathy Andrew, Barbara Sapienza, and Marsha Trent.

To Maureen Adams and Mary Shea. My gratitude for your continuing deep reading goes beyond words.

And finally, to my beloved Larry, who never grew impatient with me and never gave up.

About the Author

Janet Constantino is a former a competitive Latin Ballroom dancer and journalist, and has been a licensed psychotherapist since 1983. In 2015, she earned an MFA in Creative Writing from Pacific University, and in 2021, she won second place in the MFK Fisher Last House writing contest. A practicing Buddhist, Janet has a grown son and twin granddaughters. She and her husband of twenty-five years live in the beautiful city of Sonoma, California, with their beloved Labradoodle and tuxedo cat.

Looking for your next great read?

We can help!

Visit www.shewritespress.com/next-read
or scan the QR code below for a list
of our recommended titles.

She Writes Press is an award-winning
independent publishing company founded to
serve women writers everywhere.